DOUBLE WHAMMY

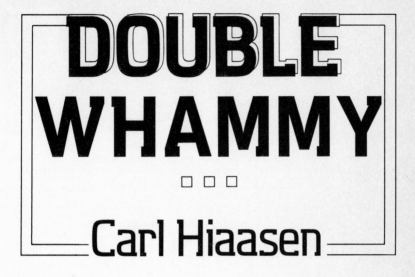

DOUBLE WHAMMY

Carl Hiaasen

G. P. PUTNAM'S SONS   NEW YORK

*This is a work of fiction. None of
the characters are based on real people.*

G. P. Putnam's Sons
Publishers Since 1838
200 Madison Avenue
New York, NY 10016

Library of Congress Cataloging-in-Publication Data

Hiaasen, Carl.
Double whammy.

I. Title.
PS3558.I217D6   1987   813'.54   87-13145
ISBN 0-399-13297-X

Printed in the United States of America
1   2   3   4   5   6   7   8   9   10

IN MEMORY OF CLYDE INGALLS

On the morning of January 6, two hours before dawn, a man named Robert Clinch rolled out of bed and rubbed the sleep from his eyes. He put on three pairs of socks, a blue flannel shirt, olive dungarees, a Timex waterproof watch, and a burgundy cap with a patch stitched to the crown. The patch said: "Mann's Jelly Worms."

Clinch padded to the kitchen and fixed himself a pot of coffee, four eggs scrambled (with ketchup), a quarter-pound of Jimmy Dean sausage, and two slices of whole-wheat toast with grape jam. As he ate, he listened to the radio for a weather report. The temperature outside was forty-one degrees, humidity thirty-five percent, wind blowing from the northeast at seven miles per hour. According to the weatherman, thick fog lay on the highway between Harney and Lake Jesup. Robert Clinch loved to drive in the fog because it gave him a chance to use the amber fog lights on his new Blazer truck. The fog lights had been a $455 option, and his wife, Clarisse, now asleep in the bedroom, was always bitching about what a waste of money they were. Clinch decided that later, when he got home from the lake, he would tell Clarisse how the fog lights had saved his life on Route 222; how a wall-eyed truck driver with a rig full of Valencia oranges had crossed the center line and swerved back just in time because he'd seen the Blazer's fancy fog lights. Robert Clinch was not sure if Clarisse would bite on the story; in fact, he wasn't sure if she'd be all too thrilled that the truck hadn't plowed into him, vanquishing in one fiery millisecond the expensive Blazer, the sleek bass boat, and Robert Clinch himself. Clarisse did not think much of her husband's hobby.

Robert Clinch put on a pair of soft-soled Gore-Tex boots and slipped into a vivid red ski vest that was covered with emblems from various fishing tournaments. He went out to the garage where the boat was kept and gazed at it proudly, running his hand along the shiny gunwale. It was a Ranger 390V, nineteen and one-half feet long. Dual livewells, custom upholstery and carpeting (royal blue), and twin tanks that held enough fuel to run all the way to Okeechobee and back. The engine on the boat was a two-hundred-horsepower Mercury, one of the most powerful outboards ever manufactured. A friend had once clocked Bobby Clinch's boat at sixty-two miles per hour. There was no earthly reason to go so fast, except that it was fun as hell to show off.

Robert Clinch loved his boat more than anything else in the world. Loved it more than his wife. More than his kids. More than his girlfriend. More than his double-mortgaged home. Even more than the very largemouth bass he was pursuing. Riding on the lake at dawn, Robert Clinch often felt that he loved his boat more than he loved life itself.

On this special morning he decided, for appearance' sake, to bring along a fishing rod. From a rack on the wall he picked a cheap spinning outfit—why risk the good stuff? As he tried to thread the eight-pound monofilament through the guides of the rod, Clinch noticed that his hands were quivering. He wondered if it was the coffee, his nerves, or both. Finally he got the rod rigged and tied a plastic minnow lure to the end of the line. He found his portable Q-Beam spotlight, tested it, and stored it under a bow hatch inside the boat. Then he hitched the trailer to the back of the Blazer.

Clinch started the truck and let it warm. The air in the cab was frosty and he could see his breath. He turned up the heater full blast. He thought about one more cup of coffee but decided against it; he didn't want to spend all morning with a bursting bladder, and it was too damn cold to unzip and hang his pecker over the side of the boat.

He also thought about bringing a gun, but that seemed silly. Nobody took a gun to the lake.

Robert Clinch was about to pull out of the driveway when he got an idea, something that might make his homecoming more bearable.

He slipped back into the house and wrote a note to Clarisse. He put it on the dinette, next to the toaster: "Honey, I'll be home by noon. Maybe we can go to Sears and look for that shower curtain you wanted. Love, Bobby."

Robert Clinch never returned.

By midafternoon his wife was so angry that she drove to Sears and purchased not only a shower curtain but some electric hair curlers and a pink throw rug too. By suppertime she was livid, and tossed her husband's portion of Kentucky fried chicken over the fence to the Labrador retriever next door. At midnight she phoned her mother in Valdosta to announce that she was packing up the kids and leaving the bum for good.

The next morning, as Clarisse rifled her husband's bureau for clues and loose cash, the county sheriff phoned. He had some lousy news.

From the air a cropduster had spotted a purplish slick on a remote corner of Lake Jesup known as Coon Bog. On a second pass the cropduster had spotted the sparkled hull of a bass boat, upside down and half-submerged about fifty yards from shore. Something big and red was floating nearby.

Clarisse Clinch asked the sheriff if the big red thing in the water happened to have blond hair, and the sheriff said not anymore, since a flock of mallard ducks had been pecking at it all night. Clarisse asked if any identification had been found on the body, and the sheriff said no, Bobby's wallet must have shaken out in the accident and fallen into the water. Mrs. Clinch told the sheriff thank you, hung up, and immediately dialed the Visa Card headquarters in Miami to report the loss.

"What do you know about fishing?"

"A little," said R. J. Decker. The interview was still at the stage where Decker was supposed to look steady and taciturn, the stage where the prospective client was sizing him up. Decker knew he was pretty good in the sizing-up department. He had the physique of a linebacker: five-eleven, one hundred ninety pounds, chest like a drum, arms like cable. He had curly dark hair and sharp brown eyes that gave nothing away. He often looked amused but seldom smiled around strangers. At times he could be a very good listener, or pretend to be. Decker was neither diffident nor particularly patient;

he was merely on constant alert for jerks. Time was too short to waste on them. Unless it was absolutely necessary, like now.

"Are you an outdoorsman?" Dennis Gault asked.

Decker shrugged. "You mean can I start a campfire? Sure. Can I kill a Cape buffalo barehanded? Probably not."

Gault poured himself a gin and tonic. "But you can handle yourself, I presume."

"You presume right."

"Size doesn't mean a damn thing," Gault said. "You could still be a wimp."

Decker sighed. Another macho jerk.

Gault asked, "So what kind of fishing do you know about?"

"Offshore stuff, nothing exotic. Grouper, snapper, dolphin."

"Pussy fish," Gault snorted. "For tourists."

"Oh," Decker said, "so you must be the new Zane Grey."

Gault looked up sharply from his gin. "I don't care for your attitude, mister."

Decker had heard this before. The *mister* was kind of a nice touch, though.

Dennis Gault said, "You look like you want to punch me."

"That's pretty funny."

"I don't know about you," Gault said, stirring his drink. "You look like you're itching to take a swing."

"What for?" Decker said. "Anytime I want to punch an asshole I can stroll down to Biscayne Boulevard and take my pick."

He guessed that it would take Gault five or six seconds to come up with some witty reply. Actually it took a little longer.

"I guarantee you never met an asshole like me," he said.

Decker glanced at his wristwatch and looked very bored—a mannerism he'd been practicing.

Gault made a face. He wore a tight powder-blue pullover and baggy linen trousers. He looked forty, maybe older. He studied Decker through amber aviator glasses. "You don't like me, do you?" he said.

"I don't know you, Mr. Gault."

"You know I'm rich, and you know I've got a problem. That's enough."

"I know you kept me suffocating in your neo-modern earth-tone lobby for two hours," Decker said. "I know your secretary's name is Ruth and I know she doesn't keep any Maalox tablets in her desk because I asked. I know your daddy owns this skyscraper and your granddad owns a sugar mill, and I know your T-shirt looks like hell with those trousers. And that's all I know about you."

Which was sort of a lie. Decker also knew about the two family banks in Boca Raton, the shopping mall in Daytona Beach, and the seventy-five thousand acres of raw cane west of Lake Okeechobee.

Dennis Gault sat down behind a low Plexiglas desk. The desk looked like it belonged in a museum, maybe as a display case for Mayan pottery. Gault said, "So I'm a sugar daddy, you're right. Want to know what I know about you, Mr. Private Eye, Mr. Felony Past?"

Oh boy, thought R. J. Decker, this is your life. "Tell me your problem or I'm leaving."

"Tournament fishing," Gault said. "What do you know about tournament fishing?"

"Not a damn thing."

Gault stood up and pointed reverently to a fat blackish fish mounted on the wall. "Do you know what that is?"

"An oil drum," Decker replied, "with eyes." He knew what it was. You couldn't live in the South and not know what it was.

"A largemouth bass!" Gault exclaimed.

He gazed at the stuffed fish as if it were a sacred icon. It was easy to see how the bass got its name; its maw could have engulfed a soccer ball.

"Fourteen pounds, four ounces," Gault announced. "Got her on a crankbait at Lake Toho. Do you have any idea what this fish was worth?"

Decker felt helpless. He felt like he was stuck in an elevator with a Jehovah's Witness.

"Seventy-five thousand dollars," Gault said.

"Christ."

"Now I got your attention, don't I?" Gault grinned. He patted the flank of the plastic bass as if it were the family dog.

"This fish," he went on, "won the Southeast Regional Bass Anglers Classic two years ago. First place was seventy-five large and a Ford Thunderbird. I gave the car to some migrants."

"All that for one fish?" Decker was amazed. Civilization was in serious trouble.

"In 1985," Gault went on, "I fished seventeen tournaments and made one hundred and seven thousand dollars, Mr. Decker. Don't look so astounded. The prize money comes from sponsors—boat makers, tackle manufacturers, bait companies, the outboard marine industry. Bass fishing is an immensely profitable business, the fastest-growing outdoor sport in America. Of course, the tournament circuit is in no way a sport, it's a cutthroat enterprise."

"But you don't need the money," Decker said.

"I need the competition."

The Ted Turner Syndrome, Decker thought.

"So what's the problem?"

"The problem is criminals," Gault said.

"Could you be more specific?"

"Cheats."

"People who lie about the size of the fish they catch—"

Gault laughed acidly. "You can't lie about the size. Dead or alive, the fish are brought back to the dock to be weighed."

"Then how can anybody cheat?"

"Ha!" Gault said, and told his story.

There had been an incident at a big-money tournament in north Texas. The contest had been sponsored by a famous plastic-worm company that had put up a quarter-million-dollar purse. At the end of the final day Dennis Gault stood on the dock with twenty-seven pounds of largemouth bass, including a nine-pounder. Normally a catch like this would have won a tournament hands down, and Gault was posing proudly with his string of fish when the last boat roared up to the dock. A man named Dickie Lockhart hopped out holding a monster bass—eleven pounds, seven ounces—which of course won first place.

"That fish," Dennis Gault recalled angrily, "had been dead for two days."

"How do you know?"

"Because I know a stiff when I see one. That fish was cold, Mr. Decker, icebox-type cold. You follow?"

"A ringer?" It was all Decker could do not to laugh.

"I know what you're thinking: Who cares if some dumb shitkicker redneck cheats with a fish? But think about this: Of the last seven big-money tournaments held in the United States, Dickie Lockhart has won five and finished second twice. That's two hundred sixty thousand bucks, which makes him not such a dumb shitkicker after all. It makes him downright respectable. He's got his own frigging TV show, if you can believe that."

Decker said, "Did you confront him about the ringer?"

"Hell, no. That's a damn serious thing, and I had no solid proof."

"Nobody else was suspicious?"

"Shit, *everybody* else was suspicious, but no one had the balls to say boo. Over beers, sure, they said they knew it was a stiff. But not to Dickie's face."

"This Lockhart, he must be a real tough guy," Decker said, needling.

"Not tough, just powerful. Most bass pros don't want to piss him off. If you want to get asked to the invitationals, you'd better be pals with Dickie. If you want product endorsements, you better kiss Dickie's ass. Same goes if you want your new outboard wholesale. It adds up. Some guys don't like Dickie Lockhart worth a shit, but they sure like to be on TV."

Decker said, "He's the only one who cheats?"

Gault hooted.

"Then what's the big deal?" Decker asked.

"The big deal"—Gault sneered—"is that Lockhart cheats in the big ones. The big deal is that he cheats against *me*. It's the difference between a Kiwanis softball game and the fucking World Series, you understand?"

"Absolutely," Decker said. He had heard enough. "Mr. Gault, I really don't think I can help you."

"Sit down."

"Look, this is not my strong suit. . . ."

"What is your strong suit? Divorces? Car repos? Workmen's comp? If you're doing so hot, maybe you wouldn't mind telling me why you're moonlighting at that shyster insurance agency where I tracked you down."

Decker headed for the door.

"The fee is fifty thousand dollars."

Decker wheeled and stared. Finally he said, "You don't need a P.I., you need a doctor."

"The money is yours if you can catch this cocksucker cheating, and prove it."

"Prove it?"

Gault said, "You were an ace photographer once. Couple big awards—I know about you, Decker. I know about your crummy temper and your run-in with the law. I also know you'd rather sleep in a tent than a Hilton, and that's fine. They say you're a little crazy, but crazy is exactly what I need."

"You want pictures?" Decker said. "Of fish."

"What better proof?" Gault glowed at the idea. "You get me a photograph of Dickie Lockhart cheating, and I'll get you published in every blessed outdoors magazine in the free world. That's a bonus, too, on top of the fee."

The cover of *Field and Stream,* Decker thought, a dream come true. "I told you," he said, "I don't know anything about tournament fishing."

"If it makes you feel any better, you weren't my first choice."

It didn't make Decker feel any better.

"The first guy I picked knew plenty about fishing," Dennis Gault said, "a real pro."

"And?"

"It didn't work out. Now I need a new guy."

Dennis Gault looked uncomfortable. "Distracted" was the word for it. He set down his drink and reached inside the desk. Out came a fake-lizardskin checkbook. Or maybe it was real.

"Twenty-five up front," Gault said, reaching for a pen.

R. J. Decker thought of the alternative and shrugged. "Make it thirty," he said.

2

To Dr. Michael Pembroke fell the task of dissecting the body of Robert Clinch.

The weight of this doleful assignment was almost unbearable because Dr. Pembroke by training was not a coroner, but a clinical pathologist. He addressed warts, cysts, tumors, and polyps with ease and certitude, but corpses terrified him, as did forensics in general.

Most Florida counties employ a full-time medical examiner, or coroner, to handle the flow of human dead. Rural Harney County could not justify such a luxury to its taxpayers, so each year the county commission voted to retain the part-time services of a pathologist to serve as coroner when needed. For the grand sum of five thousand dollars Dr. Michael Pembroke was taking his turn. The job was not unduly time-consuming, as there were only four thousand citizens in the county and they did not die often. Most who did die had the courtesy to do so at the hospital, or under routine circumstances that required neither an autopsy nor an investigation. The few Harney Countians who expired unnaturally could usually be classified as victims of (a) domestic turmoil, (b) automobile accidents, (c) hunting accidents, (d) boating accidents, or (e) lightning. Harney County had more fatal lightning strikes than any other place in Florida, though no one knew why. The local fundamentalist church had a field day with this statistic.

When news of Robert Clinch's death arrived at the laboratory,

Dr. Pembroke was staring at a common wart (*verruca vulgaris*) that had come from the thumb of a watermelon farmer. The scaly brown lump was not a pleasant sight, but it was infinitely preferable to the swollen visage of a dead bass fisherman. The doctor tried to stall and pretend he was deeply occupied at the microscope, but the sheriff's deputy waited patiently, leafing through some dermatology pamphlets. Dr. Pembroke finally gave up and got in the back of the squad car for the short ride to the morgue.

"Can you tell me what happened?" Dr. Pembroke asked, leaning forward.

"It's Bobby Clinch," the deputy said over his shoulder. "Musta flipped his boat in the lake."

Dr. Pembroke was relieved. Now he had a theory; soon he'd have a cause-of-death. In no time he could return to the wart. Maybe this wouldn't be so bad.

The police car pulled up to a low red-brick building that served as the county morgue. The building had once been leased out as a Burger King restaurant, and had not been refurbished since the county bought it. While the Burger King sign had been removed (and sold to a college fraternity house), the counters, booths, and drive-up window remained exactly as they had been in the days of the Whopper. Dr. Pembroke once wrote a letter to the county commission suggesting that a fast-food joint was hardly the proper site for a morgue, but the commissioners tersely pointed out that it was the only place in Harney with a walk-in freezer.

Peering through the plate-glass window, Dr. Pembroke saw a pudgy man with a ruddy, squashed-looking face. It was Culver Rundell, whose shoulders (the doctor remembered) had been covered with brown junctional moles. These had been expertly biopsied and found to be nonmalignant.

"Hey, doc!" Culver Rundell said as Dr. Pembroke came through the door.

"Hello," the pathologist said. "How are those moles?" Pathologists seldom have to deal with whole patients so they are notoriously weak at making small talk.

"The moles are coming back," Culver Rundell reported, "by the hundreds. My wife takes a Flair pen and plays connect-the-dots from my neck to my butthole."

"Why don't you come by the office and I'll take a look."

"Naw, doc, you done your best. I'm used to the damn things, and so's Jeannie. We make the best of the situation, if you know what I mean."

Culver Rundell ran a fish camp on Lake Jesup. He was not much of a fisherman but he loved the live-bait business, worms and wild shiners mainly. He also served as official weighmaster for some of America's most prestigious bass tournaments, and this honor Culver Rundell owed to his lifelong friendship with Dickie Lockhart, champion basser.

"Are you the one who found the deceased?" Dr. Pembroke asked.

"Nope, that was the Davidson boys."

"Which ones?" Dr. Pembroke asked. There were three sets of Davidson boys in Harney County.

"Daniel and Desi. They found Bobby floating at the bog and hauled him back to the fish camp. The boys wanted to go back out so I told 'em I'd take care of the body. We didn't have no hearse so I used my four-by-four."

Dr. Pembroke climbed over the counter into what once had been the kitchen area of the Burger King. With some effort, Culver Rundell followed.

The body of Robert Clinch lay on a long stainless-steel table. The stench was dreadful, a mixture of wet death and petrified french fries.

"Holy Jesus," said Dr. Pembroke.

"I know it," said Rundell.

"How long was he in the water?" the doctor asked.

"We were kind of hoping you'd tell us." It was the deputy, standing at the counter as if waiting for a vanilla shake.

Dr. Pembroke hated floaters and this was a beaut. Bobby Clinch's eyes were popping out of his face, milkballs on springs. An engorged tongue poked from the dead man's mouth like a fat coppery eel.

"What happened to his head?" Dr. Pembroke asked. It appeared that numerous patches of Robert Clinch's hair had been yanked raw from his scalp, leaving the checker-skulled impression of an underdressed punk rocker.

"Ducks," said Culver Rundell. "A whole flock."

"They thought it was food," the deputy explained.

"It looks like pickerel weeds, hair does. Especially hair like Bobby's," Rundell went on. "In the water it looks like weeds."

"This time of year ducks'll eat anything," the deputy added.

Dr. Pembroke felt queasy. Sometimes he wished he'd gone into radiology like his dumb cousin. With heavy stainless surgical shears he began to cut Robert Clinch's clothes off, a task made more arduous by the swollen condition of the limbs and torso. As soon as Clinch's waterlogged dungarees were cut away and more purple flesh was revealed, both Culver Rundell and the sheriff's deputy decided to wait on the other side of the counter, where they took a booth and chatted about the latest scandal with the University of Florida football team.

Fifteen minutes later, Dr. Pembroke came out with a chart on a clipboard. He was scribbling as he talked.

"The body was in the water at least twenty-four hours," he said. "Cause of death was drowning."

"Was he drunk?" Rundell asked.

"I doubt it, but I won't get the blood tests back for about a week."

"Should I tell the sheriff it was an accident?" the deputy said.

"It looks that way, yes," Dr. Pembroke said. "There was a head wound consistent with impact in a high-speed crash."

A bad bruise is what it was, consistent with any number of things, but Dr. Pembroke preferred to be definitive. Much of what he knew about forensic medicine came from watching reruns of the television show *Quincy, M.E.* Quincy the TV coroner could always glance at an injury and announce what exactly it was consistent with, so Dr. Pembroke tried to do the same. The truth was that after the other two men had left the autopsy table, Dr. Pembroke had worked as hastily as possible. He had drawn blood, made note of a golf-ball-size bruise on Bobby Clinch's skull and, with something less than surgical acuity, hacked a Y-shaped incision from the neck to the belly. He had reached in, grabbed a handful of lung, and quickly ascertained that it was full of brackish lake water, which is exactly what Dr. Pembroke wanted to see. It meant that Bobby Clinch had drowned, as suspected. Further proof was the presence of a shiny dead minnow in the right bronchus, indicating that on the way down Bobby Clinch had inhaled violently, but to no avail. Having determined this, Dr. Pembroke had wasted not another moment with the rancid body; had not even turned it over for a quick look-see before dragging it into the hamburger cooler.

The pathologist signed the death certificate and handed it to the deputy. Culver Rundell read it over the lawman's shoulder and nodded. "I'll call Clarisse," he said, "then I gotta hose out the truck."

The largemouth bass is the most popular gamefish in North America, as it can be found in the warmest waters of almost every state.

Its appeal has grown so astronomically in the last ten years that thousands of bass-fishing clubs have sprung up, and are swamped with new members. According to the sporting-goods industry, more millions of dollars are spent to catch largemouth bass than are spent on any other outdoor activity in the United States. Bass magazines promote the species as the workingman's fish, available to anyone within strolling distance of a lake, river, culvert, reservoir, rockpit, or drainage ditch. The bass is not picky; it is hardy, prolific, and on a given day will eat just about any God-awful lure dragged in front of its maw. As a fighter it is bullish, but tires easily; as a jumper its skills are admirable, though no match for a graceful rainbow trout or tarpon; as table fare it is blandly acceptable, even tasty when properly seasoned. Its astonishing popularity comes from a modest combination of these traits, plus the simple fact that there are so many largemouth bass swimming around that just about any damn fool can catch one.

Its democratic nature makes the bass an ideal tournament fish, and a marketing dream-come-true for the tackle industry. Because a large-mouth in Seattle is no different from its Everglades cousin, expensive bass-fishing products need no regionalization, no tailored advertising. This is why hard-core bass fishermen everywhere are outfitted exactly the same, from their trucks to their togs to their tackle. On any body of water, in any county rural or urban, the uniform and arsenal of the bassing fraternity are unmistakable. The universal mission is to catch one of those freakishly big bass known as lunkers or hawgs. In many parts of the country, any fish over five pounds is considered a trophy, and it is not uncommon for the ardent basser to have three or four such specimens mounted on the walls of his home; one for the living room, one for the den, and so on. The geographic range of truly gargantuan fish, ten to fifteen pounds, is limited to the humid Deep South, particularly Georgia and Florida. In these areas the quest for the world's biggest bass is rabid and ruthless; for tournament fishermen this is the big leagues, where top prize money for a two-day event might equal seventy-five thousand dollars. If the weather on these days happens to be rotten or the water too cold, a dinky four-pound bass might win the whole shooting match. More than likely, though, it takes a lunker fish to win the major tournaments, and few anglers are capable of catching lunkers day in and day out.

Weekend anglers are fond of noting that the largest bass ever caught was not landed by a tournament fisherman. It was taken by a nineteen-year-old Georgia farm kid named George W. Perry at an oxbow slough called Montgomery Lake. Fittingly, young Perry had never heard of Lowrance fish-finders or Thruster trolling motors or Fenwick graphite flipping sticks. Perry went out fishing in a simple rowboat and took the only bass lure he owned, a beat-up Creek Chub. He went fishing mainly because his family was hungry, and he returned with a largemouth bass that weighed twenty-two pounds, four ounces. The year was 1932. Since then, despite all the space-age advancements in fish-catching technology, nobody has boated a bass that comes close to the size of George Perry's trophy, which he and his loved ones promptly ate for dinner. Today an historical plaque commemorating this leviathan largemouth stands on Highway 117, near Lumber City, Georgia. It serves as a defiant and nagging challenge to modern bass fishermen and all their infernal electronics. Some ichthyologists have been so bold as to suggest that the Monster of Montgomery Lake was a supremely mutant fish, an all-tackle record that will never be bested by any angler. To which Dickie Lockhart, in closing each segment of *Fish Fever,* would scrunch up his eyes, wave a finger at the camera, and decree: "George Perry, next week your cracker butt is history!"

There was no tournament that weekend, so Dickie Lockhart was taping a show. He was shooting on Lake Kissimmee, not far from Disney World. The title of this particular episode was "Hawg Hunting." Dickie needed a bass over ten pounds; anything less wasn't a hawg.

As always, he used two boats; one to fish from, one for the film crew. Like most TV fishing-show hosts, Dickie Lockhart used videotapes because they were cheaper than sixteen-millimeter, and reusable. Film was unthinkable for a bass show because you might go two or three days shooting nothing but men casting their lures and spitting tobacco, but no fish. With the video, a bad day didn't blow the whole budget because you just backed it up and shot again.

Dickie Lockhart had been catching bass all morning, little two- and three-pounders. He could guess the weight as soon as he hooked up, then furiously skitter the poor fish across the surface into the boat. "Goddammit," he would shout, "rewind that sucker and let's try again."

During lulls in the action, Dickie would grow tense and foul-mouthed. "Come on, you bucket-mouthed bastards," he'd growl as he cast at the shoreline, "hit this thing or I'm bringing dynamite tomorrow, y'hear?"

Midmorning the wind kicked up, mussing Dickie Lockhart's shiny black hair. "Goddammit," he shouted, "stop the tape." After he got a comb from his tacklebox and slicked himself down, he ordered the cameraman to crank it up again.

"How do I look?" Dickie asked.

"Like a champ," the cameraman said thinly. The cameraman dreamed of the day when Dickie Lockhart would get shitfaced drunk and drop his drawers to moon his little ole fishing pals all across America. Then Dickie would fall out of the boat, as he often did after drinking. Afterward the cameraman would pretend to rewind the videotape and erase this sloppy moment, but of course he wouldn't. He'd save it and, when the time was right, threaten to send it to the sports-and-religion network that syndicated Dickie Lockhart's fishing show. Dickie would suddenly become a generous fellow, and the cameraman would finally be able to afford to take his wife to the Virgin Islands.

Now, with the tape rolling, Dickie Lockhart was talking man-to-man with the serious bass angler back home. Dickie's TV accent was much thicker and gooier than his real-life accent, an exaggeration that was necessary to meet the demographic of the show, which was basically male Deep Southern grit-suckers. As he cast his lure and reeled it in, Dickie Lockhart would confide exactly what brand of crankbait he was using, what pound line was on the reel, what kind of sunglasses (amber or green) worked better on a bright day. The patter carried an air of informality and friendliness, when in fact the point was to shill as many of Dickie Lockhart's sponsors' products as possible in twenty-four minutes of live tape. The crankbait was made by Bagley, the line by Du Pont, the reel by Shimano, the sunglasses by Polaroid, and so on. Somehow, when Dickie stared into the camera and dropped these bald-faced plugs, it didn't seem so cheap.

At about noon a third bass boat raced up to the fishing spot, and Dickie started hollering like a madman. "Goddammit, stop the tape! Stop the tape!" He hopped up and down on the bow and shook his fist at the man in the other boat. "Hey, can't you see we're filming a goddamn TV show here? You got the whole frigging lake but you gotta stop here and wreck the tape!" Then he saw that the other angler was Ozzie Rundell, Culver's brother, so Dickie stopped shouting. He didn't apologize, but he did pipe down.

"Didn't mean to interrupt," Ozzie said. He was a mumbler. Dickie Lockhart told him to speak up.

"Didn't mean to interrupt!" Ozzie said, a bit louder. In his entire life he had never boated a bass over four pounds, and was in awe of Dickie Lockhart.

"Well?" Dickie said.

"I thought you'd want to know."

Dickie shook his head. He kicked a button on the bow and used the trolling motor to steer his boat closer to Ozzie's. When the two were side by side, Dickie said impatiently, "Now start over."

"I thought you'd want to know. They found Bobby Clinch."

"Where?"

"Dead."

Ozzie would get around to answering the questions, but not in the order he was asked. His mind worked that way.

"How?" Dickie said.

"In Lake Harney."

"When?"

"Flipped his boat and drowned," Ozzie said.

"Goddamn," said Dickie Lockhart. "I'm sorry."

"Yesterday," Ozzie said in conclusion.

Dickie turned to the cameraman and said, "Well, that's it for the day."

Ozzie seemed thrilled just to be able to touch the deck of the champion's boat. He gazed at Dickie Lockhart's fishing gear the way a Little Leaguer might stare at Ted Williams' bat. "Well, sorry to interrupt," he mumbled.

"Don't worry about it," Dickie Lockhart said. "They stopped biting two hours ago."

"What plug you usin'?" Ozzie inquired.

"My special baby," Dickie said, "the Double Whammy."

The Double Whammy was the hottest lure on the pro bass circuit, thanks in large measure to Dickie Lockhart. For the last eight tournaments he'd won, Dickie had declared it was the amazing Double Whammy that had tricked the trophy fish. His phenomenal success with the lure—a skirted spinnerbait with twin silver spoons—had not been duplicated by any other professional angler, though all had tried, filling their tackleboxes with elaborate variations and imitations. Most of the bassers caught big fish on the Double Whammy, but none caught as many, or at such opportune times, as Dickie Lockhart.

"It's a real killer, huh?" Ozzie said.

"You betcha," Dickie said. He took the fishing line in his front teeth and bit through, freeing the jangling lure. "You want it?" he asked.

Ozzie Rundell beamed like a kid on Christmas morning. "Shoot yeah!"

Dickie Lockhart tossed the lure toward Ozzie's boat. In his giddiness Ozzie actually tried to catch the thing in his bare hands. He missed, of course, and the Double Whammy embedded its needle-sharp hook firmly in the poor man's cheek. Ozzie didn't seem to feel a thing; didn't seem to notice the blood dripping down his jawline.

"Thanks!" he shouted as Dickie Lockhart started up his boat. "Thanks a million!"

"Don't mention it," the champion replied, leaning on the throttle.

3

R. J. Decker had been born in Texas. His father had been an FBI man, and the family had lived in Dallas until December of 1963. Two weeks after Kennedy was shot, Decker's father was transferred to Miami and assigned to a crack squad whose task was to ensure that no pals of Fidel Castro took a shot at LBJ. It was a tense and exciting time, but it passed. Decker's father eventually wound up in a typically stupefying FBI desk job, got fat, and died of clogged arteries at age forty-nine. One of Decker's older brothers grew up to be a cop in Minneapolis. The other sold Porsches to cocaine dealers in San Francisco.

A good athlete and a fair student in college, R. J. Decker surprised all his classmates by becoming a professional photographer. Cameras were his private passion; he was fascinated with the art of freezing time in the eye. He never told anyone but it was the Zapruder film that had done it. When *Life* magazine had come out with those grainy movie pictures of the assassination, R. J. Decker was only eight years old. Still he was transfixed by the frames of the wounded president and his wife. The pink of her dress, the black blur of the Lincoln— horrific images, yet magnetic. The boy never imagined such a moment could be captured and kept for history. Soon afterward he got his first camera.

For Decker, photography was more than just a hobby, it was a way of looking at the world. He had been cursed with a short temper and a cynical outlook, so the darkroom became a soothing place, and the ceremony of making pictures a gentle therapy.

Much to his frustration, the studio-photography business proved unbearably dull and profitable. Decker did weddings, bar mitzvahs, portraits, and commercial jobs, mostly magazine advertisements. He was once paid nine thousand dollars to take the perfect picture of a bottle of Midol. The ad showed up in all the big women's magazines, and Decker clipped several copies to send to his friends, as a joke on himself.

And, of course, there were the fashion layouts with professional models. The first year Decker fell in love seventeen times. The second year he let the Hasselblad do the falling in love. His pictures were very good, he was making large sums of money, and he was bored out of his skull.

One afternoon on Miami Beach, while Decker was on a commercial shoot for a new tequila-scented suntan oil, a young tourist suddenly tore off her clothes and jumped into the Atlantic and tried to drown herself. The lifeguards reached her just in time, and Decker snapped a couple of frames as they carried her from the surf. The woman's blond hair was tangled across her cheeks, her eyes were puffy and half-closed, and her lips were grey. What really made the photograph was the face of one of the lifeguards who had rescued the young woman. He'd carefully wrapped his arms around her bare chest to shield her from the gawkers, and in his eyes Decker's lens had captured both panic and pity.

For the hell of it Decker gave the roll of film to a newspaper reporter who had followed the paramedics to the scene. The next day the Miami *Sun* published Decker's photograph on the front page, and paid him the grand sum of thirty dollars. The day after that, the managing editor offered him a full-time job and Decker said yes.

In some ways it was the best move he ever made. In some ways it was the worst. Decker only wished he would have lasted longer.

He thought of this as he drove into Harney County, starting a new case, working for a man he didn't like at all.

Harney was Dickie Lockhart's hometown, and the personal headquarters of his bass-fishing empire.

Upon arrival the first thing Decker did was to find Ott Pickney, which was easy. Ott was not a man on the move.

He wrote obituaries for the Harney *Sentinel,* which published two times a week, three during boar season. The leisurely pace of the small newspaper suited Ott Pickney perfectly because it left plenty of time for golf and gardening. Before moving to Central Florida, Pickney had worked for seventeen years at the Miami *Sun,* which is where Decker had met him. At first Decker had assumed from Ott's sluggish behavior that here was a once-solid reporter languishing in the twilight of his career; it soon became clear that Ott Pickney's career had begun in twilight and grown only dimmer. That he had lasted so long in Miami was the result of a dense newsroom bureaucracy that always seemed to find a place for him, no matter how useless he was. Ott was one of those newspaper characters who got passed from one department to another until, after so many years, he had become such a sad fixture that no editor wished to be remembered as the one who fired him. Consequently, Ott didn't get fired. He retired from the *Sun* at full pension and moved to Harney to write obits and grow prizewinning orchids.

R. J. Decker found Pickney in the *Sentinel*'s newsroom, such as it was. There were three typewriters, five desks, and four telephones. Ott was lounging at the coffee machine; nothing had changed.

He grinned when Decker walked in. "R.J.! God Almighty, what brings you here? Your car break down or what?"

Decker smiled and shook Ott's hand. He noticed that Ott was wearing baggy brown trousers and a blue Banlon shirt. Probably the last Banlon shirt in America. How could you not like a guy who wasn't ashamed to dress like this?

"You look great," Decker said.

"And I feel great, R.J., I really do. Hey, I know it's not exactly the big city, but I had my fill of that, didn't I?" Ott was talking a little too loudly. "We got out just in time, R.J., you and me. That paper would have killed both of us one way or another."

"It tried."

"Yeah, boy," Ott said. "Sandy, get over here! I want you to meet somebody." A wrenlike man with thick eyeglasses walked over and nodded cautiously at Decker. "R.J., this is Sandy Kilpatrick, my editor. Sandy, this is R. J. Decker. R.J. and I worked together down in the Magic City. I wrote the prose, he took the snapshots. We covered that big voodoo murder together, remember, R.J.?"

Decker remembered. He remembered it wasn't exactly a big voodoo murder. Some redneck mechanic in Hialeah had killed his wife by sticking her with pins; safety pins, hundreds of them. The me-

chanic had read something about voodoo in *Argosy* magazine and
had totally confused the rituals. He loaded his wife up on Barbancourt
rum and started pricking away until she bled to death. Then he
pretended to come home from work and find her dead. He blamed
the crime on a Haitian couple down the street, claiming they had
put a hex on his house and Oldsmobile. The cops didn't go for this
and the redneck mechanic wound up on Death Row.

As Ott was reinventing this story, Sandy Kilpatrick stared at R. J.
Decker the way visitors from Miami got stared at in this part of
Florida. Like they were trouble. Kilpatrick obviously had heard Ott's
voodoo-murder story about four hundred times and soon started to
shrink away.

"Nice meeting you," Decker said.

Kilpatrick nodded again as he slipped out of the office.

"Good kid," Ott Pickney said avuncularly. "He's learning."

Decker helped himself to a cup of coffee. His legs were stiff from
the long drive.

"What the hell brings you here?" Ott asked amiably.

"Fish," Decker said.

"Didn't know you were a basser."

"I thought I'd give it a try," Decker said. "They say Harney's a
real hotspot for the big ones."

"Lunkers," Ott said.

Decker looked at him quizzically.

"In these parts, they're not *big ones,* they're lunkers," Ott explained.
"The most mammoth bass in the hemisphere."

"Hawgs," Decker said, remembering one of Dennis Gault's phrases.

"Sure, you got it!"

"Where's the best place to try, this time of year?"

Ott Pickney sat down at his desk. "Boy, R.J., I really can't help
you much. The man to see is Jamie Belliroso, our sports guy."

"Where can I find him?"

"Maui," Ott Pickney said.

Jamie Belliroso, it turned out, was one of a vanishing breed of
sportswriters who would accept any junket tossed their way, as long
as gourmet food and extensive travel were involved. This month it
was a marlin-fishing extravaganza in Hawaii, sponsored by a company
that manufactured polyethylene fish baits. Jamie Belliroso's air fare,
room, and board would all be paid for with the quiet understanding
that the name of the bait company would be mentioned a mere eight

or ten times in his feature article, and that the name of the company would be spelled correctly—which, in Belliroso's case, was never a sure thing. In the meantime, the blue marlin were striking and Jamie was enjoying the hell out of Maui.

"When will he be back?" Decker asked.

"Who knows," Ott said. "From Hawaii he's off to Christmas Island for bonefish."

Decker said, "Anyone else who could help me? Someone mentioned a guide named Dickie Lockhart."

Ott laughed. "A *guide?* My friend, Dickie's not a guide, he's a god. A big-time bass pro. The biggest."

"What does that mean?"

"It means he wouldn't be seen in the same boat with a greenhorn putz like you. Besides, Dickie doesn't hire out."

Decker decided not to mention Dennis Gault's grave allegations. Ott was obviously a huge fan of Dickie Lockhart's. Decker wondered if the whole town was as starstruck.

"There's a couple good guides work out on the lake," Ott suggested. "Think they're up to two hundred dollars a day."

The world has gone mad, Decker thought. "That's too rich for my blood," he said to Ott.

"Yeah, it's steep all right, but they don't give the tourist much choice. See, they got a union."

"A union?" It was all too much.

"The Lake Jesup Bass Captains Union. They keep the charter rates fixed, I'm afraid."

"Christ, Ott, I came here to catch a fish and you're telling me the lake's locked up by the fucking Izaak Walton division of the Teamsters. What a swell little town you've got here."

"It's not like that," Ott Pickney said in a you-don't-understand tone. "Besides, there's other options. One, rent yourself a skiff and give it a shot alone—"

"I wouldn't know where to start," Decker said.

"Or two, you can try this guy who lives out at the lake."

"Don't tell me he's not in the union?"

"He's the only one," Ott said. "When you meet him you'll know why." Ott rolled his eyeballs theatrically.

Decker said, "I sense you're trying to tell me the man is loony."

"They say he knows the bass," Ott said. "They also say he's dangerous."

Decker was in the market for a renegade. The mystery man sounded like a good possibility.

"What does he charge?" Decker asked, still playing the rube.

"I have no idea," Ott said. "After you see him, you may want to reconsider. In that case you can hook up with one of the regulars out of Rundell's marina."

Decker shook his head. "They sound like hot dogs, Ott. I just want to relax."

Ott's brow wrinkled. "I know these folks, R.J. I like 'em, too. Now I won't sit here and tell you bassers are completely normal, 'cause that's not true either. They're slightly manic. They got boats that'll outrace a Corvette, and they're fairly crazy out on the water. Just the other day I wrote up a young man who flipped his rig doing about sixty on the lake. Hit a cypress knee and punched out."

"He died?"

"It was dawn. Foggy. Guess he was racing his pals to the fishing hole." Pickney chuckled harshly. "No brakes on a boat, partner."

"Didn't the same thing happen a few years ago in one of those big tournaments?" Decker said. "I read about it in the Orlando papers. Two boats crashed on the way out."

Ott said, "Yeah, over on Apopka. Officially it's a grand-prix start, but the boys call it a blast-off. Fifty boats taking off from a dead stop." Ott shaped his hands into two speedboats and gave a demonstration. "Kaboom! Hell, those tournaments are something else, R.J. You ought to do a color layout sometime."

"I've heard all kinds of stuff goes on. Cheating and everything."

"Aw, I heard that too, and I just can't believe it. How in the world can you cheat? Either you've got fish on a stringer, or you don't." Ott sniffed at the idea. "I know these folks and I don't buy it, not for a second. Texas, maybe, sure. But not here."

Ott Pickney acted like it was all city talk. He acted like the desk made him an authority—his desk, his newsroom, his town. Ott's ego was adapting quite well to the rural life, Decker thought. The wise old pro from Miami.

Pickney perked up. "You on expense account?"

"A good one," Decker said.

"Buy me lunch?"

"Sure, Ott."

"The guy at the lake, his name is Skink. As I said, they talk like he's only got one oar in the water, so watch your step. One time we sent a kid to write a little feature story about him and this Skink took an ax and busted the windows out of the kid's car. He lives in a cabin off the old Mormon Trail. You can't miss it, R.J., it's right on the lake. Looks like a glorified outhouse."

"Skink what?" Decker asked.

"That's his whole name," Ott Pickney said. "That's all he needs up here." He rolled his chair back and clomped his shoes up on the bare desk. "See, sport, you're not in Miami anymore."

The man named Skink said, "Go."

"I need to talk to you."

"You got thirty seconds." The man named Skink had a gun. A Remington, Decker noted. The rifle lay across his lap.

It was a large lap. Skink appeared to be in his late forties, early fifties. He sat in a canvas folding chair on the porch of his cabin. He wore Marine-style boots and an orange rainsuit, luminous even in the twilight. The shape and features of his face were hard to see, but Skink's silver-flecked hair hung in a braided rope down his back. Decker figured long hair was risky in this part of the woods, but Skink was substantial enough to set his own style.

"My name is Decker."

"You from the IRS?" The man's voice was deep and wet, like mud slipping down a drain.

"No," Decker said.

"I pay no taxes," Skink said. He was wearing a rainhat, though it wasn't raining. He was also wearing sunglasses and the sun was down. "I pay no attention to taxes," Skink asserted. "Not since Nixon, the goddamn thief."

"I'm not from the government," Decker said carefully. "I'm a private investigator."

Skink grunted.

"Like Barnaby Jones," Decker ventured.

Skink raised the rifle and aimed at Decker's heart. "I pay no attention to television," he said.

"Forget I mentioned it. Please."

Skink held the gun steady. Decker felt moisture bead on the back of his neck. "Put the gun away," he said.

"I don't know," Skink said. "I feel like shooting tonight."

Decker thought: Just my luck. "I heard you do some guiding," he said.

Skink's gun lowered a fraction of an inch. "I do."

"For bass," Decker said. "Bass fishing."

"Hundred bucks a day, no matter."

"Fine," Decker said.

"You'll call me captain?"

"If you want."

Skink lowered the rifle all the way. Decker reached into his pocket and pulled out a one-hundred-dollar bill. He unfolded it, smoothed it out, and offered it to Skink.

"Put it away. Pay when we get your fish in the boat." Skink looked annoyed. "You act like you still want to talk."

For some reason the banjo music from *Deliverance* kept tinkling in Decker's head. It got louder every time he took a good look at Skink's face.

"Talk," Skink said. "Quick." He reached over and set the rifle in a corner, its barrel pointing up. Then he removed the sunglasses. His eyes were green; not hazel or olive, but deep green, like Rocky Mountain evergreens. His eyebrows, tangled and ratty, grew at an angle that gave his tanned face the cast of perpetual anger. Decker wondered how many repeat customers a guide like Skink could have.

"Do you fish the tournaments?"

"Not anymore," Skink said. "If it's tournament fish you're after, keep your damn money."

"It's cheaters I'm after," Decker said.

Skink sat up so suddenly that his plastic rainsuit squeaked. The forest-green eyes impaled R. J. Decker while the mouth chewed hard on the corners of its mustache. Skink took a deep breath and when his chest filled, he looked twice as big. It was only when he got to his feet that Decker saw what a diesel he truly was.

"I'm hungry," Skink said. He took ten steps toward his truck, stopped, and said, "Well, Miami, come on."

As the pickup bounced down the old Mormon Trail, Decker said, "Captain, how'd you know where I was from?"

"Haircut."

"That bad?"

"Distinctive."

"Distinctive" was not a word Decker expected to hear from the captain's lips. Obviously this was not the type of fellow you could sort out in a day, or even two.

Skink steered the truck onto Route 222 and headed south. He

drove slow, much slower than he had driven on the trail. Decker noticed that he hunched himself over the wheel, and peered hawklike through the windshield.

"What's the matter?" Decker asked.

"Hush."

Cars and trucks were flying by at sixty miles an hour. Skink was barely doing twenty. Decker was sure they were about to get rear-ended by a tractor-trailer.

"You all right?"

"I pay no attention to the traffic," Skink said. He turned the wheel hard to the right and took the truck off the road, skidding in the gravel. Before Decker could react, the big man leapt from the cab and dashed back into the road. Decker saw him snatch something off the center line and toss it onto the shoulder.

"What the hell are you doing?" Decker shouted, but his voice died in the roar of a passing gasoline tanker. He looked both ways before jogging across the highway to join Skink on the other side.

Skink was kneeling next to a plump, misshapen lump of gray fur.

Decker saw it was a dead opossum. Skink ran a hand across its furry belly. "Still warm," he reported.

Decker said nothing.

"Road kill," Skink said, by way of explanation. He took a knife out of his belt. "You hungry, Miami?"

Decker said uneasily, "How about if we just stop someplace and I buy you supper?"

"No need," Skink said, and he sawed off the opossum's head. He lifted the carcass by its pink tail and stalked back to the truck. Decker now understood the reason for the fluorescent rainsuit; a speeding motorist could see Skink a mile away. He looked like a neon yeti.

"You'll like the flavor," Skink remarked as Decker got in the truck beside him.

"I think I'll pass."

"Nope."

"What?"

"We both eat, that's the deal. Then you get the hell out. Another day we'll talk fish."

Skink pulled the rainhat down tight on his skull.

"And after that," he said, turning the ignition, "we might even talk about cheaters."

"So you know about this?" Decker said.

Skink laughed bitterly. "I do, sir, but I wisht I didn't."

Clouds of insects swirled in and out of the high-beams as the truck jounced down the dirt road. Suddenly Skink killed the lights and cut the ignition. The pickup coasted to a stop.

"Listen!" Skink said.

Decker heard an engine. It sounded like a lawn mower.

Skink jumped from the truck and ran into the trees. This time Decker was right behind him.

"I told the bastards," Skink said, panting.

"Who?" Decker asked. It seemed as if they were running toward the noise, not away from it.

"I told them," Skink repeated. They broke out of the pines, onto a bluff, and Skink immediately shrank into a crouch. Below them was a small stream, with a dirt rut following the higher ground next to the water. A single headlight bobbed on the trail.

Decker could see it clearly—a lone rider on a dirt bike. Up close the motorcycle sounded like a chainsaw, the growl rising and falling with the hills. Soon the rider would pass directly beneath them.

Decker saw that Skink had a pistol in his right hand.

"What the hell are you doing?"

"Quiet, Miami."

Skink extended his right arm, aiming. Decker lunged, too late. The noise of the gun knocked him on his back.

The dirt bike went down like a lame horse. The rider screamed as he flew over the handlebars.

Dirt spitting from its rear tire, the bike tumbled down the embankment and splashed into the stream, where the engine choked and died in bubbles.

Up the trail, the rider moaned and began to extricate himself from a cabbage palm.

"Christ!" Decker said, his breath heavy.

Skink tucked the pistol in his pants. "Front tire," he reported, almost smiling. "Told you I was in the mood to shoot."

Back at the shack, Skink barbecued the opossum on an open spit and served it with fresh corn, collards, and strawberries. Decker focused on the vegetables because the opossum tasted gamy and terrible; he could only take Skink's word that the animal was fresh and had not lain dead on the highway for days.

As they sat by the fire, Decker wondered why the ferocious mosquitoes were concentrating on his flesh, while Skink seemed immune. Perhaps the captain's blood was lethal.

"Who hired you?" Skink asked through a mouthful of meat.

Decker told him who, and why.

Skink stopped chewing and stared.

"You know Mr. Gault?" Decker asked.

"I know lots of folks."

"Dickie Lockhart?"

Skink bit clean through a possum bone. "Sure."

"Lockhart's the cheater," Decker said.

"You're getting close."

"There's more?" Decker asked.

"Hell, yes!" Skink tossed the bone into the lake, where its splash startled a mallard.

"More," Skink muttered. "More, more, more."

"Let's hear it, captain," Decker said.

"Another night." Skink spit something brown into the fire and scowled at nothing in particular. "How much you getting paid?"

Decker was almost embarrassed to tell him. "Fifty grand," he said.

Skink didn't even blink. "Not enough," he said. "Come on, Miami, finish your damn supper."

4

Ott Pickney stopped by the motel before eight the next morning. He knocked loudly on R. J. Decker's door.

Groggily, Decker let him in. "So how'd it go?" Ott asked.

"A lively night."

"Is he as kooky as they say?"

"Hard to tell," Decker said. Living in Miami tended to recalibrate one's view of sanity.

Ott said he was on his way to a funeral. "That poor fella I told you about."

"The fisherman?"

"Bobby Clinch," Ott said. "Sandy wants a tearjerker for the week-end paper—it's the least we can do for a local boy. You and Skink going out for bass?"

"Not this morning." Skink had left the proposition in the air. Decker planned to meet him later.

Ott Pickney said, "Why don't you ride along with me?"

"To a funeral?"

"The whole town's closing down for it," Ott said. "Besides, I thought you might want to see some big-time bassers up close. Bobby had loads of friends."

"Give me a second to shower."

Decker hated funerals. Working for the newspaper, he'd had to cover too many grim graveside services, from a cop shot by some coked-up creep to a toddler raped and murdered by her babysitter. Child murders got plenty of play in the papers, and a shot of the grieving parents was guaranteed to run four columns, minimum. A funeral like that was the most dreaded assignment in journalism. Decker didn't know quite what to expect in Harney. For him it was strictly business, a casual surveillance. Maybe even Dickie Lockhart would show up, Decker thought as he toweled off. He was eager to get a glimpse of the town celebrity.

They rode to the graveyard in Ott Pickney's truck. Almost everyone else in Harney owned a Ford or a Chevy, but Ott drove a new Toyota flatbed. "Orchids," he explained, a bit defensively, "don't take up much space."

"It's a fine truck," Decker offered.

Ott lit a Camel so Decker rolled down the window. It was a breezy morning and the air was cold, blowing dead from the north.

"Can I ask something?" Ott said. "It's personal."

"Fire away."

"I heard you got divorced."

"Right," Decker said.

"That's a shame, R.J. She seemed like a terrific kid."

"The problem was money," Decker said. "He had some, I didn't." His wife had run off with a timeshare-salesman-turned-chiropractor. Life didn't get any meaner.

"Jesus, I'm sorry." The divorce wasn't really what Ott wanted to talk about. "I heard something else," he said.

"Probably true," Decker said. "I did ten months at Apalachee, if that's what you heard."

Pickney was sucking so hard on the cigarette that the ash was three inches long. Decker was afraid it would drop into Ott's lap and set his pants on fire, which is what had happened one day in the newsroom of the Miami *Sun*. None of the fire extinguishers had been working, so Ott had been forced to straddle a drinking fountain to douse the flames.

"Do you mind talking about it?" Ott said. "I understand if you'd rather not."

Decker said, "It was after one of the Dolphin games. I was parked about four blocks from the stadium. Coming back to the car, I spotted some jerkoff breaking into the trunk, trying to rip off the cameras. I told him to stop, he ran. He was carrying two Nikons and a brand-new Leica. No way was I going to let him get away."

"You caught up with him?"

"Yeah, he fell and I caught up to him. I guess I got carried away."

Pickney shook his head and spit the dead Camel butt out the window. "Ten months! I can't believe they'd give you that much time for slugging a burglar."

"Not just any burglar—a football star at Palmetto High," Decker said. "Three of his sisters testified that they'd witnessed the whole thing. Said Big Brother never stole the cameras. Said he was minding his own business, juking on the corner when I drove up and asked where I could score some weed. Said Big Brother told me to get lost, and I jumped out of my car and pounded him into dog meat. All of which was a goddamn lie."

"So then?"

"So the state attorney's office dropped the burglary charge on Mr. Football Hero, and nailed me for agg assault. He gets a scholarship to USC, I get felony arts-and-crafts. That's the whole yarn."

Pickney sighed. "And you lost your job."

"The newspaper had no choice, Ott." Not with the boy's father raising so much hell. The boy's father was Levon Bennett, big wheel on the Orange Bowl Committee, board chairman of about a hundred banks. Decker had always thought the newspaper might have rehired him after Apalachee if only Levon Bennett wasn't in the same Sunday golf foursome as the executive publisher.

"You always had a terrible temper."

"Luck, too. Of all the thieves worth stomping in Miami, I've got to pick a future Heisman Trophy winner." Decker laughed sourly.

"So now you're a . . ."

"Private investigator," Decker said. Obviously Ott was having a little trouble getting to the point.

The point being what in the hell Decker was doing as a P.I. "I burned out on newspapers," he said to Ott.

"With your portfolio you could have done anything, R.J. Magazines, free-lance, the New York agencies. You could write your own ticket."

"Not with a rap sheet," Decker said.

It was a comfortable lie. A lawyer friend had arranged for Decker's criminal record to be legally expunged, wiped off the computer, so the rap sheet wasn't really the problem.

The truth was, Decker had to get away from the news business. He needed a divorce from photography because he had started to see life and death as a sequence of frames; Decker's mind had started to work like his goddamn cameras, and it scared him. The night he made up his mind was the night the city desk had sent him out on what everybody figured was a routine drug homicide. Something stinky dripping from the trunk of a new Seville parked on the sky level of the Number Five Garage at Miami International. Decker got there just as the cops were drilling the locks. Checked the motor drive on the Leica. Got down on one knee. Felt the cold dampness seep through his trousers. *Raining like a bitch.* Trunk pops open. *A young woman, used to be, anyway.* Heels, nylons, pretty silk dress, except for the brown stains. *Stench bad enough to choke a maggot.* He'd been expecting the usual Juan Doe—Latin male, mid-twenties, dripping gold, no ID, multiple gunshot wounds. *Not a girl with a coat hanger wrapped around her neck.* Not Leslie. Decker refocused. *Leslie.* Jesus Christ, he knew this girl, worked with her at the paper. Decker fed the Leica more film. She was a fashion writer—who the fuck'd want to murder a fashion writer? *Her husband, said a homicide guy.* Decker bracketed the shots, changed angles to get some of the hair, but no face. Paper won't print faces of the dead, that's policy. He fired away, thinking: I know this girl, so why can't I stop? *Leica whispering in the rain, click-click-click.* Oh God, she's a friend of mind so why the fuck can't I stop. *Husband told her they were flying to Disney World, big romantic weekend, said the homicide man.* Decker reloaded, couldn't help himself. *Strangled her right here, stuffed her in the trunk, grabbed his suitcase, and hopped a plane for Key West with a barmaid from North Miami Beach.* She'd only been married what, three months? *Four, said the homicide guy, welcome to the Magic Kingdom. Haven't you got enough pictures for Chrissakes?* Sure, Decker said, but he couldn't look at Leslie's body unless it was through the lens, so he ran back to his car and threw up his guts in a puddle.

Three days later, Levon Bennett's son tried to steal R. J. Decker's cameras outside the stadium, and Decker chased him down and beat him unconscious. Those are my eyes, he'd said as he slugged the punk. Without them I'm fucking blind, don't you understand?

At Apalachee he'd met a very nice doctor doing four years for Medicare fraud, who gave him the name of an insurance company that needed an investigator. Sometimes the investigator had to take his own pictures—"sometimes" was about all Decker figured he could handle. Besides, he was broke and never wanted to see the inside of a newsroom again. So he tried one free-lance job for the insurance company—took a picture of a forty-two-foot Bertram that was supposed to be sunk off Cat Island but wasn't—and got paid two thousand dollars. Decker found the task to be totally painless and profitable. Once his rap sheet was purged, he applied for his P.I. license and purchased two cameras, a Nikon and a Canon, both used. The work was small potatoes, no Pulitzers but no pain. Most important, he had discovered with more and more cases that he still loved the cameras but could see just fine without them—no blood and gore in the darkroom, just mug shots and auto tags and grainy telescopic stills of married guys sneaking out of motels.

None of this he told Ott Pickney. Being a private detective isn't so bad, is what he said, and the pay's good. "It's just temporary," Decker lied, "until I figure out what I want to do."

Ott managed a sympathetic smile. He was trying to be a pal. "You were a fine photographer, R.J."

"Still am," Decker said with a wink. "I waltzed out of that newspaper with a trunkload of free Ektachrome."

The funeral was like nothing R. J. Decker had ever seen, and he'd been to some beauties. Jonestown. Beirut. Benghazi.

But this was one for the books. The L. L. Bean catalog, to be exact.

They were burying Bobby Clinch in his bass boat.

Actually, part of the boat. The blue metal-flake hull had been sawed up and hewn into a coffin. It wasn't a bad job, either, especially on short notice.

Clarisse Clinch thought it a ghastly idea until the Harney County Bass Blasters Club had offered to pay the bill. The funeral director was a dedicated fisherman, which made it easier to overlook certain state burial regulations concerning casket material.

R. J. Decker resisted the urge to grab an F-1 and shoot some pictures. The last thing he needed in the viewfinder was a shrieking widow.

The thirty-acre cemetery was known locally as Our Lady of Tropicana, since it had been carved out of a moribund citrus grove. The mourners stood in the sunshine on a gentle green slope. The preacher had finished the prayer and was preparing to lay Bobby Clinch's soul to rest.

"I know some of you were out on Lake Jesup this morning and missed the church service," the preacher said. "Clarisse has been kind enough to let us open the casket one more time so you boys—Bobby's fishing buddies—can pay your eternal respects."

Decker leaned over to Ott Pickney. "Which one is Lockhart?"

"Don't see him," Ott said.

A line of men, many dressed in khaki jumpsuits or bright flotation vests, a few still sloshing in their waders, filed by the sparkly blue casket. The undertaker had done a miraculous job, all things considered. The bloatedness of the body's features had been minimized by heavy pink makeup and artful eye shadows. Although the man in the casket did not much resemble the Bobby Clinch that his pals had known, it could easily have been an older and chubbier brother. While some of the fishermen reached in and tugged affectionately at the bill of Bobby's cap (which concealed what the ducks had done to his hair), others placed sentimental tokens in the coffin with their dead companion; fishing lures, mostly: Rapalas, Bombers, Jitterbugs, Snagless Sallies, Gollywompers, Hula Poppers, River Runts. Some of the lures were cracked or faded, the hooks bent and rusted, but each represented a special memory of a day on the water with Bobby Clinch. Clarisse made an effort to appear moved by this fraternal ceremony, but her thoughts were drifting. She already had a line on a buyer for her husband's Blazer.

Ott Pickney and R. J. Decker were among the last to walk by the casket. By now the inside looked like a display rack at a tackle shop. A fishing rod lay like a sword at the dead man's side.

Ott remarked, "Pearl Brothers did a fantastic job, don't you think?"

Decker made a face.

"Well, you didn't know him when he was alive."

"Nobody looks good dead," Decker said. Especially a floater.

Finally the lid was closed. The bier was cleared of flowers, including the impressive spray sent by the Lake Jesup Bass Captains Union—a leaping lunker, done all in petunias. With the ceremony concluded, the mourners broke into small groups and began to trudge back to their trucks.

"I gotta get some quotes from the missus," Ott whispered to Decker.

"Sure. I'm in no particular hurry."

Ott walked over and tentatively sat down on a folding chair next to Clarisse Clinch. When he took out his notebook, the widow recoiled as if it were a tarantula. R. J. Decker chuckled.

"So you like funerals?"

It was a woman's voice. Decker turned around.

"I heard you laugh," she said.

"We all deal with grief in our own way." Decker kept a straight face when he said it.

"You're full of shit." The woman's tone stopped just short of friendly.

Mid-thirties, dark blue eyes, light brown hair curly to the shoulders. Decker was sure he had seen her somewhere before. She had an expensive tan, fresh from Curaçao or maybe the Caymans. She wore a black dress cut much too low for your standard funeral. This dress was a night at the symphony.

"My name is Decker."

"Mine's Lanie."

"Elaine?"

"Once upon a time. Now it's Lanie." She shot a look toward Ott Pickney. Or was it Clarisse? "You didn't know Bobby, did you?" she said.

"Nope."

"Then why are you here?"

"I'm a friend of Ott's."

"You sure don't look like a friend of Ott's. And I wish you'd please quit staring at my tits."

Decker reddened. Nothing clever came to mind so he kept quiet and stared at the tops of his shoes.

Lanie said, "So what did you think of the sendoff?"

"Impressive."

" 'Sick' is the word for it," she said.

An ear-splitting noise came from the gravesite. Bobby Clinch's customized bass-boat casket had slipped off the belts and torn free of the winch as it was being lowered into the ground. Now it stood on end, perpendicular in the hole; it looked like a giant grape Popsicle.

"Oh Jesus," Lanie said, turning away.

Cemetery workers in overalls scrambled to restore decorum. Decker saw Clarisse Clinch shaking her head in disgust. Ott was busy scribbling, his neck bent like a heron's.

"How well did you know him?" Decker asked.

"Better than anybody," Lanie said. She pointed back toward the driveway, where the mourners' cars were parked. "See that tangerine Corvette? That was a present from Bobby, right after he finished second in Atlanta. I've only given two blowjobs in my entire life, Mr. Decker, and that Corvette is one of them."

Decker resisted asking about the other. He tried to remember the polite thing to say when a beautiful stranger struck up a conversation about oral sex. None of the obvious replies seemed appropriate for a funeral.

The woman named Lanie said, "Did you get a look inside the coffin?"

"Yeah, amazing," Decker said.

"That fishing rod was Bobby's favorite. A Bantam Maglite bait-caster on a five-foot Fenwick graphite."

Decker thought: Oh no, not her too.

"I gave him that outfit for Christmas," Lanie said, adding quickly: "It wasn't my idea to bury him with it."

"I wouldn't have thought so," Decker said.

They watched the cemetery workers tip Bobby Clinch's coffin back into the grave, where it landed with an embarrassing thud. Hastily the diggers picked up their shovels and went to work. Lanie slipped on a pair of dark sunglasses and smoothed her hair. Her motions were elegant, well-practiced in the kind of mirrors you'd never find in Harney. The lady was definitely out-of-town.

"It wasn't what you think. Bobby and me, I mean."

"I don't think anything," Decker said. Why did they always have this compulsion to confess? Did he look like Pat O'Brien? Did he look like he cared?

"He really loved me," Lanie volunteered.

"Of course he did," Decker said. The Corvette was proof. A greater love hath no man than an orange sports car with a T-top and mag wheels.

"I hope you find out what really happened," she said. "That's why you're here, isn't it? Well, you're going to earn your fee on this one."

Then she walked away. R. J. Decker found himself concentrating on the way she moved. It was a dazzlingly lascivious walk, with a sway of the hips that suggested maybe a little booze for breakfast. Decker had done worse things than admire a woman's legs at a funeral, but he knew he should have been thinking about something else. Why, for example, the grieving mistress knew more about him than he knew about her. He got up and strolled after her. When he called her name, Lanie turned, smiled, didn't stop walking. By the time Decker caught up she was already in the Corvette, door locked.

She waved once through the tinted windows, then sped off, nearly peeling rubber over his feet.

When Decker got back to the grave, Ott Pickney was finishing his interview.

He nodded good-bye to Clarisse. "A cold woman," he said to Decker. "Something tells me Bobby spent too much time on the lake."

As they walked to the truck, Decker asked about the fishing rod in the coffin.

"Looked like a beauty," Ott agreed.

"Yes, but I was wondering," Decker said. "Guy goes fishing early one morning, flips his boat, falls in the lake . . ."

"Yeah?"

"How'd they ever find the rod?"

Ott shrugged. "Hell, R.J., how do I know? Maybe they snagged it off the bottom."

"Thirty feet of brown water? I don't think so."

"Okay, maybe he didn't bring it with him. Maybe he left it at home."

"But it was his favorite rig."

"What are you getting at?"

"I just think it's odd."

"Bass fanatics like Bobby Clinch got a hundred fishing poles, R.J., a new favorite every day. Whatever catches a lunker."

"Maybe you're right."

"You need to relax," Ott said, "you really do."

They climbed in the Toyota and like clockwork Pickney lit up a Camel. He couldn't do it outdoors, in the fresh air, Decker thought; it had to be in a stuffy cab. He felt like getting out and hiking back to the motel. Give himself some time to think about this Lanie business.

"Clarisse didn't give me diddly for this story," Ott complained. "A bitter, bitter woman. I'd much rather have been interviewing your saucy new friend."

Decker said, "Who was she, anyway?"

"A very hot number," Ott said. "Don't tell me she's already got your dick in a knot."

"She seemed to know who I am. Or at least what I do."

"I'm not surprised."

"She said her name was Lanie."

"Lovely, lovely Lanie," Ott sang.

"Then you know her."

"R.J., everybody knows Lanie Gault. Her brother's one of the biggest bass fishermen in the country."

Dickie Lockhart missed the big funeral because he had to fly to New Orleans and meet with his boss.

The boss was the Reverend Charles Weeb, president, general manager, and spiritual commander of the Outdoor Christian Network, which syndicated Dickie Lockhart's television show.

Lockhart was not a remotely religious person—each Sunday being occupied by fishing—so he'd never bothered to ascertain precisely which denomination was espoused by the Reverend Charles Weeb. Whenever the two men met, Weeb never mentioned sin, God, Jesus Christ, the Virgin Mary, or any of the A-list apostles. Instead Weeb mainly talked about ratings and revenues and why some of Lockhart's big sponsors were going soft on him. During these discussions the Reverend Charles Weeb often became exercised and tossed around terms like "shithead" and "cocksucker" more freely than any preacher Dickie Lockhart had ever met.

Two or three times a year, Lockhart would be summoned to New Orleans for a detailed review of *Fish Fever,* Lockhart's immensely popular television show. The Reverend Charles Weeb, who naturally had his own evangelical show on the Outdoor Christian Network, seemed to possess an uncommon interest in Lockhart's low-budget fishing travelogue.

On the day of Bobby Clinch's funeral the two men met in a pink suite in a big hotel on Chartres Street. The room was full of fruit baskets and complimentary bottles of booze. On a credenza by the door stood an odd collection of tiny statuary—plastic dashboard saints that various hotel workers had dropped off so that the Reverend Weeb might bestow a small blessing, if he had time.

"Nutty Catholics," Weeb grumbled. "Only know how to do two things—screw and beg forgiveness."

"Can I have an apple?" Dickie Lockhart asked.

"No," said Charles Weeb. He wore an expensive maroon jogging suit that he'd bought for cash on Rodeo Drive in Beverly Hills. As always, his straw-blond hair looked perfect. Weeb also had straw-blond eyebrows which, Dickie Lockhart guessed, were combed with as much care as the hair.

Weeb propped his Reeboks on the coffee table, slipped on a pair of reading glasses, and scanned the latest Nielsens.

"Not too terrible," he said.

"Thank you," Lockhart said. Meetings were not his strong suit; he was already daydreaming about Bourbon Street, and what might happen later.

"You want to explain Macon?" Charlie Weeb said, peering over the rims.

Lockhart shrank into the sofa. He had no idea what the boss was talking about. Had he missed a fishing tournament? Maybe a promotional gig for one of the top sponsors? Wasn't Macon where Happy Gland Fish Scent was manufactured?

"Macon," Weeb sighed. His tone was that of a disappointed parent. "We lost Macon to that shiteating cocksucker."

"Spurling?"

"Who else!" Weeb crumpled the Nielsens.

Ed Spurling hosted a show called *Fishin' with Fast Eddie,* which was broadcast by satellite to one hundred and seventeen television stations. One more, counting Macon.

In the fierce battle for TV bass-fishing supremacy, Ed Spurling was Dickie Lockhart's blood rival.

"Macon," Dickie said morosely. Georgia was damn good bass country, too.

"So it's one hundred twenty-five stations to one-eighteen," the Reverend Charles Weeb remarked. "Too damn close for comfort."

"But we've got some overlap," Lockhart noted. "Mobile, Gulfport, and Fort Worth."

Weeb nodded. "Little Rock too," he said.

These were cable systems that carried both bass programs; a few markets could easily support more than one.

"Guess I forgot to tell you," Weeb said. "You lost the dinnertime slot in Little Rock. They bumped you to Sunday morning, after *Ozark Bowling.*"

Lockhart groaned. Spurling's lead-in was Kansas City Royals baseball, a blockbuster. It didn't seem fair.

"You see what's happening," the reverend said darkly.

"But the show's doing good. Did you see the one from Lake Jackson?"

"Shaky lens work." Weeb sneered. "Looked like your video ace had the DTs."

"We do our best," the fisherman muttered, "on a thousand lousy bucks per episode." That was the *Fish Fever* budget, excluding Dickie Lockhart's salary. Travel money was so tight that Lockhart drove a Winnebago between locations to save on motels.

Weeb said, "Your show needs a damn good jolt."

"I caught three ten-pounders at Lake Jackson!"

"Spurling's got a new theme song," Weeb went on. "Banjos. Mac Davis on the vocals. Have you heard it?"

Lockhart shook his head. He wasn't much for arguing with the boss, but sometimes pride got the best of him. He asked Charles Weeb, "Did you see the latest BBRs?"

Published by *Bass Blasters* magazine, the Bass Blasters Ratings (BBR) ranked the country's top anglers. The BBR was to bass fishing what the Nielsens were to the TV networks.

"Did you notice who's number one?" Dickie Lockhart asked. *"Again."*

"Yeah." Weeb took his sneakers off the coffee table and sat up. "It's a good fucking thing, too, because right now all we got going for us is your name, Dickie. You're a winner and viewers like winners. 'Course, I see where Mr. Spurling won himself a tournament in mid-Tennessee—"

"The minor leagues, Reverend Weeb. I smoked him at the Atlanta Classic. He finished eighth, and no keepers."

Weeb stood up and smoothed the wrinkles from his expensive jogging suit. Then he sat down again. "As I said, we're very pleased you're on top. I just hate to see you slipping, that's all. It happens, if you're not careful. Happens in business, happens in fishing too. One and the same."

Weeb tore open a fruit basket and tossed Lockhart an apple. Lockhart felt like telling Weeb how much his jogging suit looked like K-Mart pajamas.

The Reverend Charles Weeb said, "This is the majors, Dickie. If you don't win, you get benched." He took off his glasses. "I truly hope you keep winning. In fact, I strongly recommend it."

On this matter, of course, Dickie Lockhart was way ahead of him.

5

Decker honked twice as he drove up to Skink's shack. Short, polite honks. The last thing he wanted to do was surprise a man in a shooting mood.

The shack had a permanent lean, and looked as if a decent breeze could flatten it. Except for the buzz of horseflies, the place stood silent. Decker stuck his hands in his pockets and walked down to the lake. Across the water, several hundred yards away, a sleek boat drifted with two fishermen, plugging the shoreline. Every time one of them cast his lure, the shiny monofilament made a gossamer arc over the water before settling to the surface. The pointed raspberry hull of the fishermen's boat glistened under the noon sun. Decker didn't even bother to try a shout. If Skink were fishing, he'd be alone. And never in a boat like that.

Decker trudged back to the shack and sat on the porch. Seconds later he heard a cracking noise overhead, and Skink dropped out of an old pine tree.

He got up off the ground and said, "I'm beginning not to despise you."

"Nice to hear," Decker said.

"You didn't go inside."

"It's not my house," Decker said.

"Precisely," Skink grumped, clomping onto the porch. "Some people would've gone in anyway."

Daylight added no nuances or definition to Skink's appearance. Today he wore camouflage fatigues, sunglasses, and a flowered shower cap from which sprouted the long braid of silver-gray hair.

He poured coffee for Decker, but none for himself.

"I got fresh rabbit for lunch," Skink said.

"No thanks."

"I said *fresh*."

"I just ate," Decker said unconvincingly.

"How was the funeral?"

Decker shrugged. "Did you know Robert Clinch?"

"I know them all," Skink said.

"Lanie Gault?"

"Her brother's the big tycoon who hired you."

"Right." Decker had been relieved when Ott had told him that Dennis Gault was Lanie's brother. A husband would have been disconcerting news indeed.

Decker said, "Miss Gault thinks there's something strange about the way Bobby Clinch died."

Skink was on his haunches, working on the fire. He didn't answer right away. Once the tinder was lit, he said, "Good rabbit is tough to come by. They tend to get all the way smushed and there's no damn meat left. The best ones are the ones that just barely get clipped and knocked back to the shoulder of the road. This one here, you'd hardly know it got hit. Meat's perfect. Might as well dropped dead of a bunny heart attack." Skink was arranging the pieces on a frypan.

"I'll try a bite or two," Decker said, surrendering.

Only then did Skink smile. It was one of the unlikeliest smiles Decker had ever seen, because Skink had perfect teeth. Straight, flawless, blindingly white ivories, the kind nobody is born with. TV-anchorman-type teeth—Skink's were that good.

Decker wasn't sure if he should be comforted or concerned. He was still thinking about those teeth when Skink said: "I was at the Coon Bog Saturday morning."

"When it happened?"

"Right before."

"They said he must've been doing sixty knots when the boat flipped."

Skink basted the sizzling rabbit with butter. He looked up and said, "When I saw the boat, it wasn't moving."

"Was Clinch alive?"

"Hell, yes."

Decker said, "Then the accident must have happened after you left."

Skink snorted.

"Did he see you?" Decker asked.

"Nope. I was kneeling in the trees, skinning out a rattler. Nobody saw me." He handed Decker a hunk of fried meat.

Decker blew on it until it cooled, then took a small bite. It was really very good. He asked, "What made you notice Clinch?"

"Because he wasn't fishing."

Decker swallowed the meat, and out came a quizzical noise.

"He wasn't fishing," Skink repeated, "and I thought that was damn strange. Get up at dawn, race like mad to a fishing hole, then just poke around the lily pads with a paddle. I was watching because I wanted to see if he'd find what he was looking for."

"Did he?"

"Don't know. I left, had to get the snake on ice."

"Christ," Decker said. He reached into the frypan and gingerly picked out another piece of rabbit. Skink nodded approvingly.

Decker asked, "What do you make of it?"

Skink said: "I'm working for you, is that right?"

"If you'll do it, I sure need the help."

"No shit." The pan was empty. Skink poured the gloppy grease into an old milk carton.

"Bass were slapping over that morning," he said, "and not once did that fucker pick up a rod and cast. Do you find that strange?"

"I suppose," Decker said.

"God, you need a lesson or two," Skink muttered. "Guys like Clinch love to catch bass more than they love to screw. That's the truth, Miami. You put 'em on a good bass lake at dawn and they get *hard*. So the question is, why wasn't Bobby Clinch fishing on the Coon Bog last Saturday?"

Decker had nothing to offer.

"You want to hear something even stranger?" Skink said. "There was another boat out there too, and not far away. Two guys."

Decker said, "And they weren't fishing either, were they, captain?"

"Ha-ha!" Skink cawed. "See there—those rabbit glands went straight to your brain!"

Decker's coffee had cooled, but it didn't matter. He gulped the rest of it.

Skink had become more animated and intense; the cords in his neck were tight. Decker couldn't tell if he was angry or ecstatic. Using a pocket knife to pick strings of rabbit meat from his perfect teeth, Skink said: "Well, Miami, aren't you going to ask me what this means?"

"It was on my list of questions, yeah."

"You'll hear my theory tonight, on the lake."

"On the lake?"

"Your first communion," Skink said, and scrambled noisily back up into the big pine.

Ott Pickney had left Miami in gentle retreat from big-city journalism. He knew he could have stayed at the *Sun* for the rest of his life, but felt he had more or less made his point. Having written virtually nothing substantial in at least a decade, he had nonetheless departed the newspaper in a triumphant state of mind. He had survived the conversion to cold type, the advent of unions, the onslaught of the preppy cubs, the rise of the hotshot managers. Ott had watched the stars and starfuckers arrive and, with a minimum of ambition, outlasted most of them. He felt he was living proof that a successful journalist need not be innately cunning or aggressive, even in South Florida.

In Ott's own mind, Harney was the same game, just a slower track.

Which is why he half-resented R. J. Decker's infernal skepticism about the death of Bobby Clinch. A foolhardy fisherman wrecks his boat and drowns—so what? In Miami it's one crummy paragraph on page 12-D; no one would look twice. Ott Pickney was peeved at Decker's coy insinuation that something sinister was brewing right under Ott's nose. This wasn't Dade County, he thought, and these weren't Dade County people. The idea of an organized cheating ring at the fish tournaments struck Ott as merely farfetched, but the suggestion of foul play in Robert Clinch's death was a gross insult to the community. Ott resolved to show R. J. Decker how wrong he was.

After the funeral, Ott went back to the newsroom and stewed awhile. The *Sentinel*'s deadlines being what they were, he had two days to play with the Clinch piece. As he flipped through his notebook, Ott figured he had enough to bang out fifteen or twenty inches. Barely.

In an uncharacteristic burst of tenacity, he decided to give Clarisse Clinch another shot.

He found the house in chaos. A yellow moving van was parked out front; a crew of burly men was emptying the place. Clarisse had set up a command post in the kitchen, and under her scathing direction the movers were working very swiftly.

"Sorry to intrude," Ott said to her, "but I remembered a couple more questions."

"I got no answers," Clarisse snapped. "We're on our way to Valdosta."

Ott tried to picture Clarisse in a slinky, wet-looking dress, sliding long-legged into a tangerine sports car. He couldn't visualize it. This woman was a different species from Lanie Gault.

"I just need a little more about Bobby's hobby," Ott said. "A few anecdotes."

"Anecdotes!" Clarisse said sharply. "You writing a book?"

"Just a feature story," Ott said. "Bobby's friends say he was quite a fisherman."

"You saw the coffin," Clarisse said. "And you saw his friends." She clapped her hands twice loudly. "Hey! Watch the ottoman, Pablo, unless you want to buy me a new one!"

The man named Pablo mumbled something obscene.

Clarisse turned back to Ott. "Do you fish?"

He shook his head.

"Thank God there's at least one of you," she said.

Her eyes flickered to a bookcase in the living room. Ott noticed that there were no books on the shelves, only trophies. Each of the trophies was crowned with a cheap gold-painted replica of a jumping fish. Bass, Ott assumed. He counted up the trophies and wrote the number "18" in his notebook. One of the movers unfolded a big cardboard box and began wrapping and packing the trophies.

"No!" Clarisse said. "Those go in the dumpster."

The mover shrugged.

Ott followed the widow to the garage. "This junk in here," she was saying, "I've got to sell."

Bobby Clinch's fishing gear. Cane poles, spinning rods, flipping rods, bait-casting rods, popping rods, fly rods. Ott Pickney counted them up and wrote "22" in his notebook. Each of the outfits seemed to be in immaculate condition.

"These are worth a lot of money," Ott said to Clarisse.

"Maybe I should take out an ad in your newspaper."

"Yes, good idea." All Harney *Sentinel* reporters were trained in the paperwork of classified advertising, just in case the moment arose. Ott got a pad of order forms out of the glove box in the truck.

"Twenty-two fishing rods," he began.

"Three pairs of hip waders," Clarisse said, rummaging through her husband's bass trove.

"Two landing nets," Ott noted.

"Four vests," she said, "one with Velcro pockets."

"Is that an electric hook sharpener?"

"Brand new," Clarisse said. "Make sure you put down that it's brand new."

"Got it."

"And I don't know what to do about *this*." From under a work-bench she dragged what appeared to be a plastic suitcase with the word "PLANO" stamped on the top. "I can't even lift the darn thing," she said. "I'm afraid to look inside."

"What is it?" Ott asked.

"The mother lode," Clarisse said. "Bobby's tacklebox."

Ott hoisted it by the handle, then set it down on the kitchen counter. It must have weighed fifty pounds.

"He has junk in there from when he was ten years old. Lures and stuff." Clarisse's voice sounded small; she was blinking her eyes as if she were about to cry, or at least fighting the urge.

Ott unfastened the clasps on the tacklebox and opened the lid. He had never seen such an eclectic collection of gadgets: rainbow-colored worms and frogs and plastic minnows and even tiny rubber snakes, all bristling with diamond-sharpened hooks. The lures were neatly organized on eight folding trays. Knives, pliers, stainless-steel hook removers, sinkers, swivels, and spools of leader material filled the bottom of the box.

In a violet velvet pouch was a small bronze scale used for weighing bass. The numerals on the scale optimistically went up to twenty-five pounds, although no largemouth bass that size had ever been caught.

Of the scale, Clarisse remarked: "That stupid thing cost forty bucks. Bobby said it was tournament-certified, whatever that means. All the guys had the same model, he said, so nobody could cheat on the weight."

Ott Pickney carefully fitted the bronze scale back in its pouch. He returned the pouch to Bobby Clinch's tacklebox and closed the latches.

Clarisse sat down on the concrete steps in the garage and stared sadly at the bushel of orphaned fishing poles. She said, "This is what Bobby's life was all about, Mr. Pickney. Not me or the kids or the job at the phone company . . . just this. He wasn't happy unless he was out on the lake."

Finally a decent quote, Ott thought, and scribbled feverishly in his notebook. *He wasn't happy unless he was fishing on the lake.* Close enough.

It wasn't until later, as Ott Pickney was driving back to the newspaper office, that it hit him like a fist in the gut: R. J. Decker was right. Something odd was going on.

If Bobby Clinch had taken the tacklebox on his fateful trip, it surely would have been lost in the boat accident.

So why had he gone to Lake Jesup without it?

Skink's boat was a bare twelve-foot skiff with peeling oars and splinters on the seat planks.

"Get in," he told R. J. Decker.

Decker sat in the prow and Skink shoved off. It was a chilly night under a muffled sky; an unbroken mat of high gray clouds, pushed south by a cold breeze. Skink set a Coleman lantern in the center of the skiff, next to Decker's weatherproof camera bag.

"No bugs," Skink remarked. "Not with this wind."

He had brought two fishing rods that looked like flea-market specials. The fiberglass was brown and faded, the reels tarnished and dull. The outfits bore no resemblance to the sparkling masterpiece that Decker had seen displayed so reverently in Bobby Clinch's casket.

Skink rowed effortlessly; wavelets kissed at the bow as the little boat crossed Lake Jesup. Decker enjoyed the quiet ride in the cool night. He was still slightly uneasy around Skink, but he was beginning to like the guy, even if he was a head case. Decker had met a few like Skink, eccentric hoary loners. Some were hiding, some were running, some just waiting for something, or someone, to catch up. That was Skink, waiting. Decker would give him plenty of room.

"Looks like no one else is out tonight," he said to Skink.

"Ha, they're everywhere," Skink said. He rowed with his back to Decker. Decker wished he'd take off the damn shower cap, but couldn't figure a way to broach the subject.

"How do you know which way to go?" he asked.

"There's a trailer park due northwest. Lights shine through the trees," Skink said. "They leave 'em on all night, too. Old folks who live there, they're scared if the lights go off. Wild noises tend to get loud in the darkness—you ever noticed that, Miami? Pay attention now: the boat is the face of a clock, and you're sittin' at midnight. The trailer park lights are ten o'clock—"

"I see."

"Good. Now look around about two-thirty, see there? More lights. That's a Zippy Mart on Route 222." Skink described all this without once turning around. "Which way we headed from camp, Miami?"

"Looks like due north."

"Good," Skink said. "Got myself a fuckin' Eagle Scout in the boat."

Decker didn't know what this giant fruitcake was up to, but a boat ride sure beat hell out of an all-night divorce surveillance.

Skink stopped rowing after twenty minutes. He set the lantern on the seat plank and picked up one of the fishing rods. From the prow Decker watched him fiddling with the line, and heard him curse under his breath.

Finally Skink pivoted on the seat and handed Decker the spinning rod. Tied to the end of the line was a long purple rubber lure. Decker figured it was supposed to be an eel, a snake, or a worm with thyroid. Skink's knot was hardly the tightest that Decker had ever seen.

"Let's see you cast," Skink said.

Decker held the rod in his right hand. He took it back over his shoulder and made a motion like he was throwing a baseball. The rubber lure landed with a slap four feet from the boat.

"That sucks," Skink said. "Try opening the bail."

He showed Decker how to open the face of the reel, and how to control the line with the tip of his forefinger. He demonstrated how the wrist, not the arm, supplied the power for the cast. After a half-dozen tries, Decker was winging the purple eel sixty-five feet.

"All right," Skink said. He turned off the Coleman lantern.

The boat drifted at the mouth of a small cove, where the water lay as flat as a smoky mirror. Even on a starless night the lake gave off its own gray light. Decker could make out an apron of pines along the shore; around the boat were thick-stemmed lily pads, cypress nubs, patches of tall reeds.

"Go to it," said Skink.

"Where?" Decker said. "Won't I get snagged on all these lilies?"

"That's a weedless hook on the end of your line. Cast just like you were doing before, then think like a nightcrawler. Make it dance like a goddamn worm that knows it's about to get eaten."

Decker made a good cast. The lure plopped into the pads. As he retrieved it, he waggled the rod in a lame attempt to make the plastic bait slither.

"Jesus Christ, it's not a fucking *breadstick,* it's a snake." Skink snatched the outfit from Decker's hands and made a tremendous cast. The lure made a distant plop as it landed close to the shoreline. "Now watch the tip of the rod," Skink instructed. "Watch my wrists."

The snake-eel-worm skipped across the lily pads and wriggled across the plane of the water. Decker had to admit it looked alive.

When the lure was five feet from the boat, it seemed to explode. Or something exploded beneath it. Skink yanked back, hard, but the eel flew out of the water and thwacked into his shower cap.

Decker's chest pounded in a spot right under his throat. Only bubbles and foam floated in the water where the thing had been.

"What the hell was that?" he stammered.

"Hawg," Skink said. "Good one, too." He unhooked the fake eel from his cap and handed the fishing rod back to Decker. "You try. Quick now, while he's still hot in the belly."

Decker made a cast in the same direction. His fingers trembled as he jigged the rubber creature across the surface of the cove.

"Water's nervous," Skink said, drying his beard. "Slow it down a tad."

"Like this?" Decker whispered.

"Yeah."

Decker heard it before he felt it. A jarring concussion, as if somebody had thrown a cinderblock in the water near the boat. Instantly something nearly pulled the rod from his hands. On instinct Decker yanked back. The line screeched off the old reel in short bursts, bending the rod into an inverse U. The fish circled and broke the surface on the starboard side, toward the stern. Its back was banded in greenish black, its shoulders bronze, and its fat belly as pale as ice. The gills rattled like dice when the bass shook its huge mouth.

"Damn!" Decker grunted.

"She's a big girl," Skink said, just watching.

The fish went deep, tugged some, sat some, then dug for the roots of the lilies. Awestruck, Decker more or less hung on. Skink knew what would happen, and it did. The fish cleverly wrapped the line in the weeds and broke off with a loud crack. The battle had lasted but three minutes.

"Shit," Decker said. He turned on the lantern and studied the broken end of the monofilament.

"Ten-pounder," Skink said. "Easy." He swung his legs over the plank, braced his boots on the transom, and started to row.

Decker asked, "You got another one of those eels?"

"We're going in," Skink said.

"One more shot, captain—I'll do better next time."

"You did fine, Miami. You got what you needed, a jolt of the ballbuster fever. Save me from listening to a lot of stupid questions down the road." Skink picked up the pace with the oars.

Decker said, "I've got to admit, it was fun."

"That's what they say."

During the trip back to shore, Decker couldn't stop thinking about the big bass, the tensile shock of its strength against his own muscles. Maybe there was something mystical to Bobby Clinch's obsession. The experience, Decker admitted to himself, had been exhilarating and pure; the solitude and darkness of the lake shattered by a brute from the deep. It was nothing like fishing on the drift boats, or dropping shrimp off the bridges in the Keys. This was different. Decker felt like a little kid, all wired up.

"I want to try this again," he told Skink.

"Maybe someday, after the dirty work is over. You want to hear my theory?"

"Sure." Decker had been waiting all damn night.

Skink said: "Robert Clinch found out about the cheating. He knew who and he knew how. I think he was after the proof when they caught him on the bog."

"Who caught him? Dickie Lockhart?"

Skink said, "Dickie wasn't in the other boat I saw. He's not that stupid."

"But he sent somebody to kill Bobby Clinch."

"I'm not sure of that, Miami. Maybe it was a trap, or maybe Clinch just turned up in the worst place at the worst time."

"What was Bobby looking for?" Decker asked.

Skink made three swipes of the oars before answering. "A fish," he said. "A particular fish."

That was Skink's theory, or what he intended to share of it. Twice Decker asked Skink what he meant, what particular fish, but Skink never replied. He rowed mechanically. The only sounds on the lake were his husky breaths and the rhythmic squeak of the rusty oarlocks.

Slowly the details of the southern shoreline, including the crooked silhouette of the cabin, came into Decker's view. The trip was almost over.

Decker asked, "You come out here every night?"

"Only when I'm in the mood for fish dinner," Skink replied.

"And you always use that big purple worm?"

"Nope," Skink said, beaching the boat with a final stroke, "what I usually use is a twelve-gauge."

When R. J. Decker got back to the motel, he found a note from the night manager on the door. The note said Ott Pickney had called, but it didn't say why.

Decker already had the key in the lock when he heard a car pull in and park. He glanced over his shoulder, half-expecting to see Ott's perky Toyota flatbed.

What he saw instead was a tangerine Corvette.

6

Decker had a poor memory for names. Terrific eye for faces, but no name recollection whatsoever.

"It was a spring-fashion shoot," Lanie Gault prodded. "You acted like you'd rather be in Salvador."

"I think I remember now," Decker said. "On Sanibel Beach, right?"

Lanie nodded. She sat on the edge of the bed, looking relaxed. Strange motel room, strange man, but still relaxed. Decker was not nearly so comfortable.

"Must have been five, six years ago," he said. Trying to be professional, trying not to look at her legs.

"You've put on some weight," Lanie said. "It's good weight, though, don't worry."

Decker turned on the television, looking for Letterman. He stopped flipping channels when he found one of those dreadful syndicated game shows. He sat down heavily and pretended to watch the tube.

"Do I look any different?" Lanie asked. She didn't say it as if she were begging a compliment.

"You look great," Decker said, turning from the TV.

"Believe it or not, I think I've still got the swimsuit I wore for the pictures."

On this detail Decker's memory was clear. Yellow one-piece thong, the kind that required some touch-up shaving.

Lanie said, "You screwed one of the other models, didn't you?"

Decker sighed.

"She was talking about it on the drive back to Boca."

"I hope she was kind," Decker said. Diane was her name. A very nice lady. Hadn't seemed like the magpie type, but here you had it. He'd kept a phone number, except now she was married to a large Puerto Rican police captain. Her number was filed under S, for suicide.

Lanie Gault kicked her sandals off and sat cross-legged on the bedspread. She wore a fruity-colored sleeveless top and white shorts. Her arms and legs, even the tops of her feet, were a golden tan. So were her neck and chest, the part Decker could see. He wondered about the rest, wondered if it was worth a try. Bad timing, he decided.

"Can we turn that shit down, please?" Lanie said. On the television a young couple from Napa had just won an Oldsmobile Cutlass, and the audience was going nuts.

Decker twisted down the volume.

She said, "Look, I'm sorry about this morning. I'd had a couple martinis to get me going."

"Don't blame you," Decker said.

"I must have sounded like a coldhearted whore, which I'm not."

Decker went along with it. "It was a tough funeral," he said, "especially with the wife there."

"You said it."

"Before you tell me about Bobby," Decker said, "I'd like to know how you knew about me. About why I was here." He guessed it was her brother but he wanted to make sure.

"Dennis called me," Lanie said.

"Why?"

"Because he knows I've got a personal interest. Or maybe he's just feeling guilty about Bobby and wants me to know he's not giving up on it."

Or maybe he wants you to try me out, Decker thought.

Lanie said, "I met Bobby Clinch at a bass tournament in Dallas two summers ago. I was doing outdoor layouts for the Neiman-Marcus catalog—beach togs, picnic wear, stuff like that. Dennis happened to be in town for this big tournament, so I drove out to the reservoir one afternoon, just to say hi. Must have been sixty boats, a hundred guys, and they all looked exactly the same. They dressed alike, walked alike, talked alike, chewed tobacco alike. All dragging fish to be weighed. Afterward they gathered around this tall chalkboard to see who was ahead in the points. Christ, I thought I'd died and gone to redneck hell."

"Then Bobby came along."

"Right," Lanie said. "He said hello, introduced himself. It sounds corny, but I could tell he was different from the others."

"Corny" was not the word for how it sounded. Decker listened politely anyway. He figured there was a love scene coming.

Lanie said, "That night, while the rest of the guys were playing poker and getting bombed, he took me out on the reservoir in his boat, just the two of us. I'll never forget, it was a crescent moon, not a cloud anywhere." She laughed gently and her eyes dropped. "We wound up making it out on the water. In the bow of Bobby's boat was this fancy pedestal seat that spun around . . . and that's what we did. Lucky we didn't capsize."

This girl, Decker thought, has a wondrous imagination.

"Bobby wasn't one of these full-time tournament freaks," Lanie said. "He had a good job laying cable for the phone company. He fished four, maybe five pro events a year, so he wasn't a serious threat to anybody. He had no enemies, Decker. All the guys liked Bobby."

"So what made him different?" Decker asked.

"He enjoyed himself more," Lanie said. "He seemed so happy just to be out there . . . and those were the best nights for us, after he'd spent a day on the lake. Even if he hadn't caught a thing, he'd be happy. Laughing, oh brother, he'd laugh at the whole damn ritual. Bobby loved fishing, that's for sure, but at least he saw how crazy it looked from the outside. And that's more than I can say for my brother."

R. J. Decker got up and switched off the TV. This was the part he'd been waiting for.

"Did Dennis tell you exactly why he hired me?"

"No," Lanie said, "but it can only be one thing. The cheating." As if it were no secret.

"Dennis knows Dickie Lockhart's been rigging the tournaments," she said. "It's all he talks about. At first he actually tried to hire some killers. He said that's what Hemingway would have done."

"No, Hemingway would have done it himself."

"About six months ago Dennis flew down two mob guys from Queens. Offered them eighty-five grand to bump off Dickie and grind the body into puppy chow. My brother didn't know one of the creeps was working for the feds—Sal something-or-other. He blabbed the whole crazy story. Luckily no one at the FBI believed it, but for a while Dennis was scared out of his pants. At least it cured him of the urge to kill Dickie Lockhart. Now he says he'll settle for an indictment."

"So your brother's next move," R. J. Decker said, "was to hire me."

Lanie shook her head. "Bobby."

Decker had been hoping she wouldn't say that.

"Dennis met Bobby on the pro circuit and they hit it off right away. They even fished together in a few of the buddy tournaments, and always finished in the loot. Dennis told Bobby his suspicions about Lockhart and offered him a ton of money to get the proof."

"What could Bobby do that your brother couldn't do himself?"

"Snoop," Lanie said, "inconspicuously. Everybody knows Dennis has a hard-on for Dickie Lockhart. Dickie knows it too, and he's damn careful with Dennis around. So my brother's plan was to pull out of the next few tournaments—claim the family business as an excuse—and hope that Dickie got careless."

"With Bobby Clinch watching every move."

"Exactly."

Decker asked, "How much money did Dennis offer him?"

"Plenty. Bobby wasn't greedy, but he wanted enough to be able to get out of his marriage. See, he wanted Clarisse to have the house, free and clear. He'd never just walk out on her and the kids."

R. J. Decker wasn't exactly moved to tears. Lanie's story was mucky, and Decker was ready to say goodnight.

"Did your brother know about you and Bobby?" he asked.

"Sure he did. Dennis never said a word, but I'm sure he knew." Lanie Gault put her hands under her chin. "I thought he might bring it up, after Bobby was killed. Just a note or a phone call—something to let on that he knew I was hurting. Not Dennis. The sonofabitch has Freon in his veins, I'm warning you. My brother wants to nail Dickie Lockhart and if you happen to die in the chase he won't be sending a wreath to the funeral. Just another replacement. Like you."

The possibility of being murdered over a dead fish did not appeal to R. J. Decker's sense of adventure. He had photographed men who had died for less, and many who had died for more. Over the years he had adopted a carrion fly's unglamorous view of death: it didn't really matter how you got that way, it stunk just the same.

"You think Lockhart killed your boyfriend?" Decker asked Lanie.

"Who else would do it?"

"You're sure it was no accident?"

"Positive," Lanie said. "Bobby knew every log in that lake. He could've run it blindfolded."

Decker was inclined to believe her. "Who owns Dickie's TV show?" he asked.

"The Outdoor Christian Network. You heard of it?"

"TV Bible geysers," Decker said.

Lanie straightened, as if working out a crick in her spine. "More than old-time religion," she said. "OCN is quite the modern conglomerate. They're into health insurance, unit trusts, oil futures, real-estate development . . ."

"I'll check into it," Decker promised. "I'm tired, Lanie. I've got a rotten drive tomorrow."

She nodded, got up, and slipped into her sandals. She stood in front of the mirror and brushed through her hair in brisk, sure strokes.

"One more thing," Decker said. "Out at the cemetery, how did you know which one was me? Sanibel was a long time ago."

Lanie laughed. "You kidding?"

"Don't tell me I stood out."

"Yeah, you did," she said, "but Dennis wired me a picture, in case I wasn't sure."

"A picture."

Lanie reached in her purse. "Courtesy of the booking desk at the Dade County Jail."

Decker recognized the old mug shots. Cute move, Dennis. Just a touch of the hot needle.

"I've seen friendlier smiles," Lanie said, studying the police photos. "You still taking pictures, Decker?"

"Once in a while."

"Maybe you could do me sometime. I'm thinking of going back into modeling." Lanie put the purse under her arm and opened the door. "It's been so long I've probably forgotten how to pose."

You're doing just fine, Decker thought. "Good night," he said.

Decker had to go back to Miami to soup some film for an insurance-fraud trial, set for the coming week. He figured he'd use the long drive to decide what to do about Dennis Gault and the fishing scam. His instincts about the cast of characters told him to drop the case— but what about the death of Bobby Clinch?

As he packed his suitcase Decker heard himself say: So what? He hated the way he sounded because he sounded like every lazy asshole cop or P.I. he'd ever met. Big cases, big problems. Go for the easy bucks, that would be the advice.

Yet Decker knew he couldn't drop it now. Bobby Clinch got killed because he went snooping for a secret fish; such a remarkable crime couldn't easily be ignored. The idea that somebody had become homicidal over a largemouth bass was perversely appealing to Decker, and it made him want very much to get a picture of the guys who did it.

First he needed to meet with Gault again, a distasteful prospect. He could do it this evening, back in Miami; it wouldn't take long. From the motel room Decker called and made reservations for the following night on a seven-P.M. United flight to New Orleans. The Cajun Invitational Bass Classic was this week's stop on the professional fishing tour, and a good place for Decker to get his first glimpse of Dickie Lockhart in action. He had seen the famous TV angler's face on a billboard across from a bait shop on Route 222: "Dickie Lockhart Loves Happy Gland Fish Scent! So Do Lunker Bass!" Decker had been so intrigued by the billboard that he'd asked a man at the bait shop if the Happy Gland company made a formula for humans. The man at the bait shop dutifully checked behind the counter and said no.

Before leaving Harney, Decker tried to call Ott Pickney at the newspaper. Sandy Kilpatrick, the birdlike editor, said Ott had gone out early to do some interviews. The note of concern in Kilpatrick's voice suggested that pre-lunchtime enterprise was uncharacteristic behavior for Ott. Decker left a message to have Ott call him that night in Miami.

At that moment Ott Pickney was slurping down black coffee at Culver Rundell's bait shop on the southern shore of Lake Jesup. Culver Rundell was behind the counter and his brother Ozzie was out back dipping shiners. Ott was trying to strike up a conversation about Bobby Clinch. Ott had set his reporter's notebook on the counter twenty minutes earlier, and the pages were still blank.

"Sorry I'm not much help," Culver Rundell said. "Bobby was a nice guy, a pretty good basser. That's about all I can tell you. Also, he favored spinnerbaits."

"Spinnerbaits."

"Over plastic worms," Culver Rundell explained.

Ott Pickney could not bring himself to transcribe this detail.

"I understand you were here when they brought in the body," Ott said.

"I was. The Davidson boys found him. Daniel and Desi."

"How awful," Ott said.

"It was my truck that took him to the morgue."

Ott said nothing about the autopsy. Dr. Pembroke was third on his list of interview subjects.

"I hated to miss the funeral," Culver Rundell said, "but we had one hellacious busy morning."

"The casket was made out of Bobby's boat."

"So I heard!" Culver said. "What a neat idea. I wisht I coulda seen it."

Ott tapped his Bic pen on the counter and said amiably, "I was amazed how handsomely they did it."

"What I heard," said Culver Rundell, "is they got a regular oak coffin from Pearl Brothers, sanded off the finish, and paneled it with long strips from the hull of the boat. Cost another two grand, I know for a fact. The bass club is paying."

Ott Pickney said, "And who would have done the work, the funeral home?"

"Naw, it was Larkin's shop."

Larkin was a carpenter. He had done all the benches at the Harney County Courthouse, and also the front doors on the new U.S. Post Office.

"He's the best in town," Culver Rundell remarked. He thought he was doing Larkin a favor, a little free publicity for the business.

"Well, he did a damn fine job with the coffin," Ott said. He left two one-dollar bills on the countertop, said good-bye, and drove immediately to Larkin's shop. Ott hoped there would be something left to see, though he had no idea exactly what to look for.

The shop was more of an old A-frame barn with a fancy new electric garage door, the kind used on those big import-export warehouses in western Dade County. The door to the wood shop was up. Ott saw plenty of raw furniture but no carpenters. It turned out Larkin wasn't there; it was a slow morning, so he'd gone fishing. Naturally.

A young black apprentice carpenter named Miller asked the reporter what he wanted.

"I'm doing a story about Bobby Clinch, the young man who died in that terrible boating accident at the Bog."

"Yeah," Miller said. His workshirt was soaked. Sawdust and curlicued pine shavings stuck to his coal-black arms. He looked as if he were in the middle of a project, and wanted to get back to it.

Pushing things, Ott Pickney said, "This shop did the custom work on the coffin, right?"

"Yeah," Miller said, "the boat job."

"It was really something," Ott said. "How did you guys do that? You won't mind if I take some notes—"

"Mr. Larkin did it all by himself," Miller said. "I guess he knew the deceased."

That last word rattled Ott. He glanced up from the notebook to catch the cutting look in Miller's eye. The look said: Don't patronize me, pal, I got better things to do.

"Blue metal-flake casket, man. Looked like a giant fucking cough drop."

Ott cleared his throat. "I'm sure they meant well . . . I mean, it was supposed to be symbolic. Sort of a farewell gesture."

"I'll give you a farewell gesture—" Miller said, but then the phone rang in the far corner of the workshed. The apprentice hurried off, and Ott quietly poked through the shop. He wondered why he'd never gotten the hang of talking to black people, why they always looked at him as if he were a cockroach.

Miller was talking in a loud voice into the phone. Something about a walnut dining table and an unpaid bill.

Ott Pickney slipped out the front way, then walked around to the back of the shop where Miller couldn't see him. Against one wall stood two long green dumpsters filled with fresh-cut lumber remnants. They were the sweetest-smelling dumpsters Ott had ever come across. He stood on his tiptoes and looked inside. In the first he saw a pile of wooden chips, blocks, odd triangles and rectangles, a broken sawhorse, a hogshead, empty cans of resin and varnish; Mr. Larkin's predictable junk.

At the second dumpster Ott found a similar jumble of pulp, plywood, and two-by-fours, but also something else: molded chunks of blue-sparkled fiberglass. It was the remains of Bobby Clinch's Ranger bass boat, sawed to pieces in the customizing of the fisherman's coffin.

Ott boosted himself, using an empty gallon can of Formsby's

turned upside down. He stuffed the notebook into the back pocket of his trousers and stretched over the rim of the dumpster so his arms could reach the wreckage. As he sifted through the fiberglass scraps, Ott realized it was impossible to tell how these jigsawed pieces had ever comprised a nineteen-foot boat.

The one fragment he recognized was the console. Ott found it in the bottom of the dumpster.

Every expensive bass boat has a console, a recessed cockpit designed to give anglers the same sensation as if they were racing the Daytona 500 instead of merely demolishing the quietude of a lake.

To Ott Pickney, the cockpit of Bobby Clinch's fishing boat more closely resembled the pilot's deck of a 747. Among the concave dials were a compass, a sonic depth recorder, a digital tachometer, an LED gauge showing water temperature at five different depths, power-tilt adjusters, trim tabs, a marine radio and an AM-FM stereo, with a tape deck. All these electronics obviously were ruined from being submerged in the lake, but Ott was fascinated anyway. He hoisted the console out of the dumpster to take a closer look.

He set the heavy piece on his lap and imagined himself at the controls of a two-hundred-horsepower speedboat. He pretended to hunker behind the Plexiglas windshield and aim the boat along a winding creek. The only trouble was, the steering wheel wouldn't budge in his hands.

Ott turned the console over, thinking the shaft had gotten snarled in all the loose wiring. But that wasn't the problem; the problem was a short length of black nylon rope. The rope had been wrapped tightly around the base of the steering column beneath the console, where it wouldn't be seen. Ott plucked fruitlessly at the coils; the rope had been tied on with authority. The steering was completely jammed.

Which meant, of course, that the direction of Bobby Clinch's boat had been fixed. It meant that Clinch himself needn't have been at the wheel at the instant of the crash. It meant that the fisherman probably was already dying or injured when the ghost-driven bass boat flipped over and tunneled bow-first into the chilly water.

Ott Pickney did not grasp this scenario as swiftly as he might have. It was dawning on him slowly, but he became so engrossed in the contemplation that he lost track of his surroundings. He heard footsteps and looked up, expecting to see Miller, the carpenter's black apprentice. Instead there were three other men, dressed in the standard local garb—caps, jeans, flannel shirts. One of the visitors carried a short piece of lumber, a second carried a loop of heavy wire; the other just stood dull-eyed, fists at his side. Ott started to say something but his greeting died beneath the grinding whine of a carpenter's table saw; Miller back at work inside the shed. The three men stepped closer. Only one was a local, but he recognized Ott Pickney and knew that the reporter could identify him. Unfortunately for Ott, none of the men wished to see their names in the paper.

7

Dennis Gault was holding a stack of VCR cassettes when he answered the door. He was wearing salmon shorts and a loose mesh top that looked like it would have made an excellent mullet seine. Gault led R. J. Decker to the living room, which was filled with low flat-looking furniture. The predominant hue was cranberry.

Gault put a cassette in the video recorder and told Decker to sit down. "Want a drink?" Gault asked. He smelled like he was on his tenth Smirnoff.

Decker took a cold beer.

A fishing show came on the television screen. Gault used the remote control to fast-forward the tape. Two guys in a bass boat, Decker could tell; casting and reeling, casting and reeling, occasionally hauling in a small fish. Fast-forward was the only way to endure this, Decker decided.

A commercial came on and Gault abruptly hit the freeze button. "Theeeeere's Dickie!" he sang derisively.

On the screen Dickie Lockhart stood by the side of a lake, squinting into the sun. He was wearing a crisply pressed basser's jumpsuit, desert tan; his cap was off and his hair was blow-dried to perfection. He was holding up a sixteen-ounce bottle of Happy Gland Fish Scent, and grinning.

"Does that stuff really work?" Decker asked. A bit off the point, but he was curious.

"Hard to say," Gault replied. "Stinks like a sack of dead cats, that's for sure."

He speeded the tape forward until he found the segment he'd been searching for. He froze the picture as the angler in the bow of the boat hoisted a fat black bass to show the camera.

"There! Look now, pay attention!" Gault said. Excitedly he shuffled on bare knees across the floor to the television screen, one of those custom five-foot monsters that eats up the whole wall. "There, Decker, look. This fish is a ringer!"

"How can you tell?"

"See here, the eyes are flat. Not cloudy yet, but flat as tile. And the color's washed out of the flanks. No vertical stripes, not a one. Muck is the color of this fish."

"It doesn't look too healthy," Decker agreed.

"Healthy? Man, this fish is DOA. Check the dorsal. The guy is fanning the fins for the camera. Why? 'Cause they'd fold up otherwise. This fish is de-fucking-ceased."

"But they just showed the fisherman reeling it in," Decker said.

"Wrong. Now watch." Gault backed up the tape and replayed the fight. The rod was bent, the water around the boat boiled and splashed—but the angles and the editing of the video made it impossible to see the actual size of the bass. Until the fisherman lifted it for the camera.

"That rookie caught a fish," Gault said, "but not *this* fish." He hit a button and rewound the tape. "Want to watch another one?"

"That won't be necessary," Decker said.

"You see how easy it is to cheat."

"For a TV show, sure."

"It's even easier in a tournament," Gault said, "especially when your partner's in on it. And the weighmaster too. Not to mention the goddamn sponsors." He went to the kitchen and came back with a beer for Decker and a fresh vodka-tonic for himself.

"Tell me about what happened in Harney," he said.

"Met a guy named Skink," Decker said.

Gault whistled and arched his eyebrows. "A real fruitbar. I fished with him once on the St. John's."

"He's going to help me catch Lockhart."

"Not on my nickel!" Gault protested.

"I need him."

"He's a maniac."

"I don't think so."

"He eats dead animals off the road!"

"Waste not, want not," Decker said. "He's the only one up there I'd trust. Without him I quit the case."

Gault folded his hands. Decker drank his beer.

"All right," Gault said, "but be careful. That guy's got Texas Tower written all over him, and neither of us wants to be there if he ever reaches the top."

What Gault meant was: If there's trouble, don't drag my name into it.

"What else did you do?" he asked Decker.

"Went to a funeral."

Gault licked his lower lip nervously.

"Robert Clinch," Decker said, "late of your hire. Nice of you to tell me."

Gault toyed with the stack of fishing videotapes, pretending to organize them. Without looking up, he asked, "Do they know what exactly happened?"

"The coroner says it was accidental."

Gault smiled thinly. "We know that's horseshit, don't we? The only question in my mind is: How'd they do it?"

Decker said, "My question is: Who?"

"Who? Dickie Lockhart, that's who!" Gault said. "Don't be stupid, man. Dickie knew I was closing in and he knew Bobby was working for me. What do you mean—*who?*"

"You're probably right," Decker said, "but I'd like to be sure."

"Haven't you been listening? Christ, don't tell me I've hired a complete moron."

"I met your sister," Decker said. He liked to save the best for last.

"Elaine?" Gault said. He looked most uncomfortable, just as Decker had expected. It was worth the wait.

"We had a nice chat," Decker said. He wanted Gault to be the one who finished the conversation. He didn't want to be the one to take it any further, but he had to. He needed to find out if Gault knew everything.

"You didn't tell me a couple important things. You didn't tell me about Clinch and you didn't tell me you had a sister up in Harney." Decker's voice had the slightest sting of irritation.

"She gets around, my sister." Gault drained his glass. His face was getting red.

Stubborn bastard, Decker thought, have it your way.

"You knew she was having an affair with Bobby Clinch," he said evenly.

"Says who?" Gault snapped. The red became deeper.

"Lanie."

"Lanie?"

"That's what they call her."

"Oh, is it now?"

"Personally, I don't care if she's screwing the entire American Legion post," Decker said, "but I need to know what you know."

"You better shut your mouth, ace!" Gault's face was actually purple now.

Decker thought: We really hit a nerve here. But from the murderous looks he was getting, he figured now wasn't the time to pursue it. He got up and headed for the door but Gault grabbed his arm and snarled, "Wait just a minute." Decker shook free and—rather gently, he thought—guided Gault backward until his butt hit the sofa.

"Good-bye now," Decker said.

But Gault had lost it. He lunged and got Decker by the throat. Gagging, Decker felt manicured fingernails digging into the meat of his neck. He stared up the length of Gault's brown arms and saw every vein and tendon swollen. The man's cheeks were flushed but his lips twitched like bloodless worms.

The two men toppled across the low sofa with Gault on top, amber eyeglasses askew. He was spitting and hollering about what a shiteating punk Decker was, while Decker was trying to squirm free from the neckhold before he passed out. His vision bloomed kaleidoscopic and his skull roared. The blood in his head was trying to go south but Dennis Gault wouldn't let it.

A cardinal rule of being a successful private investigator is: Don't slug your own clients. But sometimes exceptions had to be made. Decker made one. He released his fruitless grip on Gault's wrists and, in a clumsy but effective pincer motion, hammered him in the ribs with both fists. As the wind exploded from Gault's lungs, Decker bucked him over and jumped on top.

Dennis Gault had figured R. J. Decker to be strong, but he was unprepared for the force now planted on his sternum. As his own foolish rage subsided, he fearfully began to wonder if Decker was just getting warmed up.

Gault felt but never saw the two sharp punches that flattened his nose, shattered his designer frames, and closed one eye. Later, when he awoke and dragged himself to the bathroom, he would marvel in the mirror that only two punches could have done so much damage. He found a pail of ice cubes waiting on the nightstand, next to a bottle of aspirin.

And a handwritten note from R. J. Decker: "The fee is now one hundred, asshole."

Harney was such a small county that it was difficult to mount a serious high-school athletic program. There was, after all, only one high school. The enrollment fluctuated from about one hundred and seventy-five to two hundred and ten, so the pool of sports talent was relatively limited. In those rare and precious years when Harney High fielded a winning team, the star athletes were encouraged to flunk a year or two in order to delay graduation and prolong the school's victory streak. A few idealistic teachers spoke out against this unorthodox display of school spirit, but the truth was that many of the top jocks were D students anyway and had fully intended to spend six or seven years in high school.

Football was the sport that Harney loved most; unfortunately, the football team of Harney High had never compiled a winning record. One season, in desperation, they even scheduled three games against the wimpiest parochial schools in Duval County. Harney lost every game. The coach was fired, and moved out of town.

Consequently the Harney High athletic department decided to concentrate on another sport, basketball. The first order of business was to build a gymnasium with a basketball court and some portable bleachers. The second move was to send a cautious delegation of coaches and teachers into the black neighborhood to recruit some good basketball players. A few old crackers in Harney huffed and swore about having to watch a bunch of skinny spooks tear up and down the court, and about how it wasn't fair to the good Christian white kids, but then it was pointed out that the good Christian white kids were mostly slow and fat and couldn't make a lay-up from a trampoline.

Once the basketball program was established, the team performed better than anyone had expected. The first year it made it to the regionals, the next to the state playoffs in the Class Four-A division. True, the star center of the Harney team was twenty-seven years old, but he looked much younger. No one raised a peep. As the team kept winning, basketball eventually captured Harney County's heart.

The Harney High basketball team was called the Armadillos. It was not the first choice of names. Originally the school had wanted its team to be the Rattlers, but a Class AA team in Orlando already claimed that nickname. Second choice was the Bobcats, except that a Bible college in Leesburg had dibs on that one. It went on like this for several months—the Tigers, the Hawks, the Panthers; all taken, the good names—until finally it came down to either the Owls or the Armadillos. The school board voted to name the team the Owls since it had six fewer letters and the uniforms would be much less expensive, but the student body rebelled and gathered hundreds of signatures on a typed petition declaring that the Harney Owls was "a pussy name and nobody'll ever go to any of the damn games." Without comment the school board reversed its vote.

Once the Harney Armadillos started kicking ass on the basketball court, the local alumnae decided that the school needed an actual mascot, something on the order of the famous San Diego Chicken, only cheaper. Ideas were submitted in a local contest sponsored by the *Sentinel,* and a winner was chosen from sixteen entries. Working on commission, one of the matrons from the Sewing Club stitched together an incredible costume out of old automobile seat covers and floormats.

It was a six-foot armadillo, complete with glossy armored haunches, a long anteater nose (salvaged from a Hoover canister vacuum), and a scaly tail.

The mascot was to be known as Davey Dillo, and he would perform at each of the home games. By custom he would appear before the opening tipoff, breakdancing to a tape of Michael Jackson's "Billie Jean." Then at halftime Davey Dillo would stage a series of clumsy stunts on a skateboard, to whatever music the band had learned that week.

Davey Dillo's was not a polished act, but the youngsters (at least those under four) thought it was the funniest thing ever to hit the Harney gymnasium. The grown-ups thought the man inside the armadillo costume had a lot of guts.

On the evening of January 12 the Harney Armadillos were all set to play the Valencia Cropdusters in a battle for first place in the midstate Four-A division. Inside the gymnasium sat two hundred fans, more than the coaches and cheerleaders had ever seen; so many fans that, when the national anthem was sung, it actually sounded on key.

The last words—"home of the brave!"—were Davey Dillo's regular cue to prance onto the basketball court and wave a single sequined glove on one of his armadillo paws. Then he would start the dance.

But on this night the popular mascot did not appear.

After a few awkward moments somebody cut off the Michael Jackson tape and put on Ricky Scaggs, while the coaches ordered the players to search the gym. In all two years of his existence, Davey Dillo had never missed a sporting event at Harney High (even the track and field), so nobody knew what to think. Soon the crowd, even the Valencia High fans, began to chant, "We want the Dillo! We want the Dillo!"

But Davey Dillo was not in the locker room suiting up. He wasn't oiling the wheels on his skateboard. He wasn't mending the pink-washcloth tongue of his armadillo costume.

Davey Dillo—rather, the man who created and portrayed Davey Dillo—was missing.

His identity was the worst-kept secret in Harney County. It was Ott Pickney, of course.

8

R. J. Decker lived in a trailer court about a mile off the Palmetto Expressway. The trailer was forty feet long and ten feet wide, and made of the finest sheet aluminum. Inside the walls were covered with cheap paneling that had warped in the tropical humidity; the threadbare carpet was the color of liver. For amenities the trailer featured a badly wired kitchenette, a drip of a shower, and a decrepit air conditioner that leaked gray fluid all over the place. Decker had converted the master closet to a darkroom, and it was all the space he needed; it was a busy week if he used it more than once or twice.

He didn't want to live in a trailer park, hated the very idea, but it was all he could afford after the divorce. Not that his wife had cleaned him out, she hadn't; she had merely taken what was hers, which amounted to practically everything of value in the marriage. Except for the cameras. In aggregate, R. J. Decker's camera equipment was worth twice as much as the trailer where he lived. He took no special steps to protect or conceal the cameras because virtually all his trailer-park neighbors owned free-running pit bulldogs, canine psychopaths that no burglar dared to challenge.

For some reason the neighbors' dogs never bothered Catherine. Decker was printing film when she dropped by. As soon as he let her in the door, she wrinkled her nose. "Yuk! Hypo." She knew the smell of the fixer.

"I'll be done in a second," he said, and slipped back into the darkroom. He wondered what was up. He wondered where James was. James was the chiropractor she had married less than two weeks after the divorce.

The day Catherine had married Dr. James was also the day Decker had clobbered the burglar. Catherine had always felt guilty, as if she'd lighted the fuse. She'd written him two or three times a month when he was at Apalachee; once she'd even mailed a Polaroid of herself in a black bra and panties. Somehow it got by the prison censor. "For old times," she'd printed on the back of the snapshot, as a joke. Decker was sure Dr. James had no idea. Years after the marriage Catherine still called or stopped by, but only at night and never on weekends. Decker always felt good for a little while afterward.

He washed a couple of eight-by-tens and hung the prints from a clothesline strung across the darkroom. He could have turned on the overheads without harm to the photographs, but he preferred to work in the red glow of the safelight. Catherine tapped twice and came in, shutting the door quickly. She knew the routine.

"Where's the mister?" Decker asked.

"Tampa," Catherine said. "Big convention. Every other weekend is a big convention. What've we got here?" She stood on her toes and studied the prints. "Who's the weight-lifter?"

"Fireman out on ninety-percent disability."

"So what's he doing hulking out at Vic Tanny?"

"That's what the insurance company wants to know," Decker said.

"Pretty dull stuff, Rage." Sometimes she called him Rage instead of R. J. It was a pet name that had something to do with his temper. Decker didn't mind it, coming from Catherine.

"I've got a good one cooking," he said.

"Yeah? Like what?"

She looked great in the warm red light. Catherine was a knockout. Was, is, always will be. An expensive knockout.

"I'm investigating a professional fisherman," Decker said, "for cheating in tournaments. Allegedly."

"Come on, Rage."

"I'm serious."

Catherine folded her arms and gave him a motherly look. "Why don't you ask the paper for your old job back?"

"Because the paper won't pay me a hundred large to go fishing."

Catherine said, "Wow."

She smelled wonderful. She knew Decker liked a certain perfume so she always wore it for him—what was the name? He couldn't remember. Something fashionably neurotic. Compulsion, that was it. A scent that probably wouldn't appeal to Dr. James, at least Decker hoped not. He wondered if Catherine was still on the same four-ounce bottle he'd bought for her birthday three years ago.

Decker tweezered another black-and-white of the goldbrick fireman out of the fixer and rinsed it down.

"No pictures of fish?" Catherine asked.

"Not yet."

"Somebody is really gonna pay you a hundred thousand?"

"Well, at least fifty. That's if I get what he wants."

She said, "What are you going to do with all that money?"

"Try to buy you back."

Catherine's laugh died in her throat. She looked hurt. "That's not really funny, R.J."

"I guess not."

"You didn't mean it, did you?"

"No, I didn't mean it."

"You've got a nasty streak."

"I was beaten as a child," Decker said.

"Can we get out of here? I'm getting high on your darn chemicals."

Decker took her to a barbecue joint on South Dixie Highway. Catherine ordered half a chicken and iced tea, he had beer and ribs. They talked about a thousand little things, and Decker thought about how much fun it was to be with her, still. It wasn't a sad feeling, just wistful; he knew it would go away. The best feelings always did.

"Have you thought about New York?" Catherine asked.

The free-lance speech. Decker knew it by heart.

"Look at Foley. He had a cover shot on *Sports Illustrated* last summer," she said.

Foley was another photographer who'd quit the newspaper and gone free-lance.

"Hale Irwin," Decker said derisively.

"What?"

"That was Foley's big picture. A golfer. A fucking golfer, Catherine. That's not what I want to do, follow a bunch of Izod shirts around a hot golf course all day for one stupid picture."

Catherine said, "It was just an example, Rage. Foley's had plenty of business since he moved to New York. And not just golfers, so don't give me that pissed-off look."

"He's a good shooter."

"But you're better, by a mile." She reached across the table and pinched his arm gently. "Hey, it doesn't have to be heavy-duty. No Salvadors, no murders, no dead girls in Cadillacs. Just stick to the soft stuff, Rage, you've earned it."

Decker guessed it was about time for the all-that-wasted-talent routine.

Catherine came through. "I just hate to see you wasting all your talent," she said. "Snooping around like a thief, taking pictures of . . ."

"Guys who cheat insurance companies."

"Yeah."

Decker said, "Maybe you're right."

"Will you think about New York?"

"Take some of these ribs, I can't eat 'em all."

"No, thanks, I'm full."

"So tell me about the quack."

"Stop it," Catherine said. "James's patients are wild about him. He's very generous with his time."

"And the spine-cracking business is good."

"Good, but it could be better," Catherine said. "James is talking about moving."

Decker grinned. "Let me guess where."

Catherine reddened. "His brother's got a practice on Long Island. It's going gangbusters, James says."

"No shit?"

"Don't look so cocky, R.J. This has nothing to do with you."

"So you wouldn't come see me," Decker said. "I mean, if I were to move to New York and you somehow wound up on Long Island, you wouldn't drop by and chat?"

Catherine wiped her hands on a napkin. "Jesus, I don't know." Her voice was different now, the airy confidence gone. "I don't know what I've done, R.J. Sometimes I wonder. James is special and I realize how lucky I am, but still . . . The man irons his socks, did I tell you that?"

Decker nodded. "You called me from your honeymoon to tell me that." From Honolulu she'd called.

"Yeah, well."

"That's okay," Decker said. "I didn't mind." It was better than losing her completely. He would miss her if the sock-ironing chiropractor whisked her away to New York.

"You know the hell of it?" Catherine said. "My back's still killing me."

Decker's telephone was ringing when he returned to the trailer. The man on the other end didn't need to identify himself.

"Hello, Miami."

"Hey, captain." Decker was surprised. Skink would do anything to avoid the phone.

"The Armadillo is dead," said Skink.

Decker figured Skink was talking about his supper.

"You listening?" Skink said.

"The armadillo."

"Yeah, your little pal from the newspaper."

"Ott?"

"Officially he's only missing. Unofficially he's dead. You better get up here. It's time to go to work."

Decker sat down at the kitchen counter. "Start at the beginning," he said. Gruffly Skink summarized the facts of the disappearance, closing with a neutral explanation of Ott Pickney's alter ego, Davey Dillo.

"They say he was very convincing," Skink said, by way of con-dolence.

Decker had a hell of a hard time imagining Ott in an armadillo costume on a skateboard. He had a harder time imagining Ott dead.

"Maybe they just took him somewhere to put a scare in him," he speculated.

"No way," Skink said. "I'll see you soon. Oh yeah—when you get to Harney, don't check in at the motel. It's not safe. You'd better stay out here with me."

"I'd rather not," Decker said.

"Aw, it'll be loads of fun," Skink said with a grunt. "We can roast weenies and marshmallows."

Decker drove all night. He shot straight up Interstate 95 and got off at Route 222, just west of Wabasso. Another ninety minutes and he was in Harney County. By the time he got to Skink's place on the lake, it was four-thirty in the morning. Already one or two bass boats were out on the water; Decker could hear the big engines chewing up the darkness.

At the sound of Decker's car Skink clumped onto the porch. He was fully dressed—boots, sunglasses, the orange weathersuit. Decker wondered if he slept in uniform.

"That's some driving," Skink said. "Get your gear and come on inside."

Decker carried his duffel into the shack. It was the first time he had ventured beyond the porch, and he wasn't sure what to expect. Pelts, maybe. Wallpaper made from rabbit pelts.

As he pushed past the screen door, Decker was amazed by what he saw: books. Every wall had raw pine shelves to the ceiling, and every shelf was lined with books. The east wall was for classic fiction: Poe, Hemingway, Dostoyevsky, Mark Twain, Jack London, Faulkner, Fitzgerald, even Boris Pasternak. The west wall was for political biographies: Churchill, Sandburg's Lincoln, Hitler, Huey Long, Eisenhower, Joseph McCarthy, John F. Kennedy, even Robert Caro's Lyndon Johnson, though it looked like a book-club edition. The south wall was exclusively for reference books: the *Britannica, Current Biography,* the *Florida Statutes,* even the *Reader's Guide to Periodic Literature.* This was the wall of the shack that leaned so precipitously, and now Decker knew why: it held the heaviest books.

The shelves of the north wall were divided into two sections. The top was philosophy and the humanities. The bottom half was for children's books. The Hardy Boys, Tom Swift, Dr. Seuss. *Charlotte's Web* and the Brothers Grimm.

"What're you staring at?" Skink demanded.

"These are great books," Decker said.

"No shit."

In the middle of the floor there was a bare mattress and army blanket, but no pillow. The Remington was propped in a corner. The Coleman lantern hung from a slat in the ceiling; it offered only a fuzzy white light that would flare or dim as the mantle burned down. Decker thought Skink must do his reading in the daytime, or else he'd go blind.

Another car pulled up outside the shack. Decker glanced at Skink. He looked as if he were expecting somebody. He pushed open the screen door and a cop walked in; a state trooper. Stiff cowboy-style hat, pressed gray uniform (long sleeves of course). On one shoulder was a patch shaped like a Florida orange. The cop was almost as big as Skink. He was younger, though—a wedge of muscle from the waist up.

Decker noticed that this state trooper was different from most.

Most were big, young, lean, and white. This trooper was black. Decker could not imagine a more miserable place than Harney County to be a black cop.

"This is Jim Tile," Skink said. "Jim, this is the guy I told you about."

"Miami," Tile said, and shook Decker's hand. Skink dragged a rocker and a folding chair in from the porch. Tile took off his hat and sat down in the rocker, Decker took the chair and Skink sat on the bare pine floor.

Decker said, "What happened to Ott?"

"He's dead," Skink said.

"But what the hell happened?"

Skink sighed and motioned to Jim Tile. "Yesterday morning," the trooper said, in a voice so deep it seemed to shake the lantern, "I was on road patrol about dawn. Out on the Gilchrist Highway where it crosses Morgan Slough."

"Some of the guys fish the slough when the water's up," Skink cut in. "You need a johnboat, and no outboard. Ten minutes from the highway and you're into heavy bass cover."

Jim Tile said, "So I see a pair of headlights back in the scrub. I can tell it's a truck. I pull off and park. Ten minutes go by and the truck hasn't moved, though the lights are still on. If it's two kids screwing they wouldn't be leaving the headlights on, so I go to check it out."

"You're alone?" Decker asked.

Tile laughed. "Nearest backup is in frigging Orlando. Yeah, I'm alone, you could say that. So I take my pumpgun and my Kevlar light and start slipping toward the truck through the scrub, moving close as I can to the big cypresses so whoever's back there won't see me. All of a sudden I hear a door slam and the truck comes tearing out of the bush. I go down in a crouch and jack a round into the shotgun, but they never slow down, just hit the highway and take off."

"Three guys," Skink said.

"In a dark green pickup," Tile said. "I'm pretty sure it was a Ford, but it wasn't local. I didn't catch the tag."

"Did the men see you?" Decker asked.

"The one on the passenger side, no doubt about it."

"Did you recognize him?"

"Let him finish, Miami," Skink said.

"So I go down to where the truck was parked," Tile said, "right on the edge of the slough. I mean, from the tire tracks you could see they'd backed right up to the water. I figure they're poaching gators or maybe jacklighting a deer that came down to drink. Makes sense, except the ground is completely dry and clean. No blood, no skin, no shells, no nothing."

"Except this," Skink said. He reached into his rainsuit and took out a notebook. He handed it to R. J. Decker. It was a news reporter's notebook, the standard pocket-size spiral. On the front, written in blue ink, were the words: "PICKNEY/CLINCH OBIT." Decker could tell from the thinness of the notebook that some of the pages had been torn out. Those that remained were blank.

"It was under some palmetto," Jim Tile said, "maybe thirty feet from where the truck was parked."

"You didn't find anything else?" Decker asked.

"No, sir."

"Did you report this?"

"Report what?" Tile said. "A truck parked in the bushes? Show me the law against that."

"But you found this notebook and it belongs to a missing person."

Skink shook his head. "The basketball team says he's missing but nobody's filed a report yet. The sheriff may or may not get around to it."

"What are you saying?" Decker asked.

"The sheriff's name is Earley Lockhart," Skink said, "as in Dickie. As in uncle. And, for what it's worth, he has a twelve-pound bass hanging behind his desk. Jim, tell Mr. Decker about your outstanding relationship with the Harney County sheriff's department."

"No relationship," Jim Tile said. "Far as they're concerned, I don't exist. Wrong color. Wrong uniform."

Skink said, "Jim and I go way back. We depend on each other, especially when there's trouble. That's why Jim brought me the Armadillo's notebook."

"But how do you know he's dead?" Decker said.

Skink stood up and turned off the Coleman. Out on the porch he picked up one of his spinning rods. "You wanna drive?" he said to Jim Tile.

"Sure," said the trooper, "give Mr. Decker a ride in a real po-leece car."

"I've had the privilege," Decker said.

*   *   *

"Who was the guy in the truck, the one who recognized you?" Decker asked.

He was sitting in the back of the patrol car, behind the steel grate. Jim Tile was at the wheel; he glanced over at Skink, a crinkled orange mass on the passenger's side, and Skink nodded that it was all right.

"Man named Ozzie Rundell," Jim Tile said.

"Halfwit," Skink grumbled.

"Has he got a brother?" R. J. Decker had heard of Culver Rundell. Ott had mentioned him at Bobby Clinch's funeral. He'd said he was surprised not to see Culver at the service.

"Yeah, Culver," Jim Tile said. "He runs a bait shop on Lake Jesup."

Decker thought it was probably the same one he'd stopped at a few days earlier. Culver could have been the man behind the counter.

"He's smarter than Ozzie," Skink remarked, "but mildew is smarter than Ozzie."

They were on a two-lane blacktop, no center line, no road signs. Decker didn't recognize the highway. Jim Tile was driving fast, one hand on the wheel. Through the grate Decker could see the speedometer prick ninety. He was glad there was no fog.

"How'd you meet the captain?" he asked Jim Tile.

"Used to work for him," the trooper said.

"In Tallahassee," Skink added. "Long time ago."

"What kind of work?" Decker asked.

"Scut work," Skink said.

Decker was too tired to pursue it. He stretched out in the back seat and started to doze. He kept thinking about Ott Pickney and wondering what he was about to see. Skink and Jim Tile were silent up front. After about fifteen minutes Decker felt the patrol car brake and pull off the pavement. Now it bounced along with the sound of sticks and leaves scratching at the undercarriage.

Decker opened his eyes and sat up. They were at Morgan Slough.

Jim Tile got out first and checked around. The cool darkness was ebbing from the swamp; another half-hour and it would be dawn. Skink took his fishing rod from the car and went to the edge of the water, which was the burned color of black tea. The slough was a tangle of lilies and hydrilla, dead branches and live cypress knees. In the tall boughs hung tangled tresses of Spanish moss. The place looked prehistoric.

Jim Tile stood with his hands on his hips. Skink started to cast, reel in, cast again.

"What's going on?" Decker said, shaking off his drowsiness. The crisp winter air had a faint smoky smell.

"The plug I'm using is called a Bayou Boogie," Skink said. "Medium-fast sinker, two sets of treble hooks. I sharpened 'em earlier, before you got here. You probably noticed I put new line on the reel since you and I went out."

"I didn't notice," Decker muttered. All this way for a goddamn fishing lesson. Didn't these people ever just come out and say something?

"Fifteen-pound test Trilene," Skink went on. "You know how much weight this stuff'll lift?"

"No idea," Decker said.

"Well—there we go!" Skink's fishing rod bent double. Instead of setting the hook, he pumped slowly, putting his considerable muscle into it. Whatever it was on the end of the line barely moved.

"You're snagged on a stump," Decker said to Skink.

"Don't think so."

Slowly it was coming up; somehow Skink was pulling the thing in. He pumped so hard that Decker was sure the rod would snap, then Skink would slack up, reel fast, and pump again. The line was stretched so tautly that it hummed.

"You're almost there," Jim Tile said.

"Get ready!" Skink's voice strained under the effort.

He gave a mighty pull and something broke water. It was an iron chain. Skink's fishing lure had snagged in one of the links. Jim Tile knelt down and grabbed it before it could sink back into the slough. He unhooked the fishing lure, and Skink reeled in.

By now Decker knew what was coming.

Hand over hand, Jim Tile hauled on the chain. The wrong end came up first; it was an anchor. A new anchor, too, made of cast iron. A clump of hydrilla weed hung like a soggy green wig from the anchor's fork.

Jim Tile heaved it on shore. Wordlessly he started working toward the other end, the submerged end of the chain.

Instinctively, R. J. Decker thought of his cameras. They were locked in his car, back at Skink's shack. He felt naked without them, like the old days. Certain things were easier to take if you were looking through a camera; sometimes it was the only protection you had, the lens putting an essential distance between the eye and the horror. The horror of seeing a dead friend in the trunk of a Seville, for example. The distance existed only in the mind, of course, but some-times the inside of a lens was a good place to hide. Decker hadn't felt like hiding there for a long time, but now he did. He wanted his cameras, longed for the familiar weight around his neck. Without the cameras he wasn't sure if he could look, but he knew he must. After all, that was the point of getting out of the business. To be able to look again, and to feel something.

Jim Tile struggled with the chain. Skink knelt beside him and loaned his weight to the tug.

"There now," Skink said, breathing hard. The other end of the chain came out of the water in his right hand.

"Get it done," said Jim Tile.

Tied to the end of the chain was a thin nylon rope. Skink's massive hands followed the rope down until the water was up to his elbows. His fingers foraged blindly below the surface; he looked like a giant raccoon hunting a crawfish.

"Ah!" he exclaimed.

Jim Tile stood up, wiped his hands on his uniform, and backed away. With a primordial grunt Skink lifted his morbid catch from the bottom of Morgan Slough.

"Oh God," groaned R. J. Decker.

Ott Pickney floated up dead on the end of a fish stringer. Like a lunker bass, he had been securely fastened through both lips.

9

They were driving back toward Harney on the Gilchrist Highway.

"We can't just leave him there," R. J. Decker said.

"No choice," Skink said from the back seat of the patrol car.

"What do you mean? We've got a murder here. Last time I checked, that's still against the law, even in a shitbucket town like this."

Jim Tile said, "You don't understand."

Skink leaned forward and mushed his face against the grating. "How do we explain being out in the slough? A spade cop and a certifiable lunatic like me." And an ex-con, Decker thought. From under the flowered shower cap Skink winked at him. "It's Jim I'm really worried about, Miami. They'd love a shot at State Trooper Jim Tile, am I right?"

Decker said, "Screw the locals, then. Go to the state attorney general and get a grand jury. We've got two dead men, first Clinch and now Ott Pickney. We can't let it lie."

"We won't," said Jim Tile.

Terrific, Decker thought, the three musketeers.

"What are you so afraid of?" he asked the trooper. "You think they'd really try to frame us?"

"Worse," said Jim Tile. "They'll ignore us. Clinch was already ruled an accident."

"But Ott's floating out there on a fish stringer," Decker said. "I think somebody might legitimately raise the question of foul play."

Jim Tile pulled the car off the pavement and stopped. They were a mile and a half outside the town limits. A pair of headlights approached from the other direction.

"Duck down," Jim Tile said.

Skink and Decker stayed low until the other car had passed. Then Skink climbed out with his fishing rod. "Come on," he said to Decker, "we'll hoof it from here. It's best that nobody sees Jim with the two of us."

Decker got out of the car. The sky in the east was turning a metallic pink.

"Explain it to him," Jim Tile said to Skink, and drove away.

Decker started trudging down the highway. He felt a hundred years old. He wished he were back in Miami, that's how rotten he felt. He was trying to remember if Ott Pickney had any kids, or an ex-wife somewhere. It was entirely possible there was nobody, just the orchids.

"I'm sorry about your friend," Skink said, "but you've got to understand."

"I'm listening."

"The body will be gone by noon, if it's not already. They'll be back for it. They saw Jim Tile out by the slough, and that was that."

Decker said, "We should've stayed there. Jim could have called for help on the radio."

Skink marched ahead of Decker and turned around, walking backward so he could face him directly. "The sheriff's office scans all police frequencies. They would've picked up the call and sent a couple marked cars. Next thing you know, the locals grab jurisdiction and they're questioning you and me, and they're calling Tallahassee about poor Jim Tile—how there's all these irregularities in his report, how uppity and uncooperative he is. Whatever bullshit they can make up, they will. You know how many black troopers there are in this whole state? Not enough for a goddamn basketball team. Jim's a good man and I'm not gonna let him get hung by a bunch of hicks. Not over a fish, for Christ's sake."

Decker had never heard Skink say so much in one breath. He asked, "So what's the plan?"

Skink stopped backward-walking. "Right now the plan is to get off the road."

Decker spun around and saw a pickup truck coming slowly down the highway. Rays from the new sun reflected off the windshield, making it impossible to see who was driving, or how many there were up front.

Skink tugged Decker's arm and said, "Let's stroll through the woods, shall we?"

They left the pavement and walked briskly into a stand of tall pine. They heard the truck speed up. When it was even with them, it stopped. A door slammed, then another.

Skink and Decker were twenty-five yards from the highway when the first shots rang out. Decker hit the ground and pulled Skink with him. A bullet peeled the bark off a tree near their feet.

Decker said, "I'm sure glad you're wearing that orange raincoat, captain. Bet they can only see us a mile or two away."

"Semiautomatic?" Skink asked through clenched teeth.

Decker nodded. "Sounds like a Ruger Mini-14." Very popular with the Porsche-and-powder set in Miami, but not the sort of bang-bang you expected upstate.

The rifle went off again, so rapidly that it was impossible to tell the fresh rounds from the echoes. The slugs slapped at the leaves in a lethal hailstorm. From where they huddled Decker and Skink couldn't see the truck on the highway, but they could hear men's voices between the volleys.

"Will they come for us?" Decker whispered.

"I expect." Skink's cheek was pressed against a carpet of pine needles. A fire ant struggled in the tangle of his mustache; Skink made no move to brush it away. He was listening to the ground.

"There's only two of them," he announced.

"Only?" One with a Ruger was plenty.

Skink's right hand fished under his rainsuit and came out with the pistol.

Decker heard twigs crackle at the edge of the pine.

"Let's run for it," he said. They wouldn't have a prayer in a shoot-out.

"You run," Skink said.

And draw fire, Decker thought. What a grand idea. At least in Beirut you had a chance because of the doorways; doorways made excellent cover. You simply ran a zigzag from one to another. Right now there wasn't a doorway in sight. Even the trees were too skinny to offer protection.

Decker heard footsteps breaking the scrub a few yards behind him. Skink motioned for him to go.

He bunched up on his knees, dug his toes into the moist dirt, and pushed off like a sprinter. He ran erratically, weaving through the pine trunks and hurdling small palmetto bushes. A man shouted and then the gunfire started again. Decker flinched as bullets whined off the tree trunks—low, high, always a few feet behind him. Whoever was shooting was running too, and his aim was lousy.

Decker didn't know the terrain so he picked his openings as they appeared. He spotted promising cover across a bald clearing and he pumped for it, holding his head low. He almost made it, too, when something struck him in the eyes and he crumpled in pain.

A rifle slug had caught a pine branch and whipped it flush across Decker's face. He lay panting on the ground, his fists pressed to his eyes. Maybe they would think he'd been hit. Maybe they would go looking for Skink.

Abruptly the shooting was over.

Decker heard honking. Somebody was leaning on the horn of the truck; long urgent blasts. From the highway a man shouted somebody's name. Decker couldn't make out the words. He took his hands from his face and was relieved to discover that he wasn't blind. His cheeks were wet from his eyes, and his eyes certainly stung, but they seemed to be working.

It was not until he heard the pickup roar away that Decker dared to move, and then he wasn't sure which way to go. The direction that made the most sense was away from the road, but he didn't want to abandon Skink, if Skink were still alive.

Decker crawled to a tree and stood up, cautiously aligning his profile with the trunk. Nothing moved in the clearing; the morning lay dead silent, the songbirds still mute with fear.

What the hell, Decker thought. At the top of his lungs he shouted, "Skink!"

Something big and pale moved at the edge of the woods across the clearing. It made a tremendous noise. "I told you to call me captain!" it bellowed.

Skink was fine. He stood stark naked except for his military boots. "Look what that asshole did to my suit!" He held up the plastic rain jacket. There were three small holes between the shoulder blades. "I got out of it just in time," Skink said. "Hung it on a limb. When I rustled the branch the guy squared around perfectly and cut loose. He was looking the wrong place, slightly."

Hairy and bare-assed, Skink led Decker to the body. The dead man had a black crusty circle between his sandy eyebrows. His mouth was set in an O.

"You were right about the Ruger," Skink said. The rifle lay at the man's side. The clip had been removed.

"To answer your question, no, I've never seen him before," Skink said. "He's hired help, somebody's out-of-town cousin. His pal stayed at the treeline as a lookout."

"I'm sure they figured one gun was enough," Decker said.

"Guy's all of thirty years old," Skink mused, looking down at the dead man. "Stupid jerkoff."

Decker said, "May I assume we won't be notifying the authorities?"

"You learn fast," Skink said.

In the mid-1970s a man named Clinton Tyree became governor of Florida. He was everything voters craved: tall, ruggedly handsome, an ex-college football star (second-team All-American lineman), a decorated Vietnam veteran (a sniper once lost for sixteen days behind enemy lines with no food or ammunition), an eligible bachelor, an avid outdoorsman—and best of all, he was native-born, a rarity at that time in Florida. At first Clinton Tyree's political ideology was conservative when it was practical to be, liberal when it made no difference. At six-foot-six, he looked impressive on the campaign trail and the media loved him. He won the governorship running as a Democrat, but proved to be unlike any Democrat or Republican that the state of Florida had ever seen. To the utter confusion of everyone in Tallahassee, Clint Tyree turned out to be a completely honest man. The first time he turned down a kickback, the bribers naturally assumed that the problem was the amount. The bribers, wealthy land developers with an eye on a particular coastal wildlife preserve, followed with a second offer to the new governor. It was so much money that it would have guaranteed him a comfortable retirement anywhere in the world. The developers were clever, too. The bribe money was to emanate from an overseas corporation with a bank account in Nassau. The funds would be wired from Bay Street to a holding company in Grand Cayman, and from there to a blind trust set up especially for Clinton Tyree at a bank in Panama. In this way the newly acquired wealth of the newly elected governor of Florida would have been shielded by the secrecy laws of three foreign governments.

The crooked developers thought this was an ingenious and foolproof plan, and they were dumbfounded when Clinton Tyree told them to go fuck themselves. The developers had naively contributed large sums to Tyree's gubernatorial campaign, and they could not believe that this was the same man who was now—on a state letterhead!—dismissing them as "submaggots, unfit to suck the sludge off a septic tank."

The rich developers were further astounded to discover that all their conversations with the governor had been secretly tape-recorded by the chief executive himself. They learned about this when carloads of taciturn FBI agents pulled up to their fancy Brickell Avenue office tower, stormed in with warrants, and arrested the whole gold-chained gang of them. Soon the Internal Revenue Service merrily leapt into the investigation and, within six short months, one of the largest land-development firms in the Southeastern United States went belly-up like a dead mudfish.

It was an exciting and historic moment in Florida history. Newspaper editorials lionized Governor Clint Tyree for his courage and honesty, while network pundits promoted him as the dashing harbinger of a New South.

Of course, the people who really counted—that is, the people with the money and the power—did not view the new governor as a hero. They viewed him as a dangerous pain in the ass. True, every slick Florida politician got up and preached for honest government, but few vaguely understood the concept and even fewer practiced it. Clint Tyree was different; he was trouble. He was sending the wrong message.

With Florida no longer virgin territory, competition was brutal among greedy speculators. The edge went to those with the proper grease and the best connections. In the Sunshine State growth had always depended on graft; anyone who was against corruption was obviously against progress. Something had to be done.

The development interests had two choices: they could wait for Tyree's term to expire and get him voted out of office, or they could deal around him.

Which is what they did. They devoted their full resources and attention to corrupting whoever needed it most, a task accomplished with little resistance. The governor was but one vote on the state cabinet, and it was a simple matter for his political enemies to secure the loyalty of an opposing majority. Money was all it took. Similarly, it was simple (though slightly more expensive) to solidify support in the state houses so that Clinton Tyree's oft-used veto was automatically overridden.

Before long the new governor found himself on the losing side of virtually every important political battle. He discovered that being interviewed by David Brinkley, or getting his picture on the cover of *Time,* meant nothing as long as his colleagues kept voting to surrender every inch of Florida's beachfront to pinky-ringed condominium moguls. With each defeat Clint Tyree grew more saturnine, downcast, and withdrawn. The letters he dictated became so dark and profane that his aides were terrified to send them out under the state seal, and rewrote them surreptitiously. They whispered that the governor was losing too much weight, that his suits weren't always pressed to perfection, that his hair was getting shaggy. Some Republicans even started a rumor that Tyree was suffering from a dreaded sexual disease.

Meanwhile the rich developers who had tried to bribe him finally went to trial, with the governor sitting as the chief witness against them. It was, as they say, a media circus. Clinton Tyree's friends thought he held up about as well as could be expected; his enemies thought he looked glazed and unkempt, like a dope addict on the witness stand.

The trial proved to be a tepid victory. The developers were convicted of bribery and conspiracy, but as punishment all they got was probation. They were family men, the judge explained; churchgoers, too.

By wretched coincidence, the day after the sentencing, the Florida Cabinet voted 6–1 to close down the Sparrow Beach Wildlife Preserve and sell it to the Sparrow Beach Development Corporation for twelve million dollars. The purported reason for the sale was the unfortunate death (from either sexual frustration or old age) of the only remaining Karp's Seagrape sparrow, the species for whom the verdant preserve had first been established. With the last rare bird dead, the cabinet reasoned, why continue to tie up perfectly good waterfront? The lone vote against the land deal belonged to the governor, of course, and only afterward did he discover that the principal shareholder in the Sparrow Beach Development Corporation was none other than his trusted running mate, the lieutenant governor.

The morning after the vote, Governor Clinton Tyree did what no other Florida governor had ever done. He quit.

He didn't tell a soul in Tallahassee what he was doing. He simply walked out of the governor's mansion, got in the back of his limousine, and told his chauffeur to drive.

Six hours later he told the driver to stop. The limo pulled into a bus depot in downtown Orlando, where the governor said goodbye to his driver and told him to get the hell going.

For two days Governor Clinton Tyree was the subject of the most massive manhunt in the history of the state. The FBI, the highway patrol, the marine patrol, the Florida Department of Law Enforcement, and the National Guard sent out agents, troops, psychics, bloodhounds and helicopters. The governor's chauffeur was polygraphed seven times and, although he always passed, was still regarded as a prime suspect in the disappearance.

The search ended when Clinton Tyree's notarized resignation was delivered to the Capitol. In a short letter released to the press, the ex-governor said he quit the office because of "disturbing moral and philosophical conflicts." He graciously thanked his friends and supporters, and closed the message by quoting a poignant but seemingly irrelevant passage from a Moody Blues song.

After Clint Tyree's resignation, the slimy business of selling off Florida resumed in the state capital. Those who had been loyal to the young governor began to give interviews suggesting that for two whole years they'd known that he was basically a nut. A few intrepid reporters depleted precious expense accounts trying to track down Clinton Tyree and get the real story, but with no success. The last confirmed sighting was that afternoon when the fugitive governor had vanished from the downtown Orlando bus depot. Using the name Black Leclere, he had purchased a one-way ticket to Fort Lauderdale, but never arrived. Along the way the Greyhound Scenic Cruiser had stopped to refuel at an Exxon station; the driver hadn't noticed that the tall passenger in a blue pinstriped suit who had gotten off to use the men's room had never come back. The Exxon station was located across from a fruit stand on Route 222, four miles outside the town limits of Harney.

Clinton Tyree had selected Harney not only because of its natural beauty—the lake and the ranchlands, the cypresses and the pines—but also because of its profound political retardation. Harney County had the lowest voter registration per capita of any county in Florida. It was one of the few places to be blacklisted by both the Gallup and Lou Harris pollsters, due to the fact that sixty-three percent of those interviewed could not correctly name a vice-president, any vice-president, of the United States. Four out of five Harney citizens had not bothered to cast ballots during the previous gubernatorial election, mainly because the annual bull-semen auction was scheduled the same day.

This was a town where Clinton Tyree was sure he'd never be recognized, where he could build himself a place and mind his own business and call himself Rajneesh or Buzz, or even Skink, and nobody would bother him.

Skink waited all day to get rid of the body. Once darkness fell, he took the truck and left R. J. Decker in the shack. Decker didn't ask because he didn't want to know.

Skink was gone for an hour. When he got back, he was regarbed in full fluorescence. He stalked through the screen door and kicked off his Marine boots. His feet were bare. He had two limp squirrels under one arm, fresh roadkills.

"The Armadillo is still there," he reported.

Immediately Decker guessed what had happened: Skink had hauled the other body out to Morgan Slough. And he probably had hooked it on the same fish stringer.

"I can't stay here," Decker said.

"Suit yourself. Sheriff cars all over the place. There's a pair of 'em parked out on the Mormon Trail, and they hate it out there, believe me. Could be something's in the wind."

Decker sat on the bare wooden floor, his back rubbing against the unvarnished planks of a bookcase. He needed sleep, but every time he closed his eyes he saw Ott Pickney's corpse. The images were indelible. Three frames, if he'd had a camera.

First: the crest of the skull breaking the surface, Ott's hair dripping to one side like brown turtle grass.

Then a shot of the bloodless forehead and the wide-open eyes focused somewhere on eternity.

Finally: a full pallid death mask, fastened grotesquely on the stringer with a loop of heavy wire, and suspended from the water by Skink's tremendous arms, visible in the lower-left-hand corner of the frame.

That was how R. J. Decker was doomed to remember Ott Pickney. It was a curse of the photographic eye never to forget.

"You look like you're ready to quit," Skink said.

"Give me another option."

"Keep going as if nothing happened. Stay on Dickie Lockhart's ass. There's a bass tournament this weekend—"

"New Orleans."

"Yeah, well, let's go."

"You and me?"

"And Mr. Nikon. You got a decent tripod, I hope."

"Sure," Decker said. "In the car."

"And a six-hundred-millimeter, at least."

"Right." His trusty NFL lens; it could peer up a quarterback's nostrils.

"So?" Skink said.

"So it's not worth it," Decker said.

Skink tore off his shower cap and threw it into a corner. He pulled the rubber band out of his ponytail and shook his long hair free.

"I got some supper," he said. "I'll eat all of it if you're not hungry."

Decker rubbed his temples. He didn't feel like food. "I can't believe they'd kill somebody over a goddamn fish."

Skink stood up, holding the dead squirrels by their hind legs. "This thing isn't about fishing."

"Well, money then," Decker said.

"That's only part of it. If we quit, we miss the rest. If we quit, we lose Dickie Lockhart, probably forever. They can't touch him on the killings, not yet anyway."

"I know," Decker said. There wouldn't be a shred of evidence. Ozzie Rundell would go to the chair before he'd rat on his idol.

Decker asked, "Do you think they know it's us?"

"Depends," Skink said. "Depends if the other guy in the pickup saw our faces this morning. Also depends if the Armadillo told 'em about you before he died. If he told 'em who you are, then you've got problems."

"Me? What about you? It was your gun that waxed the guy."

"What gun?" Skink said, raising his hands. "What gun you talking about, officer?" He flashed his anchorman smile. "Don't worry about me, Miami. If you've got the urge to worry, worry about setting up some good fish pictures."

Skink cooked the squirrels on sticks over the outdoor fire. Decker drank a cold beer and felt the night close down over Lake Jesup. They ate in silence; Decker was hungrier than he'd thought. Afterward they each popped open another beer and watched the embers burn down.

"Jim Tile is with us the whole way," Skink said.

"Is it safe?" Decker asked. "For him, I mean."

"Not for him, not for us. But Jim Tile is a careful man. So am I. And you—you're catching on." Skink balanced the beer can on one knee. "There's an Eastern nonstop to New Orleans," he said, "leaves about noon from Orlando."

Decker glanced over at him. "What do you think?"

Skink said, "Probably smart if we drive separate."

Decker nodded. They'll never let him on the plane, he thought, not dressed like that. "Then I guess I'll see you at the airport."

Skink dumped a tin of water on the last of the coals. "Where you headed tonight?" he asked.

"There's somebody I need to see," Decker said, "though I'm not sure where she's staying. Actually, I'm not even sure she's still in town. It's Dennis Gault's sister."

Skink snorted. "She's still in town." He peeled off his rainsuit. "She's at the Days Inn, least that's where the little gumdrop Vette is parked."

"Thanks, I can find it. What about the deputies up on the Trail?"

"Long gone," Skink said. "Shift ended a half-hour ago."

He walked Decker to the car.

"Be careful with that lady," Skink said. "If you get the urge to tell her your life story, I understand. Just leave out the part about today."

"I'm too damn tired," Decker sighed.

"That's what they all say."

She was still at the Days Inn. Room 135. When she answered the door she wore a nightshirt. One of those expensive silky tops; it barely came down far enough to cover her pale yellow panties. R. J. Decker noticed the color of her panties when she reached up to get a robe from a hook on the back of the closet door. Decker did a pitiful job of trying not to stare.

Lanie said, "What's in the bag?"

"A change of clothes."

"You going somewhere?"

"Tomorrow."

"Where?"

"Up north a ways."

Lanie sat in the middle of the bed and Decker took a chair. An old James Bond movie was on television.

"Sean Connery was the best," Lanie remarked. "I've seen this darn thing about twenty times."

"Why are you still in town?" Decker asked.

"I'm going tomorrow, too."

"You didn't answer the question. Why are you still here? Why didn't you go home after Bobby's funeral?"

Lanie said, "I went out to the cemetery today. And yesterday. I haven't felt like leaving yet, that's all. We each deal with grief in our own way—isn't that what you said?"

Very sharp, Decker thought. He just loved it when they filed stuff away. "Know what I think?" he said. "I think the Gault family needs to be tested. Scientifically, I mean. I think maybe there's a genetic deficiency that prevents you people from telling the truth. I think the Mayo Clinic might be very interested."

She rolled her eyes, a little ditty right out of high school. It was supposed to be cool but it came off as nervous.

"I won't stay long," Decker said, "but we need to talk."

"I don't feel like talking," Lanie said, "but you're welcome to stay as long as you like. I'm not tired."

She crossed her legs up under the robe and glanced over at him. Something in the stale motel room smelled fresh and wonderful, and it definitely wasn't Parfum de Days Inn. It was Lanie; she was one of those women who just naturally smelled like a spring day. Or maybe it just seemed that way because she looked so good. Whatever the phenomenon, Decker had the sense to realize he was in trouble, that by walking into her room and letting her hop into bed he had lost all leverage, all hope of getting any answers. He knew he was wasting his time, but he didn't feel like leaving.

"You look like hell," Lanie said.

"Been a long day."

"Hot on the trail?"

"Oh, right."

"Anything new about Bobby's death?"

"I thought you didn't feel like talking," Decker said.

"I'm curious, that's all. More than curious. I loved him, remember?"

"You keep saying that," Decker said, "like you've got to keep reminding yourself."

"Why don't you believe me?"

Lee Strasberg material. Lanie the wounded lover. Her tone of voice was exquisite—hurt but not defensive. And not a flicker of doubt in those beautiful eyes; in fact, she looked about ready to cry. It was such a splendid performance that Decker reconsidered the question: Why didn't he believe her?

"Because Bobby Clinch wasn't your type," he said.

"How do you know?"

"That Corvette parked outside. That's you, Lanie. Bobby was pure pickup truck. You might've liked him, laid him, maybe even given him that blowjob you're so proud of, but you didn't love him."

"You can tell all this from looking at a damn car!"

"I'm an expert," Decker said, "it's what I do." It was true about cars: there was no better clue to the total personality. Any good cop would tell you so. Decker hadn't thought much about the psychology of automobiles until he became a private investigator and had to spend half his time tracing, following, and photographing all kinds. On long surveillances in busy parking lots he made a game of matching shoppers to their cars, and had gotten good at it. The make, model, color, everything down to the shine on the hubcaps was a clue to the puzzle. Decker's own car was a plain gray 1979 Plymouth Volaré, stylistically the most forgettable automobile Detroit ever produced. Decker knew it fit him perfectly. It fit his need to be invisible.

"So you think I belong back in Miami," Lanie was saying sarcastically. "Who can you picture me with, Decker? I know—a young Colombian stud! Rolex, gold necklace, and black Ferrari. Or maybe you figure I'm too old for a coke whore. Maybe you see me on the arm of some silver-haired geezer playing the ponies out at Hialeah."

"Anybody but Bobby Clinch," Decker said. "Steve and Eydie you weren't."

Of course then the tears came, and the next thing Decker knew he had moved to the bed and put his arms around Lanie and told her to knock off the crying. Please. In his mind's eye he could see himself in this cheesy scene out of a cheap detective movie; acting like the gruff cad, awkwardly consoling the weepy long-legged knockout, knowing deep down he ought to play it as the tough guy but feeling compelled to show this warm sensitive side. Decker knew he was a fool but he certainly didn't feel like letting go of Lanie Gault. There was something magnetic and comforting and entirely natural about holding a sweet-smelling woman in a silken nightie on a strange bed in a strange motel room in a strange town where neither one of you belonged.

A Bell Jet-Ranger helicopter awaited the Reverend Charles Weeb at the Fort Lauderdale Executive Airport. Weeb wore a navy pinstriped suit, designer sunglasses, and lizard boots. He was traveling with a vice-president of the Outdoor Christian Network and a young brunette woman who claimed to be a secretary, and who managed to slip her phone number to the chopper pilot during the brief flight.

The helicopter carried the Reverend Charles Weeb to a narrow dike on the edge of the Florida Everglades. Looking east from the levee, Weeb and his associates had a clear view of a massive highway construction site. The land had been bulldozed, the roadbed had been poured, the pilings had been driven for the overpasses. Dump trucks hauled loose fill back and forth, while graders crawled in dusty clouds along the medians.

"Show me again," Weeb said to the vice-president.

"Our property starts right about there," the vice-president said, pointing, "and abuts the expressway for five miles to the south. The state highway board has generously given us three interchanges."

Generously my ass, thought Weeb. Twenty thousand in bonds to each of the greedy fuckers.

"Give me the binoculars," Weeb said.

"I'm sorry, sir, but I left them at the airport."

"I'm going to go sit in the helicopter," the brunette woman whined.

"Stay right here," Weeb growled. "How'm I supposed to see the lake system without the binoculars?"

"We can fly over it on the way back," the vice-president said. "The canals are almost done."

Vigorously Weeb shook his head. "Dammit, Billy, you did it again. People don't buy townhouses on *canals*. 'Canal' is a dirty word. A canal is where raw sewage goes. A canal is where ducks fuck and cattle piss. Who wants to live on a damn canal! Would you pay a hundred-fifty grand to do that? No, you'd want to live on a *lake,* a cool scenic lake, and lakes is what we're selling here."

"I understand," said the vice-president. Lakes it is. Straight, narrow lakes. Lakes you could toss a stone across. Lakes of identical fingerlike dimensions.

The company that OCN had hired was a marine dredging firm whose foremen were, basically, linear-minded. They had once dredged the mouths of Port Everglades and Government Cut, and a long stretch of the freighter route in Tampa Bay. They had worked with impressive speed and efficiency, and they had worked in a perfectly straight line—which is desirable if you're digging a ship channel but rather a handicap when you're digging a lake. This problem had been mentioned several times to Reverend Charles Weeb, who had merely pointed out the fiscal foolishness of having big round lakes. The bigger the lake, the more water. The more water, the less land to sell. The less land to sell, the fewer townhouses to build.

"Lakes don't have to be round," the Reverend Weeb said. "I'm not going to tell you again."

"Yes, sir."

Weeb turned to the west and stared out at the Glades. "Reminds me of the fucking Sahara," he said, "except with muck."

"The water rises in late spring and early summer," the vice-president reported.

"Dickie promises bass."

"Yes, sir, some of the best fishing in the South."

"He'd better be right." Weeb walked along the dike, admiring the spine of the new highway. The vice-president walked a few steps behind him while the secretary stayed where she was, casting glances toward the blue-tinted cockpit of the Jet-Ranger.

"Twenty-nine thousand units," Weeb was saying, "twenty-nine thousand families. Our very own Christian city!"

"Yes," the vice-president said. It was the name of the development that gnawed at him. Lunker Lakes. The vice-president felt that the name Lunker Lakes presented a substantial marketing problem; too colloquial, too red behind the neck. The Reverend Charles Weeb disagreed. It was his audience, he said, and he damn well knew what they would and would not buy. Lunker Lakes was perfect, he insisted. It couldn't miss.

Charlie Weeb was heading back to the chopper. "Billy, we ought to start thinking about shooting some commercials," he said. "Future Bass Capital of America, something like that. Fly Dickie down and get some tape in the can. He can use his own crew, but I'd like you or Deacon Johnson to supervise."

The vice-president said, "There's no fish in the lakes yet."

Weeb climbed into the chopper and the vice-president squeezed in beside him. The secretary was up front next to the pilot. Weeb didn't seem to care.

"I know there's no fucking fish in the lakes. Tell Dickie to go across the dike and shoot some tape on the other side. He'll know what to do."

The Jet-Ranger lifted off and swung low to the east.

"Head over that way," the vice-president told the pilot, "where they're digging those lakes."

"What lakes?" the pilot asked.

Skink was late to the airport. R. J. Decker was not the least bit surprised. He slipped into a phone booth and called the Harney

Sentinel to see if anything had broken loose about the shootings. He had a story all made up about going to meet Ott at the pancake house but Ott never showing up.

Sandy Kilpatrick got on the phone. He said, "I've got some very bad news, Mr. Decker."

Decker took a breath.

"It's about Ott," Kilpatrick said. His voice was a forced whisper, like a priest in the confessional.

"What happened?" Decker said.

"A terrible car accident early this morning," Kilpatrick said. "Out on the Gilchrist Highway. Ott must have gone to sleep at the wheel. His truck ran off the road and hit a big cypress."

"Oh Jesus," Decker said. They'd set up the wreck to cover the murder.

"It burned for two hours, started a mean brushfire," Kilpatrick said. "By the time it was over there wasn't much left. The remains are over at the morgue now, but . . . well, they're hoping to get enough blood to find out if he'd been drinking. They're big on DUI stats around here."

Ott's body would be scorched to a cinder. No one would ever suspect it had been in the water, just as no one would guess what had really killed him. The cheapest trick in the book, but it would work in Harney. Decker could imagine them already repainting the death's-head billboard on Route 222: "DRIVE SAFELY. DON'T BE FATALITY NO. 5."

He didn't know what to say now. Conversations about the newly dead made him uncomfortable, but he didn't want to seem uncaring. "I didn't think Ott was a big drinker," he said lamely.

"Me neither," Kilpatrick said, "but I figured something was wrong when he didn't show up for the basketball game night before last. He was the team mascot, you know."

"Davey Dillo."

"Right." There was a pause on the end of the line; Kilpatrick pondering how to explain Ott's armadillo suit. "It's sort of an un-written rule here at the newspaper," the editor said, "that everybody gives to the United Way. Just a few bucks out of each paycheck—you know, the company's big in civic charity."

"I understand," Decker said.

"Well, Ott refused to donate anything, said he didn't trust 'em. I'd never seen him so adamant."

"He always watched his pennies," Decker said. Ott Pickney was one of the cheapest men he'd ever met. While covering the Dade County courthouse he'd once missed the verdict in a sensational murder trial because he couldn't find a parking spot with a broken meter.

Sandy Kilpatrick went on: "Our publisher has a rigid policy about the United Way. When he heard Ott was holding back, he ordered me to fire him. To save Ott's job I came up with this compromise."

"Davey Dillo?"

"The school team needed a mascot."

"It sure doesn't sound like Ott," Decker said.

"He resisted at first, but he got to where he really enjoyed it. I heard him say so. He was dynamite on that skateboard, too, even in that bulky costume. Someone his age—the kids said he should have been a surfer."

"Sounds like quite a show," Decker said, trying to imagine it.

"He never missed a game, that's why I was worried the other night when he didn't show. Only thing I could figure is that he'd gone out Saturday night and tied one on. Maybe went up to Cocoa Beach, met a girl, and just decided to stay the weekend."

Ott sacked out with a beach bunny—the story probably was all over Harney by now. "Maybe that's it," Decker said. "He was probably on his way home when the accident happened." This was Ott's old pal from Miami, lying through his teeth. If Kilpatrick only knew the truth, Decker thought. He said, "Sandy, I'm so sorry. I can't believe he's dead." That part was almost true, and the regret was genuine.

"The service is tomorrow," Kilpatrick said. "Cremation seemed the best way to go, considering."

Decker said good-bye and hung up. Then he called a florist shop in Miami and asked them to wire an orchid to Ott Pickney's funeral. The best orchid they had.

11

Jim Tile was born in the town of Wilamette, Florida, a corrupt and barren flyspeck untouched by the alien notions of integration, fair housing, and equal rights. Jim Tile was one of the few blacks ever to have escaped his miserable neighborhood without benefit of a bus ride to Raiford or a football scholarship. He attributed his success to good steady parents who made him stay in school, and also to his awesome physical abilities. Most street kids thought punching was the cool way to fight, but Jim Tile preferred to wrestle because it was more personal. For this he took some grief from his pals until the first time the white kids jumped him and tried to push his face in some cowshit. There were three of them, and naturally they waited until Jim Tile was alone. They actually got him down for a moment, but the one who was supposed to lock Jim Tile's arms didn't get a good grip and that was that. One of the white kids ended up with a broken collarbone, another with both elbows hyperextended grotesquely, and the third had four broken ribs where Jim Tile had squeezed him in a leg scissors. And they all went to the hospital with cowshit on their noses.

After high school Jim Tile enrolled at Florida State University in Tallahassee, majored in criminal justice, was graduated, and joined the highway patrol. His friends and classmates told him that he was nuts, that a young black man with a 4.0 grade average and a college degree could write his own ticket with the DEA or Customs, maybe even the FBI. Jim Tile could have taken his pick. Besides, everybody knew about the highway patrol: it had the worst pay and the highest risks of any law-enforcement job in the state—not to mention its reputation as an enclave for hardcore rednecks who, while not excluding minority recruits, hardly welcomed them with champagne and tickertape parades.

In the 1970s the usual fate of black troopers was to get assigned to the lousiest roads in the reddest counties. This way they could spend most of their days writing tickets to foul-mouthed Klansmen farmers who insisted on driving their tractors down the middle of the highway in violation of about seventeen traffic statutes. Two or three years of this challenging work was enough to inspire most black troopers to look elsewhere for employment, but Jim Tile hung on. When other troopers asked him why, he replied that he intended someday to become commander of the entire highway patrol. His friends thought he was joking, but when word of Jim Tile's boldly stated ambition reached certain colonels and lieutenants in Tallahassee he was immediately reassigned to patrol the remote roadways of Harney County and faithfully protect its enlightened citizenry, most of whom insisted on addressing him as Boy or Son or Officer Zulu.

One day Trooper Jim Tile was told to accompany a little-known gubernatorial candidate on a campaign swing through Harney. The day began with breakfast at the pancake house and finished with a roast-hog barbecue on the shore of Lake Jesup. The candidate, Clinton Tyree, gave the identical slick speech no less than nine times, and out of utter boredom Jim Tile memorized it. By the end of the day he was unconsciously muttering the big applause lines just before they came out of the candidate's mouth. From the reactions—and penurious donations—of several fat-cat political contributors, it was obvious that they had gotten the idea that Clinton Tyree was letting a big black man tell him what to say.

At dusk, after all the reporters and politicos had polished off the barbecue and gone home, Clinton Tyree took Jim Tile aside and said:

"I know you don't think much of my speech, but in November I'm going to be elected governor."

"I don't doubt it," Jim Tile had said, "but it's because of your teeth, not your ideals."

After Clinton Tyree won the election, one of the first things he did was order Trooper Jim Tile transferred from Harney County to the governor's special detail in Tallahassee. This unit was the equivalent of the state's Secret Service, one of the most prestigious assignments in the highway patrol. Never before had a black man been chosen as a bodyguard for a governor, and many of Tyree's cronies told him that he was setting a dangerous precedent. The governor only laughed. He told them that Jim Tile was the most prescient man he'd met during the whole campaign. An exit survey taken on election day by the pollster Pat Caddell revealed that what Florida voters had liked most about candidate Clinton Tyree was not his plainly spoken views on the death penalty or toxic dumps or corporate income taxes, but rather his handsome smile. In particular, his teeth.

During his brief and turbulent tenure in the governor's mansion, Clinton Tyree confided often in Jim Tile. The trooper grew to admire him; he thought the new governor was courageous, visionary, earnest, and doomed. Jim Tile was probably the only person in Florida who was not surprised when Clinton Tyree resigned from office and vanished from the public eye.

As soon as Tyree was gone, Trooper Jim Tile was removed from the governor's detail and sent back to Harney in the hopes that he'd come to his senses and quit the force.

For some reason he did not.

Jim Tile remained loyal to Clinton Tyree, who was now calling himself Skink and subsisting on fried bass and dead animals off the highway. Jim Tile's loyalty extended so far as to driving the former governor to the Orlando airport for one of his rare trips out of state.

"I could take some comp time and come with you," Jim Tile volunteered.

Skink was riding in the back of the patrol car in order to draw less attention. He looked like a prisoner anyway.

"Thanks for the offer," he said, "but we're going to a tournament in Louisiana."

Jim Tile nodded in understanding. "Gotcha." Bopping down Bourbon Street he'd be fine. Fishing the bayous was another matter.

"Keep your ears open while I'm gone," Skink said. "I'd steer clear of the Morgan Slough, too."

"Don't worry."

Skink could tell Jim Tile was worried. He could see distraction in the way the trooper sat at the wheel; driving was the last thing on his mind. He was barely doing sixty.

"Is it me or yourself you're thinking about?" Skink asked.

"I was thinking about something that happened yesterday morning," Jim Tile said. "About twenty minutes after I dropped you guys off on the highway, I pulled over a pickup truck that nearly broke my radar."

"Mmmm," Skink said, acting like he couldn't have cared less.

"I wrote him up a speeding ticket for doing ninety-two. The man said he was late for work. I said where do you work, and he said Miller Lumber. I said you must be new, and he said yeah, that's right. I said it must be your first day because you're driving the wrong damn direction, and then he didn't say anything."

"You ever seen this boy before?"

"No," Jim Tile said.

"Or the truck?"

"No. Had Louisiana plates. Jefferson Parish."

"Mmmm," Skink said.

"But you know what was funny," Jim Tile said. "There was a rifle clip on the front seat. No rifle, just a fresh clip. Thirty rounds. Would have fit a Ruger, I expect. The man said the gun was stolen out of his truck down in West Palm. Said some nigger kids stole it."

Skink frowned. "He said that to your face? *Nigger* kids? What the hell did you do when he said that, Jim? Split open his cracker skull, I hope."

"Naw," Jim Tile said. "Know what else was strange? I saw two jugs of coffee on the front seat. Not one, but two."

"Maybe he was extra thirsty," Skink said.

"Or maybe the second jug didn't belong to him. Maybe it belonged to a buddy." The trooper straightened in the driver's seat, yawned, and stretched his arms. "Maybe the man's buddy was the one with the rifle. Maybe there was some trouble back on the road and something happened to him."

"You got one hell of an imagination," Skink said. "You ought to write for the movies." There was no point in telling his friend about the killing. Someday it might be necessary, but not now; the trooper had enough to worry about.

"So you got the fellow's name, the driver," Skink said.

Jim Tile nodded. "Thomas Curl."

"I don't believe he works at Miller's," Skink remarked.

"Me neither."

"Suppose I ask around New Orleans."

"Would you mind?" Jim Tile said. "I'm just curious."

"Don't blame you. Man's got to have a reason for lying to a cop. I'll see what I can dig up."

They rode the last ten miles in silence; Jim Tile, wishing that Skink would just come out and tell him about it, but knowing there were good reasons not to. The second man was dead, the trooper was sure. Maybe the details weren't all that important.

As he pulled up to the terminal, Jim Tile said, "This Decker, you must think he's all right."

"Seems solid enough."

"Just remember he's got other priorities. He's not working for you."

"Maybe he is," Skink said, "and he just doesn't know it."

"Yet," said Jim Tile.

R. J. Decker was pacing in front of the Eastern Airlines counter when Skink lumbered in, looking like a biker who'd misplaced all his amphetamines. Still, Decker had to admit, the overall appearance was a slight improvement.

"I took a bath," Skink said, "aren't you proud?"

"Thank you."

"I hate airplanes."

"Come on, they're boarding our flight."

At the gate Skink got into an argument with a flight attendant who wouldn't let him carry on his scuba gear.

"It won't fit under the seat," she explained.

"I'll show you where it fits," Skink growled.

"Just check the tanks into baggage," Decker said.

"They'll bust 'em," Skink protested.

"Then I'll buy you new ones."

"Our handlers are very careful," the flight attendant said brightly.

"Troglodytes!" said Skink, and stalked onto the airplane.

"Your friend's a little grumpy this morning," the flight attendant said as she took Decker's ticket coupon.

"He's just a nervous flier. He'll settle down."

"I hope so. You might mention to him that we have an armed sky marshal on board."

Oh, absolutely, Decker thought, what a fine idea.

He found Skink hunkered down in the last row of the tail section.

"I traded seats with a couple Catholic missionaries," Skink explained. "This is the safest place to be if the plane goes down, the last row. Where's your camera gear?"

"In a trunk, don't worry."

"You remembered the tripod?"

"Yes, captain."

Skink was a jangled mess. He fumed and squirmed and fidgeted. He scratched nervously at the hair on his cheeks. Decker had never seen him this way.

"You don't like to fly?"

"Spent half my life on planes. Planes don't scare me. I hate the goddamn things but they don't scare me, if that's what you're getting at." He dug into a pocket of his black denim jacket and brought out the black sunglasses and the flowered shower cap.

"Please don't put those on," Decker said. "Not right now."

"You with the fucking FAA or what?" Skink pulled the rainhat tight over his hair. "Who cares," he said.

The man looks miserable, Decker thought, a true sociopath. It wasn't the airplane, either, it was the people; Skink plainly couldn't stand to be out in public. Under the rainhat he seemed to calm. Behind the charcoal lenses of the sunglasses, Decker sensed, Skink's green eyes had closed.

"Pay no attention to me," he said quietly.

"Take a nap," Decker said. The jet engines, which seemed anchored directly over their heads, drowned Decker's words; the plane started rolling down the runway. Skink said nothing until they were airborne.

Then he shifted in his seat and said: "Bad news, Miami. The Rundell brothers are on this bird. Picking their noses up in first class, if you can believe it. Makes me sick."

Decker hadn't noticed them when he boarded; he'd been preoccupied with Skink. "Did they see you?"

"What do you think?" Skink replied mordantly.

"So much for stealth."

Skink chuckled. "Culver damn near wet his pants."

"He'll be on the phone to Lockhart the minute we're on the ground."

"Can't have that," Skink said. He stared out the window until the flight attendants started moving down the aisle with the lunch trays. Skink lowered the tabletop at his seat and braced his logger's arms on it.

"Ozzie and Culver, they don't know your face."

"I don't think so," Decker said, "but I can't be sure. I believe I stopped in their bait shop once."

"Damn." Skink smoothed the plastic cap against his skull and fingered his long braid of hair. Decker could tell he was cooking up a scheme. "Where does this plane go from New Orleans?" Skink asked.

"Tulsa."

"Good," Skink said. "That's where you're going. As soon as you get there, hop another flight and come back. You got plenty of cash?"

"Yeah, and plastic."

"It's cash you'll need," Skink said. "Most bail bondsmen don't take MasterCard."

Whatever the plan, Decker didn't like it already. "Is it you or me who's going to need bail?"

"Aw, relax," Skink said.

But now it was impossible.

When the stewardess brought the food, Skink glowered from under his cap and snapped: "What in the name of Christ is this slop?"

"Beef Wellington, muffins, a fresh garden salad, and carrot cake."

"How about some goddamn opossum?" Skink said.

The flight attendant's blue buttonlike eyes flickered slightly. "I don't think so, sir, but we may have a chicken Kiev left over from the Atlanta flight."

"How about squirrel?" Skink said. "Squirrel Kiev would be lovely."

"I'm sorry, but that's not on the menu," the stewardess said, the lilt and patience draining from her voice. "Would you care for a beverage this morning?"

"Just possum hormones," Skink said, "and if I don't get some, I'm going to tear this goddamn airplane apart." Then he casually ripped the tray table off its hinges and handed it to the flight attendant, who backpedaled in terror up the aisle.

She was calling for her supervisor when Skink rose from his seat and shouted, "You promised opossum! I called ahead and you promised to reserve a possum lunch. Kosher, too!"

R. J. Decker felt paralyzed. Skink's plan was now evident, and irreversible.

"Fresh opossum—or we all die together!" he proclaimed. By now pandemonium was sweeping the tail section; women and children scurried toward the front of the aircraft while the male passengers conferred about the best course of action. Skink's size, apparel, and maniacal demeanor did not invite heroic confrontation at thirty thousand feet.

To Decker it seemed like every passenger in the airplane had turned around to stare at the lunatic in the flowered shower cap.

The aisle cleared as a man with a badge on his shirt came out of first class and hurried toward the trouble.

"Remember, you don't know me!" Skink whispered to Decker.

"No kidding."

The sky marshal, a short stocky man with a bushy mustache, asked R. J. Decker if he would mind moving up a few rows for the remainder of the flight.

"Gladly," Decker said.

The sky marshal carried no gun, just a short billy club and a pair of handcuffs. He sat down in Decker's seat.

"Are you the man with the opossum?" Skink asked.

"Behave yourself," the sky marshal said sternly, "and I won't have to use these." He jangled the handcuffs ominously.

"Please," Skink said, "I'm a heavily medicated man."

The sky marshal nodded. "Everything is fine now. We're only a half-hour from New Orleans."

Soon the plane was calm again and lunch service was resumed. When Decker turned around he saw Skink and the sky marshal chatting amiably.

After landing in New Orleans, the pilot asked all passengers to remain seated for a few minutes. As soon as the cabin door opened, three city policemen and two federal agents in dark suits boarded the plane and led Skink away in handcuffs and leg irons. On the way out he made a point of kissing one of the flight attendants on the earlobe and warning the pilot to watch out for windshear over Little Rock.

The Rundell brothers watched in fascination.

"Where they taking him?" Ozzie wondered.

"The nuthouse, I hope," said Culver. "Let's get going."

R. J. Decker stayed on the plane to Tulsa. Except for one drunken tourist wearing a Disney World tank top and Pluto ears, it was a peaceful flight.

12

On the night of January 15, Dickie Lockhart got dog-sucking drunk on Bourbon Street and was booted out of a topless joint for tossing rubber nightcrawlers on the dancers. The worms were a freebie from a national tackle company whose sales reps had come to town for the big bass tournament. The sales reps had given Dickie Lockhart four bags of assorted lures and hooks, plus a thousand dollars cash as incentive to win the tournament using the company's equipment. Dickie blew the entire grand in the French Quarter, buying rock cocaine and rainbow-colored cocktails for exquisitely painted women, most of whom turned out to be flaming he-she's out trolling for cock. In disgust Dickie Lockhart had retreated to the strip joints, where at least the boobs were genuine. The trouble happened when he ran out of five-dollar bills for tips; finding only the slippery rubber nightcrawlers in his pockets, he began flicking them up at the nude performers. In his drunken state he was vastly entertained by the way the gooey worms clung to the dancers' thighs and nipples, and would occasionally tangle in their pubic hair. The nightcrawlers looked (and felt) so authentic that the strippers began shrieking and clawing at their own flesh; one frail acrobat even collapsed and rolled about the stage as if she were on fire. Dickie thought the whole scene was hysterical; obviously these girls had never been fishing. He was mildly baffled when the bouncers heaved him out of the joint (hadn't they seen him on TV?), but took some satisfaction when other patrons booed the rough manner in which he was expelled.

Afterward he had a few more drinks and went looking for his boss, the Reverend Charles Weeb. Drunk was the only condition in which Dickie Lockhart could have made this decision; as a rule one did not pop in on Reverend Weeb unless one was invited.

Dickie lurched up to the top-floor suite of the swank hotel on Chartres Street and pounded on the door. It was almost midnight.

"Who is it?" a female voice asked.

"DEA!" said Dickie Lockhart. "Open the fuck up!"

The door opened and a beautiful long-haired woman stood there; at least she seemed beautiful to Dickie Lockhart. An apparition, really. She was wearing canvas hip waders and nothing else. Her lovely breasts poked out in a friendly way from under the suspenders. For a moment Dickie almost forgot he was supposed to be with the DEA.

"I got a warrant for Charles Weeb," he snarled.

"What's with the fishing pole?" the naked wader asked.

Dickie Lockhart had been carrying a nine-foot boron fly rod all night long. He couldn't remember why. Somebody in a bar had given it to him; another damn salesman, probably.

"It's not a fishing rod, so shut up!"

"Yes, it is," said the woman.

"It's a heroin probe," Dickie Lockhart said. "Now stand back." He brushed past her and marched into the living room of the suite, but the reverend was not there. Dickie headed for the master bedroom, the woman clomping after him in the heavy waders.

"Have you got a warrant?" she asked.

Dickie found the Reverend Charles Weeb lying on his back in bed. Another young woman was on top of him, bouncing happily. This one was wearing a Saints jersey, number 12.

From behind Dickie Lockhart the bare-breasted wader announced: "Charlie, there's a man here to arrest you."

Weeb looked up irritably, fastened his angry eyes on Dickie Lockhart, and said: "Be gone, sinner!"

It occurred to Dickie that maybe it wasn't such a hot idea to stop by unannounced. He went back to the living room, turned on the television, and slumped on the couch. The woman in the waders fixed him a bourbon. She said her name was Ellen O'Something and that she had recently been promoted to executive secretary of the First Pentecostal Church of Exemptive Redemption, of which the Reverend Charles Weeb was founder and spiritual masthead. She apologized for answering the door half-naked, said the waders weren't really her idea. Dickie Lockhart said he understood, thought she looked darn good in them. He told her to watch out for chafing, though, said he spoke from experience.

"Nice fly rod," she remarked.

"Not for bass," Dickie Lockhart said. "The action's too fast for poppers."

The woman nodded. "I was thinking more about streamers," she said. "A Muddler Minnow, for instance. Say a four or a six."

"Sure," Dickie Lockhart said, dumbstruck, dizzy, madly in love. "Sure, with the boron you could throw a size four, you bet. Do you fish?"

At that moment the Reverend Charles Weeb thundered into the room with a mauve towel wrapped around his midsection. The apparition excused herself and clomped off to a bedroom. Dickie Lockhart's heart ached. He was sure he'd never see her again, Charles Weeb would make sure of that.

"Son, what in the name of holy fuck is the matter with you?" the clergyman began. "What demon has possessed you, what poison serpent, what diseased fucking germ has invaded your brain and robbed you of all common sense? What in the name of Our Savior Jesus were you thinking when you knocked on my door tonight?"

"I'm fairly plastered," Dickie Lockhart said.

"Well, so you are. But see what you've done. That young lady in there—"

"The quarterback?"

"Hush! That young lady was on the brink of a profound revelation when you burst in and interrupted our collective concentration. I don't appreciate that, Dickie, and neither does she."

"The night's young," Dickie Lockhart said. "You can try again."

The Reverend Weeb glowered. "Why did you come here?"

Dickie shrugged. "I wanted to talk."

"About what?" Weeb hiked up the towel to cover the pale fatty roll of shrimp-colored belly. "What was so all-fired important that you would invade my personal privacy at this hour?"

"The show," Dickie said, emboldened by Ellen's bourbon. "I just don't think you fully appreciate the show. I think you take me for granted, Reverend Weeb."

"Is that right?"

Dickie Lockhart stood up. It wasn't easy. He pointed the nine-foot boron fly rod directly at Reverend Weeb's midsection, so that the tip tickled the gray curly hair.

"Catching bass is not easy," Dickie Lockhart said, his own anger welling, fueled by a mental image of his beloved Ellen O'Something bouncing on top of this flabby rich pig. "Catching bass is not a sure thing."

Weeb said, "I understand, Dickie." He had dealt with angry drunks before and knew that caution was the best strategy. He didn't like the fishing rod poking into his tummy, but realized that only his pride was in danger. "Overall, I think you do a hell of a job with *Fish Fever*, I really do."

"Then why do you treat me like shit?"

"Now, I pay you very well," Weeb said.

With his wrist Dickie Lockhart started whipping the rod back and forth, filling the room with sibilant noise. Weeb had a hunch it would hurt like hell if the tip thwacked across his bare flesh, and he edged back a step.

"I heard," said Dickie Lockhart, "that you been talking to Ed Spurling."

"Where did you hear that?" A new look came into the minister's eyes, a look of nervousness.

"Some boys that fish with Ed. Said Ed told 'em that the Outdoor Christian Network wanted to buy his TV show."

Weeb said, "Dickie, that's ridiculous. We've got the best bass show in all America. Yours. We don't need another."

"That's what I said, but those boys that fish with Ed told me something else. They said Ed was bragging that you promised to make him number one within two years. Within two years, they said, *Fish Fever* would be out of production."

These redneck assholes, Weeb was thinking, what a grapevine they had. It was too bad Ed Spurling couldn't keep his damn mouth shut.

"Dickie," Weeb said, "somebody's pulling your leg. I never met Spurling in my life. I don't blame you for being upset, buddy, but I swear you've got nothing to worry about. Look, of all the pro bass anglers in the world, who did I ask to do the promotion footage for Lunker Lakes? Who? You, Dickie, 'cause you're the best. All of us at OCN feel the same way: you're our number-one man."

Lockhart lowered the fishing rod. His eyes were muddy, his arms like lead. If he didn't pass out soon he'd need another bourbon.

Soothingly the Reverend Charles Weeb said, "Don't worry, son, none of what you heard is true."

"Sure glad to hear it," Dickie said, "because there's no telling what would happen if I found out otherwise. No telling. Remember the guy from the zoning board down in Lauderdale, the one you told me to take fishing that time? Man, he had some wild stories about that Lunker Lagoon."

"Lunker Lakes," Weeb said tersely.

"He says he got himself a brand-new swimming pool, thanks to you. With a sauna in the shallow end!"

"I wouldn't know."

Dickie broke into a daffy grin. "And I'm trying to imagine what your faithful flock might do if they found out their shepherd was double-boffing a couple of sweet young girls from the church. I'm wondering about that, Reverend Weeb."

"I get the point."

"Do you really?" Dickie Lockhart wielded the fly rod swordlike and, with an artful flick, popped the knot on Charlie Weeb's bath towel, which dropped to his ankles.

"Aw, what a cute little thing," Dickie said with a wink. "Cute as a junebug."

Weeb flushed. He couldn't believe that the tables had turned so fast, that he had so carelessly misjudged this nasty little cracker bastard. "What do you want?" he asked Dickie Lockhart.

"A new contract. Five years, no cancellation. Plus ten percent of first-run syndication rights. Don't look so sad, Reverend Weeb. I'll make it easy for you: you don't have to announce it until after I win the tournament this week. I'll show up at the press conference with the trophy, put on a good show."

"All right," Weeb said, cupping his hands over his privates, "what else?"

"I want the budget doubled to two thousand per show."

"Fifteen hundred tops."

"Fine," Dickie said, "I'm not a greedy man."

"Anything more?" asked Reverend Weeb.

"Yeah, go get Ellen and tell her I'm giving her a ride home."

Lake Maurepas, where the Cajun Invitational Bass Classic was to be held, was a bladder-shaped miniature of the immense Lake Pontchartrain. Located off Interstate 55 northwest of New Orleans, the marshy and bass-rich Maurepas was connected to its muddy mother at Pass Manchac, a few miles south of the town of Hammond. It was there that R. J. Decker and Skink took a room at a Quality Court motel. At the Sportsman's Hideout Marina they rented a small aluminum johnboat with a fifteen-horsepower outboard, and told the lady at the cash register they'd be going out at dusk. The lady looked suspicious until Skink introduced himself as the famous explorer Philippe Cousteau, and explained he was working on a documentary about the famous Louisiana eel spawn, which only took place in the dead of night. Yes, the lady at the cash register nodded, I've heard of it. Then she asked for Philippe's autograph and Skink earnestly replied (in a marvelous French accent) that for such a beautiful woman, a mere autograph would never do. Instead he promised to name a new species of mollusk in her honor.

It had taken the better part of the morning to get Skink arraigned and bailed out of jail, and by now it was the middle of the day; not hot, but piercingly bright, the way it gets in January in the Deep South. Skink said there was no point in going out on the water now because the bass would be in thick cover. He curled up on the floor of the motel room and went to sleep while Decker read the New Orleans *Times-Picayune*. On the back page of the local section was a small item about a local man who had disappeared on a fishing trip to Florida and was presumed drowned somewhere in the murky vastness of Lake Okeechobee. The young man's name was Lemus Curl, and except for the absence of a blackened bullet hole in his forehead, the picture in the paper matched the face of the man whom Skink had shot dead near Morgan Slough; the man who had tried to murder them with the rifle. Obviously it was Lemus Curl's brother whom Jim Tile had stopped for speeding shortly afterward. Interestingly, the same Thomas Curl was quoted in the newspaper as saying that his brother had slipped off the dike and tumbled into the water on the west side of the big lake. The article reported that Lemus Curl had been tussling with a hawg bass at the time of the tragic accident. Decker thought this last detail, though untrue, lent a fine ironic touch to the story.

Skink snored away and Decker felt alone. He felt like calling Catherine. He found a pay phone outside the lobby of the Quality Court. She answered on the fifth ring, and sounded like she'd been sleeping.

"Did I wake you?"

"Hey, Rage, where you at?"

"In a motel outside New Orleans."

"Hmmm, sounds romantic."

"Very," Decker said. "My roommate is a 240-pound homicidal hermit. For dinner he's fixing me a dead fox he scraped off the highway near Ponchatoula, and after that we're taking a leaky tin boat out on a windy lake to spy on some semi-retarded fishermen. Don't you wish you were here?"

"I could fly in tomorrow, get a hotel in the Quarter."

"Don't be a tease, Catherine."

"Oh, Decker." She was stretching, waking up, probably kicking off the covers. He could tell all that over the phone. "I had to get up early and take James to the airport," she said.

"Where to now?"

"San Francisco."

"And of course he didn't want you to come along."

"That's not true," Catherine said. "Those conventions are a bore, and besides, I've got plans of my own. What are you doing out in the bayous?"

"Rethinking Darwin," Decker said. "Some of these folks didn't evolve from apes; it was the other way around."

"You should have gotten a nice room downtown."

"That's not what I meant," Decker said. "The fish people, I'm talking about."

"Take notes," Catherine said, "it sounds like it'll make a terrific movie. *Attack of the Fish People.* Now, be honest, Rage, wouldn't you rather be shooting pictures of golfers?"

Decker said, "I'd better go."

"That's it?"

"I've got a lot to tell you, but not over the phone."

"It's all right," Catherine said. "Anytime you want to talk." He wished she'd been serious about flying up to New Orleans, though it was a nutty scheme. She would have been safer in San Francisco with her chiropractor.

"I'll call you when I get back," Decker said.

"Take care," Catherine said. "Slurp an oyster for me."

At dusk Skink was ready to roll. Shower cap, weathersuit, mosquito netting, lamps, flippers, regulator, scuba tank, dive knife, speargun and, purely for show, a couple of cheap spinning rods. R. J. Decker was afraid the johnboat would sink under the weight. He decided there was no point in bringing the cameras at night; a strobe would be useless at long distance. If his theory was correct, Dickie Lockhart wouldn't be anywhere near the lake anyway.

They made sure they were alone at the dock before loading the boat and shoving off. It was a chilly night, and a northern breeze stung Decker's cheeks and nose. At the throttle, Skink seemed perfectly warm and serene behind his sunglasses. He seemed to know where he was going. He followed the concrete ribbon of I-55, which was sunk into the marshlands on enormous concrete pilings. The highway pilings were round and smooth, as big as sequoias but out of place; the cars that raced overhead intruded harshly on the foggy peace of the bayous. After twenty minutes Skink cut off the motor.

"I prefer oars," Skink said, but there were none in the boat. "You can hear more with oars," he remarked.

R. J. Decker noticed what he was talking about. Across the water, bouncing off the pilings, came the sound of men's voices; pieces of conversation, deep bursts of laughter, carried by the wind.

"Let's drift for a while," Skink suggested. He picked up one of the fishing poles and made a few idle casts. Darkness had settled in and the lake was gray. Skink cocked his head, listening for clues from the other boat.

"I think I see them," Decker said. A fuzzy pinprick of white light, rocking.

"They've got a Coleman lit," Skink said. "Two hundred yards away, at least."

"They sound a helluva lot closer," Decker said.

"Just a trick of the night."

After a few minutes the light went out. Skink and Decker heard the ignition sounds of a big engine. It was probably a bass boat. Swiftly Skink hand-cranked the outboard and aimed the johnboat toward the other craft. Legs wide, he stood up as he steered, though Decker couldn't imagine how he could safely navigate around the highway pilings, not to mention the submerged stumps and brush-piles that mined the lakeshore. Every so often Skink would cut the outboard and listen to make sure the other boat was still moving; as long as their engine was running, they'd never know they were being followed. Sitting on two hundred horses, you can't hear yourself think.

After a few minutes the other boat stopped and the Coleman lantern flickered on again. The men's voices were faint and more distant than before.

"We'll never get close," Skink muttered, "unless we walk it."

Fortuitously the wind pushed the johnboat into a stand of lily pads. Hand over hand, Skink used the roots to pull them to shore, where Decker tied the boat to a sturdy limb. He grabbed a flashlight and hopped out after Skink. They followed a ragged course along the shoreline for probably four hundred yards, taking tentative spongy steps and using the flashlight sparingly. They passed through a trailer park with particular stealth, not wishing to be mistaken for bears and blasted to oblivion. Far removed from his native territory, Skink's nocturnal instincts remained sound; his path brought them out of the bogs within thirty yards of where the bass boat floated.

The lantern illuminated two men, not the Rundell brothers. "Local boys," Skink whispered. "Makes sense. Need someone who knows the water." The anglers were not casting their fishing lines; rather, they seemed to be studying the water. The deck of the boat bristled with rods, each with a line out. In the penumbra a half-dozen red floats were visible bobbing around the sides of the boat. "Live-baiters," Skink explained. "My guess is worms."

R. J. Decker said, "It could be anybody out for a night on the lake."

"No," Skink said, "these boys are out to load the boat."

And they were. Every so often one of the poles would bend and flutter, and a bass would splash out in the pads. Quickly one of the men would snatch the rig and reel in the fish as fast as he could. The bass were quickly unhooked and put in a livewell under a hatch in the stern.

This methodical fish-collecting went on for two hours, during which Skink said little and scarcely moved a muscle. Decker's legs were cramping from sitting on his haunches, but it was impossible to stand up and stretch without being seen. Mercifully, as the wind stiffened and the temperature dropped, the two poachers finally called it quits. They reeled in the worms, stored the rods, cranked the big engine, and motored slowly—confoundingly so—up the southeastern shore of the lake. The boat stayed unusually close to the elevated highway, maneuvering in and out of the pilings; occasionally the lantern light flickered across the faces of the two men as they leaned over the gunwales, peering at something which neither Decker nor Skink could see.

Of course it was Skink who led the way back to the johnboat. By the time they got there, the marsh was empty and silent; the other men had finished their business and roared away.

Skink stripped down to his underwear and began fitting his considerable bulk into a wetsuit.

"I was afraid of this," Decker said. Pitch black, fifty degrees, and this madman was going in. Decker couldn't wait to see the look on the game warden's face.

"Can you drive the boat?" Skink asked.

"I think I can handle it."

"Take me along the pilings, the same way our buddies went."

Decker said, "I wouldn't dive in this soup."

"Who's asking you to? Come on, let's move."

They motored down the lake to the poachers' bass hole. Skink strapped on a yellow scuba tank, adjusted his headlamp, and slipped over the side. He fitted a nylon rope around his waist and tied it to the transom of the boat. One sharp tug was a signal to stop, two meant reverse, and three tugs meant trouble. "In that case do your best to haul me in," Skink advised. "If you can't manage, then get the hell out of here, I'm gator chow."

Decker steered the boat anxiously, monitoring Skink's progress by the bubbles surfacing in the foamy wake. He wondered what the fish and turtles must think, confronted in their inky element by such a hoary gurgling beast. The engine's throttle was set as low as it would go, so the johnboat moved at a crawl; Skink was a heavy load to tow.

When he found what he was searching for, Skink tugged so hard that the rope nearly pulled the stern under. Immediately Decker shifted to neutral so the propeller wouldn't be spinning perilously when Skink came up.

He burst to the surface like a happy porpoise. He held a wire cage, three feet by three. Inside the trap were four healthy largemouth bass, which flapped helplessly against the mesh as Skink hoisted their manmade cell into the bow. He turned off the regulator, spit out the mouthpiece, and tore off his mask.

"Jackpot!" he said breathlessly. "Lookit here."

Hanging from the fish cage was an eight-foot length of heavy monofilament line, transparent from more than a few feet away. Skink had cut one end with his dive knife. "They tied it to a willow branch—you'd never see it unless you knew where to look," he said. "Get the wirecutters, Miami."

Decker clipped the hinges off the fish cage. Skink reached in and took out the bass one by one, gently releasing each fish back into the lake. It was an oddly tender moment; Skink's grin was as warm as the glow from the lantern. After the bass were freed, he returned the empty cage to the water and tied it to the same dry bough.

Decker had to admit that it was an ingenious cheat. Salt the lake with pre-caught fish and scoop them out on tournament day. Dennis Gault was right: these boys would do anything to win. The more he thought about it, the more disgusted Decker got. The poachers had corrupted this beautiful place, polluted its smoky mystery. He couldn't wait to see their faces when they discovered what had happened, couldn't wait to take their pictures.

Probing the waters around the highway pilings, Decker and Skink located three more submerged cages, each stocked with the freshly caught bass. They counted eleven fish in all, four in the final trap; lifting the largest by its lower lip, Skink estimated its weight at nine and a half pounds. "This bruiser would have bought dirty Dickie first place," he gloated. "*Adiós,* old girl." And he let the fish go.

That left two smaller bass flopping in the mesh, their underslung jaws snapping in mute protest while starved burgundy gills flared in agitation.

"Sorry, fellas," Skink said. "You're the bait." With a pair of blunt-nosed pliers he carefully clipped the first two spines of the dorsal fin on each bass.

"What're you doing?" R. J. Decker asked.

"Marking them," Skink replied, "that's all."

With the fish still trapped, he securely rewired the door of the cage and eased it below the surface. He made sure it was tied securely to the concrete beam where Dickie Lockhart would be looking for it. By that time, of course, the bass champion would be in a state of desperate panic, wondering not only who was sabotaging his secret fish cages but also how in the world he would ever win the tournament now.

13

The day the Cajun Invitational Bass Classic was to begin, Dennis Gault was hundreds of miles away in Miami. Though it nettled him to miss the competition, strategy dictated that he sit out the tournament. He wanted Dickie Lockhart to feel safe and secure, knowing his archenemy wasn't around to spy on him. He wanted Dickie and his gang to let their guard down.

Gault spent most of the morning in a surly mood, barking at secretaries and hanging up on commodity brokers who wanted the scoop on the new cane crop. In the morning paper he checked the weather in New Orleans and was elated to see that it was windy and cold; this meant rugged fishing. R. J. Decker called briefly to say things were going well, but offered no details. The other thing he didn't offer was an apology for smashing Dennis Gault's nose. Gault was miffed at Decker's icy attitude but thrilled by the idea that the drama finally had begun. Gault's hatred for Dickie Lockhart consumed him, and he would not rest until the man was not just broken but scandalized.

The cheating was only part of it; Gault would have rigged some bass tournaments himself, had he found trustworthy conspirators. The more virulent seed of Dennis Gault's resentment was knowing that a dumb hick like Dickie was part of the bass brotherhood—the Good Old Boy that Gault himself could never be. Dickie was the champ, the TV personality, the world-famous outdoorsman; he could scarcely balance a checkbook or tie a Windsor, but he knew Curt Gowdy personally. In a man's world, that counted for plenty.

Losing to Lockhart in a bass tournament was bad enough, but watching impotently while the asshole outsmarted everybody else was intolerable. Dennis Gault's venom toward Dickie and his crowd spilled from a deep well. It was the way they looked at him when he showed up for the tournaments; he was the outsider, the dilettante with the money. Their eyes said: You don't belong on this lake, mister, you belong on a golf course. He was constantly referred to as The Rich Guy from Miami. Coral Gables would have been fine, but *Miami*. He might as well have dropped in from Bolivia as far as the other bassers were concerned. To a man they were rural Deep Southerners, with names like Jerry and Larry, Chet and Greg, Jeb and Jimmy. When they talked it was bubba-this and brother-that, between spits of chaw. When Dennis Gault opened his mouth and all that get-me-my-broker stuff came out, the bassers looked at him as if he were a peeling leper.

Naively Gault had thought this antagonism might abate as his angling skills improved and he began to win a few tournaments. Things only got worse, of course, due in large measure to his own absymal judgment. For instance, Dennis Gault insisted on driving his burgundy Rolls Corniche to all the fishing tournaments. The purple vision of such a car towing a bass boat down the Florida Turnpike was enough to stop traffic, and it positively ruined the bucolic ambience of any dockside gathering. Many times Gault would return from a hard day of fishing to find his tires flattened, or see that some mischiefmaker had parked his burgundy pride beneath a tree filled with diarrhetic crows. But Gault was a peculiar man when it came to personal tastes; his father had driven a Rolls and by God that's what Dennis would drive. He did not like pickup trucks, but a pickup would have helped him crack the bass clique. With the Corniche he stood no chance.

The incident with the helicopters is what sealed his excommunication.

Long before he had collected any evidence against Dickie Lockhart, Dennis Gault had proposed a monitoring program to deter cheating in the big-money tournaments. Rumors of flagrant bass-planting had surfaced even in the usually booster-minded outdoor magazines, and a few unseemly scandals had come to light. Consequently, professional tournament organizers were in a mood to mend their tarnished image. More as a public-relations gambit than anything, they had agreed to try Dennis Gault's unusual experiment.

This was his plan: to have independent spotters in helicopters follow the fishermen and keep an eye on them during the competition. Gault even offered to pay for the chopper rentals himself, an offer which was snapped up immediately.

The problem with the plan was that largemouth bass don't much care for noise, and helicopters make plenty. The fish didn't like the penetrating thrum of the big machines, nor the waves the aircraft kicked up on the water. This was quickly evident in the Tuscaloosa bass tournament, where Gault's airborne scheme was tried for the first and last time. Whenever the helicopters would appear and hover over the bass boats, the fish would go deep and quit eating. The wind from the rotors made it impossible to cast a lure, and blew the caps and forty-dollar Polaroid sunglasses off several irritated contestants. The whole thing was a truly terrible idea, and on the second day of the experiment two of the helicopters were actually shot out of the sky by angry bass fishermen. Because no one was seriously injured, the offenders were assessed only ten penalty pounds apiece off their final stringers. Dennis Gault finished in fourteenth place and was banished from the national Competition Committee forever.

Which was probably just as well. Soon afterward Gault had come to suspect Dickie Lockhart of cheating, and his obsession took root like a wild and irrational vine. It twisted itself so ferociously around Gault's soul that even knowing of R. J. Decker's progress in Louisiana only agitated him; Gault itched to be there to share in the stalk, though he knew it would have been a grave mistake. On the telephone Decker had addressed him in the same cold tones as the fishermen always did, as if he were a spoiled wimp, and this began to bother Gault too. Sometimes Decker seemed to forget he was hired help.

The way this is going, Gault thought, I'll be the last to know if something shakes loose.

So he made a call and asked Lanie for another favor.

Decker got up before dawn, struggled into his blue jeans, and threw on a musty blue pea jacket. The DJ on the clock radio announced that it was forty-eight degrees in downtown Hammond. Decker shivered, and put on two pairs of socks; living in the South Florida heat turned your blood to broth.

Skink sat on the floor of the motel room and flossed his teeth. He wore only Jockey shorts, sunglasses, and the flowered bathcap. Decker asked if he wanted to go along but Skink shook his head no. The twang of the floss against gleaming bicuspids sounded like a toy ukulele.

"Want me to bring back some coffee?" Decker asked.

"A rabbit would be good," Skink said.

Decker sighed and said he'd be back before ten. He got in the rental car and headed for the dock at Pass Manchac. On old Route 51 he encountered a steady stream of well-buffed Jeeps, Broncos, and Blazers, all towing bass boats to Lake Maurepas. Many of the trucks had oversize tires, tinted windows, and powerful fog lights that shot amber spears through the soupy-dark bayous. These vehicles served as the royal carriages of the top bass pros, who had won them in various fishing tournaments; a tournament wasn't even worth entering unless a four-wheel-drive was one of the prizes. Many of the bassers won three or four a year.

At the fish camp the mood was solemn and businesslike as the sleek boats were backed off galvanized trailers into the milky-green water. The anglers all wore caps, vests, and jumpsuits plastered with colorful patches advertising their sponsors' products; everything from bug spray to chewing tobacco to worms was shilled in this manner. Most of the fishermen wore Lucite goggles to protect their faces during the breakneck race to the bass hole. This innovation had recently been introduced to the bassing world after one unlucky angler died hitting a swarm of junebugs at fifty knots; one of the brittle beetles had gone through his left eyeball like a bullet and tunneled straight into his brain.

R. J. Decker sipped coffee from a Styrofoam cup and stood among a throng of wives, girlfriends, and mechanics waiting for the tournament to begin. A tall chalk scoreboard posted outside the Sportsman's Hideout displayed the roster of forty entrants, which included some of the most famous bass fishermen of all time: Jimmy Houston of Oklahoma, Larry Nixon of Texas, Orlando Wilson of Georgia, and of course the legendary Roland Martin of Florida. Revered in the world of fishing, these names meant absolutely nothing to R. J. Decker, who recognized only one entry on the Cajun Invitational chalkboard: Dickie Lockhart.

But where was the sonofabitch? As the headlights of the trucks sporadically played across the water, Decker scrutinized the faces of the anglers, now hunkered behind the consoles of their boats. They looked virtually identical with their goggles and their caps and their puffed ruddy cheeks. Dickie's boat was out there somewhere, Decker knew, but he'd have to wait until the weigh-in to see him.

At precisely five-thirty a bearded man in khaki trousers, a flannel shirt, and a string tie strode to the end of the dock and announced through a megaphone: "Bass anglers, prepare for the blast-off!" In unison the fishermen turned their ignitions, and Lake Maurepas boiled and rumbled and swelled. Blue smoke from the big outboards curled skyward and collected in an acrid foreign cloud over the marsh. The boats inched away from the crowded ramp and crept out toward where the pass opened its mouth to the lake. The procession came to a stop at a lighted buoy.

"Now the fun starts," said a young woman standing next to R. J. Decker. She was holding two sleeping babies.

The starter raised a pistol and fired into the air. Instantly a wall of noise rose off Maurepas: the race was on. The bass boats hiccuped and growled and then whined, pushing for more speed. With the throttles hammered down, the sterns dug ferociously and the bows popped up at such alarming angles that Decker was certain some of the boats would flip over in midair. Yet somehow they planed off perfectly, gliding flat and barely creasing the crystal texture of the lake. The song of the big engines was that of a million furious bees; it tore the dawn all to hell.

It was one of the most remarkable moments Decker had ever seen, almost military in its high-tech absurdity: forty boats rocketing the same direction at sixty miles per hour. In darkness.

Most of the spectators applauded heartily.

"Doesn't anyone ever get hurt?" Decker asked the woman with the two babies, who were now yowling.

"Hurt?" she said. "No, sir. At that speed you just flat-out die."

Skink was waiting outside the motel when Decker returned. "You got the cameras?" he asked.

"All ready," Decker said.

They drove back to the Sportsman's Hideout and rented the same johnboat from the night before. This time Decker asked for a paddle. The cashier said brightly to Skink: "Are you finding enough of those eels, Mr. Cousteau?"

"*Sí,*" Skink replied.

"*Oui!*" Decker whispered.

"Oui!" Skink said. "Many many eels."

"I'm so glad," the cashier said.

Hastily they loaded the boat. Decker's camera gear was packed in waterproof aluminum carriers. Skink took special care to distribute the weight evenly, so the johnboat wouldn't list. After the morning's parade of lightning-fast bass rigs, the puny fifteen-horse outboard seemed slow and anemic to Decker. By the time they got to the secret spot, the sun had been up an hour.

Skink guided the johnboat deep into the bulrushes. The engine stalled when the prop snarled in the thick grass. Skink used his bare hands to pull them out of sight, away from the pass. Soon they seemed walled in by cattails, sawgrass, and hyacinth. Directly overhead was the elevated ramp of Interstate 55; Decker and Skink were hidden in its cool shadow. Wordlessly Skink shed the orange rainsuit and put on a full camouflage hunting outfit, the type deer hunters use. He threw one to R. J. Decker and told him to do the same. The mottled hunting suit was brand-new, still crinkled from the bag.

"Where'd you get this?" Decker asked.

"Borrowed it," Skink said. "Put the tripod up front." By swinging the plastic paddle he cleared a field of view through the bullrushes. He pointed and said, "That's where we pulled the last trap."

Decker set the tripod in the bow, carefully tightening the legs. He attached a Nikon camera body with a six-hundred-millimeter lens; it looked like a snub-nosed bazooka. He had decided on black-and-white film; as evidence it was much more dramatic than a tiny Kodachrome slide. Color was for vacation snapshots, black-and-white was for the grit of reality. With a long lens the print would have that grainy texture that seemed to convey guilt, seemed proof that somebody was getting caught in the act of something.

Decker closed one eye and expertly focused on the strand of monofilament tied to the concrete piling.

"How long do we wait?" he asked.

Skink grunted. "Long as it takes. They'll be here soon."

"How can you be sure?"

"The fish," Skink said. He meant the two bass he had left in the fish trap, the ones he had marked with the pliers. "The longer you leave 'em, the worse they look. Bang their heads against the wire, get all fucked up. They'd stand out bad at the weigh-in. The trick is to get 'em fresh."

"Makes sense," Decker said.

"Well, these boys aren't stupid."

On this point Decker and Skink disagreed.

After fifteen minutes they heard the sound of another boat. Skink slid to his knees and Decker took his position at the tripod camera. A boat with a glittering green metal-flake hull drifted into the Nikon's frame; the man up front held a fishing rod and used a foot pedal to control a small electric motor. The motor made a purring sound; it was designed to maneuver the boat silently, so as not to frighten the bass. The angler seated in the stern was casting a purple rubber worm and working the lure as a snake, the way Skink had showed Decker that night on Lake Jesup.

Unfortunately, neither of the men in the green boat happened to be Dickie Lockhart searching for his traps; they were just ordinary fishermen. After a while they glided away, still working the shoreline intently, seldom speaking to one another. Decker didn't know if the men were contestants in the big tournament, but thought they probably must be, judging by the grim set to their jawlines.

An hour passed and no other boats went by. Skink leaned back, propping his shoulders against the plastic cowling of the outboard motor. He looked thoroughly relaxed, much happier than he had seemed in the motel room. A blue heron joined them in the shade of the highway. Head cocked, it waded the shallows in slow motion, finally spearing a small bluegill. Skink laughed out loud and clapped his hands appreciatively. "Now, that's fishing!" he exclaimed, but the noise startled the gangly bird, which squawked and flapped away, dropping the bluegill. No bigger than a silver dollar, the wounded fish swam in addled circles, flashing in the brown water. Skink leaned over and snatched it with one sure swipe.

"Please," Decker protested.

Skink shrugged. "Gonna die anyway."

"I promise, we'll get a big lunch at Middendorf's—"

But it was too late. Skink gulped the fish raw.

"Christ." Decker looked away. He hoped like hell they wouldn't see any snakes.

"Protein," Skink said, muffling a burp.

"I'll stick to Raisin Bran."

Stiffly Decker stood up to stretch his legs. He was beginning to think Dickie Lockhart wouldn't show up. What if he'd gotten spooked by finding the other traps empty? What if he'd decided to play it safe and fish honestly? Skink had assured him that no such change of plans was possible, too much was at stake. Not just first-place prize money but crucial points in the national bass standings—and don't forget the prestige. Damn egos, Skink had said, these boys make Reggie Jackson seem humble by comparison.

"Any sign of the Rundell brothers this morning?" Skink asked.

"Not that I saw," Decker said.

"You can bet your ass they'll show up at the weigh-in. We'll have to be careful. You look worried, Miami."

"Just restless."

Skink sat forward. "You been thinking about the dead guy back in Harney, am I right?"

"Dead guys, plural."

"See why Bobby Clinch got killed in the Coon Bog," Skink said. "He was looking for fish cages, same as we were last night. Only Bobby wasn't too careful. The Bog is probably where Dickie hides some big mother hawgs."

Decker said, "It's not just Clinch that bothers me, it's the other two."

Skink propped his chin in his hands. He was doing his best to appear sympathetic. "Look at it like this: the creep I killed probably killed your pal the Armadillo."

"Is that how you look at it?"

"I *don't* look at it," Skink said, "period."

"He shot at us first," Decker said, almost talking to himself.

"Right."

"But we should have gone to the cops."

"Don't be a jackass. You want your fucking name in the papers? Not me," Skink said. "I got no appetite for fame."

Decker had been dying to ask. "What exactly did you do," he said to Skink, "before this?"

"Before this?" Skink plucked off his shades. "I made mistakes."

"Something about you does look familiar," Decker said. "Something about the mouth."

"Used to leave it open a lot," Skink said.

"I think it's the teeth," Decker was saying.

Skink's forest-green eyes sparkled. "Ah, the teeth." He grinned, quite naturally.

But R. J. Decker couldn't make the connection. The brief governorship of Clinton Tyree had occurred before Decker's newspaper days and before he paid much attention to statewide politics. Besides, the face now smiling at him from beneath the flowered bathcap was so snarled and seamed that the governor's closest friends might have had trouble recognizing him.

"What's the story?" Decker asked earnestly. "Are you wanted somewhere?"

"Not wanted," Skink said. "Lost."

But before Decker could press for more, Skink raised a fishy brown finger to his lips. Another boat was coming.

Coming fast, and from the opposite direction. Skink motioned to Decker and they shrank to the deck of the narrow johnboat. The sound of the other outboard stopped abruptly, and Decker heard men's voices behind them. The voices seemed very close, but he was afraid to get up and look.

"You have a talk with that fuckin' guy tonight!" said one man.

"I said I would, didn't I?" Another voice.

"Find out if he was followed or what."

"He woulda said somethin'."

"Mebbe. Mebbe he's just bean a smardass. Ever thoughta that?"

"I'll talk to him. Christ, was it the third piling or the fourth?"

"The fourth," said the first voice. "See, there's the line."

The fishermen had spotted the submerged trap. Decker carefully lifted himself from the bottom of the johnboat and inched toward the camera in the bow. Skink nodded and motioned that it was safe to move. The poachers' voices bounced back and forth off the concrete under I-55.

" 'Least the fuckers didn't find this one."

"Pull it up quick."

Decker studied the two men through the camera. They had their backs toward him. Under the caps one looked blondish and one had thick black hair, like Dickie Lockhart's. Both seemed like large men, though it was difficult to tell how much of the bulk was winter clothing. The bass boat itself was silver and blue, with an unreadable name in fancy script along the side. Decker kept the camera trained on the fishermen. His forefinger squeezed the shutter button while his thumb levered the rewind. He had snapped six frames and still the men had not turned around.

It was maddening. Decker could see that they had the fish cage out of the water. "They won't turn around," he whispered to Skink. "I haven't got the picture yet."

From the back of the boat Skink acknowledged with a grunt. He flipped his sunglasses down. "Get ready," he said.

Then he screamed, a piercing feral cry that made Decker shiver. The unhuman quavering echo jolted both fishermen and caused them to drop the wire cage with a commotion. Clutching their precious captive bass, they wheeled to face a screeching bobcat, or maybe even a panther, but instead saw only the empty mocking glades. Swiftly, Decker fired away. His camera captured every detail of bewilderment in the two men's faces, including the bolt of fear in their eyes.

Two men who definitely were not Dickie Lockhart.

14

"So what now?"

"Eat," Skink said through a mouthful of fried catfish. They sat at a corner table in Middendorf's. No one seemed to notice their camouflage suits.

Decker said, "Wait till Gault hears we tailed the wrong guys."

Skink had momentarily turned his attention to a bowl of drippy coleslaw. "Maybe not," he said. "Maybe they work for Lockhart."

Decker had considered that possibility. Perhaps Dickie was too cautious to pull the fish traps himself. All he'd have to do was recruit some pals for the deed, and rendezvous later on the lake to pick up the purloined bass. Some of those boys would do anything Dickie Lockhart told them, as long as he promised to put them on TV.

The other possible explanation of what had happened that morning made just as much sense: R. J. Decker had simply photographed the wrong gang of cheaters.

Either way, the faces on film were not the ones Dennis Gault wanted to see.

"You know damn well Dickie's got the tournament rigged."

"Of course," Skink said. "But there's a billion places to hide the bass around here. Bayous far as the eye can see. Shit, he could sink the traps out on Pontchartrain and we'd grow old lookin' in that soup."

"So we staked out the obvious place," Decker said gloomily.

"And got ourselves some obvious assholes." Skink signaled a waitress for more catfish. "It'll all work out, Miami. Go to the weigh-in, see what happens. And eat your goddamn hush puppies, all right? Worse comes to worst, I'll just shoot the motherfucker."

"Pardon?"

"Lockhart," Skink said.

"Come on." Decker vainly searched Skink's face for some sign that he was joking.

"Gault would love it," Skink said. "Damn, I got a mouthful of bones here. How hard is it to properly fillet a fish? Doesn't take a fucking surgeon, does it?" A waitress warily approached the table but Decker motioned her away.

"We're not killing Dickie," he whispered to Skink.

"I've been thinking about it," Skink said, not lowering his voice even a little. "Who gives a shit if Lockhart croaks? His sponsors? The network? Big deal." Skink paused to chew.

"I'll get the damn photograph," Decker said.

"Be lots easier just to shoot his ass. Fella I know in Thibodaux, he'd lend me a deer rifle."

"No!" Decker snapped, but he saw that the idea had already lodged itself like a tick, somewhere behind those infernal sunglasses. "It's crazy," Decker said. "You mention it again and I'm gone, captain."

"Oh, relax," Skink said.

"I mean it!"

Skink reached over and speared a hush puppy from Decker's plate. "I warned you," he said playfully. "You had your chance."

The bass boats were as haphazard in their return as they had been regimented in departure. The weigh-in was set for four-thirty, and the fishermen cut wild vectors across Lake Maurepas to beat the deadline. They came from all directions; wide open seemed to be the only speed they knew. The ramp at Pass Manchac was bustling with spectators, sponsors, and even a local television crew. A monumental glass aquarium—a grudging concession to conservationists—had been erected near the scoreboard, ostensibly to keep the caught bass alive so they could be freed later. As the catches were brought in, the fish were weighed, measured, and photographed by a Louisiana state biologist. Then they were dropped into the greenish tank, where most of them promptly turned belly-up and expired in deep shock.

The all-important weight totals went up on the big scoreboard. The angler with the biggest fish would receive ten thousand dollars; heaviest stringer was twenty grand, plus a new bass boat, a vacation trailer, and a Dodge Ram four-by-four, which would most likely be traded back for cash.

Decker waited alone because Skink had gone back to the motel. He had mumbled something about not wanting to bump into the Rundell brothers—and there they were, slurping beer by the gas pumps. Ozzie was such a pitiable dolt, yet it was he who'd driven the getaway truck from the scene of Ott Pickney's murder. Decker played with the idea of sneaking up to Ozzie and whispering something terrifying into his ear, just to get a reaction. A fatal angina attack, maybe.

But Decker decided to keep a safe distance, on the off-chance Culver might remember him from the bait shop.

The ritual of the weigh-in—the handshakes, the hushed gathering around the scales, the posting of the results—held Decker's attention at first, but after a while his thoughts drifted back to Skink. It occurred to him that Skink was starting to unravel, or maybe just finishing the process, and that for all his backwoods savvy the man might become a serious liability. Decker wished Jim Tile were around to settle Skink down, or at least advise Decker how to handle him.

A burst of applause sprang from around the stage and the rest of the crowd rose on tiptoes, straining to see. A lean, tan, and apparently well-known fisherman was parading a stringer of three immense bass the way a triumphant boxer brandishes the championship belt. The scorer climbed a stepladder and wrote "21-7" in chalk next to the name of Ed Spurling. By four pounds he had become the new leader of the Cajun Invitational Bass Classic.

Grinning handsomely, Fast Eddie Spurling slipped the fat fish into the gigantic aquarium and clasped his hands over his head. Reflexively, and without purpose, Decker snapped a few pictures.

The cheaters in the green boat arrived ten minutes before the deadline. They wore no smiles for the fans. Only four bass hung on their stringer, including the two wan specimens that Skink had marked the previous night in the fish trap. Decker got off four frames before the cheaters slung their catch onto the scale and trudged off in a sulk. "Eight-fourteen," the weighmaster droned through a megaphone. Tenth place, Decker noted; it wasn't Lockhart, but it still felt good.

Dickie's boat was the last one to reach the dock. The crowd rustled and shifted; some of the other anglers craned their necks and muttered nervously, but a few pretended not to notice the champ's arrival. Ed Spurling popped a Budweiser and turned his back on the scene. He was talking to a bigshot from the Stren line company.

Dickie Lockhart pulled off his goggles, smoothed his jumpsuit, and ran a comb through his unnaturally shiny hair. All this, before bounding out of the boat. "Hey," he said when a fan called out his name. "How you? Hey there! Nice to see ya," as he threaded through the spectators. A crew from *Fish Fever* filmed the victory march.

Dickie's driver, a local boy, remained on his knees in the back of the bass boat, trying to grab the fish out of the livewell. He seemed to be taking a long time. Eventually even Ed Spurling turned to watch.

There were five bass in all, very nice ones. Decker figured the smallest to be four pounds; the biggest was simply grotesque. It had the color of burnt moss and the shape of an old stump. The eyes bulged. The mouth was as wide as a milkpail.

Dickie Lockhart's helper carried the stringer of fish through the murmuring throng to the weighmaster, who dumped them in a plastic laundry basket. The hawg went on the scale first: twelve pounds, seven ounces. When the weight flashed on the official Rolex digital readout, a few in the crowd whistled and clapped.

Ten grand, Decker thought, just like that. He snapped a picture of Dickie cleaning his sunglasses with a bandanna.

The entire stringer went next. "Thirty-oh-nine," the weighmaster bellowed. "We've got us a winner!"

Decker noticed that the applause was neither unanimous nor ebullient, save for the beer-drooling Rundells, Dickie's most loyal worshipers.

"Polygraph!" a basser from Reserve shouted angrily.

"Put him on the box," yelled another, one of Ed Spurling's people.

Dickie Lockhart ignored them. He grabbed each end of the stringer and lifted the bass for the benefit of the photographers. True-life pictures, he knew, were the essence of product-endorsement advertisements in outdoor magazines. Each of Dickie's many sponsors desired a special shot of their star and the prizewinning catch, and Lockhart effusively obliged. By the time he had finished posing and deposited the big fish into the tank, the bass were so dead that they sank like stones. The scorer chalked "30-9" next to Dickie's name on the big board.

R. J. Decker's camera ran out of film, but he didn't bother to reload. It was all a waste of time.

The weighmaster handed Lockhart two checks and three sets of keys.

"Just what I need," the TV star joked, "another damn boat."

R. J. Decker couldn't wait to get out, and he pushed the rental car, an anemic four-cylinder compact, as fast as it would go. On Route 51 a gleaming Jeep Wagoneer passed him doing ninety, minimum. The driver looked like Ed Spurling. The passenger had startling straw-blond hair and wore a salmon jogging suit. They both seemed preoccupied.

At the motel the skinny young desk clerk flagged Decker into the lobby.

"I gave the key to your lady friend," he said with a wink. "Didn't think you'd mind."

"Of course not," Decker said. Catherine—she'd come after all. He almost ran to the room.

The moment he opened the door Decker realized that Skink could no longer be counted among the sane; he had vaulted the gap from eccentric to sociopath.

Lanie Gault was tied up on the floor.

Not just tied up but tightly wrapped—wound like a mummy from shoulders to ankles in eighty-pound monofilament fishing line.

She was alive, at least. Her eyes were wide open, but upside-down it was hard to read the emotions. Decker noticed that she was naked except for bikini panties and gray Reebok sneakers. Her mouth was sealed; Skink had run a strip of hurricane tape several times around Lanie's head, gumming her curly brown hair. Decker decided to save the tape for last.

"Don't move," he said. As if she'd be going out for cigarettes.

Decker dug a pocket knife from his camera bag. He knelt next to Lanie and began sawing through the heavy strands. Skink had wrapped her about four hundred times, spun her like a top, evidently; cutting her free took nearly thirty minutes. He took extra care with the tape over her mouth.

"Christ," she gasped, examining the purple grooves in her flesh. Decker helped her to the bed and handed her a blouse from her overnight bag.

"You know," Lanie said, cool as ever, "that your friend is totally unglued."

"What did he do to you?"

"You just saw it."

"Nothing else?"

"This isn't enough?" Lanie said. "He strung me up like a Christmas turkey. The weird thing was, he never said a word."

Decker was almost afraid to ask: "Why'd he take your clothes off?"

Lanie shook her head. "He didn't, that was me. Thought I'd surprise you when you got back. I was down almost to the bare essentials when Bigfoot barged in."

"We're sharing the room," Decker said lamely.

"Cute."

"He sleeps on the floor."

"Lucky for you."

Decker said, "He didn't act angry?"

"Not really. Annoyed, I guess. He tied me up, grabbed his gear, and took off. Look at me, Decker, look what he did! I got stripes on my tits, stripes all over."

"They'll go away," Decker said, "once the circulation comes back."

"That line cut into the back of my legs," Lanie said, examining herself in the mirror.

"I'm sorry," Decker said. He was impressed that Lanie was taking it so well. "He didn't say where he was going?"

"I told you, he didn't say a damn thing, just sang this song over and over."

Decker was past the point of being surprised. "A song," he repeated. "Skink was singing?"

"Yeah. 'Knights in White Satin.' "

"Ah." Moody Blues. The man was a child of the Sixties.

"He's not much of a crooner," Lanie grumbled.

"As long as he didn't hurt you."

She shot him a look.

"I mean, besides tying you up," Decker said.

"He didn't try to pork me, no," Lanie said, "and he didn't stick electrodes into my eyeballs, if that's what you mean. But he's still totally nuts."

"I'm aware of that."

"I could call the cops, you know."

"What for? He's long gone."

Not so long, Lanie thought, maybe fifteen minutes. "Mind if I take a shower?"

"Go ahead." Decker slumped back on the bed and closed his eyes. Soon he heard water running in the bathroom. He wished it were rain.

Lanie came out, still dripping. Already the purple ligature bars were fading.

"Well, here we are," she said, a bit too brightly. "Another night, another motel. Decker, we're in a rut."

"So to speak."

"Remember the last time?"

"Sure."

"Well, don't get too damn excited," she said, scowling. She wrapped herself in the towel.

Decker had always been a sucker for fresh-out-of-the-shower women. With considerable effort he pushed ahead with purposeful conversation. "Dennis told you I was here."

"He mentioned it, yeah."

"What else did he mention?"

"Just about Dickie and the tournament, that's all," Lanie said. She sat on the bed and crossed her legs. "What's with you? I came all this way and you act like I've got a disease."

"Rough day," Decker said.

She reached over and took his hand. "Don't worry about your weird friend, he'll find his way back to Harney."

Decker said, "He forgot his plane ticket." Not to mention the insistent New Orleans bail bondsman; the airline disturbance was a federal rap.

"He'll be fine," Lanie said. "Put him on a highway and he'll eat his way home."

Decker perked up. "So you know about Skink?"

"He's a legend," Lanie said. She started unbuttoning Decker's shirt. "One rumor is he's a mass murderer from Oregon. Another says he's ex-CIA, helped kill Trujillo. One story goes he's hiding from the Warren Commission."

"Those are first-rate," Decker said, but he had nothing more plausible to offer in the way of Skink theories. A bomber for the Weather Underground. Owsley's secret chemist. Lead singer for the Grass Roots. Take your pick.

"Come under the covers," Lanie said, and before Decker knew it the towel was on the floor and she was sliding between the muslin sheets. "Come on, you tell me about your rough day."

This, thought Decker, from a woman who'd just been strung up nude by a madman. Good old irrepressible Lanie Gault.

Later she got hungry. Decker said there was a good burger joint down the street, but Lanie nagged him into driving all the way to New Orleans. She tossed her overnight bag in the back seat and announced that she'd get her own room in the Quarter because she didn't want to stay at the Quality Court, in case Skink returned. Decker didn't blame her one bit.

They went to the Acme for raw oysters and beer. Lanie kept making suggestive oyster remarks while Decker smiled politely, wishing like hell he were back in Miami, alone in his trailer. He had enjoyed rolling around in bed with her—at least he'd thought so at the time—but was having difficulty recalling any of the prurient details.

Shortly after midnight he excused himself, went to a pay phone on Iberville, and called Jim Tile in Florida. Decker told him what had happened with Skink, Lanie, and the bass tournament.

"Man," the trooper said. "He tied her up?"

"And took off."

"Come on home," Tile said.

"What about Skink?"

"He'll be all right. He gets these moods."

Decker told Tile about Skink's histrionics on the airplane. "He has arraignment tomorrow," Decker said. "In the federal building on Poydras. If he calls, Jim, please remind him."

Tile said, "Don't hold your breath."

Lanie had ordered another dozen on the half-shell while Decker was on the phone.

"I'm stuffed," he said, but ate one anyway.

"Dennis says you're getting close to Lockhart."

She'd been trying all night to find out what happened with the tournament. Decker hadn't said much.

Lanie said, "I heard on the radio that Dickie won."

"That's right." Radio? What kind of radio station covers a fish tournament? Decker wondered.

"Did he cheat again?" Lanie asked.

"I don't know. Probably." Decker paused. "I'll send your brother a full report."

"He'll be pissed."

Tough shit, Decker wanted to say. But instead: "We're not giving up."

"You and Bigfoot?"

"He's got a particular talent."

"Not with women," Lanie said.

Decker dropped her off at the Bienville House. His feelings were not the least bit wounded when she didn't invite him to stay the night.

He took his time driving back to Hammond. It was past two in the morning, but I-10 was loaded with big trucks and semis, city-bound. Their headlights made Decker's eyes water.

At the junction near Laplace he decided to take Route 51 instead of the new interstate. The bumpy unlit two-lane was Skink's kind of highway. Decker flicked on his brights and drove slowly, hoping against all reason to spot the big orange rainsuit skulking roadside. By the time Decker reached Pass Manchac all he'd seen was a gray fox, two baby raccoons, and a fresh-dead water moccasin.

Decker pumped the brakes as he drove by the Sportsman's Hide-out. Someone had left the spotlights on at the dock. It made no sense; the tournament was over, the bassers long gone. Decker ne-gotiated a sleepy U-turn and went back.

When he got out of the car, he noticed that the lake air was not nearly as chilly as the night before. Too late for the fishermen, the wind had finally shifted from north to south; it was a balmy Gulf breeze that made the spotlights tremble on the poles.

One of the beams aimed at the tournament scoreboard, another more or less at the giant aquarium.

Decker wondered if anyone had remembered to free the bass. He strolled down to the docks to see.

The aquarium pump labored, grinding noisy bubbles. The water had turned a silty shade of brown. With the back of his hand Decker wiped a window in the condensation and peered into the glass tank. Right away he spotted three dead fish, gaping and jelly-eyed, rolling slow-motion with the current along the bottom. Decker felt like a tourist at some Charles Addams rendition of Marineland.

The shadow of something larger drifted over the dead bass. Decker glanced toward the top of the ten-foot tank, but looked away when the spotlight caught him flush in the eyes.

To escape the glare he climbed the wooden stairs to the weighmaster's platform, which overlooked both the scoreboard and the release tank. From this vantage Decker spotted more dead bass floating on the surface, and something else, whorling slowly in the backwash of the pump. The form was big-shouldered and brown—at first Decker thought it might be a sea cow, somebody's sick idea of a joke.

When the thing drifted by, he got a better look.

It was a man, floating facedown; a chunky man dressed in a brown jumpsuit.

Decker watched the corpse go around the tank again. This time, when it floated by, he grabbed the stiff cold shoulders and flipped it over with a splash.

Dickie Lockhart's eyes stared wide but were long past seeing. He wore a plum-sized bruise on his right temple. If the blow hadn't killed him outright, it had definitely rendered him unfit for a midnight swim.

The killer's final touch was diabolical, and not without wit: a fishing lure, the redoubtable Double Whammy, had been hooked through Dickie Lockhart's lower lip. It hung off Dickie's face like a queer Christmas ornament. Unfortunately, being just as dead as Dickie, none of the bass in the aquarium could appreciate the piquancy of the killer's gesture.

R. J. Decker lowered the corpse back into the water and walked quickly to the car. The scene screamed for a photograph, but it screamed something else too. Decker heard it all the way back to the motel and even afterward, deep into fitful dreams.

According to his official church biography, Charles Weeb had turned to God after an anguished boyhood of poverty, abuse, and neglect. His father had died a drunk and his mother had died a dope fiend, though not before selling Charlie's two sisters to a Chinese slavery ring in exchange for sixty-five dollars and three grams of uncut opium.

The imagined fate of the missing Weeb sisters was a recurring theme in Charlie's TV sermons on the Outdoor Christian Network; nothing sucked in money faster than a lingering close-up of those snapshots of the two little girls, June-Lee and Melissa, under the plaintive caption: "WHAT HAS SATAN DONE WITH THESE ANGELS?"

The Reverend Charles Weeb knew, of course. The angels in question were both alive and well, and presumably still working for Mr. Hugh Hefner in the same capacity that had first attracted Reverend Weeb's attention. He had personally clipped their childhood photographs from the pages of *Playboy* magazine—that hokey section featuring family pictures of the centerfold as a little girl. Charlie Weeb had long since forgotten the real names of these models, or even what month and year they had starred in the publication. However, he wasn't the least bit worried that the pictures would be recognized and his scheme revealed, since no devout OCN viewer could ever admit to looking at such a magazine. The Reverend Charles Weeb made sure to regularly warn his flock that *Playboy* was a passport to hell.

In fact Charlie Weeb had no sisters, just an older brother named Bernie, who had been busted selling phony oil leases from a North Miami boiler room and was now doing seven years for wire fraud. Weeb's father had been a shoe salesman with an ulcer intolerant of alcohol; his mother was not a dope fiend but a successful real-estate agent, and from her Charlie Weeb had drawn the inspiration for his dream project in Florida, Lunker Lakes.

The Weeb family had never been particularly religious, so neighbors were surprised, even somewhat skeptical, to learn that little Charlie had grown up to become a fundamentalist preacher. The Weebs, after all, were Jewish. Acquaintances were even more puzzled to turn on the television and see Charlie going on about his wretched parents and kidnapped sisters. Bernie the Bum was the only one whom the neighbors remembered.

Charles Weeb's path to religious prominence had been a curious and halting one. After being expelled from the Citadel for moral turpitude, he had spent ten years chasing fads, hoping to hit it big. "Eighteen-to-twenty-five alive!" was Charlie's slogan, because that was always his target market. His schemes were always about two years too late and fifty percent undercapitalized. For a while he ran a health-food store in Tallahassee, then a disco in Gulf Shores, then a hot-tub factory in Orlando. Though his track record made him look like a loser, Charlie Weeb was basically a clever man; no matter how catastrophically his enterprises failed, Weeb's bank account always prospered. In the late 1970s the IRS expressed an avid interest in Charlie Weeb's fortunes; this he took as a signal to find God, and quickly. Thus was born the First Pentecostal Church of Exemptive Redemption.

Charlie Weeb didn't own an actual church, but he had something even better: a TV station.

For two million dollars he had purchased a small UHF operation whose programming consisted entirely of game shows, Atlanta Braves baseball, and *The Best of Hee-Haw*. Nothing changed for four months, until one Sunday morning a man with straw-blond hair and messianic eyebrows stood behind a cardboard pulpit and introduced himself as the Most Holy Reverend Charles Weeb. From now on, he said, WEEB-TV would be the voice of Jesus Christ.

Then, live on the air, Charlie Weeb healed a crippled cat.

Hundreds of viewers saw it. The calico kitten limped to the stage and—after a tremulous Reverend Weeb prayed for its soul and passed a hand over its furry head—the animal scampered away, cured.

The following Sunday Charlie Weeb performed the same miracle on a gimpy beagle. The Sunday after that, a shoat. Two weeks later, a baby llama, on loan from a traveling circus.

Weeb saved the master coup for Christmas Sunday, the start of a ratings-sweep week. Before his biggest TV audience ever, he healed a lamb.

It was a magnificent performance, full of biblical symbolism. Few viewers who saw the nappy dull-eyed critter rise off the floor were not deeply moved. No one in Charlie Weeb's flock seemed to mind that the miracle took about an hour longer than expected; they figured that, it being a busy Christmas, God was running a little late. In fact, the reason for the delay in the much-promoted lamb healing was that Charlie Weeb's assistant had injected way too much lidocaine into the animal's hind legs before the show, so it took an extra long time for the effect of the drug to wear off.

The Reverend Weeb nearly preached himself hoarse over that lamb, and after the Christmas miracle he swore off healings forever. By then it didn't matter; his reputation had been made. Soon stations all over the South were airing Weeb's show, *Jesus in Your Living Room,* and weekly mail donations were topping in the six figures. In TV evangelism Charlie Weeb finally had hooked into a popular trend before it tapped out.

This time he decided to take a chance. This time he funneled the profits into expansion instead of Bahamian bank accounts. With Weeb's preacher hour as its blockbuster leadoff, the Outdoor Christian Network was inaugurated with sixty-four stations as prepaid subscribers. The OCN format was simple: religion, hunting, fishing, farm-stock reports, and country-music-awards shows. Even as Charlie Weeb branched the OCN empire into real estate, investment banking, and other endeavors, he could scarcely believe the rousing success of his TV formula; it confirmed everything he had always said about the state of the human race.

Initially Weeb had refused to believe that grown men would sit for hours watching fishing programs on cable TV. In person the act of fishing was boring enough; watching someone else do it seemed like a form of self-torture. Yet Weeb's market researchers convinced him otherwise—Real Men tuned in to TV fishing, and the demographics were rock-solid for beer, tobacco, and automotive advertising, not to mention the marine industry.

Weeb scanned the projections and immediately ordered up a one-hour bass-fishing program. He personally auditioned three well-known anglers. The first, Ben Geer, was rejected because of his weight (three hundred and ninety pounds) and his uncontrollable habit of coughing gobs of sputum into the microphone. The second angler, Art Pinkler, was witty, knowledgeable, and ruggedly handsome, but burdened with a squeaky New England accent that spelled death on the Q meter. The budget was too lean for speech lessons or overdubbing, so Pinkler was out; Charlie Weeb needed a genuine redneck.

Which left Dickie Lockhart.

Weeb thought the first episode of *Fish Fever* was the worst piece of television he had ever seen. Dickie was incoherent, the camera work palsied, and the tape editors obviously stoned. Still Dickie had hauled in three huge largemouth bass, and the advertisers had loved every dirt-cheap minute. Baffled, Weeb stuck with the show. In three years, *Fish Fever* became a top earner for the Outdoor Christian Network, though in recent months it had lost ground in several important markets to Ed Spurling's rival bass show. Spurling's program was briskly edited and slickly packaged, which appealed to Charlie Weeb, as did anything that made wads of money and was not an outright embarrassment. Sensing that Dickie Lockhart's days as the Baron of Bass might be numbered, the Reverend Weeb had quietly approached Fast Eddie Spurling to see if he could be bought. The two men were still haggling over salaries by the time the Cajun Invitational fishing tournament came along, when Dickie found the preacher with two nearly naked women.

Lockhart's demand for a lucrative new contract was an extortion that Reverend Weeb could not afford to ignore; competition had grown cutthroat among TV evangelicals—the slightest moral stain and you'd be off the air.

As he had vowed, Dickie Lockhart won the New Orleans tournament easily. Charlie Weeb didn't bother to show up at the victory party. He scheduled a press conference for the next morning to announce Dickie Lockhart's new cable deal, and phoned the TV writer of the *Times-Picayune* to let him know. Then he called a couple of hookers.

At five-thirty in the morning, a city policeman knocked on the double door to Charlie Weeb's hotel suite. The cop recognized one of the hookers but didn't mention it. "I've got bad news, Reverend," the policeman said. "Dickie Lockhart's been murdered."

"Jesus help us," Charlie Weeb said.

The cop nodded. "Somebody beat him over the head real good.

Stole his truck, his boat, all his fishing gear. The cash he won in the tournament, too."

"This is terrible," said Reverend Weeb. "A robbery."

"We'll know more tomorrow, when the lab techs are done," the cop said on his way out. "Try to get some rest."

"Thank you," said Charlie Weeb.

He was wide-awake now. He paid off the hookers and sat down to write his Sunday sermon.

R. J. Decker was not exactly flabbergasted to wake up in the motel room and find that Skink had not returned. Decker had every reason to suspect that it was he who had murdered Dickie Lockhart—first of all, because Skink had talked so nonchalantly about doing it; second, the perverse details of the crime seemed to carry his stamp.

Decker showered in a daze and shaved brutally, as if pain would drive the fog from his brain. The case had turned not only more murderous but also more insane. The newspapers would go nuts with this stuff; it was probably even a national story. It was a story from which Decker fervently wished to escape.

After checking out of the motel, he packed his gear into the rental car and drove toward Pass Manchac. It was nine in the morning— surely somebody had discovered the gruesome scene by now.

As he drove across the water Decker's heart pounded; he could see blue lights flashing near the boat ramp. He pulled in at the Sportsman's Hideout, got out of the car, and wedged into the crowd that encircled the huge bass aquarium. There were five police cruisers, two ambulances, and a fire truck, all for one dead body. It had been three whole hours since Dickie's remains had been fished from the tank, strapped to a stretcher, and covered with a green woolen blanket; no one seemed in a hurry to make the trip to the morgue.

The crowd was mostly men, some of whom Decker recognized even without their caps as contestants from the bass tournament. Two local detectives with pads and pencils were working the spectators, hoping to luck into a witness. A pretty young woman leaned against one of the squad cars. She was sobbing as she talked to a uniformed cop, who was filling out a pink report. Decker heard the girl say her name was Ellen. Ellen O'Leary. She had a New Orleans accent.

Decker wondered what she knew, what she might have seen.

In the back of his mind Decker harbored a fear that Skink might show up at the dock to admire his own handiwork, but there was no sign of him. Decker slipped into a phone booth and called Dennis Gault at home in Miami. He sounded half-asleep.

"What do you want?"

What do you want? All charm, this guy.

"Your pal Dickie's landed his last lunker," Decker said.

"What do you mean?"

"He's dead."

"Shit," Gault said. "What happened?"

"I'll tell you about it later."

"Don't leave New Orleans," Gault said. "Stay put."

"No way." Just what I need is that asshole jetting up for brunch at Brennan's, Decker thought. He's probably icing a Dom Perignon already.

In an oddly stiff tone Gault asked, "Do you have those pictures?" As if it made a difference now.

Decker didn't answer. Through the pane in the phone booth he was watching Thomas Curl and the Rundell brothers in the parking lot of the marina. One of the local detectives was interviewing the three men together; when Ozzie talked, his head bobbed up and down like a dashboard puppy. The cop was scribbling energetically in his notebook.

"What number you at?" Dennis Gault asked over the phone.

"Seventy," Decker replied. "As in miles per hour."

The tire blew on Interstate 10, outside of Kenner. The spare was one of those tiny toy tires now standard equipment on new cars. To get to the spare Decker had to empty the trunk of his duffel and camera gear, which he stacked neatly by the side of the highway. He had gotten the rental halfway jacked when he heard another car pull up behind him in the emergency lane; by the emphysemic sounds of the engine, Decker knew it wasn't a cop.

Not even close. It was a brown 1974 Cordoba, its vinyl roof puckered like a sun blister. Two-for-four on the hubcaps. Three men got out of the rusty old tank; judging by their undershirts and tattoos, Decker assumed they were not from the Triple-A. He pried the crowbar out of the jack handle and held it behind him.

"Gentlemen," he said.

"Whatsamatter here?" said the largest of the trio.

"Flat tire," Decker said. "I'm fine."

"Yeah?"

"Yeah. Thanks anyway."

The men didn't exactly take the hint. Two of them ambled over to where Decker had laid the camera bag, tripod, and galvanized lens cases. One of the jerks poked at the cameras with the toe of his boot.

"Whatsis?" he said.

"Beer money," said the other.

Decker couldn't believe it. Broad daylight, cars and trucks and Winnebagos cruising by on the interstate—and these pussbuckets were going to roll him anyway. Damned Nikons, he thought; sometimes they seemed to be the root of all his troubles.

"I'm a professional photographer," Decker said. "Want me to take your picture?"

The two thinnest men looked expectantly toward the bigger one. Decker knew the idea appealed to them, although their leader needed a little convincing. "A nice eight-by-ten," Decker said affably, "just for fun." He knew what the big guy was thinking: Well, why not—we're going to steal the damn things anyway.

"Stand in front of the car and I'll get a shot of all three of you together. Go ahead, now."

Decker walked over to the camera bag and inconspicuously set the crowbar inside. He picked up a bare F-3 camera body, didn't even bother to screw on a lens. These morons wouldn't know the difference. Shrugging, murmuring, slicking their hair with brown bony hands, the highwaymen struck a pricelessly idiotic pose in front of the dented Cordoba. As he pressed the shutter, Decker almost wished there were film in the camera.

"That's just great, guys," he said. "Now let's try one from the side."

The big man scowled.

"Just a joke," Decker said. The two thin guys didn't get it anyway.

"Enougha this shit," the leader of the trio said. "We want your goddamn car."

"What for?"

"To go to Florida."

Of course, Decker thought, Florida. He should have known. Every pillhead fugitive felon in America winds up in Florida eventually. The Human Sludge Factor—it all drips to the South.

"One more picture," Decker suggested. He had to hurry; he didn't want to get mugged, but he didn't want to miss his plane, either.

"No!" the big man said.

"One more picture and you can have the car, the cameras, everything."

Decker kept one eye on the interstate, thinking: Don't they have a highway patrol in Louisiana?

"You guys got some cigarettes? That would be a good shot, have a cigarette hanging from your mouth."

One of the thin guys lighted a Camel and wedged it into his lips at a very cool angle. "Oh yeah," Decker said. "That's what I mean. Let me get the wide-angle lens."

He went back to the camera bag and fished out a regular fifty-millimeter, which he attached to the Nikon. He picked up the crowbar and slipped it down the front of his jeans. The black iron felt cold against his left leg.

When he turned around, Decker saw that all three men now sported cigarettes. "The girls down in Florida are gonna love this picture," he said.

One of the thin guys grinned. "Good pussy in Florida, right?"

"The best," Decker said. He moved up close, clicking away. The men stunk like stale beer and tobacco. Through the lens Decker saw rawboned ageless faces; they could have been twenty years old, or forty-five. Classic cons. They seemed mesmerized by the camera, or at least by Decker's hyperactive choreography. The leader of the trio plainly was getting antsy; he couldn't wait to kick Decker's ass, maybe even kill him, and get moving.

"Almost done," Decker said finally. "Move a little closer together ... that's good ... now look to my right and blow some smoke ... great! ... keep looking out at the water ... that-is-perfect!"

Staring obediently at Lake Pontchartrain, the three men never saw Decker pull out the crowbar. With both hands he swung as hard as he could, a batter's arc. The iron blade pinged off the top of their skulls one by one, as if Decker were playing a human xylophone. The robbers fell in a wailing cross-eyed heap.

Decker had expected less noise and more blood. As the adrenaline ebbed, he looked down and wondered if he had hit them more than once. He didn't think so.

Now it was definitely time to go; the flat tire was Hertz's problem. Decker quickly loaded his stuff into the Cordoba. The key was in the ignition. A blue oily pistol lay on the front seat. He tossed it out the window on his way to the airport.

The first person R. J. Decker called when he got back to Miami was Lou Zicutto. Lou was branch claims manager of the mammoth insurance company where Decker worked part-time as an investigator. Lou was a spindly little twit, maybe a hundred twenty pounds, but he had a huge florid head, which he shaved every day. As a result he looked very much like a Tootsie Pop with lips. Despite his appearance, Lou Zicutto was treated respectfully by all employees and coworkers, who steadfastly believed that he was a member of the Mafia who could have them snuffed with a single phone call. Lou himself did nothing to discourage this idea, even though it wasn't true. Except for the fancy stationery, Decker himself didn't see much difference between the mob and an insurance company, anyway.

"Where ya been?" Lou Zicutto asked. "I left a jillion messages." Lou had a raspy cabdriver voice, and he was always sucking on menthol cough drops.

"I've been out of town on a case," Decker said. He could hear Lou slurping away, working the lozenges around his teeth.

"We got Núñez this week, remember?"

Núñez was a big fraud trial the company was prosecuting. Núñez was a stockbroker who stole his own yacht and tried to scuttle it off Bimini for the insurance. Decker had shot some pictures and done surveillance; he was scheduled to testify for the company.

"You're my star witness," Lou said.

"I can't make it, Lou, not this week."

"What the hell you mean?"

Decker said, "I've got a conflict."

"No shit you got a conflict. You got a big fucking conflict with me, you don't show up." The cough drops were clacking furiously. "Two million bucks this creep is trying to rip us for."

"You got my pictures, the tapes, the reports—" Decker said.

"Your smiling face is what the lawyers want," Lou Zicutto said. "You be there, Mr. Cameraman." Then he hung up.

The second person Decker tried to call was Catherine. The first time, the line was busy. He tried again two minutes later and a man answered. It sounded like James, the chiropractor; he answered the phone the way doctors do, not with a civil hello but with a "Yes?" Like it was a pain in the ass to have to speak to another human being.

Decker hung up the phone, opened a beer, and put a Bob Seger album on the stereo. He wondered what Catherine's new house looked like, whether she had one of these sunken marble tubs she'd always wanted. A vision of Catherine in a bubble bath suddenly swept over Decker, and his chest started to throb.

He was half-asleep on the sofa when the phone rang. The machine answered on the third ring. Decker sat up when he heard Al García's voice.

"Call me as soon as you get in."

García was a Metro police detective and an old friend. Except he didn't sound so friendly on the machine; he sounded awfully damn professional. Decker was a little worried. He drank two cups of black instant coffee before calling back.

"Hey, Sarge, what's up?"

García said, "You at the trailer?"

"No, I'm in the penthouse of the Coconut Grove Hotel. They're having a Morgan Fairchild lookalike contest and I'm the judge for the swimsuit competition."

Normally García would have donated some appropriately lewd counterpunchline, but today all he offered was a polite chuckle.

"We need to talk," the detective said mildly. "See you in about thirty."

García was sitting on something, that much was certain. Decker shaved and put on a fresh shirt. He could easily guess what must have happened. A Louisiana cop probably had found those three dirtbags that Decker had clobbered along the interstate. They would have sworn that this scoundrel from Miami had flagged them down and robbed them, of course. A tracer on the Hertz car would have yielded Decker's name and address, and from then on it was only a matter of professional courtesy. Al García was probably bringing a bench warrant from St. Charles Parish.

Decker was not especially eager to return, or be returned, to Louisiana. He figured he could beat the phony assault rap from the highway robbers, but what if the Lockhart case broke open in the meantime? Decker didn't want to be around if Skink got arrested.

Skink was the big problem. If Decker hadn't enlisted the mad hermit into the case, Dickie Lockhart would still be alive. On the other hand, it was probably Lockhart who had arranged the murders of Robert Clinch and then Ott Pickney. Decker didn't know exactly what to do next; it was a goddamn mess. He had come to like Skink and he hated the thought of him going to the gas chamber over a greedy sleazoid such as Lockhart, but murder was murder. As he straightened up the trailer—a week's worth of moldy laundry, mainly—Decker toyed with the idea of telling García the whole story; it was so profoundly weird that even a Miami cop might be sympathetic. But Decker decided to hold off, for the moment. There appeared to be a good chance that Skink might never be found, or even identified as a suspect. Decker also understood that Skink might see absolutely nothing wrong in what he did, and would merely appear one day to take full credit for the deed. This was always a possibility when dealing with the chronically unraveled.

The news from Louisiana was relatively sparse. In the two days Decker had been back in Florida, the local newspapers had run only a couple of four-paragraph wire stories about Dickie Lockhart's murder at the bass tournament—robbery believed to be the motive; no prints, no suspects; services to be held in Harney County. The stories probably would have gotten better play had it not been for the biannual mass murder in Oklahoma; this time it was twelve motorists shot by a disgruntled toll-booth operator who was fed up with people not having exact change.

After trying Catherine, Decker had made three attempts to reach Dennis Gault. Various disinterested secretaries had reported that the sugarcane baron was on long distance, in a conference, or out of town. Decker had not left his name or a message. What he had wanted to tell Gault was that the case was over (obviously) and that he was pocketing twenty grand of the advance for time and expenses. Gault would bitch and argue, but not too much. Not if he had any brains.

Al García showed up right on time. Decker heard the car door slam and waited for a knock. Then he heard another car pull up the gravel drive, and another. He looked out the window and couldn't believe it: Al's unmarked Chrysler, plus two green-and-whites—a whole damn posse for a lousy agg assault. Then a terrible thought occurred to him: What if it were something more serious? What if one of those Louisiana dirtbags had actually died? That would explain the committee.

The cops were out of their squad cars, having a huddle in front of Decker's trailer. García's cigarette bobbed up and down as he talked to the uniformed officers.

"Shit," Decker said. The neighbors would be absolutely thrilled; this was good for a year's worth of gossip. Where were the pit bulls when you needed them?

Decker figured the best way to handle the scene was to stroll outside and say hello, as if nothing were out of the ordinary. He was two steps from opening the door when something the approximate consistency of granite crashed down on the base of his neck, and he fell headlong through a dizzy galaxy of white noise and blinding pinwheels.

When he awoke, Decker felt like somebody had screwed his skull on crookedly. He opened his eyes and the world was red.

"Don't fucking move."

A man had him from behind, around the neck. It was a military hold, unbreakable. One good squeeze and Decker would pass out again. A large gritty hand was clapped over his mouth. The man's chin dug into Decker's right shoulder, and his breath whistled warmly in Decker's ear.

Even when Decker's head cleared, the red didn't go away. The intruder had dragged him into the darkroom, turned on the photo light, and locked the door. From somewhere, remotely, Decker heard Al García calling his name. It sounded like the detective was outside the trailer, shouting in through a window. Probably didn't have a search warrant, Decker thought; that was just like García, everything by the bloody book. Decker hoped that Al would take a chance and pop the lock on the front door. If that happened, Decker was ready to make some serious noise.

Decker's abductor must have sensed something, because he brutally tightened his hold. Instantly Decker felt bug-eyed and queasy. His arms began to tingle and he let out an involuntary groan.

"Ssshhh," the man said.

Forced to suck air through his nose, Decker couldn't help but notice that the man smelled. Not a stink, exactly, but a powerful musk, not altogether unpleasant. Decker tuned out García's muffled shouts, closed his eyes, and concentrated. The smell was deep swamp and animal, sweet pine tinged with carrion. Mixed in were fainter traces of black bog mud and dried sweat and old smoke. Not tobacco smoke, either, but the woodsy fume of campfires. Suddenly Decker felt foolish. He abandoned all thought of a struggle and relaxed in the intruder's bearlike grip.

The voice in his ear whispered, "Nice going, Miami."

R. J. Decker was right. Al García didn't have a search warrant. What he had, stuffed in an inside pocket of his J. C. Penney suit jacket, was a bench warrant for Decker's arrest, which had been Federal Expressed that morning all the way from New Orleans. The warrant was as literate and comprehensible as could be expected, but it did not give Al García the right to bust down the door to Decker's trailer.

"Why the hell not?" asked one of the uniformed cops.

"No PC," García snapped. PC was probable cause.

"He's hiding in the can, I bet."

"Not Decker," García said.

"I don't want to wait around," the other cop said.

"Oh, you got big plans, Billy?" García said. "Late to the fucking opera maybe?"

The cop turned away.

García grumbled. "I don't want to wait either," he said. He was tired of hollering through Decker's window and he was also pissed off. He had driven all the way out here as a favor, and regretted it. He hated trailer parks; trailer parks were the reason God invented tornadoes. García could have sent only the green-and-whites, but Decker was a friend and this was serious business. García wanted to hear his side of it, because what the Louisiana people had told him so far was simply not believable.

"You want me to disable his vehicle?" asked the uniformed cop named Billy.

"What are you talking about?"

"Flatten the tires, so he can't get away."

García shook his head. "No, that won't be necessary." The standards at the police academy had gone to hell, that much was obvious. Anybody with an eighteen-inch neck could get a badge these days.

"He said he'd be here, right?" the other cop asked.

"Yeah," García mumbled, "that's what he said."

So where was he? Why hadn't he taken his own car? García was more miffed than curious.

The cop named Billy said, "Suppose the jalousies on the back door suddenly fell out? Suppose we could crawl right in?"

"Suppose you go sit under that palm tree and play with yourself," García said.

Christ, what a day. It began when the Hialeah grave robbers struck again, swiping seven human skulls in a predawn raid on a city cemetery. At first García had refused to answer the call on the grounds that it wasn't really a murder, since the victims of the crime were already dead. One of them in particular had been dead since before Al García was born, so he didn't think it was practical, or fair, that he should have to reinvestigate. Everybody in the office had agreed that technically it wasn't a homicide; more likely petty larceny. What could a crumbly old skull be worth on the street? they had asked. Fifteen, twenty bucks, tops. Unfortunately, it developed that one of the rudely mutilated cadavers belonged to the uncle of a Miami city commissioner, so the case had hastily been elevated to a priority status and all detectives were admonished to keep their sick senses of humor to themselves.

About noon García had to drop the head case when a real murder happened. A Bahamian crack freak had carved up his male roommate, skinned him out like a mackerel, and tried to sell the fillets to a wholesale seafood market on Bird Road. It was one of those cases so bent as to be threatened by the sheer weight of law-enforcement bureaucracy—the crime scene had been crawling not just with policemen, but with deputy coroners, assistant prosecutors, immigration officers, even an inspector from the USDA. By the time the mess was cleaned up, García's bum shoulder was throbbing angrily. Pure, hundred-percent stress.

He had spotted the express packet from New Orleans when he

got back to the office. A perfectly shitty ending to a shitty day. Now R. J. Decker had made like a rabbit and García was stuck in a crackerbox trailer park trying to decide if he should leave these moron patrolmen to wait with the warrant. He was reasonably sure that, left unsupervised, they would gladly shoot Decker or at least beat the hell out of him, just to make up for all the aggravation.

"Screw it," García said finally, "let's go get some coffee and try again later."

"He'll be back," Decker said when he heard the police cars pull away.

Skink had let go of his neck. They were still in the darkroom, where Skink's fluorescent rainsuit shone almost white in the wash of the red bulb. Skink appeared more haggard and rumpled than Decker remembered; twigs and small pieces of leaf hung like confetti in his long gray braid. His hair stuck out in clumps from under the shower cap.

"Where have you been?" Decker asked. His neck was torturing him, like someone had pounded a railroad spike into the crown of his spine.

"The girl," Skink said. "I should have known."

"Lanie?"

"I got back to the room and there she is, half-undressed. She said you'd invited her to fly up—"

"No way."

"I figured," Skink said. "That's why I tied her up, so you could decide for yourself what to do. You cut her loose, I presume."

"Yeah."

"And screwed her too?"

Decker frowned.

"Just what I thought," Skink said. "We've got to get the hell out of here."

"Listen, captain, that cop is a friend of mine."

"Which one?" With one blackened finger Skink scratched absently at a brambly eyebrow.

"The Cuban detective. García's his name."

"So?"

"So he's a good man," Decker said. "He'll try to get us a break."

"*Us?*"

"Yeah, with the New Orleans people. Al could make it as painless as possible."

Skink studied Decker's face and said, "Hell, I guess I squeezed too tight."

They went to a Denny's on Biscayne Boulevard, where Skink fit right in with the clientele. He ordered six raw eggs and a string of pork sausages. Decker's neck had stiffened up, and he had the worst headache of his life.

"You could have just tapped me on the shoulder," he complained.

"No time to be polite," Skink said, without a trace of apology. "I did it for your own good."

"How'd you get in, anyway?"

"Slim-jimmed the back door. Two minutes later and your bosom buddy García would have had you in bracelets. Eat something, all right? We got a long damn ride."

Decker had no intention of taking a long damn ride with Skink, and no intention of getting picked up as an accessory to murder. He had decided not to turn Skink in to the police, but the man would have to make his own escape; the partnership was over.

Skink said, "Your neighbors'll raise hell about the dead dogs."

"Oh?"

"Couldn't be helped," Skink said, slurping a drip of yolk from his mustache. "Self-defense."

"You killed the pit bulldogs?"

"Not *all* of them. Just the ones that were chasing me."

Before Decker could ask, Skink said, "With a knife. No one saw a thing."

"God." Decker's brainpan felt like the bells of Notre Dame. He noticed that his fingers twitched when he tried to butter a biscuit. It dawned on him that he was not a well person, that he needed to go to a doctor.

But before he abandoned Skink he wanted to ask about Dickie Lockhart. He wanted to hear Skink's version, in case it never came out.

"When you left the motel in Hammond," Decker began, "where'd you go?"

"Back to the lake. Borrowed a boat and found Dickie's fish traps."

"You're kidding."

Skink beamed. A brown clot of sausage was stuck between his

two front teeth. "The boat I took was Ozzie Rundell's," he said. "Dumb fucker left the keys in the switch and a map in the console."

"A depth chart of Lake Maurepas," Decker guessed, "with the trap sites marked."

"Marked real clear, too," Skink said, "in crayon, just for Ozzie."

It made sense. While Dickie Lockhart was celebrating his victory, the Rundells would sneak out on the lake to clean up the evidence. Dickie was so cheap he probably used the same traps over and over.

"Those fish he won with were Florida bass," Skink was saying. "Probably trucked in from Lake Jackson or maybe the Rodman. That mudhole Maurepas never saw bass that pretty, you can bet your ass—"

"What'd you do after you found the traps?" Decker cut in.

Skink set down his fork. "I pulled the plug on Ozzie's boat and swam to shore."

"Then?"

"Then I stuck out my thumb, and here I am."

Two cops came in, walking the cowboy walk, and took a booth. Cops ate at Denny's all the time, but still they made Decker nervous. They kept glancing over at Skink—hard glances—and Decker could tell they were dreaming up an excuse for a hassle and ID check. He laid a ten on the table and headed for the car; Skink shuffled behind, shoving a couple of biscuits into the pockets of his rainsuit. No sooner were they back on the boulevard than Decker spotted another patrol car in the rearview. The patrol car was following closely, and Decker could only assume that Al García had put out the word. When the blue lights came on, Decker dutifully pulled over.

"Hell," Skink said.

Decker waited until both cops were out of the car, then he punched the accelerator and took off.

Skink said, "Sometimes I like your style."

Decker guessed he had a three-minute lead. "I'm going to turn on Thirty-sixth Street," he said, "and when I hit the brakes, you bail out."

"Why?" Skink asked calmly.

Decker was pushing the old Plymouth beyond its natural limits of speed and maneuverability. It was one of those nights on the boulevard—every other car was either a Cadillac or a junker, and nobody was going over thirty. Decker was leaving most of his tread on the asphalt, and running every stoplight. The rearview was clear, but he knew it wouldn't take long for the cops to radio for backup.

"You might want to try another road," Skink suggested.

"You're a big help," Decker said, watching a bus loom ahead. He took a right on Thirty-fifth Street and braked the car so hard he could smell burnt metal. "Get going," he said to Skink.

"Are you crazy?"

"Get out!"

"*You* get out," Skink said. "You're the dumb shit they're after."

Impatiently Decker jammed the gearshift into park. "Look, all they got me for is agg assault and, after this, a misdemeanor resisting. Meanwhile you're looking at murder-one if they put it all together."

With a plastic crunch Skink turned in his seat. "What the hell are you talking about?"

"I'm talking about Dickie Lockhart."

Skink cackled. "You think *I* killed him?"

"It crossed my mind, yeah."

Skink laughed some more, and punched the dashboard. He thought the whole thing was hilarious. He was hooting and howling and kicking his feet, and all Decker wanted to do was push him out of the car and get going.

"You really don't know what happened, do you?" Skink asked, after settling down.

Decker killed the headlights and shrank down in the driver's seat. He was a nervous wreck, couldn't take his eyes off the mirrors. "What don't I know?" he said to Skink.

"What the goddamn warrant says, you don't even know. Jim Tile got a copy, airmail. He read it to me first thing this morning and you should hear what it says, Miami. Says you murdered Dickie Lockhart."

"Me?"

"That's what it says."

Decker heard the first siren and went cold.

Skink said, "You got set up, buddy, set up so good it's almost a thing of beauty. The girl was bait."

"Go on," Decker said thickly. He was trying to remember Lanie's story, trying to remember some of the holes.

"Don't even think about turning yourself in," Skink said. "García may be your pal but he's no magician. Now please let's get the hell out of here while we still can. I'll tell you the rest as we go."

17

They ditched the Plymouth back at the trailer park and took a bus to the airport, where Decker rented a white Thunderbird from Avis. Skink did not approve; he said they needed a four-by-four truck, something on the order of a Bronco, but the Avis people only had cars.

Sticking in the heavy traffic, they drove around Little Havana for two hours while Decker quizzed Skink about what had happened at Lake Maurepas.

"Who whacked Lockhart?" he asked.

"I don't know that," Skink said. "This is what I do know, mostly from Jim Tile and a few phone calls. While you were banging Gault's sister, somebody clubbed Dickie to death. First thing the next morning, Gault himself flies to New Orleans to offer the cops a sworn statement. He tells them an ex-con photographer named Decker was trying to blackmail Dickie over the bass cheating. Says you approached him with some photographs and wanted a hundred K—he even had a note in your handwriting to that effect."

"Jesus," Decker groaned. It was the note he had written the night Gault had fought with him—the note raising his fee to one hundred thousand dollars.

Skink went on: "Gault tells the cops that he told you to fuck off, so then you went to Lockhart. At first Dickie paid you—thirty grand in all, Gault says—"

"Cute," Decker muttered. Thirty had been his advance on the case.

"—but then Dickie gets tired of paying and says no more. You go to New Orleans to confront him, threaten to expose him at the big tournament. There's an argument, a fight . . . you can script the rest. The cops already have."

"And my alibi witness is the real killer's sister."

"Lanie wasted no time giving an affidavit," Skink said. "A very helpful lady. She says you poked her, drove her back to New Orleans, and dropped her at a hotel. Says you told her you had to go see Dickie on some business."

"I can pick 'em," Decker said mordantly.

Skink fidgeted in the car; his expression had grown strained. The press of the traffic, the din of the streets, bothered him. "Almost forgot," he said. "They got the blackmail photographs too."

"What photographs?"

"Of Dickie pulling the fish cages," Skink replied. "Beats me, too. You're the expert, figure it out."

Decker was astounded. "They got actual pictures?"

"That's what the DA says. Very sharp black-and-whites of Dickie doing the deed."

"But who took 'em?"

"The DA says you did. They traced an empty box of film to a wholesale shipment of Kodak that went to the photo lab at the newspaper. The newspaper says it was part of the batch you swiped on your way out the door."

"I see." Skink was right: it was almost a thing of beauty.

Skink said, "Are you missing any film?"

"I don't know."

"The junk we shot in Louisiana, where's that?"

"Still in my camera bag," Decker said, "I guess."

"You guess." Skink laughed harshly. "You better damn well find out, Miami. You're not the only wizard with a darkroom."

Decker felt tired; he wanted to close his eyes, cap the lens. Skink told him they should take U.S. 27 up to Alligator Alley and go west.

"We'd be safer in the city," Decker said. He didn't feel like driving the entire width of the state; the drumbeat pain on his brainstem was unbearable. The Alley would be crawling with state troopers, too; they had an eye for sporty rental cars. "Where exactly did you want to go?" he asked Skink.

"The Big Cypress is a good place to hide." Skink gave him a sideways glance.

"Not the swamp-rat routine," Decker said, "not tonight. Let's stay in town."

"You got somewhere that's safe?"

"Maybe."

"No hotels," Skink hissed.

"No hotels."

Decker parked at the curb and studied the house silently for several moments. It seemed impressively large, even for Miami Shores. There were two cars, a Firebird and a Jaguar sedan, parked in a half-circle gravel driveway. The sabal palms and seagrape trees were bathed by soft orange spotlights mounted discreetly around the Bermuda lawn. A Spanish archway framed the front door, which was made of a coffee-colored wood. There were no iron bars across the front window, but Decker could see a bold red sticker advertising the burglar alarm.

"You gonna sit here and moon all night?" Skink said.

They got out and walked up the driveway, the gravel crunching noisily under their feet. Skink had nothing to say about the big house; he'd seen plenty, and most were owned by wealthy and respectable thieves.

Indelicately Decker asked him to stand back a few steps from the door.

"So they don't die of fright, is that it?" Skink said.

Catherine answered the bell. "Rage," she said, looking more than a little surprised.

She wore tight cutoff jeans and a sleeveless lavender top, with no brassiere. Decker was ticked off that James the doctor had let her answer the door in the middle of the night—they could have been any variety of nocturnal Dade County creep: killers, kidnappers, witch doctors looking for a sacrificial goat. What kind of a lazy jerk would send his wife to the door alone, with no bra on, at eleven-thirty?

"I would've called," R. J. Decker said, "but it's kind of an emergency."

Catherine glanced at Skink and seemed to grasp the seriousness of the situation.

"Come on in, guys," she said in a friendly den-mother tone. Then she leaned close and whispered to Decker: "James is here."

"I know." The Jag was the giveaway.

A snow-white miniature poodle raced full speed into the foyer, its toenails clacking on the tile. The moment it saw Skink, the dog began to snarl and drool deliriously. It chomped the cuff of his orange rainsuit and began tearing at the plastic. Wordlessly Skink kicked the animal once, sharply, skidding it back down the hall.

"Sorry," Decker said wanly.

"It's okay," Catherine said, leading them into the kitchen. "I hate the little bastard—he pees in my shoes, did I tell you that?"

Out of nowhere Skink said: "We need a place for the night."

Catherine nodded. "There's plenty of room." An emergency is right, she thought; that would be the only thing to get Decker to stay under the same roof.

Skink said: "Decker's hurt, too."

"I'm all right."

"What is it?" Catherine asked.

"I almost broke his neck," Skink said, "accidentally."

"It's just a sprain," Decker said.

Then James the doctor—Catherine's husband—walked into the kitchen. He wore a navy Ralph Lauren bathrobe that stopped at his pale hairless knees; he also wore matching blue slippers. Decker was seized by an urge to repeatedly slap the man in the face; instead he just froze.

James studied the two visitors and said, "Catherine?" He wanted an explanation.

Both Catherine and Decker looked fairly helpless, so Skink stepped forward and said, "This is your wife's ex-husband, and I'm his friend."

"Oh?" In his lifetime James had never seen anything like Skink up close, but he was doing his best to maintain a man-of-the-house authority. To Decker he extended his hand and said, "R.J., isn't it? Funny we haven't met before."

"Uproarious," Decker said, giving the doctor's hand an exceedingly firm shake.

"They're spending the night," Catherine told her husband. "R.J.'s trailer flooded."

"There's been no rain," James remarked.

"A pipe broke," Catherine said impatiently.

Good girl, Decker thought; still quick on her feet.

"I'm going to fix these fellows some tea," she said. "Everybody into the living room, now, scat."

The living room had been designed around one of those giant seven-foot televisions of the type Decker had seen at Dennis Gault's

condominium. Every chair, every sofa, every bar stool had a view of
the screen. James the chiropractor had been watching a videocassette
of one of the "Star Wars" movies. "I've got all three on tape," he
volunteered.

Decker was calming down. He had no reason to hate the guy,
except maybe for the robe; anyway, it was Catherine who had made
the choice.

James was slender and somewhat tall—taller than Decker had
expected. He had a fine chin, high cheekbones, and quick aggressive-
looking eyes. His hair was reddish-brown, his skin fair. His long
delicate hands were probably a competitive advantage in the world
of chiropractic. On the whole he was slightly better-looking than
Decker had hoped he would be.

"I've seen some of your photographs, and they're quite good,"
James said, adding: "Catherine has an old album."

A double beat on the word *old*. In a way Decker felt a little sorry
for him, having two surly strangers in the house, and a wife expecting
him to be civil. The man was nervous, and who wouldn't be?

Bravely James smiled over at Skink, a dominating presence in his
fluorescent rainsuit. James said, "And you must be a crossing guard!"

Catherine brought cinnamon tea on a plain tray. Skink took a cup
and drank it down hot. Afterward his dark green eyes seemed to
glow.

As Catherine poured him another cup, Skink said: "You're quite
a beautiful girl."

Decker was dumbstruck. James the doctor was plainly mortified.
Skink smiled luminously and said, "My friend was an idiot to let you
go."

"Thank you," Catherine said. She didn't act put out at all, and she
certainly didn't act threatened. The look on her face was charmed
and knowing. It was, Decker thought irritably, as if she and Skink
were sharing a secret, and the secret was about him.

"Catherine," James said sternly, changing the subject, "have you
seen Bambi?"

"He was playing in the hall a few minutes ago."

"He looked a little tired," Decker offered.

"Bambi?" Skink made a face. "You mean that goddamn yappy
dog?"

James stiffened. "He's a pedigreed."

"He's a fucking rodent," Skink said, "with a perm."

Catherine started to laugh, caught herself. Even in his jealous snit, Decker had to admit they made a comical foursome. He was glad to see that Skink's momentary charm had evaporated; he was much more likable as a heathen.

James glared at him and said, "I didn't get your name."

"Ichabod," Skink said. "Icky for short."

Decker suspected, and fervently hoped, that Ichabod was not Skink's real name. He hoped that Skink had not chosen this particular moment, in front of these particular people, to bare the murky secrets of his soul. Catherine was known to have that effect on a man.

Inanely Decker said to James, "This is quite a place. Your practice must be going great guns."

"Actually," James said, "I picked up this house before I became a doctor." He seemed relieved not to be talking about the poodle or his wife's good looks. "Back when I was in real estate," he said, "that's when I lucked into the place."

"What kinda real estate?" Skink asked.

"Interval-ownership units," James replied, without looking at him.

"Timeshares," Catherine added helpfully.

On the sofa Skink shifted with an audible crinkle. "Timeshares," he said. "Wherebouts?"

Catherine pointed to several small plaques hanging on one of the walls. "James was the top salesman three years in a row," she said. It didn't sound like she was bragging; it sounded like she said it to get it out of the way, knowing James would have mentioned it anyway.

"And where was this?" Skink pressed.

"Up the coast north of Smyrna," James said. "We did very well for a stretch in the late seventies. Then Tallahassee cracked down, the media went sour on us, and the interval market dried up. Same old tune. I figured it was time to move along to something else."

"Boom and bust," Decker played along. "That's the story of Florida." Was it purely the money, he wondered, that had attracted Catherine to this lanky twit? In a way he hoped it was that simple, that it was nothing more.

Skink got up and crunched over to examine the plaques. Catherine and James couldn't take their eyes off him; they had never had such a wild-looking person roaming their house.

"What was the name of your project?" Skink asked, toying with his silvery braid.

"Sparrow Beach," James said. "The Sparrow Beach Club. Seems like ancient history now."

Skink gave no reply, but let out a soft and surprising noise. It sounded to R. J. Decker like a sigh.

"Is your friend all right?" Catherine asked later.

"Sure," Decker said. "He prefers to sleep outdoors, really."

In the middle of James's monologue about his sales triumphs at Sparrow Beach, Skink had turned to Catherine and asked if he could spend the night in the backyard. Decker could tell he was brooding, but had no private moment to ask what was wrong. Catherine had loaned Skink an old blanket and in a flat voice Skink had thanked her for the hospitality and lumbered out the back door. He had ignored James completely.

Skink settled in under a tall avocado tree, and from the window Decker could see him sitting upright against the trunk, facing the narrow waterway that ran behind Catherine's house. Decker had an urge to join him there, under the stars.

"Let James have a look at your neck," Catherine said.

"No, I'll be fine."

"Lie down here," James instructed, making room on the sofa. "Lie down on your stomach."

The next thing Decker knew, James was hunched over him with one knee propped on the sofa for leverage. Intently he kneaded and probed the back of Decker's neck, while Catherine watched cross-legged on an ottoman.

"That hurt?" James asked.

Decker grunted. It did hurt, but the rubbing helped; James seemed to know what he was doing.

"Brother, you're really out of alignment," he said.

"That's a medical term?"

"Full traction is what you need. Slings and weights. Thermal therapy. Ultrasound. You're too young for Medicare, otherwise I'd fix you right up with a twelve-week program." James worked his fingers along Decker's spine. He seemed at ease now, enjoying the role of expert. "Have you got any insurance?" he asked.

"Nope," Decker said.

"Workmen's comp? Maybe you're in an HMO."

"Nope." The guy was unbelievable; the pitchman's spark was probably left over from his days of peddling condos.

"I must caution you," James went on, "that injuries such as this should never go untreated. Your neck has been wrenched badly."

"I'm aware of that," Decker said, wincing under the chiropractor's explorations. "Tell me, what's the difference between this and a massage?"

"I'm a doctor, that's the difference. Don't move now, I think I've got an extra brace in the trunk of the car."

After James had left the room, Catherine came over and knelt down on the floor next to Decker. "Tell me what's happened, Rage."

"Somebody's trying to frame me for a murder."

"Who? Not the Fish People!"

"Afraid so," Decker said. He was ready for a trenchant scolding—this was Catherine's specialty—but for some reason (probably pity) she refrained.

"The guy out back, Grizzly Adams—"

"He's all right," Decker said.

"James is scared of him."

"So am I, but he's all I've got."

Catherine kissed him lightly on the ear. "Is there anything I can do?"

For one flushed moment Decker felt his heart stop. Bump, bump—then dead air. All from a whiff of perfume and a silly peck on the earlobe. It was so wonderful that Decker almost forgot she'd dumped him for a guy who wore ninety-dollar bathrobes.

Catherine said, "I want to help."

"Does James have a broker?" Decker asked.

"Yes. Hutton, Shearson, somebody big like that. It's a VIP account, that much I know. They sent us a magnum of champagne last Christmas."

Decker said, "This is what I need. Tell James you got a tip at the beauty parlor—"

"Oh, please."

"Or wherever, Catherine, just tell him you got a tip on a stock. It's traded as OCN, I think. The Outdoor Christian Network. See if your husband's broker can send over a prospectus. I need a copy as soon as possible."

She said, "He'll think it's odd. We never talk about his investments."

"Try it," Decker said. "Play dumb and sweet and just-trying-to-help. You can do it."

"You're still an asshole, Rage."

"And you're still a vision, Catherine. Would your husband get too terribly upset if you and I took off our clothes and hopped in the shower? We can tell him it's part of my medical treatment. Hot-water traction, they call it."

At that moment James walked in, too preoccupied to notice his wife scooting back to the ottoman. James was carrying a foam-padded brace, the kind that fastens around the neck like a collar.

"That man," he said indignantly, "has built a bonfire in our back-yard!"

Catherine went to the window. "For heaven's sake it's not a *bonfire*," she said. "It's just a barbecue, honey, no worse than you and your hibachi."

"But the hibachi is gas," James protested.

R. J. Decker pushed himself off the sofa and went to see for himself. Skink huddled in a familar pose beneath the avocado tree; crouched on his haunches, tending a small campfire.

"He looks like a damn hobo," James said.

"That's enough," Catherine snapped. "He's not hurting anybody."

Decker observed that Skink had fashioned a rotisserie spit out of dead branches. He was cooking a chunk of gray meat over the fire, rotating it slowly by hand.

"What do you suppose he's got there?" Catherine said.

"Probably something gross he scrounged from the garbage," James said. "Or maybe a duck out of that filthy canal."

In the flickering shadows Decker couldn't be sure, but he had a pretty good idea what his friend was fixing for dinner. It was Bambi, of course. Skink was serenely roasting the doctor's pet poodle.

R. J. Decker took a bed in one of the guestrooms, but he couldn't sleep. Dancing on the walls were cartoon sheep in red tuxedos—wallpaper for a baby's room, obviously, but Catherine had never been too wild about kids. On this matter the chiropractor had failed to change her mind. Still, Decker admired his optimism for leaving the nursery wallpaper up.

When Decker closed his eyes, the tuxedoed sheep were replaced by the face of Dennis Gault: the seething visage of a man trying to strangle him. Decker wondered if the fistfight at Gault's condominium had been an act like everything else; he wondered if Gault were really that clever or ballsy, or if things had just fallen right. Decker couldn't wait to meet up with Gault and ask him. Afterward it would be nice to choke the sonofabitch so decisively that his eyeballs would pop out of his skull and roll across his fancy glass desk like a couple of aggies.

At about three o'clock Decker gave up on sleep and got out of bed. From the window there was no sign of Skink's campfire, or of Skink himself. Decker assumed—hoped, at least—that he was curled up in the bushes somewhere.

For Decker, being in the same house with Catherine was unnerving. Though it was also the house of James, Catherine's tastes predominated—smart and elegant, and so expensive that Decker marveled how such a destitute mongrel as himself had managed to keep her as long as he had. If only he could steal a few moments alone with her now, but how? Skink wanted to be on the road before dawn— there was little time.

Barefoot, and wearing only his underwear, Decker made his way through the long hallways, which smelled of Catherine's hair and perfume. A couple of times, near doorways, Decker had to step carefully over the white beams of photosensitive alarm units, which were mounted at knee-level throughout the house.

Photoelectronic burglar alarms were the latest rage among the rich in Miami, thanks to a widely publicized case in which a whole gang of notorious cat burglars was captured inside a Star Island mansion after tripping the silent alarm. The gang had comprised bold Mariel refugees relatively new to the country and unschooled in the basic skills and technology of modern burglary. While looting the den of the mansion, one of the Cuban intruders had spotted a wall-mounted photoelectronic unit and naturally assumed it was a laser beam that would incinerate them all if they dared cross it. Consequently, they did not. They sat there all night and, the next morning, surrendered sheepishly to police. The incident made all the TV news. Photo- electronic burglar alarms became so popular that burglars soon began to specialize in stealing the alarms themselves. In many of the houses where such devices were installed, the alarm itself was more valuable than anything else on the premises. For a while, all the fences in Hialeah were paying twice as much for stolen burglar alarms as they were for Sony VCRs, but even at five hundred a pop it was virtually impossible for thieves to keep up with the demand.

Tiptoeing around the alarm beams, Decker found the master bed- room at the far west end of Catherine's house. He listened at the door to make sure nothing was going on, and was greatly relieved to hear the sound of snoring.

Decker slipped into the room. He stood at the door until his eyes adjusted; the window shades were drawn and it was very dark. Grad- ually he inched toward the source of the snoring until his right foot stubbed a wooden bed poster. Decker bit back a groan, and one of the two forms in the big bed stirred and turned slightly under the covers. Decker knelt by the side of the bed, and the form snored directly into his face.

"Catherine," he whispered.

She snored again, and Decker remembered how difficult it was to wake her up. He shook her gently by the shoulder and said her name again. This time she swallowed, sighed, and groggily opened her eyes. When she saw who it was, she sat up immediately.

She put her hand on the back of Decker's head and pulled him close. "What are you doing here?"

"Hey, careful with the neck," Decker whispered back.

Catherine glanced at her husband to make sure he was still dozing. Decker had counted on James being a sound sleeper; unlike surgeons or obstetricians, chiropractors rarely had to go tearing off to the hospital in the middle of the night. Back spasms could wait. James was probably accustomed to getting a full nine hours.

"What is it, Rage?" Catherine said into his ear. Her hair was tangled from sleep, and her eyes were a little puffy, but Decker didn't care at all. He kissed her on the mouth and boldly slipped a hand under her nightshirt.

During the kiss Catherine sort of gulped, but still she closed her eyes. Decker knew this because he peeked; he had to. Some women closed their eyes during kissing just to be polite, but Catherine never did unless she was honestly enjoying herself. Decker was pleased to see her eyes shut. The activity beneath the nightshirt was another matter. With an elbow Catherine deftly had pinned his hand to her left breast; obviously that was as far as Mr. Hand would be allowed to go. It was all right with Decker; the left one had always been his favorite, anyway.

Catherine pulled away and said, "You're nuts. Get outta here."

"Come to my room," Decker said.

Catherine shook her head and gestured toward her husband.

"Leave him here," Decker said playfully.

"He'll notice if I get out of bed."

"Just for a few minutes."

"No—"

So he kissed her again. This time she gave a shy purr, which Decker correctly read more as tolerance than total surrender. The second kiss lasted longer than the first, and Decker was getting fairly heated up when James suddenly rolled over, snorted, and said, "Cath?"

Carefully she lay down on the pillow, Decker's hand still resting on her breast. "Yes, hon?" she said.

Cath.

Hon.

Very sweet, Decker thought, a regular goddamn testimonial to marital bliss. He started to remove his hand but Catherine wouldn't let him. Decker smiled in the dark.

"Cath," James said torpidly, "did Bambi ever come in?"

"No, honey," she said. "He's probably out on the porch. Go back to sleep now."

Catherine held motionless until James's breathing grew thick and regular. Then she turned her back to him so that she and Decker were face-to-face at the edge of the bed.

"Go back to your room," she whispered. "Give me about ten minutes."

"Thatta girl," Decker said, rising off his knees. "One more kiss."

Catherine said, "Ssshhh," but she kissed him back. This time she let her tongue sneak into his mouth.

"We'll need your boat."

Catherine and Decker opened their eyes mid-kiss and stared at each other. The whisper did not belong to James.

"The boat," Skink said.

Catherine saw his tangled face looming impassively over Decker's shoulder.

"I don't mean to interrupt," Skink said, "but there's some cops out front."

Decker stood up and fought back a panic. It had to be Al García. He knew about the divorce, and Catherine would have been high on his list of interviews. The surprising thing was that he'd come in the dead of night—unless, of course, he knew Decker was inside the house.

Which any nitwit could have figured out from the rental car out front. Decker wondered if maybe deep down he wanted to go back to jail—what else could explain such carelessness? Skink took care of survival in the boonies, but the city was Decker's responsibility and he kept making dumb mistakes.

"Your boat," Skink said again to Catherine, "it's tied up out back."

She whispered, "I don't know where the keys are."

"I don't need the keys," Skink said, no longer making an effort to talk quietly. "We'll leave 'er up at Haulover, but don't go looking right away."

The doorbell rang, followed by three sharp knocks.

James sat up in bed and reached for a lamp on the nightstand. Blearily he eyed Decker and Skink. "What's going on?"

Catherine was out from the covers, brushing her hair in the mirror. "You better get moving," she said to Decker's reflection. "I'll keep them at the door."

"We'll need a head start."

"Don't worry, Rage."

The doorbell rang again. The knocks turned to pounding.

Skink handed Decker his jeans and shoes.

"What's going on?" James the doctor wondered. "Where's the damn dog?"

Since the truck they'd been driving was registered to Dickie Lockhart, and since the New Orleans police had temporarily impounded it along with everything else belonging to Dickie, the Rundell brothers had been forced to take a Trailways all the way back to Florida. On the trip they talked primarily about two things—how their hero had died, and what had happened to their precious bass boat.

Dim as they were, even the Rundells realized that not much could be done for Dickie, but the boat was another issue. It had been stolen and then scuttled in the middle of Lake Maurepas, where it had turned up as bottom clutter on Captain Coot Hough's Vexilar LCD Video sonic fish-finder. Once the lost boat had been pinpointed, the Rundells had recruited an amateur salvage team made up of fellow bass anglers, who raised the vessel with a hand-cranked winch mounted on a borrowed construction barge. The sight of their sludge-covered beauty breaking the surface was the second saddest thing Ozzie Rundell had ever seen—the first being Dickie Lockhart's blue-lipped corpse in the big fish tank.

On the long bus ride back to Harney, Ozzie and Culver puzzled over who might have stolen their boat and why. The prime suspect seemed to be the violent hermit known to the Rundells only as Skink. A peculiar and vividly garbed man matching his description had been spotted on the lake by several other anglers, though no one had reported witnessing the actual sinking of the boat. What Skink was doing in Louisiana was a mystery that the Rundells did not contemplate for long—he was there, that's all that mattered. They clearly remembered the sky marshals leading him off the airplane in New Orleans, and they remembered the look of latent derangement in his eyes. Certainly the man was capable of stealing a boat; the riddle was finding a plausible motive. With a fellow like Skink, unadulterated malice might have been enough, but the Rundells remained doubtful. Culver in particular suspected revenge, or a plot hatched by one of Dickie Lockhart's jealous competitors. In the world of professional bassing it was well known that the Rundell brothers were the most loyal of Dickie's retinue, and in Culver's mind it made them likely targets.

If Culver were outwardly angry about the destruction of their prized fishing boat, Ozzie seemed more wounded and perplexed. He was particularly incredulous that Skink would commit such an atrocity against them for no apparent reason. In the ten-odd years since the shaggy woodsman had come to live on Lake Jesup, Ozzie had probably not exchanged a half-dozen words with him. On the rare occasions when Skink came to town, he purchased lumber and dry goods and used books from the Faith Farm—or so Mrs. Coot Hough had gossiped—but never once had he come into the bait shop for tackle or lures (though he was reputed to be an expert angler). Ozzie's only close encounters with the man were the many times he'd had to swerve to avoid the crouched figure plucking animal carcasses off the Gilchrist Highway or Route 222. Nearly all the citizenry of Harney had occasionally come across Skink and his fresh roadkills, and the general assumption was that he ate the dead critters, though no one could say for a fact. The only person known to have a friendly relationship with Skink was Trooper Jim Tile of the state highway patrol. Occasionally fishermen out on Lake Jesup would see Jim Tile sitting at Skink's campfire, but none of them knew the trooper well enough to ask about it. Actually no one in Harney, not even the blacks, knew Jim Tile much better than they knew Skink.

Which was why Ozzie was so stunned to hear his brother announce that they would visit the trooper as soon as they got home.

"We'll get some answers out of that nigger," Culver said.

"I don't know," Ozzie mumbled. He wasn't keen on confrontations. Neither was Culver, usually, but Dickie's murder had set him on edge. He was talking big and mean, the way he sometimes did after drinking.

Ozzie Rundell had a perfectly good reason for not wanting to see Jim Tile face-to-face: Jim Tile had been out at Morgan Slough the night Ott Pickney was killed, the night Ozzie was driving Tom Curl's truck. As they were speeding out from the trail, Ozzie had spotted the trooper on foot. What he didn't know was whether or not Jim Tile had spotted him too. Ozzie had assumed not, since nothing terrible had happened in the days that followed, but he didn't want to press his meager luck. He felt he should explain to his brother the risks of visiting Jim Tile, but as usual the words wouldn't come out. The day after the newsman's death, Ozzie had assured Culver that everything had gone smoothly at the slough, and hadn't mentioned the black trooper. If Ozzie revealed the truth now, Culver would be furious, and Ozzie was in no mood to get yelled at. The closest thing to a protest he could muster was: "A trooper is the law. Even a nigger trooper."

Culver scowled and said, "We'll see about that."

Jim Tile lived alone in a two-bedroom apartment on Washington Drive, in the black neighborhood of Harney. He had been married for three years until his wife had gone off to Atlanta to become a big-time fashion model. Jim Tile could have gone with her, since he had been offered an excellent job with the Georgia Bureau of Investigation, but he had chosen to stay with the highway patrol in Florida. His loyalty had been rewarded with a protracted tour of duty in the most backward-thinking and racist county in the state. To stop a car for speeding in Harney was to automatically invite a disgusting torrent of verbal abuse—the whites hated Jim Tile because he was black, and the blacks hated him for doing a honky's job. Rough words were expected, and occasionally somebody would sneak up and cut the tires on his patrol car late at night, but it seldom went any further. In all the years only one person had been foolhardy enough to try to fight Trooper Jim Tile. The boy's name was Dekle, and he was eighteen, as big and white as a Frigidaire, and just about as intelligent. Dekle had been doing seventy in a school zone and had run down a kitten before Jim Tile caught up and forced him off the road. At the time Jim Tile was new to Harney, and the Dekle boy remarked how he had never seen a chocolate state trooper before. Now you have, said Jim Tile, so turn around and put your hands on the roof of the car. At which point Dekle punched Jim Tile with all his strength and was astounded to see the trooper merely rock back slightly on his heels, when any other human being would have fallen flat on his back, out cold. The fight did not last long, perhaps thirty seconds, and years afterward Dekle's right arm still hung like a corkscrew and he still got around with the aid of a special Lucite cane, which his mother had purchased from a mail-order house in Tampa. Even in a place where there was no shortage of booze or stupidity, no one in Harney had since gotten drunk enough or dumb enough to take a poke at the black trooper. Most folks, including Ozzie Rundell, wouldn't consider giving the man any lip.

They found the apartment on Washington Drive easily; Jim Tile's black-and-tan Ford police cruiser was out front.

Culver parked his mother's truck. He got a pistol from under the front seat and tucked it into the back of his dungarees.

"What's that for?" Ozzie asked worriedly.

"It's a bad neighborhood, Oz."

"I ain't going in there with a gun," Ozzie said in a brittle voice. "I ain't!"

"Fine," Culver said. "You sit out here in the parking lot with all these jigaboos. I'm sure they'll love the prospect of a fat little cracker boy like you."

Ozzie looked around and knew that his brother was right. The streets were full of black faces, including some frightfully muscular teenagers slam-dunking basketballs through a rusty hoop nailed to a telephone pole. Ozzie decided he didn't want to stay in the truck after all. He followed Culver up to Jim Tile's apartment.

The trooper was finishing dinner, and getting ready to go out on the night shift. He came to the door wearing the gray, sharply pressed trousers of his uniform, but no shirt. The Rundell brothers were awestruck by the dimensions of his chest and arms.

After stammering for a second, Culver finally said, "We need to talk about the guy lives up on the lake."

"Our boat got sunk," Ozzie warbled, without explanation.

Jim Tile let them in, motioned toward two chairs at the dinette. The Rundell brothers sat down.

"Skink is his name, right?" Culver said.

"What's the connection," Jim Tile asked mildly, "between the man on the lake and your boat?"

Ozzie started to say something, got lost, and looked to his brother for help. Culver said, "We heard Mr. Skink is the one who sunked it."

Jim Tile said, "Well, Mr. Skink is out of town."

"It happened out of town," Culver said. "At a tournament up in Louisiana."

"Did you go to the police?" Jim Tile asked.

"Not yet," Culver said. He had wanted to, but Thomas Curl had said it was a bad idea. He said the police would be busy with Dickie's murder, and it wouldn't be right to bother them over a bass boat. Besides, the boat *had* been recovered out of the water, and it was Thomas Curl's opinion that it could be repaired. Ozzie said great, but Culver didn't like the idea. Culver wanted a brand-new boat, and he wanted the man named Skink to buy it for him.

"Well, if you haven't talked to the police in Louisiana,

then I suggest you do," Jim Tile said. "Once there's a warrant, one of Sheriff Lockhart's deputies can go out to Lake Jesup and arrest him."

Culver Rundell doubted if Sheriff Earley Lockhart was much interested in a boat theft, not with his famous nephew turning up murdered in Louisiana. Earley had caught a flight to New Orleans two days after the killing, and had not yet returned. Before leaving, the sheriff dramatically informed the Harney *Sentinel* that his presence had been requested to assist in the homicide investigation, but in reality the Louisiana authorities merely wanted somebody to accompany Dickie's autopsied body back to Florida.

"It's a jurisdictional problem," Trooper Jim Tile said to the Rundell brothers. "I really can't help."

"You can take us to see Mr. Skink," Culver said.

"Why? You know where he lives—drive out there yourself."

To Ozzie's ear, Jim Tile's response sounded as close to a definite no as you could get. But Culver wasn't giving up.

"No way," Culver said. "I heard he's got a big gun, shoots at people just for the fun of it. He doesn't know me or my brother, and he might just open fire if we was to drive up unannounced. You, he knows. Even if he's crazy as they say, he won't shoot a damn police car."

The low, even tone of Jim Tile's voice did not change. "I told you, he's out of town."

"Well, let's go see."

"No," said Jim Tile, rising. "I have to go to work."

"Momma's truck," Ozzie blurted. "Maybe we oughta go, Culver."

Annoyed, Culver glanced at his brother. "What are you talking about?"

"I'm worried about Momma's truck out there. Maybe we should go."

"The truck'll be fine," Culver said.

"I don't know," Jim Tile said, parting the venetian blinds. "It's a pretty rough neighborhood."

Ozzie looked stricken.

"Oh, settle down," Culver said angrily. Then, to Jim Tile: "You, why won't you help us? I lost a twenty-thousand-dollar rig because of that bastard!"

Jim Tile was still looking out the window. "So that's your mother's pickup?"

"Ours is in the impound, up New Orleans," Ozzie said.

"The red one," Jim Tile said.

"Yeah," Culver grunted, secretly impressed that the trooper would remember the color.

Then Jim Tile said to Ozzie: "What about the green one?"

The color washed out of Ozzie's cheeks. His eyelids fluttered, as if he were about to faint.

"What green one?" Culver said, slow to put it together.

"The one your brother was driving week before last," Jim Tile said, "out on the Gilchrist. About dawn, one morning."

"When?" Ozzie hiccuped. "Wasn't me. Our truck is red."

"You and two other guys," Jim Tile said, "and the truck was green. Out-of-state tags."

Finally Culver was picking up on the train of conversation. He tried to help Ozzie as best he could, even though he felt like strangling him.

"I remember that day," Culver improvised, watching his brother's eyes grow big. "You and some boys went fishing up at the slough. I remember 'cause you took a couple Shakespeare plug rods out of the shop, along with some Johnson spoons and purple skirts."

Ozzie's lips were like chalk. His bottom jaw went up and down until finally he said, "Oh, yeah."

Culver said, "I remember 'cause you didn't want to try live shiners, even though I told you to. You said there was too much heavy cover, so you'd prefer dragging those damn weedless spoons."

Jim Tile was buttoning his shirt. "So, Ozzie," he said, "you guys catch anything?"

"Sure," Ozzie said, glancing at the door, as if he were about to run.

"What'd you catch?"

"Our truck is red," Ozzie Rundell said, licking his lips. His shoulders twitched and his eyes rolled up and fixed on the ceiling. His cheeks puffed out, like he was trying to fart.

"Pardon me?" Jim Tile said, bending over to tie his shoes.

"That's Momma's pickup outside," Ozzie said in a very high voice. He was gone, unglued, lost in a pathetic blubbering panic. Culver shook his head disgustedly.

"I asked what you caught," Jim Tile said, "out at Morgan Slough."

Ozzie smiled and smacked his lips. "One time Dickie gave me a tacklebox," he said.

"All right, that's enough," Culver broke in.

"Ozzie?" said Jim Tile.

"The day in the truck?"

"The green truck, yes."

"I was driving, that's all. I didn't drown nobody."

"Of course not," Jim Tile said.

"That's it," said Culver Rundell. "Shut the fuck up, Oz."

Culver had the gun out. He was holding it with two hands, pointing it at Jim Tile's heart. Jim Tile glanced down once, but seemed to pay no more attention to the gun than if it were just Culver's fly unzipped.

"Let's go," Culver said in a husky whisper.

But Jim Tile merely walked into the bedroom, stood at the dresser, and adjusted his trooper's Stetson.

"Now!" Culver shouted. Ozzie stared at the handgun and covered his ears.

Jim Tile reached for a bottle of cologne.

Culver exploded. "Nigger, I'm talking to you!"

Only then did Jim Tile turn to give Ozzie Rundell's brother his complete and undivided attention.

The boat was an eighteen-foot Aquasport with a two-hundred-horse Evinrude outboard; smooth trim, dry ride, very fast. Skink liked it quite a bit. He liked it so much he decided not to ditch it at Haulover docks after all, but to drive it up the Intracoastal Waterway all the way to Pier 66, in Fort Lauderdale. The morning was biting cold, and R. J. Decker would have preferred to travel by car, but there was no point to raising the issue. Skink was having a ball, his silvery ponytail strung out behind him like a rope in the breeze. At the Dania Beach bridge he cut the throttle down to idle speed and the Aquasport coasted into a slow crawl.

"What's up?" Decker asked.

Skink said, "Manatee zone."

In the wintertime giant manatees migrate with their young to congregate sluggishly in the warm sheltered waters of the Intracoastal. During manatee season boaters are required by law to go slow, but each year dozens of the gentle mammals are run down and sliced to ribbons by reckless tourists and teenagers. The fine for such a crime costs the offending boater no more than a new pair of Top-Siders, and is not much of a deterrent. During the last days of his governorship, Clinton Tyree had lobbied for a somewhat tougher law. His version would have required anyone who killed a manatee to immediately forfeit his boat (no matter how luxurious) and pay a ten-thousand-dollar fine or go to jail for forty-five days. The Tyree amendment would have also required the manatee killer to personally bury the dead animal himself, at a public ceremony.

Not surprisingly, the governor's proposal was quietly rejected.

R. J. Decker knew none of this, so he was somewhat perplexed when Skink took a hawklike interest in another boat, speeding south down the waterway in the predawn twilight. It was a gaily colored ski boat full of young men and women returning from a night of serious dockside partying. Skink waved furiously and shouted for them to slow down, watch out for the sea cows, but the kids just stared back with radish-colored eyes—except for the driver, who made the awful mistake of flipping Skink the magic digit. Later the girls from the ski boat would tell the marine patrol that their boy-friends had gravely underestimated the size and temperament of the old hippie, just as they had underestimated the speed of the Aqua-sport. Were it not for the other stranger dragging the old hippie off them, the girls said, their boyfriends might have been seriously killed. (At this point the girls were doing all the talking because the young men were still being X-rayed at Broward General Hospital for broken bones. The doctors marveled that they had been able to swim so far in such a traumatized condition.)

To convince Skink to quit pummeling the speeders, Decker had had to agree to let him sink their ski boat, which he did by shooting three holes in the hull. Then he scrupulously idled the Aquasport all the way to the Port Everglades inlet, and from there it was full throttle again to Pier 66. By now Decker was cold and wet and eternally grateful to be off the water. They caught a cab to the Harbor Beach Marriott, got a room, and fell asleep—Decker splayed on the king-size bed, Skink in a ball on the floor. At noon they woke up and started working the phones.

Jim Tile got off the road at nine in the morning. When he got back to the apartment, he fixed himself four poached eggs, three hunks of Canadian bacon, and a tumbler of fresh-squeezed orange juice. Then he took off his trousers, went to the bathroom, and changed the dressing on the bullet wound in his right thigh. After-ward he put on a gray sweatsuit, fixed himself some hot tea, and sat down with the newspaper. He did all this without saying a word to the Rundell brothers, who were still bound and gagged on the floor. In truth Culver didn't feel slighted (he had passed out from pain many hours before), but Ozzie was dying to talk. Ozzie was scared out of his mind.

"Thur?" he said.

Jim Tile lowered the newspaper, reached down, and yanked the towel from Ozzie's mouth.

"Sir, is my brother dead? Thank you. For taking the towel, I mean, thanks."

Jim Tile said, "Your brother's not dead."

"What's wrong with him? His face don't look right."

"His jaw's broken," Jim Tile said. "And all his fingers too." It had happened when Jim Tile had wrenched the pistol away, after Culver had shot him and ruined a perfectly good uniform.

"He needs a doctor, bad," Ozzie said plaintively.

"Yes, he does." Jim Tile hadn't meant to break Culver's jaw in so many places, and he was annoyed at himself for punching the man too hard. Culver wouldn't be doing any chatting for a long time, so now the information would have to come from Ozzie, one of the most witless and jumble-headed crackers that Jim Tile had ever met.

Culver moaned and strained against the ropes. Ozzie said, "Oh Jesus, he's hurt bad."

"Yes, he is," Jim Tile said. "You can take him to the doctor after we have our talk."

"Promise?"

"You've got my word."

"Is Culver going to jail?"

"Well, I don't know. Attempted murder of a police officer, that's a life term here in Florida. Agg assault, use of a firearm in the commission of a felony, and so on. I just don't know."

Ozzie said, "What about me?"

"Oh, same goes for you. You're his partner, right?"

Ozzie's eyes got wet. "Momma 'spects the truck back long time ago."

"She'll be worried," Jim Tile said.

"Can we go soon?"

Jim Tile folded up the newspaper and leaned forward. "First you answer some questions."

"Okay, but go slow."

"Did Dickie Lockhart get you boys to kill Bobby Clinch?"

"No, Jesus! Honest we didn't." Ozzie's nose was running. "I liked Bobby, so'd Culver—"

"Then who killed him?" Jim Tile asked.

"I don't know." Ozzie sniffed loudly, trying to get the snot off his upper lip. "I got no idea," he said.

Jim Tile believed him. He said, "Tell me about Mr. Pickney."
"Who? Help me out."
"The guy who played Davey Dillo at the high school."
"Oh, the reporter," Ozzie said. "Sir, I didn't drown nobody."
"Who did?"

Culver made a gurgling sound, opened his eyes—showing the whites—and shut them slowly again. Ozzie cried and said, "We gotta get the truck back to Momma."

"Then tell me about Morgan Slough." Jim Tile held a teacup to Ozzie Rundell's lips. He took a loud sip, swallowed twice, and began to talk. Jim Tile sat back and listened, saving his questions for the end. He figured the least interruption would confuse Ozzie beyond redemption.

"Okay, a few days after Bobby Clinch died, Tom and Lemus came by the bait shop for coffee. They were saying how somebody was trying to make it look like Dickie done it, except it was an accident—Doc Pembroke even said so. But Tom and Lemus, they said how somebody went to the newspaper with a made-up story that Dickie kilt Bobby, and now this detective from Miami was goin' around asking about Bobby and what happened at the Coon Bog. Culver ast who would try to set Dickie Lockhart up like that, but Tom said there were about a million guys jealous of Dickie would do it in a flash. He said they'd try to make it look like Bobby caught Dickie cheating in some tournament.

"So Culver hears all this and gets worried because, right before the Curl boys come by, this reporter fella had been in asting about Bobby's boat and the funeral and such—see, they sawed up his Ranger into a coffin. Mr. Pinky, he seemed real interested so Culver told him Larkin's place had done the carpenter work. The man said thanks and went off.

"Jeez, when Tom and Lemus hear all this they say we've got to get over to Larkin's right away. Culver was busy with some customers so he told me to ride along in the truck, which I did. On the way over Tom and Lemus said if we don't do something fast, the newspaper's gonna do a big write-up about how Dickie murdered Bobby Clinch, which we all knew was a lie, but still it would ruin Dickie and make him lose the TV show. They said we better stop this guy and I said yeah, but that was before I knew what they meant. What they meant by stopping him. Sir, can I have some more tea?"

Jim Tile held the cup for Ozzie.

"The green truck, that was Tom and Lemus's," Ozzie said.

"Oh," said Jim Tile.

"Anyway, we get to Larkin's and there's the guy out back by the dumpster. Ott Pinky. I recognized him right off, and Lemus says: Is that the guy? And I say yeah, it is." Ozzie paused. "I got in the back of the truck, the green truck."

Jim Tile said, "And Mr. Pickney rode up front? Between the Curl boys."

"Yes, sir. There's a deer camp on the Sumter property. Maybe sixteen miles out. We took him there for the rest of the day. See, I thought mainly they was just gonna ast him questions."

Jim Tile said, "What did you see, Ozzie?"

"Mainly I stayed in the truck."

"Then what did you hear?"

Ozzie looked down. "Jesus, I don't know. Mainly some yelling. . . ." The words tumbled slowly, trailed off. Jim Tile imagined Ozzie's fevered brain cells exploding like popcorn.

The trooper said, "What did Ott tell them?"

"We made a fire, drank some beer, fell asleep. About three hours before dawn we headed for the slough."

"Was Mr. Pickney still alive?"

"He didn't tell them hardly nothing, according to Tom and Lemus." Ozzie was untracked again, answering Jim Tile's questions in no particular sequence.

Jim Tile said, "You were the driver, that's all?"

"He was still alive when we got there. Banged up but still alive. See, I thought they was gonna let him go. I thought they was through with him. Tom and Lemus, they said to stay in the truck and I did. But it got cold and I couldn't figure what was takin' so long. Finally I got out to whizz and that's when I heard the splash."

Jim Tile said, "You didn't see anything?"

"It was a damn big splash." Ozzie sneezed, and more gunk came out of his nose. He said, "Truth is, I didn't really want to look."

Jim Tile untied Ozzie's wrists and ankles and helped him to his feet. Together they carried Culver out to the pickup and laid him on the flatbed. Ozzie put the tailgate back up. Jim Tile got an extra pillow and a blanket from his apartment.

"Think you'd best get him over to the hospital in Melbourne," Jim Tile said. "Nobody here in town can fix that jawbone."

Ozzie nodded glumly. "I gotta go by the house and fetch Momma." He got in the truck and started the ignition.

Jim Tile leaned in the driver's window and said, "Ozzie, you understand what happens if I have to arrest you."

"Culver goes to jail," Ozzie said wanly.

"For the rest of his natural life. When he gets to feeling better, please remind him, would you?"

"I will," said Ozzie. "Sir, I swear I don't think he meant to shoot you."

"Of course he did," said Jim Tile, "but I'm inclined to let the whole thing slide, long as you boys stay out of my way for a while."

Ozzie was so relieved that he nearly peed his pants. He didn't even mind that the black man had called *them* boys. Basically Ozzie was happy to still be alive. The trooper could have killed them both and gotten away with it, yet here he was, being a true Christian and letting them go.

"Just one favor,' Jim Tile said, resting a coal-black arm on the door of the truck.

"Sure," Ozzie said.

"Where can I find Thomas Curl?"

Richard Clarence Lockhart was buried on January 25 at the Our Lady of Tropicana cemetery outside Harney. It was a relatively small turnout, considering Dickie's fame and stature in the county, but the low attendance could be explained easily enough. By unfortunate coincidence, the day of the funeral was also opening day of the Okeechobee Bass Blasters Classic, so almost all Dickie's friends and colleagues were out fishing. Dickie would certainly forgive them, the preacher had chuckled, especially since the tournament required a nonrefundable entry fee of two thousand dollars per boat.

Dickie Lockhart was buried in a handsome walnut coffin, not a bass boat. The hearse bearing the coffin was escorted to Our Lady of Tropicana by three police cars, including a trooper's cruiser driven, none too happily, by Jim Tile. Dickie Lockhart's casket was closed during the eulogy, since the mortician ultimately had been frustrated in his cosmetic efforts to remove the Double Whammy spinnerbait from Dickie's lip; in the clammy New Orleans morgue the lure's hook had dulled, while Dickie's skin had only toughened. Rather than further mutilate the facial features of the deceased, the mortician had simply advised Dickie's sisters to keep the coffin closed and remember him as he was.

Ozzie Rundell was extremely grateful. He couldn't have borne another glimpse of his murdered idol.

Culver Rundell did not attend the funeral, since he was hospitalized with thirty-nine linear feet of stainless-steel wire in his jaws. On Culver's behalf, the bait shop had ordered a special floral arrangement topped by a ceramic jumping fish. Unfortunately the ceramic fish was a striped marlin, not a largemouth bass, but no one at the funeral was rude enough to mention it.

The Reverend Charles Weeb also did not attend the funeral, but on behalf of the Outdoor Christian Network he sent a six-foot gladiola wreath with a white ribbon that said: "Tight Lines, Old Friend." This was the hit of the graveside service, but the best was yet to come. The next morning, at the closing of the regular Sunday broadcast of *Jesus in Your Living Room,* Charlie Weeb offered a special benediction for the soul of his dear, dear friend Dickie Lockhart, the greatest bass fisherman in the history of America. Then Dickie's face appeared on the big screen behind the pulpit, and the assembled flock lip-synched to a Johnny Cash recording of "Nearer, My God, to Thee." At the end of the song everybody was weeping, even Charlie Weeb, the man who had so often privately referred to Dickie Lockhart as a shiftless pellet-brained cocksucker.

Twenty-five minutes after the church show was over and the audience was paid, the Reverend Charles Weeb strolled into a skybox in the Superdome, which had been rented for the big press conference. If Charlie Weeb was disappointed in the sparse turnout of media, he didn't show it. He wore his wide-bodied smile and a cream-colored suit with a plum kerchief in the breast pocket. At his side stood a rangy tanned man with curly brown hair and a friendly, toothy smile. Right away the man reminded some of the photographers of Bruce Dern, the actor, but it wasn't. It was Eddie Spurling, the fisherman.

"Gentlemen," said Charlie Weeb, still in character, "am I a happy man today! Yes indeed, I am. It is my pleasure to announce that, beginning this week, Eddie Spurling will be the new host of *Fish Fever.*"

There were only two print reporters in the room, but Weeb politely waited for them to jot the big news in their spiral notebooks.

Weeb continued: "As you know, for some time Eddie's been the host of his own popular bass show on a competing network. We are most pleased to have stolen him away, since it means—as of yesterday—an additional seventy-four independent cable stations switching to the Outdoor Christian Network for the upcoming fishing season." Charlie Weeb allowed himself a brief dramatic pause. "And let me say that although all of us will miss Dickie Lockhart and his special brand of outdoor entertainment, I'm certain that his fans will find Eddie Spurling just as exciting, just as informative, and just as much fun to fish with every week. All of us here in the OCN family couldn't be more pleased!"

Eddie stepped forward and tipped an invisible cap. He was looking pretty pleased himself, and for good reason. January had been a fabulous month. Without winning a single bass tournament he had doubled both his salary and his national TV exposure, and had also landed the lucrative six-figure endorsement contract for Happy Gland Fish Scent products. The Happy Gland package (entailing print, TV, billboard, and radio commercials) was the envy of the professional bass-fishing circuit, a prize held exclusively for the past five years by Dickie Lockhart. With Lockhart's sudden death, the Happy Gland people needed a new star. The choice was an obvious one; the ad agency didn't even bother to hold auditions. Henceforth every bottle of Bass Bolero, Mackerel Musk, and Catfish Cum would bear the grinning likeness of Fast Eddie Spurling.

"Any questions?" asked Charlie Weeb.

The reporters just looked at one another. Each of them was thinking he would go back to the newsroom and kill the editor who sent him on this assignment.

Weeb said, "I've saved the best for last. Girls, bring out the visuals."

Two young women in opalescent bathing suits entered the skybox carrying an immense gold-plated trophy. The trophy easily stood five feet off the ground. On the corners of the base of the trophy were toy-size figures of anglers holding fishing rods, bent in varying degrees of mythic struggle. At the crown of the trophy was an authentic largemouth bass in a full body mount. As bass went, it was no hawg, but poised on the trophy it did look impressive.

"Well, there!" said the Reverend Weeb.

"What did you win it for?" one of the reporters asked Eddie Spurling.

"I didn't win it," Fast Eddie said, "not yet."

"Gentlemen, read what it says on the trophy, look closely," said Charlie Weeb. "This is probably the biggest trophy most of you ever saw, including Eddie here, who's won some pretty big ones."

"None this big," Eddie Spurling said admiringly.

"Damn right," Weeb said. "That's because it's the biggest trophy ever. And it's the biggest trophy ever because it goes to the winner of the biggest fishing tournament ever. Three weeks from today, gentlemen, on the edge of the legendary Florida Everglades, fifty of the best bass anglers in the world will compete for a first prize of two hundred and fifty thousand dollars."

"Christ," said one of the reporters. Finally something to scribble.

"The richest tournament ever," Charlie Weeb said, glowing. "The Dickie Lockhart Memorial Bass Blasters Classic."

Ed Spurling said, "At Lunker Lakes."

"Oh yes," said the Reverend Weeb, "how could I forget?"

Al García was dog-tired. He'd been up since six, and even after four cups of coffee his tongue felt like mossy Styrofoam. His bum left shoulder was screaming for Percodans but García stuck with plain aspirin, four at a pop. It was one of those days when he wondered why he hadn't just retired on full disability and moved quietly to Ocala; one of those days when everything and everybody in Miami annoyed the shit out of him. The lady at the toll booth, for instance, when she'd snatched the dollar bill out of his hand—a frigging buck, just for the matchless pleasure of driving the Rickenbacker out to Key Biscayne. And the doorman at the Mayan high-rise condo. *Let's see some identification, please.* How about a sergeant's badge, asshole? The thing was, the doorman—dressed in a charcoal monkey suit that must have cost four bills—the doorman used to work for fucking Somoza. Used to pulverize peasant skulls on behalf of the Nicaraguan National Guard. García knew this, and still he had to stand there, dig around for his shield *and* a driver's license, before the goon would let him inside.

To top it off, the rich guy he's supposed to interview comes to the door wearing one of those faggy thong bathing suits (candy-apple red) that make it look like you've got a python between your legs.

"Come on in, Sergeant," said Dennis Gault. "Tell me the news."

"What news?" García looked the place over before he sat down.

Nice apartment. Thick, fluffy carpet—no rug-burn romances for this stud. Swell view of the Atlantic, too. Got to cost a million-three easy, García thought. You can't buy a toilet on the island for under two-fifty.

Gault said, "About Decker—didn't you catch him?"

"Not yet."

"Grapefruit juice? O.J.?"

"Coffee if you got it," García said. "You must be headed down to the beach."

"No," Gault said, "the sauna." After he poured García's coffee, he said, "I thought that's why you called—Decker, I mean. I figured you boys would've found him by now."

You boys. Fine, be that way, García thought. "We almost had him last night, but he got away."

"Got away?" Dennis Gault asked.

"As in, eluded us," García said. "Stole a boat and took off across the bay. By the time we got a chopper up, it was too late."

"Sounds like you boys fucked up."

"We prefer to think of it as a missed opportunity." García smiled. "Very good coffee. Colombian?"

"Yeah," Dennis Gault said. He dumped a squirt of vodka into his grapefruit juice.

"The reason I'm here," García said, "is I need you to tell me everything about what happened with Decker."

Gault sat down, tugged irritably at his cherry swimtrunks. García figured they must be riding clear up the crack of his buttocks.

"Hell, I flew to New Orleans and gave a full statement," Gault said. "How many times do I have to go over it?"

García said, "I've read your statement, Mr. Gault. It's fine as far as it goes. But, see, working the Miami angle, I need a few more details."

"Such as?"

"Such as how did Decker choose you?" García was admiring the empty coffee cup. It looked like real china.

Gault said, "My feelings about Dickie Lockhart were no secret, Sergeant. I'm sure Decker talked to some fishermen, heard the stories. Once he took those photographs, I was the logical choice for a buyer—he knew I hated Dickie, knew I wanted to see him discredited. Plus he knew I was a man of means. He knew I could afford his price, no matter how ludicrous."

Man of means. García was in hog heaven. "He told you all this, Decker did?"

"No, I don't recall that he did. You asked how he picked me and I'm telling you it wasn't too damn difficult."

García said, "How did he first contact you?"

"He called."

"Your secretary just patched him right through?"

"Of course not," Gault said. "He left a message. Left about seventeen messages before finally I got fed up and picked up the phone."

"That's good," García said. From the inside of his tan suit coat he produced a small notebook and wrote something down. "Seventeen messages—your secretary's bound to remember the name, don't you think? She probably wrote his number in a desk calendar somewhere. Even a scrap of paper would be a help."

"I don't know," Gault said. "That was weeks ago. She probably tossed it by now."

Al García left his notebook open on his lap while Gault repeated his story that R. J. Decker had demanded one hundred thousand dollars for the photographs of Dickie Lockhart cheating.

"I told him he was nuts," Gault said. "I told him to take a flying fuck."

"But you saw the pictures."

"Yeah, and it was Dickie, all right, pulling fish cages in a lake somewhere. Illegal as hell."

García said, "So why didn't you buy them?"

"For the obvious reasons, that's why." Gault pretended to be insulted.

"Too much money," García said. "That's the most obvious one."

"Forget the money. It would have been wrong."

"Wrong?"

"Don't look at me like that," Gault said. "You're looking at me like I was a common criminal."

Maybe worse, García thought. He had already decided that Dennis Gault was a liar. The question was, how far did it go?

"The note," the detective said. "Asking for a hundred grand—"

"I gave it to the cops in New Orleans."

"Yes, I know. But I was wondering what Decker meant—remember he used the word 'fee'. Like it was a real case. He said, 'The fee is now a hundred grand,' something like that."

Gault said, "Hell, I knew exactly what he meant."

"Sure, but I was thinking—why he didn't use the word 'price'? I mean, he was talking about the price of the photographs, wasn't he? It just seemed like a funny choice of words."

"Not to me," Gault said.

"When did he give you the note?"

"Same day he showed me the pictures. January 7, I guess it was." Gault got up and went to the bathroom. When he came back he was wearing a monogrammed terrycloth robe over the skimpy red thong. It had gotten chillier in the apartment.

"After I told Decker to get lost, he went right to Lockhart for all the marbles. It was pure blackmail: Pay me or I give the picures to my pals at the newspaper. Naturally Dickie paid—the poor schmuck had no choice."

García said, "How do you know all this?"

Gault laughed caustically and slapped his hands on his knees. "From R. J. Decker!" he said. "Decker told my sister Elaine. Turns out he was banging her—I'm sure New Orleans must've filled you in. Anyway, Decker told Elaine he squeezed thirty grand out of Dickie before Dickie cut him off. At the tournament Decker went to see him about it, and you know the rest."

"Decker doesn't sound too bright."

"Then why haven't you caught him?"

"What I meant," García said evenly, "is that it wasn't too bright for him to blab all this shit to your sister."

Dennis Gault shrugged and stood up. "You know how it is—in the sack you'll say anything. Besides, you never met Elaine. Talking is her second-favorite thing." Gault flashed García a sly, frat-house sort of look. García thought this showed real class, a millionaire pimping his own sister. With each passing minute the homicide detective was growing to doubt Mr. Gault's character.

He said, "Maybe Decker was just bragging."

"Bragging, passing the time, waiting for his dick to get hard again, I don't know. Whatever the reason, he told Elaine." Gault took García's coffee cup. "What about Decker's partner, this Skink maniac?"

"We don't even know his real name," García said.

"He's a nut case, I've met him. Tell your boys to be damn careful."

"You bet," García said, rising. "Thanks for the coffee. You've been most helpful."

Gault twirled the sash of his robe as he walked the detective to the door. "As you can tell, I had no love for Dickie Lockhart. If anything else had happened to him—a plane crash, prostate cancer, AIDS—you wouldn't have heard a peep out of me. Hell, I would've thrown a party. But murder—not even a cheating motherfucker like Dickie deserved to be murdered in cold blood. That's why I went to the police."

"Sort of a civic duty," García said.

"Exactly." Before Gault said good-bye, something occurred to him: It would be best to end the interview on a light and friendly note. He said to García, "You're from Cuba, right?"

"A long time ago."

"There's some hellacious fishing down there, south of Havana. Castro himself is a nut for largemouth bass, did you know that?"

"I read something about it."

Gault said, "For years I've been trying to pull some strings and wrangle an invitation, but it's damn tough in my position. I'm in the sugar business, as you know. The Bearded One doesn't send us many valentines."

"Well, you're the competition," García said.

"Still, I'm dying to try for a Cuban bass. I've heard stories of sixteen-, eighteen-pound hawgs. What's the name of that famous lake?"

García said, "I forget."

"Did you do much fishing," Gault asked, "when you lived there?"

"I was just a small boy," García said. "My great-uncle did some fishing, though."

"Is that right?"

"He was a mullet man."

"Oh."

"He sold marlin baits to Hemingway."

"No shit!" Dennis Gault said. Now he was impressed. "I saw a movie about Hemingway once," he said. "Starred that Patton guy."

Back at police headquarters, Al García sat down at his desk and slipped a cassette into a portable tape recorder. The date of January 7 had been written in pencil on the label of the cassette. It was one of three used in R. J. Decker's answering machine. García had picked them up at the trailer after he got the search warrant.

He closed the door to his office, and turned the volume on the tape machine up to number ten on the dial. Then he lit a cigarette and pressed the Play button.

There were a few seconds of scratchy blank tape, followed by the sound of a phone ringing. The fourth ring was interrupted by a metallic click and the sound of R. J. Decker's voice: "I'm not home now. Please leave a message at the tone."

The first caller was a woman: "Rage, it's me. James is on another trip and I'm in the mood for pasta. How about Rita's at nine?"

In his notebook García wrote: *Ex-wife*.

The second caller was also a woman: "R.J., it's Barbara. I'm sorry about canceling the other night. How about a drink later to make up for it?"

García wrote: *Some girl*.

The third caller was a man: "Mr. Decker, you probably don't know me but I know of you. I need a private investigator, and you come highly recommended. Call me as soon as possible—I guarantee it'll be worth your time. The number is 555-3400. The name is Dennis Gault."

In his notebook Al García wrote: *Bad guy*.

For several days Decker and Skink stayed inside the hotel room, waiting for things to cool off. Decker had done what he could over the phone, and was eager to get on the road. For his part, Skink had shrunk into a silent and lethargic melancholy, and exhibited no desire to do anything or go anywhere.

Finally, the afternoon Catherine arrived, Skink briefly came to life. He went outside and stood on the beach and started shooting at jetliners on final approach to the Fort Lauderdale-Hollywood airport.

Catherine had shown up with a recent stock prospectus from the Outdoor Christian Network, which was listed on the New York exchange as Outdoor ChristNet. Decker was no whiz when it came to stocks, so he had telephoned a reporter friend on the business desk of the Miami *Sun*. The reporter had done a search on OCN in the newsroom computer and come up with some interesting clips, which Catherine had picked up before she left Miami. From the file it was obvious that OCN's rapid growth in the Sun Belt cable market had flooded the company with fluid capital, capital which the Reverend Charles Weeb and his advisers were plowing pell-mell into Florida real estate. The prospectus made several tantalizing references to an "exciting new waterfront development targeted for middle-income family home buyers" but neglected to mention the protracted and somewhat shady process by which Lunker Lakes had escaped all zoning regulations known to man. The word "kickback," for example, appeared nowhere in the stock brochure. The newspaper articles dwelt on this aspect of the controversial project, and indeed it was the only angle that seemed to interest Skink in the slightest. He asked where exactly Lunker Lakes would be located, then took the prospectus and newspaper clippings from Decker's hands and read them closely.

Then he pulled the flowered shower cap down tight on his hair, excused himself with a mumble, walked outside, and waited on the beach. The first incoming jet was an Eastern 727 from La Guardia; the second was a United DC-10 from Chicago via St. Louis; the third was a Bahamas Air shuttle carrying day gamblers back from Freeport. None of the airliners went down or even smoked, though Skink was sure he dinged the bellies a couple of times. The noise of the gunfire was virtually smothered by the roar of the jets and the heavy-metal wail of Bon Jovi from some teenybopper's boom box. In all Skink got off eleven rounds from the nine-millimeter Browning before he spied the lifeguard's Jeep speeding toward him down the beach. The Jeep was at least three-quarters of a mile away, giving Skink plenty of time to jog back to the hotel, duck into a john in the lobby, and work on his appearance.

When he got back to the room, the shower cap and sunglasses were in his pocket, the orange rainsuit was folded under one arm, and his long braid of hair was tucked down the back of his shirt. R. J. Decker asked what happened and Skink told him.

"Excellent," Decker said. "Let's see, by my estimate that means we're now wanted by the Metro-Dade police, the highway patrol, the marine patrol, and now the FAA and FBI. Am I leaving anybody out?"

Skink settled listlessly on the floor.

Catherine said, "R.J., you've got to get him out of the city."

Decker said, "My father, rest his soul, would be so proud to know that he raised a fugitive. Not every FBI man can make that claim."

"I'm sorry," Skink sighed.

It was the most pathetic thing Decker had ever heard him say— and in one way the scariest. Skink acted like he was on the brink of losing it. Decker leaned over and said, "Captain, why were you shooting at airplanes?"

"Look who they're bringing," Skink said. "They're bringing the suckers to Lunker Lakes. The Reverend Weeb's lucky lemmings." He seemed out of breath. He motioned for Catherine to hand him the OCN prospectus. With a brown crusty finger he went down the names of directors.

"These guys," he said hoarsely. "I know a few."

"From where?" Catherine asked.

"It's not important. Twenty-nine thousand units in the Everglades is what's important. Christian city, my ass. It's the crime of the damn century. These guys are like cockroaches, you can't fucking get rid of 'em."

Decker said, "It's too late, captain. Dredging started a year ago."

"Jesus," Skink said, biting his lip. He put on his sunglasses and bowed his head. He didn't look up for some time. Decker glanced over at Catherine. She was right: they had to get Skink back to the woods.

From the hallway came sounds of men talking but trying not to be heard. Then a knock on the door to the next room; another knock across the hall.

"Hotel security," a male voice said.

R. J. Decker motioned Skink toward the bathroom. He nodded and crab-walked across the floor, shutting the door behind him. Quickly Decker peeled off his shirt and drew the shades. "Take off your shoes," he whispered to Catherine, "and lie down here on the bed." She figured out the plan immediately. She was down to bra and panties and under the covers before Decker even got a good peek.

A man knocked three times on the door.

"Whoze it?" Decker hollered. "Go 'way."

"Hotel security, please open up."

"We're sleeping!"

Another voice: "Police!"

Decker stomped to the door as noisily as possible. He cracked it just enough to give the men a narrow view of Catherine in the bed.

"What's the problem?" Decker demanded.

A blue-suited young man with a walkie-talkie stood next to a disinterested uniformed cop. The security man said, "Sir, there was an incident out on the beach. A man with a gun—nobody was hurt."

"That's damn good to hear," Decker said impatiently.

The cop said, "You haven't seen anyone unusual up on this floor?"

"For the last couple hours I haven't seen nuthin'," Decker said, "except stars." He nodded over his shoulder, toward Catherine. The security man looked a little embarrassed.

The policeman said, "Big scruffy guy with a bright hat and pony-tail. Witnesses saw him run into this hotel, so we're suggesting that all guests stay in their rooms for a while."

"Don't you worry," Decker said.

"Just for a while," the security man added, "until they catch him."

When Decker shut the door, Catherine sat up in bed and said, "Stars? You saw stars?"

"Don't you dare move," Decker said, diving headfirst into the sheets.

Thomas Curl was not a happy man. In the past few weeks he had made more money than he or three previous generations of Curls had ever seen, yet Thomas was not at peace. First of all, his brother Lemus was dead, and for a while Thomas had been stuck with the body. Since he had told everyone, including his daddy, that Lemus had accidentally drowned on a fishing trip to Florida, there was no way he could bring back a body with a bullet hole in the head. People would ask many questions, and answering questions was not Thomas Curl's strong suit. So, after discovering Lemus' turtle-eaten corpse on the fish stringer in Morgan Slough, and mulling it over for two days, Thomas decided what the hell and just buried his brother in a dry sandy grave on some pastureland east of the Gilchrist. The whole time he worked with the shovel, he had a feeling that every turkey buzzard in Florida was wheeling in the sky overhead, waiting to make a smorgasbord of Lemus' remains. Afterward Thomas took off his bass cap and stood by the grave and tried to remember a prayer. The only one he could think of began: "Now I lay me down to sleep. . . ." Close enough.

Almost every night Thomas Curl reflected sadly on how Lemus had died, how he had let him dash off into the scrub by himself, and how all of a sudden he didn't hear Lemus' Ruger anymore. And how Thomas had panicked and leapt into the green pickup and taken off, pretty sure that his brother was already dead—and how he'd returned with a borrowed coon dog and found some heavy tracks and blood, but no body. At that moment he had expected never to see his brother again, and later at the slough was horrified to the point of nausea. On orders Thomas had gone there to check on things, just to make sure the nigger cop hadn't found Ott Pickney's body. But there was poor Lemus, strung up in the black water with the other one, and it was then Thomas Curl realized the dangerous magnitude of the opposition. Thomas was not the brightest human being in the world, but he knew a message when he saw one.

So he had buried Lemus, torched Ott Pickney's body in a phony truck accident, and driven straight back to New Orleans, where, again, things didn't go as smoothly as he'd hoped. Thomas expressed the view that he shouldn't be blamed for every little loose end, and was curtly instructed to return to Florida immediately. Not Harney, either, but Miami.

Thomas Curl was not wild about Miami. Back when he was still boxing he had trained one summer at the Fifth Street Gym, out on the beach. He remembered staying in a ratty pink hotel with two other middleweights, and he remembered getting drunk on Saturday nights and, out of sheer boredom, beating the shit out of skinny Cuban refugees who lived in the city parks. Thomas remembered Miami as a hot and unfriendly place, but then again, he was young and homesick and broke. Now he was grown-up, thirty-five pounds heavier, and rolling in new money.

To boost his spirits, Thomas Curl splurged and got a room at the Grand Bay Hotel. The room came with a fruit basket and a sunken bathtub. He was sucking on a nectarine and soaking in the tub when Dennis Gault called back.

Thomas Curl said, "Hey, they got a phone in the goddamn john."

"Welcome to the city, Jethro." Gault was in a brusque mood. Dealing with this moron was at least two notches below dealing with Decker. Gault said, "A cop came to see me."

Thomas Curl spit the nectarine pit into his soapy hand. "Yeah? They caught 'em yet?"

"No," Gault said, "but the way things are shaping up, maybe it's best if they don't."

"Hell you mean?"

Gault said, "This cop, fucking Cuban, he doesn't believe a word I say."

"Who cares, long as New Orleans believes you."

"Ever heard of extradition?" Gault snapped. "This guy can cause us major problems, son. He can keep Decker away from the Louisiana people a long time. Sit on him for weeks, listen to his story, maybe even buy it."

"No way," Curl said.

"We can't take the chance, Thomas."

"I done enough for you."

Gault said, "This one's not for me, it's for your brother."

In the tub Thomas reached over and turned on the hot water. He was careful not to get the telephone wet, in case it might electrocute him.

Gault said, "I need you to find Decker. Before the cops."

"What about that crazy gorilla?"

"They probably split up by now."

"I don't want to fuck with him. Culver said he's mean as a moccasin."

Gault said, "Culver's afraid of a tit in the dark. Besides, from what Elaine says, Skink isn't the type to stick with Decker. They probably split up, like I said."

Thomas Curl was not convinced. He remembered the neatly centered bullet hole in his brother's forehead.

"What's the pay?"

"Same as before," Gault said.

"Double if I got to deal with the gorilla."

"Hell, you ought to do it for free," Gault said. Greed was truly a despicable vice, he thought. "For Christ's sake, Thomas, these are the guys who killed Lemus. One or both, it's up to you. Decker's the one that worries me most. He's the one that could hurt us in court. We're talking hard time, too."

Thomas Curl did not like the idea of being sent to the state penitentiary even for a day. There was also something powerfully attractive, even romantic, about avenging his brother's death.

"Where do I start?" he asked.

"Way behind, unfortunately," Gault said. "Decker's already running. The trick is to find out where, because he sure as hell won't be coming your way."

"Not unless I got somethin' he wants," said Thomas Curl.

Catherine said: "This won't work, not with him in the bathroom." She got out of bed and began to dress.

From behind the bathroom door, a voice grumped: "Pay no attention to me."

Decker dolefully watched Catherine button her blouse. This is what I get, he thought; exactly what I deserve. He said to her, "This man's a distraction, you're right."

"I don't know what I was thinking," Catherine said, stepping into a pink slip. "James is furious as it is, and now I'm an hour late."

"Sorry," Decker said.

"Here, give me a hand with this zipper."

"Nice skirt," Decker said. "It's silk, isn't it?"

"I can't stand these damn zippers on the side."

Decker peeked at the label. "Jesus, Catherine, a Gucci."

She frowned. "Stop it, R.J. I know what you're up to."

As always.

Decker rolled out of bed and groped around the floor for his jeans. It was dark outside, time to go. Muffled scraping noises emanated from the bathroom. Decker couldn't imagine what Skink was doing in there.

Catherine brushed out her hair, put on some pale pink lipstick.

"You look positively beatific," Decker said. "Pure as the driven snow."

"No thanks to you." She turned from the mirror and took his hands. "I'd give anything to forget about you, you bastard."

Decker said, "Could try hypnosis. Or hallucinogens."

Catherine put her arms around him. "Cut the bullshit, pal, it's all right to be scared. This is the most trouble you've ever been in."

"I believe so," Decker said.

Catherine kissed him on the neck. "Watch out for yourself, Rage. And him too."

"We'll be fine." He handed Catherine her Louis Vuitton purse and her one-hundred-percent-cashmere sweater.

Before she walked out the door she said, "I just want you to know, it wouldn't have been a mercy fuck. It would have been the real thing."

Decker said, "I got that impression, yeah."

He couldn't believe how much he still loved her.

Somehow Skink had wedged himself between the bathroom sink and the toilet, compressed his bulk into a massive, musty cube on the tile floor. At first Decker couldn't even pinpoint the location of his head; the wheezing seemed to come from under the toilet tank. Decker knelt down and saw Skink's scaly face staring out from behind the water pipes. He looked like a bearded iguana.

"Why'd you turn on the light?" he asked.

"So I wouldn't step on your vital organs."

"Worse things could happen," Skink said.

Freud would have a picnic, Decker thought. "Look, captain, we've got to get going."

"I'm safe right here," Skink observed.

"Not really," Decker said. "You're hiding under a toilet in a hundred-dollar beachfront hotel room. Someone's bound to complain."

"You think?"

Decker nodded patiently. "It's much safer back in Harney," he said. "If we leave now, we'll be back at the lake by midnight."

"You mean it?"

"Yes."

"I'll kill you, Miami, if this is a trap. I'll fucking cut out your bladder and wring it in your hair."

"It's no trap," Decker said. "Let's go."

It took forty-five minutes to disengage Skink from the plumbing. In the process the sink snapped clean off its legs; Decker left it lying on the bed.

In the lobby of the hotel he rented a Ford Escort. He got it out of the underground parking and pulled around back to the hotel's service entrance, where Skink was waiting by the dumpsters. As Skink got in the car, Decker noticed something white tucked under one arm.

"Whatcha got there?" he said.

"Seagull." Skink held up the limp bird by its curled orange feet. "Hasn't been dead more than ten minutes. I scarfed it off the grille of that seafood truck."

"Lucky us," Decker said thinly.

"You hungry? We can stop and make a fire once we get out of this traffic."

"Let's wait, okay?"

"Sure," Skink said. "It'll keep for a couple hours."

Decker headed west from the beach on the Seventeenth Street Causeway, past Port Everglades and the Ocean World aquarium. It was typical January beach traffic, bumper-to-bumper nitwits as far as the eye could see. Every other car had New York plates.

Skink fit the dead bird into the glove compartment and covered it with a copy of the rental agreement. He seemed in a much better mood already. He put on his sunglasses and flowered shower cap, and turned around to get his fluorescent rainsuit from the back seat. Through the rear window he noticed a dark blue Chrysler sedan following two car-lengths behind. He spotted a plastic bubble on the dashboard; not flashing, but a bubble just the same. The driver's face was obscured by the tinted windshield, but a red dot bobbed at mouth-level.

"Your buddy García smoke?"

Decker checked the rearview. "Oh, shit," he said.

Skink struggled into the rainsuit, adjusted his sunglasses, and said, "Well, Miami, what's it going to be?"

The blue light on the Chrysler's dashboard was flashing now. Hopelessly Decker scanned the traffic on the causeway; it was jammed all the way to the next traffic signal, and beyond. There was nowhere to go. Al García was up on his bumper and flashing his brights. Decker figured he had a better chance one-on-one, with no Fort Lauderdale cops. He decided to stop before it turned into a convoy.

He pulled into the parking lot of a liquor store. With the big Chrysler García easily blocked off the little Escort, parked, kept the blue light turning. A bad sign, Decker thought.

He turned to Skink: "I don't want to see your gun."

"Relax," Skink said. "Mr. Browning sleeps with the fishes."

Al García approached the car in a bemused and almost casual manner. At the driver's window he bent down and said, "R.J., you are the king of all fuckups."

"Sorry I stood you up the other day," Decker said.

"Everyone but the National Guard is looking for you."

"Now that you mention it, Al, aren't you slightly out of your jurisdiction? I believe this is Broward County."

"And you're a fleeing felon, asshole, so I can chase you wherever I want. That's the law." He spit out his cigarette and ground it into the asphalt with his shoe.

Decker said, "So what'd you do, follow Catherine up from Miami?"

"She's a slick little driver, she gave it her best."

Decker said, "I didn't kill anybody, Al."

"How about Little Stevie Wonder there?"

Skink blinked lizardlike behind his sunglasses.

"Come on, R.J., let's all of us go for a ride." García was so smooth he didn't even unholster his gun. Decker was impressed; you had to be. Now if only Skink behaved.

Skink retrieved his dead seagull from the glove box and Decker locked up the rental car. García was waiting in the Chrysler. "Who wants to ride shotgun?" he asked affably.

Decker said, "I thought you'd want both us ruthless murderers to sit back in the cage."

"Nah," Al García said, unplugging the blue light. He got back into traffic, turned off Seventeenth Street on Federal Highway, then cut back west on Road 84, an impossible truck route. Decker was surprised when he didn't turn south at the Interstate 95 exchange.

"Where are you going?"

"The Turnpike's a cleaner shot, isn't it?" the detective said.

"Not really," Decker said.

"He means north," Skink said from the back seat. "To Harney."

"Right," Al García said. "On the way, I want you guys to tell me all about bass fishing."

The news from Lunker Lakes was not good.

"They died," reported Charlie Weeb's hydrologist, some pinhead hired fresh out of the University of Florida.

"Died?" said the Reverend Weeb. "What the fuck are you talking about?"

He was talking about the bass—two thousand yearling large-mouths imported at enormous cost from a private hatchery in Alabama.

"They croaked," said the hydrologist. "What can I say? The water's very bad, Reverend Weeb. Tannic acid they can tolerate, but the current phosphate levels are lethal. There's no fresh oxygen, no natural water flow. Whoever dredged your canals—"

"*Lakes,* goddammit!"

"—they dredged too deep. The fish don't last more than two days."

"Jesus Christ Almighty. So what're we talking about here—stinking dead bass floating all over the place?"

The hydrologist said, "I took the liberty of hiring some local boats to scoop up the kill. With this cool weather it's not so bad, but if a warm front pushes through, they'd smell it all the way to Key West."

Weeb slammed down the phone and groaned. The woman lying next to him said, "What is it, Father?"

"I'm not a priest," Weeb snapped. He didn't have the energy for a theology lesson; it would have been a waste of time anyway. The girl worked at Louie's Lap-Dancing Palace in Gretna. She said her whole family watched him every Sunday morning on television.

"I never been with a TV star before," she said, burrowing into his chest. "You're a big boy, too."

Charlie Weeb was only half-listening. He missed Ellen O'Leary; no one else looked quite as fine, topless in the rubber trout waders. No one soothed him the way Ellen did, either, but now she was gone. Took off after Dickie Lockhart's murder. One more disappointment in a week of bleak disappointments for the Reverend Charles Weeb.

"How much do I owe you?" he asked the lap dancer.

"Nothing, Father." She sounded confused. "I brought my own money."

"What for?" Weeb looked down; he couldn't see her face, just the top of her head and the smooth slope of her naked back.

"I got a favor to ask," the lap dancer said, whispering into his chest hair. "And I wanna pay for it."

"What on earth are you talking about?"

"I want you to heal my poppa." She looked up shyly. "He's got the gout, my poppa does."

"No, child—"

"Some days he can't barely get himself out of bed."

Weeb shifted restlessly, glanced at his wristwatch.

"I'll give you two hundred dollars," the girl declared.

"You're serious?"

"Just one little prayer, please."

"Two hundred bucks?"

"And a hum job, if you want it, Father."

Charlie Weeb stared at her, thinking: It's true what they say about the power of television.

"Come, child," he said softly, "let's pray."

Later, when he was alone, the Reverend Charles Weeb thought about the girl and what she'd wanted. Maybe it was the answer he'd been looking for. It had worked before, in the early years; perhaps it would work again.

Charlie Weeb drank a Scotch and tried to sleep, but he couldn't. In recent nights he had been kept awake by the chilling realization that Lunker Lakes, his dream city, was in deep trouble. The first blow had come from the Federal Deposit Insurance Corporation, whose auditors had swept into the offices of First Standard Eurobank of Ohio and discovered that the whole damn thing was on the verge of insolvency. The problem was bad loans, huge ones, which First Standard Eurobank apparently handed out as freely as desk calendars. The Outdoor Christian Network, doing business as Lunker Lakes Ltd., had been the beneficiary of just such unbridled generosity— twenty-four million dollars for site planning and construction. On paper there was nothing unusual about the loan or the terms of repayment (eleven percent over ten years), but in reality not much money ever got repaid. About six thousand dollars, to be exact. Wanton disorganization ruled First Standard Eurobank's collections department—as patient and amiable a bunch of Christian soldiers as Charlie Weeb had ever met. He kept missing the bimonthly payments and they kept saying don't worry and Charlie Weeb *didn't* worry, because this was a fucking bank, for God's sake, and banks don't go under anymore. Then the FDIC swooped in and discovered that First Standard Eurobank had been just as patient and flexible with all its commercial customers, to the extent that virtually nobody except farmers were being made to repay their loans on time. Suddenly the president of the bank and three top assistants all moved to Barbados, leaving Uncle Sam to sort out the mess. Pretty soon the bad news trickled out: First Standard Eurobank was calling in its bad loans. All over the country big-time land developers headed for the tall grass. Charlie Weeb himself had been dodging some twit from *The Wall Street Journal* for five days.

What aggravated Weeb was that he had intended all along to pay back the money, but at a pace commensurate with advance sales at Lunker Lakes. Unfortunately, sales were going very slowly. Charlie Weeb couldn't figure it out. He fired his marketing people, fired his advertising people, fired his sales people—yet nothing improved. It was maddening. The lakefront models were simply beautiful. Three bedrooms, sunken bath and sauna, cathedral ceilings, solar heating, microwave kitchens—"Christian town-home living at its finest!" Charlie Weeb was fanatical about using the term "town home," which was a fancy way of saying two-story condo. The problem with using the word "condo" was, as every idiot in Florida knew, you couldn't charge a hundred and fifty thousand for a "condo" fourteen miles away from the ocean. For this reason any Lunker Lakes salesman who spoke the word was immediately terminated. Condos carried a hideous connotation, Charlie Weeb had lectured—this wasn't a cheesy high-rise full of nasty old farts, this was a *wholesome family community*. With fucking bike paths!

And still the dumb shits couldn't sell it. A hundred-sixty units in the first four months. A hundred-sixty! Weeb was beside himself. Phase One of the project called for eight thousand units. Without Phase One there would be no Phase Two, and without Phase Two you could scrap the build-out projections of twenty-nine thousand. While you're at it, scrap the loans, the equity, even the zoning permits. The longer the project lagged, the greater the chances that all the county commissioners who had so graciously accepted Charlie Weeb's bribes would die or be voted out of office, and a whole new set would have to be paid off. One white knight could gum up the works.

The Reverend Charles Weeb had even deeper concerns. He had been so confident of Lunker Lakes that he had broken a cardinal rule and sunk three million dollars of his own personal, Bahamian-sheltered money into the project. The thought of losing it made him sick as a dog. Lying in bed, juggling the ghastly numbers in his head, Weeb also realized that the Outdoor Christian Network itself was probably not strong enough to survive if Lunker Lakes were to go under.

So he had to do something to raise money, lots of it. And fast. This was the urgency behind scheduling the new Dickie Lockhart

Memorial Bass Blasters Classic on such short notice. Lunker Lakes was starving for publicity, and the TV coverage of the tournament was bound to boost sales—provided they could paint some of the buildings and get a few palm trees planted in time.

Trucking in two thousand young bass had been, Weeb thought, dastardly clever. For authenticity he had also planned to salt the lakes with a dozen big Florida hawgs a few days before the tournament. And, of course, he fully intended for Eddie Spurling to win the whole shebang with the fattest stringer of monster bass conceivable. Charlie Weeb had yet to discuss the importance of this matter with Eddie, but he was sure Eddie would understand. Certain details had to be arranged. Nothing could be left to chance—not on live cable television.

Charlie Weeb was feeling downright optimistic until he learned about the fish kill. He never imagined that all the bass would die, but he really didn't care to hear some elaborate scientific explanation. He knew this: Under no circumstances would the fishing tournament be canceled. If necessary he would simply purchase another truckload of bass, and somehow slip them into the lake the day of the tournament. Maybe the pinhead hydrologist could work a few miracles, buy him a few extra hours. It could be done, Charlie Weeb was sure.

As a long-term sales gimmick, the big bass tournament held much promise. However, the short-term fiscal crisis demanded immediate attention.

To this end the lap dancer from Louie's had given Charlie Weeb new spiritual inspiration.

He sat up in bed and reached for the phone.

"Deacon Johnson, please."

A sleepy voice came on the line.

Weeb said, "Izzy, wake up. It's me."

"It's three in the morning, man."

"Tough shit. Are you listening?"

"Yeah," said Deacon Johnson.

"Izzy, I want to do a healing on Sunday's show."

Deacon Johnson coughed up something in his throat.

"You sure?" he said.

"Positive. Unless you got any other brilliant ideas to solve the cash-flow problem."

Deacon Johnson said, "Healings are tricky, Charles."

"Hell, you don't have to tell me! That's why I quit doing 'em. But these are desperate times, Izzy. I figure we tape a couple fifteen-second promos tomorrow, start pushing the thing hard. Goose the ratings by the weekend—I bet we'll do a million-two."

"A million-two?" Deacon Johnson said. "For a sheep?"

"Screw the sheep. I'm talking about a real person."

Deacon Johnson didn't respond right away. The Reverend Weeb said, "Well?"

"We've never done a human being before, Charles."

"We've never dropped twenty-four mill before, Izzy. Look, I want you to set it up the same as we did with the animals. Find me a good one."

Deacon Johnson was not enthusiastic, but he knew better than to balk.

"Get me a little kid if you can," Charlie Weeb was saying, "or a teenager. No geezers and no housewives."

"I'll try," said Deacon Johnson. The logistics of the feat would be formidable.

"Blond, if possible," Weeb went on. Every heartbreaking detail spelled more money—he knew this from his experience promoting the tragic tale of June-Lee and Melissa, the two mythical Weeb sisters sold into Chinese slavery. "No redheads," Weeb instructed Deacon Johnson. "You get me a little blond kid to heal, Izzy, and I swear we'll do a million-two."

Deacon Johnson said, "I guess you wouldn't consider a practice run. Say, with a goat."

An hour out of Fort Lauderdale, Skink started to pluck the dead seagull in the back seat. Every so often he threw a handful of gray-white feathers out the window. García adjusted the rearview and watched, disbelieving. After R. J. Decker explained the custom, García decided to pull off the Turnpike for a dinner break. They dropped Skink near the Delray Beach overpass to let him roast the bird in private. García offered some matches, but as he got out of the car Skink mumbled, "Don't need any."

Decker said, "We're driving into town for some burgers. Meet you back here in about an hour."

"Fine," Skink said.

"You'll be waiting, right?"

"Most likely."

A hunching ursine shape in the darkness, Skink gathered kindling as they drove away.

Waiting in a line of cars at the Burger King drive-through, García said to Decker, "So the bottom line is, these Gomers are murdering each other over fish."

"It's money too, Al. Prizes, endorsements, TV contracts. Fishing's just the sizzle. And not all these guys are dumb peckerwoods."

The detective chuckled. "Guess not. They tricked your ass, didn't they?"

"Nicely," Decker said. On the trip he had told García about Dennis

Gault, the photographs, Dickie Lockhart, and Lanie. The part about Lanie was not Decker's favorite. "All I can figure," he said, "is she remembered my name from that fashion shoot in Sanibel. Probably read about the Bennett case too—it made all the papers." The *Sun's* unsparing headline had read: "STAFF PHOTOG CONVICTED IN BEATING OF PREP FOOTBALL STAR."

García said, "Gault must've creamed when his sister suggested you for the mark. Big ex-con photographer with a bad temper, down on his luck."

"Made to order," Decker agreed glumly.

"What about the pictures of Lockhart cheating? New Orleans sent Xerox copies, but still they look pretty good."

Decker said, "They've got to be tricked up."

"Just so you know, I served a warrant on your trailer. Took every single roll from your camera bag—had our lab soup the film."

"And?"

"Garbage. Surveillance stuff for that insurance case, that's all. No fish pictures, R.J."

There you had it. Lanie had probably swiped the good stuff out of his bag at the motel in Hammond. Her brother would've had no trouble finding a good lab man to doctor the prints. Decker said, "Jesus, Al, what the hell do I do now?"

"Well, in my official capacity as a sworn law-enforcement officer of the state of Florida, I'd advise you to turn yourself in, agree to the extradition, and trust your fate to the justice system. As a friend, I'd advise you to stay the fuck out of Louisiana until we get you some alibi witnesses."

"*We?*" Decker was surprised. "Al, you'll get in all kinds of trouble if they find out you're helping me. You're probably already in the jackpot for taking a duty car out of Dade County."

García smiled. "Didn't I tell you? I went on sick leave two days ago. Indefinite—doctor says my damn shoulder's out of whack again. The lieutenant wasn't thrilled, but what's he gonna do? Half the guys retire they get a lousy hangnail. Me, I get popped point-blank with a sawed-off and I only miss twenty-three days. They can't bitch about a week here and there for therapy."

"Sick leave," Decker mused. "That explains your unusually charming disposition."

"Don't be a smartass. Right now I'm the only friend you got."

"Not quite," Decker said.

*　　*　　*

According to Ozzie Rundell, Thomas Curl's Uncle Shawn lived just outside of Orlando. He ran a moldy roadside tourist trap called Sheeba's African Jungle Safari, located about four miles west of the Disney World entrance on U.S. 92. Ozzie had offered to draw a map, but Jim Tile said no thanks, he didn't need directions.

The broken-down zoo wasn't hard to find. In the six years since Shawn Curl had purchased the place from Leroy and Sheeba Barnwell, the once-exotic menagerie had shrunk to its current cheerless census of one emaciated lion, two balding llamas, three goats, a blind boa constrictor, and seventeen uncontrollably nasty raccoons. A big red billboard on U.S. 92 promised a "DELIGHTFUL CHILDREN'S PETTING ZOO," but in actuality there was nothing at Sheeba's to pet; not safely, anyway. Shawn Curl's insurance company had summarily canceled his policy after the ninth infectious raccoon bite, so Shawn Curl had put up a twelve-foot hurricane fence to keep the tourists away from the animals. The only consistent money-making enterprise at the African Jungle Safari was the booth with plastic palm trees where, for $3.75, tourists could be photographed draping the blind boa constrictor around their necks. Since snakes have no eyelids, the tourists didn't know that the boa constrictor was blind. They were also unaware that, except for a tiny space where the feeding tube fit, the big snake's mouth had been expertly stitched shut with a Singer sewing machine. In these litigious times, Shawn Curl wasn't taking any more chances.

He didn't know what to think when the musclebound black state trooper walked into the gift shop; Shawn Curl had never seen a black trooper in Orlando before. He noticed that the man walked with a slight limp, and thought probably he had been hired for just that reason—to fill some stupid minority handicap quota. Shawn Curl decided he'd better be civil, or else the big spade might snitch on him to the Fish and Game Department for the way the wild animals were being treated.

"What ken we do you for, officer?"

Jim Tile stood at the counter eyeing a display of bootleg Mickey Mouse dolls. Each stuffed Mickey had a Confederate flag poking out of its paw. Jim Tile picked up one of the Mickeys and turned it over.

" 'Made in Thailand,' " he read aloud.

Shawn Curl coughed nervously.

"Nine-fifty for one of these?" the trooper asked.

Shawn Curl said, "Not for you. For you, half-price."

"A discount," Jim Tile said.

"For all peace officers, yessir. That's our standard discount."

Jim Tile put the mouse doll back on the counter and said, "Does Disney know you're selling this crap?"

Shawn Curl worked his jaw sideways. "Far as I know it's all legal, officer."

Jim Tile looked around the gift shop. "They could sue you for everything," he said, "such as it is."

"Hey, I ain't dune nuthin' nobody else ain't dune."

After scanning the shelves—cluttered with painted coconut heads, rubber alligators, chipped conch shells, bathtub sharks, and other made-for-Florida rubbish—Jim Tile's disapproving brown eyes settled again on the bogus Mickey Mouse doll. "The Disney people," he said, "they won't go for this. That rebel flag is enough to get their lawyers all excited."

Exasperated, Shawn Curl puffed out his cheeks. "Who sent you here, anyway?"

"I'm looking for young Thomas."

"He ain't here."

The trooper said, "Tell me where I can find him."

"S'pose you got a warrant."

"What I got," said Jim Tile, "is his uncle. By the balls."

A family of tourists walked in, the kids darting underfoot while the mother eyed the merchandise uneasily. The father peered tentatively at the zoo grounds through a window behind the cash register. Jim Tile guessed they wouldn't stay long. They didn't. "Raccoons, that's all," the father had reported back to his wife. "We've got zillions of raccoons back in Michigan."

When they were alone again, Jim Tile said, "Shawn, give me your nephew's address in New Orleans. Right now."

"I'll give it to you," Shawn Curl said, scribbling on the back of a postcard, "but he ain't there."

"Where can I find him?"

"Last time he come through he was on his way to Miami."

"When was that?"

"Few days ago," said Shawn Curl.

"Where's he staying?"

"Some big hotel."

"You're a big help, Shawn. I guess I'll have to call Disney headquarters after all."

Shawn Curl didn't like that word. *Headquarters*. In a sulky voice he said, "The hotel is the Grand Biscayne Something. I don't remember the whole name."

"Why was Thomas going down to Miami?"

"Business, he said."

"What business is he in?"

Shawn Curl shrugged. "Promotion is what he calls it."

Jim Tile said, "I couldn't help but notice that big Oldsmobile out front, the blue Niney-Eight. It looks brand-new."

Warily Shawn Curl looked at the trooper. "No, I had it awhile."

"Still got the sticker in the window," Jim Tile remarked, "and the paper license tag from the dealer."

"So?"

"Did Thomas give you that new car?"

Shawn Curl drew a deep breath. What was the world coming to, that a nigger could talk to him like this? "Maybe he did give it to me," Shawn Curl said. "There's no law 'ginst it."

"No, there isn't," Jim Tile said. He thanked Shawn Curl for his time, and walked toward the door. "By the way," the trooper said, "that lion's humping one of your llamas."

"Shit," said Shawn Curl, scrambling to find his pitchfork.

The three boys went to the high-school basketball game but they didn't stay long. Kyle, the one with the phony driver's license, had three six-packs in the trunk, along with his stepfather's .22-caliber rifle. Jeff and Cole, both of whom were on the verge of flunking out anyway, cared even less about high-school basketball than Kyle. The game was just their excuse to get out of the house, something to tell the parents. The teenagers left before the first half was over. Kyle drove to the usual spot, a county dumpsite miles west of the city, and there they gulped down the six-packs while plinking bottles, soda cans, and the occasional hapless rat. Once the beer and ammunition were used up, there was only one thing left to do. Jeff and Cole called it "bum-bashing," though it was Kyle, the biggest one, who claimed to have invented both the phrase and the sport. That's what everyone at the high school said, anyway: It must have been Kyle's idea.

Every winter transients flock to Florida as sure as the tourists and turkey buzzards. Their numbers are not so great, but often they are more visible; sleeping in the parks and public libraries, panhandling the street corners. The weather is so mild that there is almost no outdoor place that a bum would find uninhabitable in southern Florida. Paradise is how many of them would describe it. Some towns address the problem with less tolerance than others (Palm Beach, for example, where loitering is treated the same as ax-murder), but usually the bums get by with little fear of incarceration. The reason is simple, and in it lies another prime attraction for the nation's wandering winos: there is no room for them in South Florida's jails because the jails already are too crowded with dangerous criminals.

Beginning in late December, then, the transients start appearing on the streets. Rootless, solitary, and unwelcome, they are ideal victims for the randomly violent. Kyle and his high-school friends discovered this the very first time. On a five-dollar bet from Cole, Kyle slugged a wino under a bridge. The boys ran away, but nothing happened. Of course the transient never reported the attack—the local cops would have laughed in his face. A week later the teenagers tried it again when they discovered an old longhair sleeping on a golf course in Boca Raton. This time Jeff and Cole pitched in, while Kyle added a few whacks with his stepfather's four-iron. This time when they ran away, the kids were laughing.

Soon bum-bashing became part of the weekly recreation; a thrill, something to do. The boys were easily bored and not all that popular at school, shunned by the jocks, dopers, and surfers alike. So whenever Kyle could get the car and swipe some beer money, Jeff and Cole were raring to go. Shooting the rifle always seemed to put them in the right mood.

As soon as they left the dump they started scouting for bums to bash. It was Jeff who spotted the guy curled up beneath the Turnpike overpass. Kyle drove by once, turned the car around, and drove past again. This time he parked fifty yards down the road. The three teenagers got out and walked back. Kyle liked the way it was shaping up—a dark stretch of highway with practically no traffic.

Skink was nearly asleep, stretched out halfway up the concrete embankment and faced away from the road. He heard someone coming, but assumed it was only Decker and the Cuban detective. As the men got closer, their footsteps did not alarm Skink nearly so much as their whispering. He was turning over to take a look just as Kyle ran up and kicked him brutally in the head.

Skink rolled down the embankment and lay still, facedown on the flat ground.

"Hey, Mr. Hobo," said Kyle, "sorry I busted your shades." He held up the broken sunglasses for the others to see.

Jeff and Cole each took a turn kicking Skink in the ribs. "I like his outfit," Jeff said. He was a bony kid with volcanic pustular acne. "This'd be great for hunting," he said, fingering the rainsuit.

"Then take it," Kyle said.

"Yeah, go ahead," Cole said, "even though it's about ten sizes too big."

"You'll look like an orange tepee," Kyle teased.

Jeff knelt and tried to roll Skink on his back. "He's a big sumbitch," he said. "Gimme a hand."

They turned Skink over and stripped him.

"He looks dead," Cole remarked.

"Check out the ponytail," Jeff said. He had climbed into Skink's enormous rainsuit. The hood flopped down over his eyes, and the legs and arms were way too long. The other boys laughed as Jeff did a little jig under the highway bridge. "I'm Mr. Hobo!" he sang. "Dead Mr. Hobo! Have a drink, make a stink—"

Jeff stopped singing when he saw the stranger. The man was sprinting toward them from across the road. Jeff tried to warn Kyle but it was too late.

The man took down both Kyle and Cole with a diving knee-high tackle. On the ground it was madness. The man hit Cole three times, crushing his nose and shattering his right cheekbone with an eggshell sound that made Jeff want to gag. While this was going on, Kyle, who was taller than the stranger, managed to get on his feet and grab the man around the neck, from behind. But the stranger, still on his knees, merely brought both elbows up sharply into Kyle's groin. Sickened, Jeff watched his other friend crumple. Then the man was on top of Kyle, aiming tremendous jackhammer punches at the meat of his throat.

Jeff turned from the scene to run but he stumbled inside the baggy rainsuit, got up, faltered again. A hand gripped the back of his neck and something cold pressed against the base of his skull. A gun.

"Don't move, you little fuckwad." A tough-looking dark man with a mustache.

He dragged Jeff back to the overpass, where the bigger stranger was still straddling Kyle and wordlessly redesigning the young man's face.

"Stop it!" yelled the dark man with the gun. "Decker, stop!"

But R. J. Decker couldn't stop; he couldn't even hear. Al García's voice echoed under the bridge but not a word reached Decker's ears. All that registered in his consciousness was the sight of a face and the need to punish it. Decker was working mechanically, his knuckles raw and bloody and numb. He stopped punching only when heavy damp arms encircled his chest and lifted him in the air, as if he were weightless, and suspended him there for what seemed like a very long time. Coming down, unwinding finally, the first thing Decker could hear was the furious sound of his own breathing. The second thing, from the beast with the big arms, was a tired voice that said, "Okay, Miami, I'm impressed."

23

Skink slipped unconscious in the back seat. His head sagged against R. J. Decker's shoulder and the breath rattled deep in his ribs. Decker felt warm drops seeping through his shirt.

"He's lost that eye," Al García said grimly, chewing on a cigarette as he drove.

Decker had seen it too. Skink's left eye was a jellied mess—Kyle, the big kid, had been wearing Texas roach-stomper boots. A whitish fluid oozed down Skink's cheek.

"He needs a doctor," Decker said.

So did the teenage thugs, García thought, but they would live— no thanks to Decker. Barehanded he would have killed them all if Skink hadn't stopped him. García felt certain that the kids wouldn't tell the police about the beating—Jeff, the acne twerp, was the type to spill the beans and the others knew it. Together they'd invent some melodramatic story of what had happened under the bridge, something that would play well at school. García was pretty sure two of them would spend the rest of the semester in the hospital, anyway.

Decker felt exhausted and depressed. His arms ached and his knuckles stung. He touched Skink's face and felt a crust of blood on the big man's beard.

"Maybe I ought to give up," Decker said.

"Don't be a moron."

"Once we get him to a doctor, you drop me off on the highway and haul ass back to Dade County. Nobody'll know a thing."

"Fuck you," García said.

"Al, it's not worth it."

"Speak for yourself." It was Skink. He raised his head and wiped his face with the sleeve of his rainsuit. With a forefinger he probed his broken eye socket and said, "Great."

"There's a hospital near the St. Lucie exit," García said.

Skink said, "Naw, just keep driving."

"I'm sorry, captain," Decker said. "We shouldn't have left you alone."

"Alone is how I like it." He slid over to the corner of the back seat. His face sank into the shadow.

García pulled off the Turnpike at Fort Pierce and stopped at a Pic 'n' Pay convenience store. Decker got out to make a phone call. While he was gone Skink stirred again and straightened up. In the washhouse light his face looked pulpy and lopsided; García could tell he was in agony.

He said, "Hang in there, Governor."

Skink stared at him. "What, you lifted some fingerprints?"

García nodded. "From a brass doorknob. That night at the chiropractor's house. Got a solid match from the FBI on an ancient missing-persons case."

"A closed case," Skink said.

"A famous case."

Skink gazed out the window of the car.

"Who else knows?" he said.

"Nobody but me and some G-7 clerk at the Hoover Building."

"I see."

García said, "For what it's worth, I don't like quitters, Mr. Tyree, but I suspect you had your reasons."

"I'll make no goddamn apologies," Skink said. After a pause he added: "Don't tell Decker."

"No reason to," said Al García.

Decker came back with hot coffee and Danish. Skink said he wasn't hungry. "Keep your eyes out, though," he added when they were back on the road.

"I got you something." Decker handed him a brown bag.

Skink opened it and grinned what was left of his TV smile.

Inside the bag was a new pair of black sunglasses.

Just before midnight he suddenly groaned and passed out again. Decker tore up his own shirt for a compress bandage and wrapped the bad eye. He held Skink's head in his lap and told García to drive faster.

Minutes after they crossed the county line into Harney, a highway-patrol car appeared in the rearview mirror and practically glued itself to the Chrysler's bumper.

"Oh hell," Al García said.

But R. J. Decker was feeling much better.

Deacon Johnson was proud of himself. He had gone down to the welfare office near the Superdome and found a nine-year-old blond girl who was double-jointed at the elbows. When she popped her bony arms out they looked magnificently grotesque, an effect that would be amplified dramatically by Charlie Weeb's television cameras. Deacon Johnson asked the girl's mother if he could rent her daughter for a couple of days and the mother said sure, for a hundred bucks—but no funny business. Deacon Johnson said don't worry, ma'am, this is a wholesome Christian enterprise, and led the little girl to his limousine.

At the downtown production studios of the Outdoor Christian Network, Deacon Johnson took the little girl, whose name was Darla, to meet the famous Reverend Charles Weeb.

Twirling his eyeglasses in one hand, Weeb looked relaxed behind his desk. He wore a powder-blue pullover, white parachute pants, and a pair of black Nike running shoes. A young woman with astounding breasts was trimming his famous cinnamon-blond eyebrows.

Deacon Johnson said, "Darla, show the preacher your little trick."

Darla took one step forward and extended both arms, as if awaiting handcuffs.

"Well?" said Charlie Weeb.

Darla closed her eyes, strained—and chucked her elbows out of joint at preposterous angles. The sockets emitted two little pops as they disengaged.

The statuesque eyebrow barber nearly wilted.

"Bravo!" said Charlie Weeb.

"Thank you," said Darla. Her pale arms hung crookedly at her sides.

"Izzy, whadya think?" Weeb said. "I think we're talking the big P."

"Polio?" Deacon Johnson frowned.

"Why the hell not?"

Deacon Johnson said, "Well, it's very uncommon these days."

"Perfect."

"Except everybody knows there's a vaccine."

"Not in the bowels of Appalachian coal country," Charlie Weeb said. "Not for a poor little orphan girl raised on grubworms and drainwater."

Darla spoke up. "I live in a 'partment on St. Charles," she said firmly. "With my momma."

"Talk to this child," Charlie Weeb said to Deacon Johnson. "Explain how TV works."

It was a good thing for Charlie Weeb that there was no audience for the dress rehearsals. At first Darla insisted on popping her elbows in and out, in and out—just to show off—and it took Deacon Johnson quite some time to make her understand the theatrical importance of timing. At a given cue Darla was supposed to roll her eyes, loll her tongue, and fall writhing onto the stage; when she rose again to face the cameras and audience, her polio would be cured. To demonstrate the success of his ministrations, the Reverend Charles Weeb would then toss her a beach ball.

The cue for Darla's fit was to be when Weeb raised his arms and implored: "Lord Jesus, mend this poor Christian creature!" The first few times, Darla jumped the gun badly, collapsing on the word "Jesus" so that the sound of her limp form hitting the stage stepped all over Charlie Weeb's big climax. Once Deacon Johnson had coached Darla past this problem, the next challenge was teaching her to catch the beach ball. The first few times she simply let the ball bounce off her chest, and the noise of it smacking the lanyard mike nearly blew out the engineer's eardrums. Darla dropped the ball so many times in rehearsal that the Reverend Weeb lost his Christian temper and called her a "palsied little twat"—a term which, fortunately, the child did not understand. When Weeb demanded that they go back to the lidocaine-injection method, Deacon Johnson quickly intervened and suggested now was a good time for lunch.

Miraculously, the live Sunday broadcast went off without a hitch. The crew did an extraordinary job making Darla appear sallow and gray and mortally ill. When the cue came, she collapsed perfectly and—after much thrashing—arose beaming and cherubic and healed. Reviewing the videotapes later, the Reverend Weeb marveled aloud at how deftly and invisibly little Darla had reengaged her elbow joints. Only on slo-mo could you see her do it. And, at the end, she even caught the beach ball. Charlie Weeb had been so genuinely overjoyed that he hadn't even needed the glycerine tears.

They ran the 800 number for five full minutes on the TV screen following Darla's performance. That evening, when Charlie Weeb got the final figures from the phone bank, he called Deacon Johnson at home.

"Guess the totals, Izzy."

"I really don't know. A million?"

Weeb cackled and said, "Guess again, sucker."

Deacon Johnson was too tired to guess. "I don't know, Charles," he said.

"How does a million-four sound?" the Reverend Weeb exulted.

The deacon was amazed. "Holy shit," he said.

"Exactly," said Charlie Weeb. "Are you thinking what I'm thinking?"

Thomas Curl had been thoroughly enjoying himself at the Grand Bay Hotel and was annoyed that he had to depart so suddenly. One morning, while eating eggs Benedict in the sunken bathtub, he had received a strange and unsettling phone call. Thomas Curl could tell by the scratchy connection that it was long distance, and he could tell by the voice that it wasn't either Dennis Gault or his Uncle Shawn, the only two men who knew where to find him. The voice sounded to Thomas Curl like it might belong to a nigger, but Curl couldn't be sure. Whoever it was had called him by name, so Curl had hung up the phone immediately and decided to check out of the hotel. He was worried that the black-sounding voice might turn out to be Decker's crazy gorilla friend Skink, who would think nothing of breaking into a fancy suite and drowning somebody in a sunken tub.

Thomas Curl took a more modest room at the Airport Marriott and shrewdly registered under the name "Juan Gómez," which he figured was the Miami equivalent of John Smith. The fact that Thomas Curl looked about as Hispanic as Cale Yarborough didn't stop him, and his Juan Gómez signature drew scarcely a raised eyebrow from a desk clerk named Rosario.

That evening, after a room-service steak, Thomas Curl went to work. R. J. Decker's address was in the phone book, and now it was only a matter of finding a decent map of Dade County.

The Palmetto Expressway, Thomas Curl decided, was worse than anything in New Orleans, worse even than Interstate 4 in Orlando. Thomas Curl had always considered himself a fast and sharp-witted driver, but the Palmetto shattered his confidence. It was as if he'd stalled out in the center lane, with bleating semis and muffler-dragging low-riders and cherry Porsches speeding past on both sides. Thomas Curl had heard the wild tales about Miami drivers, and now he could go back home and say it was all true. They were moving so damn fast you couldn't even flip them the finger.

He was delighted when he found his exit and got on a street with actual traffic lights. The trailer park was at the dark end of a dead-end street. Thomas Curl poked the car around slowly until he found the mailbox to R. J. Decker's mobile home. The lights were off and the trailer looked empty, as Thomas Curl knew it would be. An older grey sedan, a Dodge or Plymouth, sat in the gravel drive; the rear tires looked low on air, as if the car hadn't been driven recently. Curl parked behind it and cut off his headlights. He took a sixteen-inch flathead screwdriver from under the front seat. He was not the world's greatest burglar but he knew the fundamentals, including the fact that trailers usually were a cinch.

Another cardinal rule of burglary was: Leave your gun in the car unless you want another nickel tacked onto your prison sentence. Thomas Curl began to have second thoughts about this rule after he had gotten the screwdriver stuck in Decker's back door, and after a neighbor's sixty-five-pound pit bulldog came trotting over to investigate the racket. As the dog bared its teeth and emitted a tremulous rumble, Thomas Curl could not help thinking how nice it would have been to be holding either the shotgun or the pistol, both locked in the trunk of his car.

The pit bull got a running start before it leapt, so it landed on Thomas Curl with maximum impact. He crashed against the aluminum wall and lost his wind, but somehow kept his balance. The dog crouched at his feet and snarled hotly. The animal seemed genuinely surprised that it had failed to knock its victim down, but Thomas Curl was a muscular and stocky fellow with a low center of gravity.

The next time the dog jumped, Thomas Curl recoiled and tried to shield his face with his right arm, which is where the animal sank its yellow fangs. At first Thomas Curl felt no pain, only an unbelievable pressure. He stared at the dog and couldn't believe it. Eyes wide, its pale muzzle splotched with Curl's blood, the frenzied animal twisted and turned as it dangled from the arm; it was trying to tear the flesh from Thomas Curl's bone.

Curl swallowed his scream. With his left hand he feverishly groped for the long screwdriver, still wedged in the doorjamb. He found it, grunted as he yanked it free, and poised it firmly in his good fist.

With all his strength Thomas Curl lifted his right arm as high as his head, so that the pit bull hung before him at eye level, squirming and frothing. With one jagged downward thrust Thomas Curl disemboweled the animal. Its wild eyes went instantly dull and the legs stopped kicking, but still the powerful jaws held fast to Curl's thick arm. Moments passed and Curl stood rigid, waiting for the animal's muscles to slacken in death. Yet even as its guts dripped on the cold doorstep, steaming the night air, the dog's jaws would not let go.

Thomas Curl braced against waves of nausea. The screwdriver slipped from his good hand and pinged off the concrete stoop.

At a nearby trailer the porch light came on, and an elderly man in a long undershirt poked his head out. Thomas Curl quickly turned his back so that the neighbor would not see the dead dog on his arm. By the fresh light Curl noticed that in his panic he had succeeded in breaking the doorjamb. With his good hand he turned the knob, and lurched inside R. J. Decker's trailer.

Curl lay faceup on a sofa, the big dog across his chest. He stayed there for what seemed like an hour, until he could no longer tolerate the weight of the animal and the raw odor of its blood. In the darkness he could only imagine what his right arm looked like; he felt the first stinging tickle of a vile infection, and the burning throb of torn muscles. He realized that before long the dog's body would stiffen, and it would become virtually impossible to pry its jaws. Angrily Thomas Curl balled his left fist and tested his strength. Still supine, he aimed a fierce upper cut at the pit bull's head. The punch made little noise and had no effect, but Thomas Curl did not stop. He shut his eyes and imagined himself on the bag at the Fifth Street Gym, and punched left-breathe-left in a steady tempo. For the heavy bag drill his ex-manager used to play "Midnight Rambler" on the PA, so Curl ran the tune through his skull while he pounded on the pit bull. With each impact a ferocious bolt shot from his mangled arm into the vortex of his neck. The pain was miserable, but his alone; like any punching bag, the dog felt nothing. Its grip was immovable and, Thomas Curl began to fear, supernatural.

He dragged himself off the sofa, flipped on the kitchen lights, and began to tear Decker's trailer apart, looking for a tool. A wooden broom handle proved impotent against the demonic mandibles; a hammer satisfying to the grip, but messy and ineffectual. Finally, hanging from a pegboard in a utility closet, Thomas Curl found what he was looking for: a small hacksaw. He struggled into the narrow bathroom and knelt down. With his deadening right arm he slung the dog carcass into the shower stall, and gazed numbly at the livid mess. Thomas Curl didn't know whether he was just exhausted or going crazy, but he found it difficult to distinguish which flesh was his and which belonged to the animal. From the knotted muscle of his shoulder to the pinkish tail of the dog corpse seemed a single evil mass. Thomas Curl's left hand searched the tile until his fingers found the steel teeth of the hacksaw. He took a breath, and did what he had to.

Catherine was alone in bed when the doorbell rang.

James the doctor was gone again, this time to Montreal for a big trade show. He and several other chiropractors had agreed to endorse a new back-pain product called the Miracle VibraCouch, and the Canadian trade show was to be the scene of its unveiling. Saying good-bye at the car, James had promised to bring back videotapes of all the excitement, and Catherine had said that'll be wonderful and pecked him on the cheek. James had asked her which model VibraCouch would go best in the Florida room, the tartan or the dusty rose, and Catherine had said neither, I don't want an electric couch in my house, thank-you. James was pouting as he drove away.

When the bell rang, Catherine slipped into a short chiffon robe and padded barefoot to the door. The house was bright, and the clock in the alcove said nine-thirty. She'd overslept again.

Through a window she saw the gray Plymouth Volaré parked in the driveway. Catherine smiled—here we go again. She checked herself in the mirror and said what the hell, it's hopeless this early in the morning. When she opened the door she said, "Great timing as usual, Rage."

But the man turned around and it wasn't R.J. It was a heavyset stranger wearing R.J.'s brown leather coat. Catherine had bought the coat for him at a western shop near Denver. The stranger wore it on his shoulders like a cape. Maybe it wasn't R.J.'s coat after all, Catherine thought anxiously; maybe it was one just like it.

" 'Scuze me," said the man, "you Mrs. Decker?"

"Stuckameyer," Catherine said. "I used to be Mrs. Decker."

The man had thin sandy hair, a flat crooked nose, and tiny dull eyes. He handed Catherine a crisp brown office envelope containing a sheaf of legal papers. Catherine scanned them and looked up quizzically.

"So?" she said. "These are my old divorce papers."

"But that *is* you? Catherine Decker."

"Where'd you get this stuff?" she said irritably.

"I found it," the man said, "at Mr. Decker's."

Catherine studied him closely. She saw that he was also wearing one of R.J.'s knit shirts. She tried to slam the door but the man blocked it with a black round-toed boot.

"Don't be a dumb cunt," he said.

Catherine was turning to run when she saw the pistol. The man pointed it with his right hand extended from under the leather coat. Something round and mottled and awful was attached to the stranger's arm. It looked like a football with ears.

"Oh Jesus," Catherine cried.

"Don't mind him," the man said, "he don't bite."

He pushed his way into the house and shut the door. He shifted the pistol to his other hand, and tucked the dog-headed arm back under the coat.

"Decker's in some deep shit," said the stranger.

"Well, I don't know where he is." Catherine pulled her robe tight in the front.

Thomas Curl said, "You know why I'm here?"

"No, but I know who you are," Catherine said. "You're one of the Fish People, aren't you?"

Jim Tile's patrol car passed García on Route 222 and led them into town, which was as dark as a mortuary. The trooper took them directly to the house of an old black doctor, who packed and dressed Skink's seeping eye wound. Silently Decker and García watched the old man dance a penlight in front of Skink's haggard face and peer into the other eye for quite a long time. "He needs a neurologist right away," the doctor said finally. "Gainesville's your best bet."

Skink himself said nothing. When they got back to the cabin, he curled up on a mattress and went to sleep. Jim Tile got the campfire going. Al García selected an oak stump of suitable width and sat down close to the flames. "Now what?" he said. "We tell ghost stories?"

R. J. Decker said, "This is where he lives."

"Unbelievable," the detective muttered.

Jim Tile went to the car and came back with two black-and-white photographs, eight-by-tens. "From our friends in the bayou," he said, handing the pictures to R. J. Decker.

"Christ," Decker mumbled. They were the caught-in-the-act shots of the bass cheaters in the reeds at Lake Maurepas—except that Dickie Lockhart's head had been supered onto one of the other men's bodies. Decker recognized the mug of Dickie from the bunch he'd shot at the Cajun Classic weigh-in. Looking at the doctored photographs made him feel angry and, in a way, violated.

"Somebody swiped my film and had some fun in the darkroom," he said to Jim Tile. "I've seen better phonies."

"Sure fooled New Orleans homicide."

"It's still bush," Decker snapped. "I can find a half-dozen expert witnesses to say these are tricked."

Al García took the prints from Decker and studied them. "Nifty," he said. "That's how they do it, huh?"

"In cages, yeah."

"And how long will those fish stay alive?"

Decker shrugged. "Couple days, I guess."

Jim Tile said, "There's some other things you ought to know." He told them about his conversation with Ozzie Rundell, and Ozzie's version of Ott Pickney's murder.

"He also says Lockhart didn't kill Robert Clinch."

"You believe that?" Decker asked.

Jim Tile nodded.

García said, "Had to be Gault."

"That's my guess too," the trooper agreed, "but I'm not sure why he'd do it."

R. J. Decker thought about it. Why would Dennis Gault order the murder of a man he had recruited to work for him? Lanie might know; she might even be part of the reason.

Jim Tile said, "There's a guy named Thomas Curl, a real shitkicker. He and his brother killed your friend Ott. My bet is they did Bobby Clinch too."

"The Louisiana boys," Decker said.

Jim Tile said, "It just so happens that Lemus Curl is missing. Family says he fell into Lake Okeechobee."

García looked curiously at Decker, who tried not to react.

"But the other Curl," Jim Tile went on, "Thomas Curl, is in Miami."

"Fuck me," said Al García.

Decker said, "Let me guess: Curl is looking for me."

"Most likely," Jim Tile said. "By phone I tracked him to some ritzy hotel in the Grove, but then he took off."

"What's the connection to Gault?"

"He paid for Curl's room," Jim Tile said.

He took a piece of paper from his left breast pocket, unfolded it carefully and handed it to Decker. "Meanwhile," Jim Tile said, "Mr. Gault is going fishing."

It was a promotional flier for the Dickie Lockhart Memorial Bass Blasters Classic. In the firelight García read it aloud over Decker's shoulder: "The richest tournament in history. Entry fee is only three thousand dollars, but hurry—the field will be limited to fifty boats."

Decker couldn't believe it, the ballsiness of these guys. "Three thousand bucks," he said.

"It is amazing," Jim Tile remarked. Long ago he had given up trying to understand the cracker mentality. He wondered if the Cuban cop would have the same difficulty.

García said, "Dennis Gault I can figure out. He's a greedy little egomaniac who wants trophies for his penthouse. But what's the rest of the shit with this tournament?"

Decker explained the Outdoor Christian Network and its vast stake in the Lunker Lakes development. "They're going to use the TV fish hype to sell townhouses. Everybody does it these days. Mazda has golf, Lipton has tennis, OCN has bass. The demographics match up nicely."

Al García looked extremely amused. "You're telling me," he said, "that grown men will sit down for hours in front of a television set and watch other men go fishing."

"Millions," Decker said, "every weekend."

"I don't ever want to hear you talk about crazy Cubans," García said, "never again."

A flicker of a smile crossed Jim Tile's face, and then he grew serious. "Gault is the big problem," he said. "He's the one who can put Decker in prison."

"He'd rather have him dead," García noted.

Decker knew the detective was right. By now Dennis Gault surely understood that a trial could be disastrous; the evidence against Decker was entirely circumstantial, and Gault couldn't risk taking the witness stand himself. There were neater ways to close a murder case, and one was to make the prime suspect vanish. That, Decker thought, would be Thomas Curl's department.

García said to Decker, "We need to get to Gault before Curl gets to you."

"That's brilliant, Al."

"Any ideas, smartass?"

"Yes, as a matter of fact. My idea is that you plant your lazy Cuban butt right here for a day or so, and keep an eye on our sick friend." Decker turned to Jim Tile. "I need a favor from you."

"Starting tonight," the trooper said, "I'm on vacation."

"Good," Decker said. "You feel like taking a drive to the beach?"

Jim Tile chuckled. "My Coppertone's already packed."

Crescent Beach is a few miles south of St. Augustine. The broad expanse of sand is sugary white, but packed so hard you could drive a truck to the water's edge without fear of getting stuck. For a long time Crescent Beach and adjacent communities existed in a rare and splendid quiet. To the south, Daytona got all the publicity and the crowds to go with it; to the north, the beach at Jacksonville was still clean enough to keep the city folks home on weekends. As the condo market boomed in the seventies, though, developers scouted and scoured all of the state's oceanfront possibilities, and spied lovely Crescent Beach as a promoter's wet dream—the perfect escape. See Florida as it used to be! Enjoy the solitude of long romantic walks, the Atlantic nipping at your toes! Lie down among the dunes! The dunes became a crucial selling point for North Florida's long-ignored beaches, because the people in South Florida didn't know what a dune was—the developers had flattened them all back in the fifties. True, by Northern standards Florida dunes weren't much to write home about—stubbled little hillocks, really—but the condo salesmen made the most of them and customers thought they were quaint. Once the building boom took hold south of Jacksonville and the beachfront became clogged with exclusive resorts and high-rises and golf communities, the state was forced to start buying up the remaining dunes, making parks, and nailing boardwalks every which-way to keep the dunes from getting leveled. Mysteriously, tourists would drive for miles and pay admission just to see a three-foot crest of sand with a few strands of sea oats—a genuine touch of wilderness among the cabanas.

Lanie Gault had not chosen Crescent Beach for its dunes. She hadn't chosen it at all; a lover had bought the condo and given it to her for Valentine's Day in 1982. He was a wonderful and basically harmless man, had his own insurance company, and Lanie didn't mind that he was married. He wasn't the sort of guy you wanted to have around *all* the time anyway. Every other weekend was just fine. It lasted for about two years until his wife found out—somebody called her up with the juicy details. The insurance man couldn't figure out who would do such a thing, but Lanie knew. It was her brother. Dennis never admitted to making the phone call, but Lanie had no doubt he was the one. Dennis couldn't stand the insurance man (nothing new) and for months had been telling her to clear the deed and dump the guy, he's bad news. He *isn't* bad news, Lanie had argued, thinking: He's just slightly boring. When the wife found out, Lanie was angry with her brother but also a little relieved. A few days later the insurance man came to the condo and told her he was moving back to St. Louis and kissed her good-bye. Lanie cried and said she understood and asked if he wanted her to give the condo back. The insurance man said heavens no, it's all yours, just don't tell anyone where you got it. A week later Lanie put in brand-new wine carpeting and decided maybe her heart wasn't truly broken after all.

Lanie's condominium was on the east wing of the ninth floor, and featured a scallop-shaped balcony with an ocean view. One of the things she liked about the building was the security—not only a gatehouse at the entrance, but an armed guard in the lobby and a closed-circuit TV bank. Nobody got upstairs without clearance, and the security people had strict instructions to phone ahead, no matter what. Given such procedures, Lanie was understandably alarmed to be awakened by someone knocking on the door. She squirmed across the king-size bed and snatched the phone off the nightstand and called the desk. The guard said, "It's the police, Miss Gault, we had to let them up."

When she opened the door, she saw the problem. Jim Tile was wearing his state trooper's uniform.

"Can I help you?" Lanie asked.

"Not me," Jim Tile said, "my friend."

R. J. Decker peeked around the corner of the doorway. "Remember me? We exchanged bodily fluids not long ago."

Lanie looked stunned to see him. "Hi," she said tentatively.

The two men walked in; Jim Tile courteously removing his Stetson, Decker closing the door behind them. "I can see you're wondering how to play this scene," he said to Lanie, "because you don't know how much I know."

"What do you mean?"

Decker opened the living-room curtains without remarking on the view. "Lovey-dovey is one way to go. You know the bit: *Where you been? I missed you. Why haven't you called?* But that's only good if I don't know that you went to the New Orleans cops. And if I don't know you helped your brother set me up."

Lanie sat down and fiddled with her hair. Jim Tile went to the kitchen and fixed three glasses of orange juice.

"Another way to go," Decker continued, "is the Terrified Witness routine. Murder suspect barges into your apartment, scares the shit out of you. *Please don't hurt me. I'll do anything you want, just don't hurt me.* That's if you're trying to sell me the idea that you really believe I killed Dickie Lockhart. Which is horseshit."

Lanie smiled weakly. "Any other choices?"

"Try the truth," said Decker, "just as an experiment."

"You got a tape player?" Jim Tile asked.

Lanie said, "On the balcony, with the beach stuff." She shook her head no when Jim Tile offered a glass of juice.

The trooper went outside and got the portable stereo. He came back and set it up on the coffee table in the living room. There was already a cassette in the tape player.

Jim Tile punched the Record button. He said, "You don't mind?"

"Hey, that's my Neil Diamond you're erasing," Lanie complained.

"What a loss," Decker said.

Jim Tile fiddled with the volume dial. "Nice box," he said. "Graphic equalizers and everything."

"Let's start with Dennis," Decker said.

"Forget it, R.J."

Jim Tile said, "She's right. Let's don't start with her brother. Let's start with Robert Clinch."

Lanie stared coldly at the big black man. "I could get you in a lot of trouble."

"Don't flatter yourself," said Jim Tile.

Decker was impressed at how unimpressed Jim Tile was. He said, "Okay, princess, guess who killed Bobby."

"Dickie Lockhart did."

"Wrong."

"Then who?"

Jim Tile got up and opened the glass doors to the balcony. A cool breeze stirred the curtains. Lanie shivered.

Decker said, "Dennis didn't think much of your affair with Bobby Clinch, did he? I mean, a sexy high-class girl like you can't be sneaking off with a grotey redneck bass fisherman."

"What?" Lanie looked aggravated, not cool at all.

Jim Tile said, "Your brother had Robert Clinch killed. He hired two men to do it. They waited for him at the Coon Bog that morning, jumped him, then rigged his boat for a bad wreck. Dennis wanted everyone to think Dickie was behind it."

"No," said Lanie, glassy-eyed.

She really doesn't know, Decker thought. If she's acting, it's the performance of her life.

"Bobby wasn't getting anywhere on the cheating," she said numbly. "Dickie's people were too slick. Dennis was impatient, he was riding Bobby pretty hard. Then . . . well."

"He found out you and Bobby were involved."

Lanie gave a shallow laugh. "The sportfucking, he didn't mind. A different fella each night and he'd never say a word to me. Whenever things got serious is when he acted weird. Like when Bobby said he was going to leave his wife and go away with me, Dennis got furious. But still he would never do what you say. Never!"

Decker said, "Lanie, he needed you more than he needed Bobby."

"For what, Decker? Needed me for what?"

Decker tapped his chest. "For me."

By now Lanie was crying. Not the best job of crying Decker had ever seen, but still pretty convincing. "What are you saying?" she hacked between sobs. "You think I was whoring for my own brother! I cared for Bobby, you don't believe me but it's true."

Jim Tile was not moved. In years of writing traffic tickets, he'd heard every imaginable tale of woe. With his usual remoteness he said, "When's the last time you spoke to him?"

"Bobby? I saw him the night before he died. We had a drink at a shrimp place over in Wabasso."

"Did he tell you he was going to the lake?"

"Of course he did—he was so excited. He'd gotten a tip that Dickie was hiding his fish cages in the Coon Bog. Bobby was thrilled as anything. He couldn't wait to find the bass and call Dennis."

Decker said, "Where did the tip come from?"

"Some guy who called up Bobby, wouldn't give his name."

"It was a setup," Jim Tile said, "the phone call."

"Now, wait," Lanie said. She kept looking down at the tape player.

Time's up, Decker thought. He sat next to Lanie and said, "Call me nosy, but I'd like to know why you framed me."

Lanie didn't answer. Decker took one of her hands and held it very gently, as if it were a baby animal he was afraid of squeezing. Lanie looked frightened.

"It was your brother's idea, wasn't it?"

"At first he talked about blackmail," she said. "He asked if I knew any good photographers who could follow Dickie and get the pictures without him knowing. I thought of you, and Dennis said fine. He said to keep you interested and I said okay, anything to get back at Dickie for what he did."

"What you *thought* he did," Decker interjected.

"Dennis said it was Dickie who killed Bobby. I believed him, why shouldn't I? It made sense."

Jim Tile said, "So Dickie's murdered, then what?"

"Dennis calls me in New Orleans."

Decker said, "Just what the hell were you doing there anyway?"

"He sent me," Lanie said. "To make sure you weren't goofing off, he said. He was pissed off because you weren't telling him much on the phone."

"So you drag me into bed, then steal my film?"

"Who dragged who?" Lanie said sharply. "About the film, I'm sorry. It was a shitty thing to do. Dennis said he was dying to see what you'd got. Said the stuff belonged to him anyway."

Decker held her hand just a little tighter. "And you actually believed all this?" he asked agitatedly. "These errands didn't strike you as a little odd? No light bulb flashed on in your beautiful size-four brain?"

"No," Lanie snapped, "no light bulbs."

Jim Tile said, "Getting back to Dickie's murder . . ."

"Yeah," Lanie said, shifting her eyes to the trooper. "That morning Dennis called me in New Orleans, all upset. He said Decker had gone and killed Lockhart. Dennis was afraid."

Jim Tile said, "He told you he might be a suspect."

"Right. He said Decker was trying to frame him, and he asked me to go to the police."

"And lie?"

"He's my brother, for God's sake. I didn't want him to go to jail over a crazy goddamn fish murder. Bobby's death was bad enough, I didn't want to lose Dennis too. So I went down and gave a very brief statement." She looked at Decker again. "I said you dropped me off on your way to see Dickie Lockhart. That's all."

"It was plenty," Decker said. "Thanks a heap."

"Dennis sounded desperate."

"And with good reason."

"I still don't believe you," Lanie said.

"Yes, you do," said Jim Tile.

It was all Decker could do to hold his temper. "Any other little Dennis favors we should know about?"

Lanie said, "Can you turn that thing off?"

Jim Tile stopped the tape machine.

Lanie got up and led them through the apartment to the second bedroom. She opened the door as quietly as she could. The room was totally dark; the shades were not only drawn, but the cracks were sealed with hurricane tape. Lanie turned on the ceiling light.

A young long-haired woman lay in bed, a pink cotton blanket pulled up to her chin. Her bluish eyelids were half-closed and she breathed heavily, with her mouth open. Some pills and a half-empty bottle of Dewar's sat on the nightstand.

Jim Tile looked at R. J. Decker, who said, "I've seen her before. At the tournament in New Orleans."

"Name's Ellen O'Leary," Lanie said in a dull voice. "She's not feeling well."

In a fury Decker pushed Lanie Gault to the wall, pinned her arms. "No more games," he said. "Who's this girl?"

"I *don't* know," Lanie cried.

"You just came home one night and there she was, passed out in bed?"

"No, a man brought her. Dennis asked me to look after her."

Decker said, "You're a very sick lady, Elaine."

"Easy, man," said Jim Tile. He sat down on the bed next to Ellen O'Leary and studied the labels on the pill bottles. "Nembutals," he said to Decker.

"Swell, a Norma Jean cocktail."

"Just to make her sleepy," Lanie insisted. "She'll be all right, R.J. Every night I give her soup. Would you get off me, please?"

Decker grabbed Lanie's arm and led her out of the bedroom. Jim Tile flushed the pills down the toilet and went to the kitchen to fix coffee for the woman named Ellen. He was wondering how much stranger things would get.

Decker himself was frazzled. Lanie was impossible.

"What did your brother say about this woman?" he asked her.

"He said to keep an eye on her, that's all. Keep her sleepy and out of trouble. He said she was a danger to herself and others."

"I'll bet."

Lanie asked if she could get dressed. Decker said yes, but he wouldn't let her out of his sight. Lanie didn't object. Casually she stripped off her nightgown and stood naked in front of the mirror, brushing out her hair while Decker watched impassively. Finally she put on jeans and a University of Miami sweatshirt.

Decker said, "You know a man named Thomas Curl?"

"Sure, that's the guy who brought Ellen," Lanie answered. "He works for Dennis."

By the way she said it, Decker could tell she really didn't know. Even Lanie wasn't that good.

"Thomas Curl killed Bobby," he said.

"Stop it," Lanie said, "right now." But it was obvious by her expression that she was putting it all together.

In the other room Jim Tile carried Ellen to the shower. He propped her under a cold drizzle for ten minutes until she spluttered and bent over to vomit. Then he toweled her off and put her back in bed. Once her stomach settled, she sat up and sipped some coffee.

Jim Tile closed the door and said, "You want to talk?"

"Where am I?" Ellen asked thickly.

"Florida."

"I must've got sick—did I miss it?"

"Miss what?" Jim Tile asked.

"Dickie's funeral."

"Yes, it's over."

"Oh." Ellen's eyes filled up.

Jim Tile said, "Dickie was a friend of yours?"

"Yes, officer, he was."

"How long did you know him?"

"Not long," answered Ellen O'Leary, "just a few days. But he cared for me."

"When's the last time you saw him?"

Ellen said, "Right before it happened."

"The murder?"

"Yes, officer. I was up in the hotel with him, celebrating after the bass tournament, when Thomas Curl came to the door and said he needed to see Dickie right away."

"Then what happened, Ellen?"

"They went off together and Dickie didn't come back. I fell asleep—we'd had an awful lot of champagne. The next morning I heard on the radio what happened."

Jim Tile refilled her coffee cup. "What did you do then?" he asked.

"I was so upset, I called Reverend Weeb," she said, "and I asked him to say a prayer for Dickie's soul. And Reverend Weeb said only if I came over and knelt down with him."

"I bet you weren't in the mood for *that*."

"Right," Ellen said. She didn't understand how the black trooper could know about Reverend Weeb's strange ways, but she was grateful for the compassion.

Jim Tile opened the bedroom door and asked Decker and Lanie to come in.

"Ellen," he said, "tell Miss Gault who came and got Dickie Lockhart the night he was killed."

"Thomas Curl," said Ellen O'Leary.

Lanie looked stricken. "Are you sure?"

"I've known him since high school."

"God," Lanie said dejectedly.

Ellen tucked an extra pillow under her head. "I'm feeling lots better," she said.

"Well, I feel like hell," said Lanie.

The phone rang. Jim Tile told her to answer it, and motioned Decker to pick up the kitchen extension.

The caller was Dennis Gault.

"Hi," Lanie said, with the trooper standing very close behind her.

"How's it going, sis?" Gault asked.

"Fine," Lanie said. "Ellen's still sleeping."

"Excellent."

"Dennis, I'd like to go out, catch some sun, do some shopping. How much longer with the babysitting?"

"Look, Elaine, I don't know. The cops still haven't caught Decker."

"Oh, great." Perfect sarcasm. Decker listened admiringly—she really could have been a star of stage and screen.

"What if they don't catch him?" she said.

"Don't be ridiculous."

"Dennis, I want Tom to come get this girl."

"Soon," Gault promised. "I sent him down to Miami on some business. He'll pick up Ellen when he gets back. Relax, wouldya, sweet thing?"

"Miami," Lanie repeated.

"Yeah," her brother said, "we're getting ready for the big tournament."

"Oh boy," said Lanie, thinking: I hope you drown, you murdering bastard.

25

The fire died slowly, and as it did Al García poked and speared the embers in a feeble attempt to revive the flames. Soon a gray curling mist cloaked the lake and settled over the detective's shoulders like a damp shroud. Small creatures scuttled unseen through the woods, and each crackling twig reminded García that he was desperately removed from his element, the city. Even from the lake there were noises—what, he couldn't imagine—splashes and gurgles of all dimensions. García wondered about bears; what kind, how big. The weight of the Colt Python under his arm was a small comfort, but he knew the gun was not designed to kill bears. García was no outdoorsman, his main exposure to the wilderness being old reruns of *The American Sportsman*. Two things he remembered most vividly about the TV show were ferocious bears the size of Pontiacs, and convivial campfire scenes where all the men slugged down beers and feasted on fresh venison. García seemed to recall that there were always at least ten heavily armed guys around Curt Gowdy at the camp, plus a camera crew. And here he was, practically all alone with a dead fire.

Halfheartedly García collected some kindling and tossed it into the embers. He put his cigarette lighter to the pile, but the wood sparked and in a moment went cold. The detective unscrewed the top of his disposable lighter and dumped the fluid on the sticks. Then he leaned over and touched a match to the fire, which promptly blew up in his face.

After García picked himself off the ground, he sat down lugu-briously by the smoldering campfire. Gingerly he explored his face and found only minimal damage—his eyebrows were scorched and curlicued, and his mustache gave off an acrid smell. García jumped at the low rumble of laughter—it was Skink, hulking in the doorway of the shack.

"Honest to God," the big man said. In three minutes the fire was ablaze again. Skink made coffee, which García accepted gratefully. There was something odd about the governor's appearance, and it took the detective several moments to figure it out.

"Your eye," he said to Skink.

"What of it?"

A new eye stared from the socket where the heavy gauze had been packed. The new eye was strikingly big, with a startling yellow iris and a pupil as large as a half-dollar. García couldn't help but notice that the new eye was not a perfect fit for the hole in Skink's face.

"Where did you get it?" García asked.

"Does it look okay?"

"Fine," the detective said. "Very nice."

Skink clomped into the shack and came back with a stuffed barn owl, an erect, imperious-looking bird. "I tie this on the roof to keep the crows and grackles away," he said. Admiring the taxidermied owl at arm's length, Skink said, "If looks could kill."

García asked, "Will it still scare the birds? With one eye, I mean."

"Hell, yes," Skink said. "Even more so. Just look at that vicious fucker."

The owl's frozen gaze was still fierce, García had to admit. And Skink himself looked exceptional; while his new eye did not move in concert with its mate, it still commanded attention.

"I'll give it a try," Skink said, and put on his sunglasses.

After they finished the coffee, Skink got the Coleman lantern and led García down to the water. He told him to get in the rowboat. García shared the bow with an old tin bucket, a nylon castnet folded inside. Skink rowed briskly across the lake, singing an old rock song that García vaguely recognized: *No one knows what it's like to be the bad man, to be the sad man. . . .* More like the madman, García said to himself.

He was impressed by Skink's energy, after the savage beating he'd taken. The wooden boat cut the water in strong bolts, Skink pulling at the oars with a fervor that bordered on jubilation. Truly he was a different man than the bloodied heap wheezing in the back seat of

García's car. If the pain still bothered him, Skink didn't show it. He was plainly overjoyed to be home, and on the water.

After twenty minutes Skink guided the rowboat into a cove on the northern shore, but he didn't break his pace. With his good eye he checked over his shoulder and kept a course for the mouth of a small creek that emptied into the lake between two prehistoric live oaks. To García the creek seemed too narrow even for the little skiff, yet it swallowed them easily. For fifty yards it snaked through mossy bottomland, beneath lightning-splintered cypress and eerie tangled beards of Spanish moss. García was awestruck by the primordial beauty of the swamp but said nothing, afraid to disturb the silence. Skink had long stopped singing.

Eventually the creek opened to a blackwater pond rimmed by lily pads and mined with rotting stumps.

Skink removed his sunglasses and tucked them into the pocket of his weathersuit. He turned from the oars and motioned for the cast-net. Awkwardly García handed it to him; the lead weights were heavy and unwieldly. Standing wide-legged, Skink clenched the string in his teeth and hurled the net in a smooth low arc; it opened perfectly and settled to the water like a gossamer umbrella. When he dragged the net back into the boat, it was spangled with fish, flashing in the mesh like pieces of a shattered mirror. Skink filled the tin bucket with water and emptied the fish into it. Then he refolded the net and sat down, facing Al García.

"Golden shiners," he announced. Skink plucked one out of the bucket and swallowed it alive.

García stared at him. "What do they taste like?" he asked.

"Like shiners." Skink took another fish from the bucket and thwacked it lightly against the gunwale, killing it instantly. "Watch here," he said to García.

Leaning over the side of the skiff, Skink slapped the palm of his hand on the water, causing a loud concussion. He repeated this action several times until suddenly he pulled his hand from the pond and said, "Whooo, baby!" He dropped the dead shiner and beneath it the black water erupted—a massive fish, as bronze and broad as a cannon, engulfed the little fish where it floated.

"*Cristo!*" gasped Al García.

Skink stared at the now-silken surface and grinned proudly. "Yeah, she's a big old momma." He tossed another shiner, with the same volcanic result.

"That's a bass?" García asked.

"Hawg," Skink said. "The fucking monster-beastie of all time. Guess her weight, Sergeant."

"I've got no idea." In the fickle light of the lantern García looked hard for the fish but saw nothing; the water was impenetrable, the color of crude oil.

"Name's Queenie," Skink said, "and she weighs twenty-nine pounds, easy."

Skink tossed three more shiners, and the bass devoured them, soaking the men in her frenzy.

"So this is your pet," García said.

"Hell, no," Skink said, "she's my partner." He handed the bucket to Al García. "You try," he said, "but watch your pinkies."

García crippled a shiner and tossed it into the pond. Nothing happened, not a ripple.

"Spank the water," Skink instructed.

García tried, timidly, making more bubbles than noise.

"Louder, dammit!" Skink said. "That's it. Quick, now, drop a shiner."

No sooner had the tiny fish landed—still wriggling, this one—than the monster-beastie slurped it down. The noise was obscene.

"She likes you," Skink said. "Do it again."

García tossed another baitfish and watched it disappear. "You learn this shit from Marlin Perkins?" he said.

Skink ignored him. "Give me the bucket," he said. He fed the big fish the rest of the dying shiners, save one. Skink held it between his thumb and forefinger, tickling the water. He used the fish as a silvery wand, tracing figure-eights by the side of the rowboat. From its unseen lair deep in the pond, the big fish rose slowly until its black dorsal punctured the velvet surface. As the fish hung motionless, García for the first time could see its true size, and appreciate the awesome capacity of its underslung jaw. The bass glided slowly toward Skink's teasing shiner; frenzy had been replaced by a delicate deliberation. Skink's fingers released the baitfish, which disappeared instantly into the white maw—yet the fish did not swim away, nor did Skink withdraw his hand. Amazingly, he took the bass by its lower lip, hoisted it from the pond, and laid it carefully across his lap. "There now, momma," Skink said. Dripping in the boat, the fish flared its gills and snapped at air, but did not struggle. It was, García thought, a magnificent gaping brute—nearly thirty pounds of iridescent muscle.

"Sergeant," Skink said, "say hi to Queenie."

García did not wish to seem rude, but he didn't feel like talking to a fish.

"Come on," Skink prodded.

"Hey, Queenie," said the detective, without conviction. He was very glad his lieutenant couldn't see him.

Skink kept a thumb curled in the bass's lower lip, and slipped the other hand under its bloated pale belly. He lifted the bass and propped it long-wise on his shoulder, like a barrel. Skink's face was side-by-side with that of the monster bass, and Al García found himself staring at (from left to right) the eyes of a fish, a man, and a stuffed owl.

As if cuddling a puppy, Skink pressed his cheek against Queenie's scaly gillplates. "Meet the new boss," he whispered to the fish, "same as the old boss."

Al García didn't know what the hell he was talking about.

The Reverend Charles Weeb arrived at Lunker Lakes just in time to see the second batch of fish die. The hydrologist was crestfallen but said there was nothing to be done. Under a gray sky Weeb stood on the bank next to the young scientist and counted the fish as they bobbed to the surface of the bad water. At number seventy-five, Weeb turned and stalked back to the model town-home that was serving as tournament headquarters.

"Cancel tomorrow's press tour," he snapped at Deacon Johnson, who obediently lunged for his Rolodex.

To the hydrologist Weeb said: "So how long did this bunch live?"

"Eighteen hours, sir."

"Shit. And the trip down from Alabama was . . . ?"

"About two days," the hydrologist said.

"Shit." Lunker Lakes had now claimed four thousand young bass, and Charlie Weeb was deeply worried. For now he was thinking in the short-term.

"I can get another two thousand," he said to the hydrologist.

"I wouldn't recommend it," the man said. "The water's still sub-standard."

"*Substandard?* What you're really saying is these fish stand a better chance in a sewer, is that right?"

"I wouldn't go quite that far," the hydrologist said.

"Okay, pencil-neck, let's hear the bad news." Weeb shut the door to his private office and motioned the young man to a Chippendale chair. "You like this unit? We've got your atrium doors, your breakfast bay, your cathedral ceiling—did I mention solar heat? See, I've got to sell twenty-nine thousand of these babies and right now they're moving real fucking slow. It's gonna get slower if I got a dead-fish problem, you understand?" Charlie Weeb inhaled two Chiclets. "I'm selling a *new* Florida here, son. The last of the frontier. My buyers are simple folks who'd rather go fishing than get fried to raisins on the beach. Lunker Lakes is their kind of place, an outdoor community, see? Walk out the back door with your fishing pole and reel in a whopper. That's the way I dreamed it, but right now . . . well."

"We're talking cesspool," the hydrologist said bluntly. "I did some more tests, very sophisticated chemical scans. You've got toxins in this water that make the East River seem like Walden Pond. The worst concentration is in the bottom muck—we're talking Guinness-record PCBs."

"How?" Charlie Weeb yowled. "How can it be poisoned if it's pre-dredged!"

The hydrologist said, "I was puzzled too, until I checked down at the courthouse. This used to be a landfill, Reverend Weeb, right where the lakes are."

"A dump?"

"One of the biggest—and worst," the hydrologist reported grimly. "Four hundred acres of sludge, rubbers, dioxins, you name it. EPA never did find out."

Charlie Weeb said, "Lord God!"—an exclamation he almost never used off the air.

"In layman's terms," the hydrologist concluded, "when you dredged Lunker Lakes, you tapped into twenty-four years' worth of fermented battery acid."

Charlie Weeb coughed his gum into the trashcan. His mind was racing. He visualized the disastrous headlines and rubbed his eyes, as if to make the nightmare go away. Silently he cursed himself for succumbing to the South Florida real-estate disease when he could have played it safe and gone for tax-free muni bonds—the OCN board *had* left it up to him. Through his befogged paroxysm of self-pity Weeb remotely heard the hydrologist explaining how the lakes could be cleansed and made safe, but the project would take years and cost millions. . . .

First things first, thought Charlie Weeb. The poster on the wall reminded him that the big tournament was only four days away. The immediate priority was getting some new fish.

"If I could get the tanker truck here before dawn," Charlie

Weeb said, "get the bass in the water early, would they live until sunset?"

"Probably."

"Thank God it's a one-day tournament," Weeb said, thinking aloud.

"Can't say how healthy they'd be," the hydrologist cautioned. "They may not feed at all."

"They don't need to," Weeb said, leaving the man thoroughly confused. "Get those fucking dead fish out of my sight, every one," the preacher ordered, and the hydrologist fled to round up some boats.

Fast Eddie Spurling was next on Charlie Weeb's agenda. Eddie came in wearing a Happy Gland fishing cap and a shiny silver Evinrude jacket. Tucked into his cheek was a plug of Red Man tobacco so big it would have gagged a hyena. It was all Weeb could do to conceal his disgust; Eddie Spurling was about the biggest Gomer he'd ever met.

"The fish are dying," Eddie said, his voice pained.

"You noticed."

"Why?"

"Don't worry about it," Weeb said. "Sit down, please."

"I hate to see 'em dying like that."

Not half as much as I do, Weeb thought morosely. "Eddie," he began, "have you given much thought to the big tournament? Have you got a plan for winning?"

Eddie Spurling shifted the tobacco to his other cheek. Chewing hard, he said, "Truthfully, I figured buzzbaits would do it, but now I don't know. There's not much cover in this water. 'Fact, there's not much *anything* in this water. I didn't even see any garfish down there, and those suckers could live in a toilet bowl."

Weeb frowned.

"Jelly worms," Eddie declared through his chaw. "Rig 'em Texas-style, I think that'll be the ticket, sir."

Charlie Weeb sat forward and put on his eyeglasses. "Eddie, it's very important that you win this tournament."

"Well, I'll damn sure try." He flashed a mouthful of wet brown teeth. "Prize money like that—you kidding?"

"Trying is fine," Weeb said, "very admirable. But this time we may need to do more. A little insurance."

Weeb was not surprised that Eddie looked confused.

"You're the new star at OCN, we got a lot riding on you," Charlie

Weeb said. "If you win, we all win. And Lunker Lakes too. This is a tremendous opportunity, Eddie."

"Well, sure."

"Opportunities like this don't come along every day." Weeb rocked back and folded his hands behind his head. "I've been having this dream, Eddie, and you're in it."

"Yeah?"

"That's right. In my dream, the sun is shining, the lakes are clear and beautiful. Thousands of happy home-buyers are gathered around, and the TV is there too, waiting for the end of the big tournament. All the other fishermen are back at the dock except you, Eddie."

"Ugh."

"Then, only seconds before the deadline, I see your boat cutting across the water. You pull up with a big smile on your face, get out, wave at the cameras. Then you reach down and pull up the biggest stringer of largemouth bass anyone's ever seen. The whole joint goes wild, Eddie. There you are, standing under the Lunker Lakes sign, holding up these giant mother fish. God, it's a vision, don't you agree?"

"Sure, Reverend Weeb, it'd be a dream come true."

Charlie Weeb said, "Eddie, it *will* come true. I'm trucking in some big fucking bass from Alabama. They're yours, partner."

"Wait a minute."

"With the water this bad, I can't chance keeping the biggest ones in Lunker Lakes," Weeb said. He unrolled a map across the kitchen counter. "Here we are," he said, pointing, "and here's the Everglades dike. All you got to do is tie the boat at the culvert, hop the levee, and pull the cages."

"Cages—fish cages?"

"No, *tiger* cages, Eddie—Christ, what do you think?"

Eddie Spurling said, "I ain't gone cheat."

"Pardon me?"

"Lookit, I'll scout the lakes and dump some brush piles a few days ahead. Stock 'em with bass before tournament day and mark the spots. Hell, everybody does that—how about it?"

Charlie Weeb shook his head. "The fish will croak, Eddie, that's the problem. I got two thousand yearlings coming in the night before and I'll be lucky if they hang on until dusk. Worse comes to worst, you might be the only guy in the tournament to bring in a live bass."

"But I ain't gone cheat."

Reverend Weeb smiled patiently. "Eddie, you just bought that big place outside Tuscaloosa—what, sixty acres, something like that. And I notice your wife's driving a new Eldorado . . . well, Eddie, I look at you and see a man who's enjoying himself, am I right? I see a man who likes being number one, for a change. Some men get a chance like this and they blow it—think of Dickie Lockhart."

Eddie Spurling didn't want to think about that fool Dickie Lockhart. What happened to Dickie Lockhart was a damn fluke. Eddie ground his Red Man to a soggy pulp. "You got a place I could spit this?" he asked.

"The sink is fine," Weeb said. Angrily Eddie Spurling drilled the wad straight into the disposal.

"So what's it gonna be," Charlie Weeb said. "You want to be a star, or not?"

Later that afternoon, Deacon Johnson knocked on the door to Reverend Weeb's private office. Inside, Reverend Weeb was getting a vigorous back rub and dictating a Sunday sermon for transcription.

"Who you got lined up for the healing?" Weeb grunted, the masseuse kneading his freckled shoulder blades.

"No kids," Deacon Johnson reported glumly. "Florida's different from Louisiana, Charles. The state welfare office threatened to shut us down if we use any kids on the show."

"Pagan assholes!"

Charlie Weeb had planned a grand healing for the morning of the big bass tournament. A lavish pulpit was being constructed as part of the weigh station.

"Now what?" he said.

"I'm going down to the VA tomorrow to look for some cripples," Deacon Johnson said.

"Not real cripples?"

"No," said the deacon. "With some of the vets, it comes and goes. They stub their toe, they get a wheelchair—it's all in their head. I think we can find one to play along."

"Be careful," Reverend Weeb said. "All we need is some fruitcake Rambo flashing back to Nam on live TV."

"Don't worry," Deacon Johnson said. "Charles, I thought you'd like to hear some good news."

"Absolutely."

Deacon Johnson said, "The tournament's full. Today we got our fiftieth boat."

"Thank God." The hundred-fifty grand in entry fees would almost cover costs. "Anybody famous?" Weeb asked.

"No, couple of brothers," Deacon Johnson said. "In fact, Eddie said he never even heard of them. Tile is the name. James and Chico."

The preacher chuckled and rolled over on his back. "Long as the check cleared," he said.

Catherine was astonished when they went through the Golden Glades interchange and the toll-booth lady hardly looked twice at Lucas.

"I can't believe it," Catherine said as they drove away.

Behind the wheel, Thomas Curl scowled. "What the hell *would* she say?"

When they had pulled up to the booth, Curl had reached out with his dog-headed arm to get the ticket. The toll-booth lady glanced benignly at the pit bull, which was decomposing rather noticeably.

"Have a nice day," the toll-booth lady said. "I'm all out of Milk-bones."

"Thanks just the same," said Thomas Curl, driving on.

He had named the dead dog head Lucas.

"Why not Luke?" Catherine asked.

"What a dumb name for a dog."

Thomas Curl held the pistol tightly with his left hand; that's why he'd had to reach for the toll ticket with his right arm, the dog arm. That's the one he steered with. Catherine could see that it was grossly swollen with infection. The pus-lathered flesh had turned gray, with lightning streaks of crimson.

"You should see a doctor."

"After I see Dennis," Thomas Curl said. "And after I see your goddamn husband." Curl was sweating like a pig.

Catherine said, "He's not my husband anymore."

"I still plan to kill him, on account of Lemus."

"See if I care," said Catherine, staring out the window, seemingly enjoying the ride.

Thomas Curl didn't know what to make of her. The girl should have been frightened to death.

"Wait'll he finds out where you are."

"Decker? What makes you think he still cares?" she bluffed.

Thomas Curl laughed coarsely. "He's only got about a million fucking pitchers."

"Of me?"

"Fucking A. Under the bed, in the closet, probably in his underpants drawer too. Didn't you know that?"

Catherine didn't know about the pictures. She wondered which ones R.J. had kept, which ones he liked best.

"My husband's a doctor. He could take a look at that arm when he gets back tonight." Another bluff. James would have passed out at the sight.

"No way," Thomas said. "We're headed for Lauderdale." He looked down at the dog head and smiled. "Ain't that right, Lucas boy?"

Catherine was not surprised when Lucas made no reply, but Thomas Curl frowned unhappily. "Lucas, you hear me? Goddammit, puppy, speak!"

The festering dog head clung mutely to his arm.

Thomas Curl shoved the barrel of the pistol into one of the animal's piebald ears.

"Please don't," Catherine cried, raising her arms.

No longer paying even cursory attention to the highway, Thomas glared down at Lucas and bared his own teeth. "My daddy said you got to show 'em who's boss. Dogs is like wives, he said, you can't let 'em have their way once else they run wild. Ain't that right, Lucas boy?"

Again nothing.

Thomas Curl cocked the pistol. "Bad dog, Lucas!"

Catherine covered her mouth and let out a muffled little bark.

Curl grinned and leaned closer. "Hear that?"

Catherine barked again. It was better than having him fire a gun inside the car, doing seventy.

"That's my puppy," Curl said, oblivious. He laid the pistol in his lap and patted the crown of the dead dog's head. "You good boy, Lucas, I knew all along."

"Ruff!" said Catherine.

Skink netted more shiners and made Al García practice with the fish until nearly dawn. Finally they let the monster-beastie rest, and Skink rowed back across Lake Jesup. As they dragged the skiff ashore, García noticed two cars parked behind Skink's truck at the shack. One belonged to Trooper Jim Tile. The other was a tangerine Corvette.

"Company," Skink said, removing his raincap.

The four of them were sitting around the campfire: Decker, Tile, Lanie Gault, and a woman whom Skink did not recognize. Decker introduced her as Ellen O'Leary.

"How's the eye?" Jim Tile asked.

Skink grinned and took off his sunglasses. "Good as new," he said. Everyone felt obliged to say something nice about the owl eye.

"You hungry?" Skink said. "I'll take the truck and find some breakfast."

"We hit the Mister Donut on the way in," Decker said.

"Thank you anyway," Lanie added.

Skink nodded. "I am, sort of," he said. "Hungry, I mean. You please move the cars?"

"Take mine," Lanie said, fishing the keys out of her jeans. "Better yet, I'll go with you."

"Like hell," Decker said.

"I don't mind," said Skink, "if you don't."

"No more rope tricks," Lanie said. It was her cockteasing voice; Decker recognized it. She got in the passenger side of the Corvette. Skink squeezed himself behind the wheel.

"Hope she likes possum omelets," Decker said.

Skink and Lanie were gone a long time.

Al García told Decker the plan, beginning with: "The man's totally crazy."

"Thanks for the bulletin."

Jim Tile said, "He knows about things. You can trust him."

Skink's plan was to crash the big bass tournament and ruin it. His plan was to sabotage the Lunker Lakes resort on national television.

García said to Jim Tile: "You and me are fishing together."

"In the tournament?"

"He's already paid our entry fee," García said. "The best part is, we're supposed to be *hermanos*. Brothers."

Jim Tile shook his head. He was smiling. "I like it. I don't know why, but I do."

In a faint voice Ellen O'Leary said, "You don't look that much alike."

"In the eyes we do," García said, straight-faced. "This is going to be fun."

"Fun" is not the word R. J. Decker would have chosen. Things had gotten dangerously out of hand; suddenly a one-eyed roadside carnivore with possible brain damage was running the whole program. Even more astounding, García was going along with it. Decker couldn't imagine what could have happened while he and Jim Tile were up at Crescent Beach.

"This is all fascinating," Decker said, "and I wish both of you the best of luck in the tournament, but my immediate problem is Dennis Gault. Murder-one, remember?"

By way of interagency updating, Jim Tile said to García: "The sister is taken care of. As a state's witness, forget it." He held up the tape cassette.

"Good work," García said. He turned to Ellen O'Leary. "What about you, miss?"

Ellen looked worriedly at Jim Tile. The trooper said, "She can put Tom Curl with Dickie Lockhart right before the murder."

"Not bad," García said. "R.J., I can't figure what you're so worked up about. Sounds to me like an easy *nolle prosse*."

"If you don't mind," Decker said. "Gault set me up on a murder charge. He also arranged to kill my friend Ott. At this very moment he's got some halfwit redneck hitman out looking for me. I would prefer not to wait three or four months for the New Orleans district attorney to settle the issue."

García raised a fleshy brown hand. "Yeah, I hear you, *chico*. Why don't I just pop big Mr. Gault at the fish tournament? Irritate the hell out of him, wouldn't it?"

"Good TV, too," Jim Tile remarked.

"Pop him for what?" Decker asked.

García paused to light a cigarette. "Filing false information, for starters. He lied to me—I don't like that. Obstruction, that's another good one. I haven't used it in years, so why not."

Decker said, "It's chickenshit, Al."

"Better than nothing," Jim Tile said.

García watched a blue smoke ring float into the oaks. "Best I can do," he said, "until we find Tom Curl and have a serious chat with the boy."

"You think he'll flip?" Decker said.

"Sure." Al García smiled. "If I ask real nice."

Skink jacked the Corvette up to ninety on the Gilchrist. He felt obliged to do it, seeing as how he'd probably never get another chance. It truly was quite a car. He loved the way its snout sucked up the road.

In the passenger seat Lanie tucked her long legs beneath her bottom and turned sideways to watch him drive. Skink didn't like being watched, but he said nothing. It had been a long time since he had shared a moment with a beautiful woman; that was one price of hermitage. He remembered how good judgment went out the window in such times, so he warned himself to be careful, there was work to do. His head was killing him, too; the pain had returned as soon as he'd gotten off the lake. A specialist was out of the question. There was no time.

Lanie popped a Whitney Houston tape in the cassette player and started keeping time with her bare feet. Without looking away from the road, Skink reached over and jerked the tape out of the dash. Then he threw it out the window.

"Got any Creedence?" he said.

In the seat Lanie whirled and, through the rear window, watched Whitney Houston bounce and shatter and unspool on the highway. "You're crazy," she snapped at Skink. "You're buying me a new tape, buster."

Skink wasn't paying attention. He had spotted something far ahead in the road; a motionless brown lump. He started braking the sports car, pumping slowly so it wouldn't leave rubber or spin out. When it finally came to a stop on the shoulder, he flicked on the emergency flashers and got out. He made sure to take the keys.

The thing in the road was a dead armadillo. After a brief examination Skink carried it by its scaly tail back to the Corvette.

Lanie was aghast. Skink tossed the carcass in the back and started the car.

"Ever had one?"

Lanie shook her head violently.

"Makes one hell of a gumbo," he said. "Use the shell as a tureen, if you do it right. Holds about two gallons."

Lanie leaned back to see where the armadillo had landed, how much of a mess had been made on the upholstery.

"It's fresh, don't worry," Skink said. He wheeled the Corvette around and headed back.

"Okay, who are you? Really."

Skink said, "You've seen who I am."

"Before this," Lanie said. "You must have been . . . *somebody*. I mean, you didn't grow up on roadkills."

"Unfortunately, no."

Lanie said, "I like you. Your hands especially. The day we first met I noticed them, when you were tying me with that plastic rope."

"Fishing line," Skink said, "not rope. I'm glad there's no hard feelings."

"You can't blame me for being curious."

"Sure I can. It's none of your damn business who I am."

"Shit," Lanie said, "you're impossible."

Skink hit the brakes hard and downshifted. The sports car fishtailed severely and spun off the Gilchrist and came to rest in a field of crackling dry pastureland.

"My Vette is now parked in cowshit," Lanie observed, more perturbed than frightened.

Skink took his hands off the steering wheel.

"Want to know who I am? I'm the guy who had a chance to save this place, only I blew it."

"Save what?"

Skink made a circular gesture. "Everything. Everything that counts for anything. I'm the guy that could have saved it, but instead I ran. So there's your answer."

"Clue me in, please."

"Don't worry, it's ancient history."

Lanie said, "Were you famous or something?"

Skink just laughed. He couldn't help it.

"What's so funny?" she asked. He had a terrific smile, no doubt about it.

"No more damn questions."

"Just one," Lanie said, moving in. "How about a kiss?"

It didn't stop at just one, and it didn't stop with just kissing. Skink was impressed by both her energy and agility—unless you had circus experience, it wasn't easy getting naked in the bucket seat of a Corvette. Skink himself tore the inseam of his orange weathersuit in the struggle. Lanie had better luck with her jeans and panties; somehow she even got her long bare legs wrapped around him. Skink admired her tan, and said so. She hit a button and the seat slid down to a full recline.

Once she was on top Lanie allowed her breasts to brush back and forth against Skink's cheeks. She looked down and saw that he seemed to be enjoying himself. His huge boots were braced against the dashboard.

"What do you like?" she asked.

"Worldly things."

"You got it," Lanie said. "We're going to do it and then we're going to lie here together and talk, all right?"

"Sure."

She pressed down hard and began to rock her hips. "Get to know each other a little better."

"Fine idea," Skink said.

Then she leaned down, snuck her tongue in his ear, and said, "Leave the sunglasses on, okay?"

Even for Lanie Gault, the owl eye would have been a glaring distraction.

Later that afternoon, after Lanie was gone and Jim Tile had stashed Ellen O'Leary at his apartment, Skink took the truck to town. He came back towing a dented old boat trailer with a sagging rusty axle. In the flatbed of the pickup truck was a six-horsepower Mercury outboard that had seen brighter days. There was also a plastic forty-gallon garbage bucket, eight feet of aquarium tubing, and four dozen D-size batteries, which Skink had purchased at Harney Hardware.

He was fiddling with his trash-bucket contraption when Decker came up and said, "Why'd you let her go?"

"No reason to keep her."

To Decker the reason seemed obvious. "She'll run straight to her brother."

"And tell him what?"

"Where I am, for starters."

"You won't be here that long," Skink said. "We're all heading south. Jim Tile and the Cuban—they been practicing?"

"All day," Decker said. "García's hopeless."

"He can play captain, then."

Decker needed to ask something else but he didn't want to set Skink off.

"She doesn't know the plan, does she?"

It was another way of asking what had happened in the Corvette. Skink clearly didn't want to talk about it.

"Some of us know how to get laid with our mouths shut," he said sourly. "No, she doesn't know the damn plan."

Decker was getting ominous vibrations; maybe the beating in Delray had loosened a few more bolts in the big man's brainpan. Skink was forever pulling guns, and he looked like he wanted to pull one now. Decker asked Jim Tile for a ride to town, to make some phone calls. Al García went along; he was out of cigarettes.

"Town's a bad idea," Jim Tile said, heading away from Harney on Route 222. "The three of us shouldn't be seen together. There's a Zippy Mart about eight miles along here."

Decker said, "This idea of his . . . I don't know, Jim."

"It's his last chance," the trooper said. "You saw how bad he looks."

"Then let's get him to a hospital."

"It's not the eye, Decker. Or what those kids did to him. He's all beat up inside. He's done it to himself, you understand? Been doing it for years."

Al García leaned forward in the back seat and said, "What's the harm, R.J.? The man wants to make a point."

Decker said, "Skink I almost understand. But why are you guys going along?"

"Maybe we got a point to make, too," Jim Tile said.

After that, Decker left it alone.

"Relax," García told him. "Couple old road cops like us need a break in the monotony, that's all."

At the Zippy Mart, Jim Tile waited in the car while García went to buy his cigarettes and Decker used the pay phone. It had been several days since he had left Miami and, assuming he'd still have to make a living when this case was over, he thought it a wise idea to check his messages. He dialed his number, then punched the playback code for the tape machine.

The first voice made him wince. Lou Zicutto from the insurance company: "Hey, douche-bag, you're lucky Núñez came down with mono. We got a two-week postponement from the judge, so this time no excuses—be there with your negatives. Otherwise just go ahead and buy yourself some fucking crutches, got it?"

What a prince to work for.

Decker didn't recognize the second voice, didn't need to: "I got your wife, Mr. Decker, and she's just as pretty as the pitchers. So we're gonna trade: her tight little ass for yours. Call me . . . make it Friday at the Holiday Inn, Coral Springs. We'll be registered Mr. and Mrs. Juan Gómez."

Decker hung up and sagged against the wall.

Al García, who'd come out of the store whistling, grabbed Decker by the arm. "What is it, man?"

Jim Tile came up and took the other side.

"He's got Catherine," Decker said tonelessly.

"Fuck." García spit on the pavement.

"It's Tom Curl," said the trooper.

R. J. Decker sat on the fender of Jim Tile's car and said nothing for five minutes, just stared at the ground. Finally he looked up at the other two men.

"Is there a place around here to buy a camera?" he asked.

When they got back to Lake Jesup, Jim Tile told Skink what Thomas Curl had done.

The big man sat down heavily on the tailgate of the truck and wrapped his arms around his head. R. J. Decker took a step forward but Jim Tile motioned him back.

After a few moments Skink looked up and said, "It's my fault, Miami."

"It's nobody's fault."

"I'm the one who shot—"

"It's nobody's fault," Decker said again, "so shut up." The less said about Lemus Curl, the better. Especially in the presence of cops.

Skink pulled painfully at his beard. "This could screw up everything," he said hoarsely.

"I would say so," Al García grunted.

Skink took off the sunglasses. His good eye was red and moist. He gazed at Decker, and in a small brittle voice, said: "The plan can't be changed, it's too late."

"Do what you have to," Decker said.

"I'll kill him afterward," Skink said, "I promise."

"Thanks anyway, but it won't come to that."

"This thing—" Skink paused, raked feverishly at his beard. He was boiling inside. He pounded his fists against the fender of the truck. "This thing I have to do—it's so important."

Decker said, "I know, captain."

"You'd understand better if you knew everything." Skink spoke solemnly. "If you knew it all, then you'd see the point."

"It's all right," Decker said. "Go ahead with your plan. I've got one of my own."

Skink grinned and clapped his hands. "That's the spirit!" he said. "That's what I like to hear."

Al García and Jim Tile exchanged doubtful glances. In its own way, R. J. Decker's scheme was every bit as loony as Skink's.

Like a surgeon inspecting his instruments, Dennis Gault laid out his tournament bass tackle on the pile carpet and took inventory: six Bantam Magnumlite 2000 GT plugging reels, eight Shimano rods, four graphite Ugly Stiks, three bottles of Happy Gland bass scent, a Randall knife, two cutting stones, Sargent stainless pliers, a diamond-flake hook sharpener, Coppertone sunblock, a telescopic landing net, two pairs of Polaroid sunglasses (amber and green), a certified Chatillion scale and, of course, his tacklebox. The tacklebox was the suitcase-size Plano Model 7777, with ninety separate compartments. As was everything in Dennis Gault's tournament artillery, his bass lures were brand-new. For top-water action he had stocked up on Bang-O-Lures, Shad Raps, Slo Dancers, Hula Poppers, and Zara Spooks; for deep dredging he had armed himself with Wee Warts and Whopper Stoppers and the redoubtable Lazy Ike. For brushpiles he had unsheathed the Jig-N-Pig and Double Whammy, the Bayou Boogie and Eerie Dearie, plus a rainbow trove of Mister Twisters. As for that most reliable of bass rigs, the artificial worm, Dennis Gault had amassed three gooey pounds. He had caught fish on every color, so he packed them all: the black-grape crawdad, the smoke-sparkle lizard, the flip-tail purple daddy, the motor-oil moccasin, the blueberry gollywhomper, everything.

Gault arranged them lovingly; there was plenty of room.

The most critical decision, the one over which he pondered longest, was what strength fishing line to put on the reels. Good line is paramount; the slenderest of plastic threads, it is all that ties the angler to his wild and precious trophy. The longer a bass stays on the line, the greater its chances of escape. Since every fish that breaks off or throws the hook is money down the drain, the goal of the professional bass angler is to lose no fish whatsoever. Consequently, in tournaments there is not even the pretense of an actual battle between fisherman and fish. The brutish deep dives and graceful acrobatics of a hooked largemouth bass are not tolerated in the heat of serious angling competition. In fact, the standard strategy is to strike the fish with all your might and then drag the stunned creature into the boat as rapidly as possible. In tournaments it is not uncommon to see five-pound bass being skipped helplessly across the water in this manner.

Obviously, heavy line was essential. For the Dickie Lockhart Memorial Classic, Dennis Gault selected a twenty-pound pink Andes monofilament—limp enough to cast the lure a modest distance in a light wind, yet sturdy enough to straighten the spine of any mortal largemouth.

Gault was ironing a Bass Blasters patch onto the crown of his cap when the phone rang. It was Lanie, calling from a truck stop halfway between Harney and Fort Lauderdale.

"Ellen O'Leary is gone," she said. "Decker came to the condo and got her."

"Nice work," her brother said snidely.

"What'd you expect me to do? He had that big black guy with him, the trooper."

Gault was determined not to let anything spoil the tournament for him.

"Don't worry about it," he said.

"What about New Orleans?" Lanie asked.

"Forget about it," Gault said, "and forget about Decker. Tom Curl is taking care of it."

Lanie knew what that meant, but she swept the thought from her mind. She pretended it meant nothing. "Dennis, I told them about the affidavit, about how I lied."

She thought he would be furious, but instead he said: "It doesn't really matter."

Lanie wanted Dennis to say something more, but he didn't. She wanted to hear all about the tournament, what tackle he planned to use, where he'd be staying. She wanted him at least to sound pleased that she'd called, but he sounded only bored. With Dennis, everything was business.

"I've got to pack," he said.

"For the tournament?"

"Right."

"Could I come along?"

"Not a good idea, Elaine. Lots of tension, you know."

"But I have a surprise."

"And what might that be?"

"Not much, big brother. Just a tip that'll guarantee you win the Lockhart Memorial."

"Really, Elaine." But she had him hooked.

Lanie said, "You know of a man they call Skink?"

"Yes. He's crazy as a bedbug."

"I don't think so."

There was an edgy pause on the other end of the line. Dennis Gault was thinking sordid and unpleasant thoughts about his sister and the hermit. He wondered where his mother had gone wrong raising Elaine.

"Dennis, he's got a huge fish."

"Is that what he calls it? His fish?"

Lanie said, "Be that way. Be an asshole."

"Finish your fairy tale."

"He's raised this giant mutant bass, he's very proud of it. He makes it sound like a world record or something."

"I seriously doubt that."

Lanie said, "Then later he mentions he's got friends fishing in this tournament."

"*Later?* You mean after tea and crumpets?"

"Drop it, Dennis. It wasn't exactly easy getting this guy to open up. He'd make Charles Bronson seem like the life of the party."

"What else did he say?"

"That he and the fish were going on a trip this weekend."

Gault snorted. "He and the fish. You mean like a date?"

Lanie let him think about it. Dennis Gault didn't take a long time.

"He's going to plant the bass at Lunker Lakes," he said, "so his friends can win the tournament."

"That's what I figured."

"Not a bad day's work, even if you've got to split the prize money three ways."

"Instead of just two," Lanie said.

"What?"

"You and me, half and half," she said, "if you win with Skink's fish."

Dennis Gault had to laugh. She was something, his sister. If she were a man, she'd have steel ones.

"Deal?" Lanie said.

"Sure, fifty-fifty." Gault really didn't give a damn about the money anyway.

"I'm not riding in it," Al García said.

"It's all I could find, with a trailer hitch," Jim Tile explained.

García said, "It's a fucking garbage truck, Jim. An eleven-ton diesel garbage truck!"

"It's perfect," Skink said. "It's you."

He had strapped the wooden skiff to the secondhand trailer; even with the outboard engine it was a light load. He one-handed the tongue of the trailer and snapped it down on the ball of the hitch.

García stared in dismay. The peeling old boat was bad enough by itself, but hitched to the rump of a garbage truck it looked like a flea-market special. "Gypsies wouldn't ride in this fucking caravan," the detective said. "What happened to your cousin's lawn truck?"

"Axle broke," said Jim Tile.

"Then let's rent a regular pickup."

"No time," Skink said.

"Then let's all ride with you," García said.

"No way," Skink said. "We can't be seen together down there. From this moment on, you don't know me, I don't know you. Bass is the name of the game, no socializing. It's just you and Jim Tile, brothers. That's all."

García said, "What if something happens—how do we reach you?"

"I'll be aware. You got the map?"

"Yep." To demonstrate, García patted a trouser pocket.

"Good. Now, remember, get one of those big Igloos."

"I know, the sixty-gallon job."

"Right. And an aquarium pump."

Jim Tile said, "We've got it all written down."

Skink smiled tiredly. "So you do." He tucked his ropy gray braid down the back of his weather jacket. The trooper had advised him to do this to reduce his chances of getting pulled over for no reason on the Turnpike; long hair was a magnet for cops.

As Skink climbed into the truck, he said, "Decker make his phone call?"

"Yeah," Jim Tile said, "he's already gone."

"God, that's the one thing I'm worried about," Skink said. "I really like that boy." He pulled the raincap tight on his skull. He lifted the sunglasses just enough to fit a finger underneath, working the owl eye back into its socket.

"How you feeling?" Jim Tile asked.

"Better and better. Thanks for asking. And you, Señor Smartass Cuban, remember—"

"I'll be gentle with her, governor, don't worry."

"—because if she dies, I'll have to kill somebody."

With that Skink started the ignition, and the truck jostled down the dirt cattle path toward the Mormon Trail.

Tied upright in the flatbed was the big plastic garbage pail, criss-crossed with ropes and elastic bungy cords. Fastened crudely to the top of the pail was a battery-powered pump, obviously rebuilt, from which sprouted clear life-giving tubes. Inside the plastic container was precisely thirty gallons of Lake Jesup's purest, and in that agitated but freshly oxygenated water was the fish called Queenie, flaring her fins, jawing silent fulminations. The hugest largemouth bass in all the world.

After they checked in at the motel, Thomas Curl told Catherine to take off her clothes. She got as far as her bra and panties and said that was it.

"I want you nekked," Curl said, brandishing the pistol. "That way you won't run off."

Catherine said, "It's too cold."

Curl got a thin woolen blanket from the closet and threw it at her. "Now," he said.

Catherine fingered the blanket. "Awfully scratchy," she complained.

Thomas Curl cocked the pistol. He didn't aim it directly at her, but- pointed it up, drawn back over his left shoulder, gunslinger-style. "Strip," he said.

Reluctantly she did as she was told. The fact that Thomas Curl's minimal brain was racked by infection weighed heavily in Catherine's decision. Anyone else she would have tried to talk out of it, but this was not a well person; he had become febrile, rambling, alternately manic and torpid. He had given up all attempts to prize the dead dog head from his arm. It was his friend now.

Thomas Curl watched intently as Catherine wrapped herself twice around in the blanket and sat down at the head of her bed.

"You got the nicest tits," he said.

"Bet you say that to all your kidnap victims."

"I think I might like to poke you."

"Some other night," said Catherine.

Slowly, like a sleepy chameleon, Thomas Curl closed his puffy eyes by degrees. His head drooped to one side, and would have drooped even more except that his temple came to rest on the muzzle of the pistol. For a moment Catherine was sure she'd be rinsing brains out of her hair, but abruptly Thomas Curl woke up. He uncocked the gun and slid it into his belt. With his dog arm he motioned to the telephone on the nightstand. "Call your doctor husband," he said. "Tell him everything's peachy."

Catherine dialed the number of the hotel in Montreal, but James was not in his room. She hung up.

"I'll try later," she said.

Unsteadily Thomas Curl made his way to the bed. The stench from the dead dog head was overpowering.

"Can we open a window?" Catherine asked.

"Lie down."

"What for?"

With his good arm he flattened her on the bed. Using torn strips of bed linen, he tied her to the mattress. Catherine was impressed by the strength of the knots, considering his limited dexterity.

Thomas Curl unplugged the phone and tucked it under his right arm. "Don't try nuthin' funny," he said to Catherine.

"Are you leaving?"

"Lucas has to go for a walk."

Catherine nodded.

"I'm taking the phone," said Curl.

"Could you pick up some food?" she asked. "I'm starving."

Thomas Curl threw R. J. Decker's coat over his shoulders. "Burger King'll have to do," he said.

"Wendy's has a salad bar," Catherine suggested.

"All right," Curl said, "Wendy's."

He wasn't very hungry. He picked at some french fries while Catherine ate her salad and sipped a Diet Coke. Curl had had so much trouble untying her that he'd just cut the linen with a pocket-knife.

"Did Lucas enjoy his walk?" she said.

"He was a good boy," Curl said, patting the dog head. "A good boy for daddy."

He put the phone back in the wall and told Catherine to try Montreal again. This time James answered.

"How's the convention?" Catherine said. "Lots of laughs?"

Thomas Curl moved close to her on the bed and took out the gun, as a reminder.

Catherine said to James: "Just so you won't worry, I'm going up to my sister's in Boca for a few days. In case you called home and I wasn't there." They talked for a few minutes about the weather and the encouraging advance orders for the electric vibrating chiropractic couch, and then Catherine said good-bye.

"That was good," Thomas Curl said, munching a cold french fry. "You like him as much as Decker?"

"James is a sweetheart," Catherine said. "If it's money you're after, he'd pay anything to get me back."

"It's not money I'm after."

"I know," she said.

"So now he won't be worried, your doctor won't? When you're not home?"

"No, he's having a ball," Catherine said. "He got interviewed for *Vertebrae Today*."

Curl burped.

"A chiropractic magazine," Catherine explained. She herself was not overwhelmed with excitement.

The phone rang. Catherine started to reach for it, but Curl thwacked her arm with the butt of the gun. When he answered, a man's voice said: "It's me. Decker."

"You here yet?"

"On the way," Decker said. He was at a service plaza in Fort Pierce, gassing up Al García's car.

"You ready to trade?"

"Absolutely," Decker said. "How's Mrs. Gómez?"

Curl put the receiver to Catherine's cheek. "Tell him you're fine," he said.

"R.J., I'm fine."

"Catherine, I'm sorry about this."

"It's okay—"

Curl snatched the phone back and said: "This is the way we're going to do it: a straight-up trade."

"Fair enough, but I choose the place."

"Fuck you, bubba."

"It's the only way, Tom. It's the only way I can make sure the lady walks free."

Curl rubbed his brow. He wanted to stand firm, but his mind could not assemble an argument. Every thought that entered his head seemed to sizzle and burn up in the fever. As Decker instructed him when and where to go, Thomas Curl repeated everything aloud in a thick, disconnected voice. Luckily Catherine jotted the directions on a Holiday Inn notepad, because Curl forgot everything the instant he hung up.

"Hungry, Lucas?" He opened the brown grocery bag. He had stopped at the store and bought the dog a little treat.

Catherine eyed the package. "Gaines Burgers?"

"His favorite," Curl said. He unwrapped one of the patties and mashed it between the dog's jaws, still fixed obdurately to his own arm. The red meat stuck to the animal's dried yellow fangs. "You like that, dontcha, boy?"

Catherine said, "He's not hungry, Tom. I can tell."

"Guess you're right," Curl said. "Must be all the traveling."

28

Deacon Johnson tapped lightly on the door. For once, Reverend Weeb was alone.

"Charles, you'd better come see."

"What now?" the preacher said irritably.

He followed Deacon Johnson out of the townhouse office, through the courtyard, down a sloping walk to a boat ramp on the newly sodded shore of Lunker Lake Number One. Many of the anglers had begun to arrive, so the ramp was crowded with needle-shaped bass boats, each attached to a big candy-colored Blazer, Jeep, or Bronco. In the midst of the gleaming congregation was an immense army-green garbage truck with a warped old skiff hitched to its bumper.

Two men leaned impassively against the truck; one was tall and muscular and black, the other roundish and Latin-looking. The rest of the bass fishermen studied the unusual newcomers from a distance, and chuckled in low tones.

Charlie Weeb approached the men and said, "If you're looking for the dump, it's out Road 84." He pointed west, toward the dike. "That way."

Jim Tile said, "We're here for the bass tournament."

"Is that right?" Weeb eyed the rowboat disdainfully. "Sorry, son, but this event's not open to the general public."

Al García said, "We're not the general public, son. We're the Tile

Brothers." Coolly he handed Charlie Weeb the receipt for the registration fee. Without a glance, Weeb passed it to Deacon Johnson.

"It's them, all right," Deacon Johnson reported. "Boat number fifty, all paid up."

"You don't look like brothers," Reverend Weeb said accusingly.

"*Sí, es verdad,*" Jim Tile said.

"Fo sho," added Al García. "We true be bros."

They had practiced the routine on the long ride down. Jim Tile had done much better learning Spanish than Al García had done learning jive. Still, it achieved the desired effect.

Charlie Weeb puckered his cheeks and anxiously ran a manicured hand through his perfect blond hair. "Gentlemen, excuse me for a sec," he said, and took Deacon Johnson aside.

"This is some fucking joke."

"It's no joke, Charles."

"Spic and spade brothers? I'd call that a joke." Weeb was spitting, he was so exasperated. "Izzy, tonight we're flying in one thousand loyal Christian prospective homesite buyers. I promised them to do a healing, I promised them to have some world-class bass fishing, and I promised to get their shining faces on national cable TV. All this, Izzy, in order to *sell some fucking lots.*"

"Keep your voice down, Charles." Even at a whisper, Reverend Weeb could rattle the china.

Deacon Johnson took him by the arm and edged away from the newcomers. Standing in the rank shadow of the garbage truck, Deacon Johnson said, "We've taken their money, Charles, we've got to let them fish."

"Screw the entry fee. Give it back."

"Oh fine," Deacon Johnson said, "and when the newspapers call, you explain why you did it."

The thought of bad publicity sent a cold razor down Charlie Weeb's spine.

Almost plaintively he said: "These folks I'm bringing down, Izzy, they don't want to see a spic and a spade in this family-oriented development. The folks at home who watch my show, they don't want to see 'em either. I'm not here to pass judgment, Izzy, I'm here for the demographics. Fact is, my people are the whitest of the white. Soon as they spot those two guys, that's the ball game. They'll think everything they heard about South Florida is true, niggers and Cubans everywhere. Even on the bass lakes."

Deacon Johnson said, "There's forty-nine other boats in this tournament, Charles. Just tell your camermen to stay off the little wooden one. As for the garbage truck, we'll park it out back in the construction lot. Loan these guys a decent rental car to get around the property. Anyone asks, tell 'em they work here."

"Good idea," Weeb said. "Say they pour asphalt or something. Excellent." Sometimes he didn't know what he'd do without Izzy.

Deacon Johnson said, "Don't worry, Charles, just look at them— they don't have a chance. It'll be a holy miracle if that termite bucket doesn't sink at the dock."

All Charlie Weeb could say was: "Whoever heard of a spic and a spade in a pro bass tournament?"

But the mysterious Tile Brothers were already putting their boat in the water.

The next day was practice day, and in keeping with tradition the anglers gathered early at the boat ramp to exchange theories and cultivate possible excuses. Because no one had fished Lunker Lakes before, the talk was basically bullshit and idle speculation. The bass would be schooled by the culverts. No, they'd be holding deep. No, they'd be bedded in the shallows.

Only Charlie Weeb and his men knew the truth: there were no bass except dead ones. The new ones were on the way.

Eddie Spurling realized that something was terribly wrong, but he didn't say a word. Instead of mingling with his pals over coffee and biscuits, he strolled the shore alone in the predawn pitch. A couple of the other pros sidled up to make conversation, but Eddie was unresponsive and gloomy. He didn't show the least interest in Duke Puffin's deep-sonic crankbait or Tom Jericho's new weedless trolling motor.

While the mockingbirds announced sunrise, Eddie Spurling just stared out at the still brown canals and thought: This water's no damn good.

Al García and Jim Tile were the last to get started. They'd been briefly delayed when Billie Radcliffe, a very white young man from Waycross, Georgia, said to Jim Tile: "Where's your cane pole, Uncle Remus?" Jim Tile had felt compelled to explain the importance of good manners to Billie Radcliffe, by way of breaking every single fishing rod in Billie Radcliffe's custom-made bass boat. This had been done in a calm and methodical way, and with no interference, since

Al García and his Colt Python had supervised the brief ceremony. From then on, the other fishermen steered clear of the Tile Brothers.

It was just as well. All the practice at Lake Jesup had been in vain: Al García proved to be the world's most dangerous bass angler. On four occasions he snagged Jim Tile's scalp with errant casts. Three other times he hooked himself, once so severely that Jim Tile had to cut the barbs off the hooks just to remove them from García's thigh.

Casting a heavy plug rod required a sensitive thumb, but invariably García would release the spool too early or too late. Either he would fire the lure straight into the bottom of the boat, where it shattered like a bullet, or he would launch it straight up in the air, so it could plummet dangerously down on their heads. In the few instances when the detective actually managed to hit the water, Jim Tile put down his fishing rod and applauded. They both agreed that Al García should concentrate on steering the boat.

With the puny six-horse outboard, it took them longer to get around the canals, but by midday they reached the spot Skink had told them about, at the far western terminus of Lunker Lake Number Seven. Charlie Weeb's landscapers had not yet reached this boundary of the development, so the shores remained as barren white piles of dredged-up fill. The canal ended at the old earthen dike that separated the lush watery Florida Everglades from concrete civilization. Charlie Weeb had pushed it to the brink. This was the final barrier.

Jim Tile and Al García had the Number Seven hole to themselves, as Skink had predicted they would. It was too sparse, too bright, and too remote for the other bassers.

García nudged the skiff to shore, where Jim Tile got out and collected several armfuls of dead holly branches from a heap left by the bulldozers. Hidden under a tarp in the boat were three wooden orange crates, which they had brought from Harney in the bin of the garbage truck. García tied the crates together while Jim Tile stuffed the dead branches between the slats. Together they lowered the crates into the water. With a fishing line, Al García measured the depth at thirteen feet. He marked the secret spot by placing two empty Budweiser cans on the bank.

This was to be Queenie's home away from home.

"Oldest trick in the book," Skink had told the detective two nights before. "These big hawgs love obstructions. Lay back invisible in the bush, sucking down dumb minnows. Find the brushpile, you find the fish. Make the brushpile, you win the damn tournament."

That was the plan.

Jim Tile and Al García felt pretty good about pulling it off; there wasn't another boat in sight.

There was, however, a private helicopter.

The Tile Brothers hadn't bothered to look up, since it flew over only once.

But once was all that Dennis Gault's pilot needed to mark his map. Then he flew back to the heliport to radio his boss.

That evening, after the practice day, the mood at the boat ramp ranged from doubtful to downhearted. No one had caught a single bass, though none of the fishermen would admit it. It was more than a matter of pride—it was the mandatory furtiveness of competition. With two hundred and fifty thousand dollars at stake, lifelong friendships and fraternal confidences counted for spit. No intelligence was shared; no strategies compared; no secrets swapped. As a result, nobody comprehended the full scope of the fishless disaster that was named Lunker Lakes. While scouting the shoreline, a few anglers had come across dead yearling bass, and privately mulled the usual theories—nitrogen runoff, phosphate dumping, algae blooms, pesticides. Still, it wasn't the few dead fish as much as the absence of live ones that disturbed the contestants; as the day wore on, optimism evaporated. These were the best fishermen in the country, and they knew bad water when they saw it. All morning the men tried to mark fish on their Humminbird sonars, but all that showed was a deep gray void. The banks were uniformly steep, the bottom uniformly flat, and the lakes uniformly lifeless. Even Dennis Gault was worried, though he had an ace up his L. L. Bean sleeve.

At dusk the anglers returned to the boat ramp to find banners streaming, canned country music blaring, and an elaborate rectangular stage rising—a pink pulpit at one end, the bass scoreboard at the other. The whole stage was bathed by hot kliegs while the OCN cameramen conducted their lighting checks. Over the pulpit hung a red-lettered banner that said: "JESUS IN YOUR LIVING ROOM—LIVE AT FIVE!" And over the scoreboard hung a blue-lettered banner that said: "Lunker Lakes Presents the Dickie Lockhart Memorial Bass Blasters Classic." Every possible camera angle was cluttered with the signs and logos of the various sponsors who had put up the big prize money.

Once all the bass boats had returned to the dock, the Reverend Charles Weeb ambled centerstage with a cordless microphone.

"Greeting, sportsmen!"

The tired anglers grumbled halfheartedly.

"Understand it was tough fishing out there today, but don't you worry!" shouted Charlie Weeb. "The Lord tells me tomorrow's gonna be one hell of a day!"

The PA system amplified the preacher's enthusiasm, and the fishermen smiled and applauded, though not energetically.

"Yes, sir," Charlie Weeb said, "I talked to the Lord this afternoon, and the Lord said: 'Tomorrow will be good. Tomorrow the hawgs will be hungry!'"

Duke Puffin shouted, "Did he say to use buzzbaits or rubber worms?"

The bass fishermen roared, and Reverend Weeb grinned appreciatively. Anything to loosen the jerks up.

"As you know," he said, "tonight is barbecue night at Lunker Lakes. Ribs, chicken, Okeechobee catfish, and all the beer you can drink!"

The free-food announcement drew the first sincere applause of the evening.

"So," Reverend Weeb continued, "I got two air-conditioned buses ready to take y'all to the clubhouse. Have a good time tonight, get plenty of rest, and tomorrow you put some big numbers on that bass board, because the whole country'll be watching!"

Eagerly the anglers filed onto the buses. Jim Tile and Al García made a point of sitting in the very front. No one spoke a word to them.

As soon as the buses pulled away, Weeb tossed the microphone to an OCN technician, grabbed the young hydrologist backstage, and said: "It's here, I hope."

"Yes, sir, just give the word."

To the grips Weeb yelled: "Turn those kliegs around! Light the ramp—hurry up, asshole, while we're still young!"

Out of the settling darkness a gleaming steel tanker truck appeared. Although it looked like an ordinary oil-company truck, it was not. The driver backed cautiously down the slick boat ramp, and three feet from water's edge he braked the tanker with a gaseous hiss.

"Nice park job," the hydrologist said.

The driver hopped out waving a clipboard.

"Two thousand fresh basserinos," he said. "Who signs for these?"

After the barbecue Jim Tile and Al García drove the loaner car back to the lodge, where they got the bad news.

The raid had failed.

The Broward SWAT team had swept with lethal certainty into Room 1412 of the Coral Springs Holiday Inn and brusquely arrested one Mr. Juan Gómez, suspected kidnapper. Unfortunately he turned out to be a genuine Juan Gómez, computer software salesman. Furthermore, the young lady he had been diddling in his motel room turned out not to be the missing Catherine Stuckameyer, but rather the nineteen-year-old daughter of the founder of Floppy World, one of Juan Gómez's biggest retail clients.

By the time the confusion was sorted out and the SWAT team returned to the Holiday Inn, the other Juan Gómez, the one whose real name was Thomas Curl, had fled his room for parts unknown. Evidence technicians spent hours analyzing the Gaines Burger particles.

Al García had arranged the raid without telling R. J. Decker, who had fiercely rejected the idea of a police rescue attempt. He had insisted on handling Thomas Curl himself because Catherine's life was at stake, so Jim Tile and Al García had backed off and pretended to go along with it. As soon as Decker left Harney, García got on the phone to his lieutenant in Miami, who got on the phone to the Broward sheriff's office. There was a delay of several hours in the police bureaucracy, mainly because no Catherine Stuckameyer had officially been reported missing and the authorities suspected it was just another lonely rich wife skipping out. By the time the SWAT team moved, and found the right motel room, it was too late.

"They fucked it up," García said, slamming down the phone. "Can you believe it, now they're pissed off at me! Some pinhead *gringo* captain's saying I made 'em look bad, says there's still no evidence of a kidnap. Fucking GI Joes with their greasepaint and their M-16s hit the wrong damn room, it's not my fault."

"Meanwhile," Jim Tile said, "we've lost Curl, Decker's ex, and even Decker himself."

"So the hotshot gets his way after all. It's his ball game now."

García threw down his bass cap and cursed. "What the hell else can we do?"

"Go fishing," the trooper said. "That's all."

It was half-past midnight when someone knocked on the door of Dennis Gault's room. He couldn't imagine who it might be. He had elected not to stay at the Lunker Lakes Lodge with the others because all the parties would be raucous and distracting, and because the other anglers would ignore him as always. Besides, there was sawdust all over the carpets, and the walls reeked of fresh paint; obviously the place had been slapped together in about two weeks, just for the tournament.

So Gault had taken a suite at the Everglades Hilton, where he always stayed in Fort Lauderdale. Only Lanie, his secretaries, and a few lady friends knew where to find him. Which was why he was puzzled by the midnight visitor.

He listened at the door. From the other side came the sound of a man's labored breathing and a faint buzzing noise. "Who is it?"

"Me, Mr. Gault."

He recognized the voice. Angrily Gault opened the door, but what he saw stole his breath away. "Mother of Jesus!"

"Hey, chief," said Thomas Curl, "nice pajamas." He swayed in and crashed down into an armchair.

"Uh, Tom—"

"What's the matter, chief?"

Gault stared numbly. What could he say? Curl looked like death on a bad day. His eyes were swollen slits, his face streaked with purple. Sweat glistened on his gray forehead and a chowder-white ooze flecked the corners of his lips.

"What happened to you, Tom?"

"Mrs. Decker's safe in the trunk, don't worry." Curl wiped his mouth on the sleeve of his jacket. "Say, chief, those the shiniest damn pajamas I ever saw."

Dennis Gault's gaze fixed on Curl's right arm. "What . . . what the fuck is that?" he stammered.

"Lucas is his name," Curl said. "He good boy."

"Oh, Christ." Now Gault realized where the buzzing sound had come from. From the flies swarming around the dog head.

"I's raised around puppies," Curl said, "mostly mutts."

Gault said, "It's not good for you to be here."

"But I got a few hours to kill."

"Before you meet Decker?"

"Yep." Curl spotted a decanter of brandy on a sideboard. Mechanically Gault handed it to him. Curl drew three hard swallows from the bottle. His eyes glowed after he put it down. "I'll need a bass boat," he said, smacking his lips.

Gault scribbled a phone number on a napkin. "Here, this guy's got a Starcraft."

"Anything'll do."

"You all right?" Gault asked.

"I'll be fine. Clear this shit up once and for all." Curl noticed Gault's fishing gear laid out meticulously on the carpet. "Nice tackle, chief. Looks straight out of the catalog."

"Tom, you'd better go. I've got to be up early tomorrow."

"I ain't been sleepin much, myself. Lucas, he always wants to play."

Dennis Gault could scarcely breathe, the stink was so vile. "Call me day after tomorrow. I'll have a little something for you."

"Real good."

"One more thing, Tom, it's very important: everything's set for tonight, right? With Decker, I mean."

"Don't you worry."

Gault said, "You can handle it alone?"

"It's my rightful obligation."

At the door, Thomas Curl drunkenly thrust out his right hand. "Put her there, chief." Gault shook the rotted thing without daring to look.

"Well, tight lines!" said Curl, with a sloppy but spirited sailor's salute.

"Thank you, Tom," said Dennis Gault. He closed the door, dumped the brandy, then bolted into a scalding shower.

29

The phone calls started as soon as they turned in.

When Al García answered, the voice on the other end said: "Why don't you go back to Miami, spic-face?"

When Jim Tile answered, the message was: "Don't show your lips on the lake, nigger."

After the fourth call, García turned on the light and sat up in bed. "It's bad enough they give us the worst damn room in the place, and now this."

"Nice view of the dumpster, though," Jim Tile said. When he swung his bare brown legs out from under the covers, García noticed the bandage over Culver Rundell's bullet hole.

"It's nothing, just a through-and-through," the trooper said.

"One of these bass nuts?"

Jim Tile nodded.

"Well, shit," García said, "maybe we oughta take the phone calls more seriously."

"They're just trying to scare us."

The phone started ringing again. Jim Tile watched it for a full minute before picking up.

"You're gator bait, spook," the caller drawled.

The trooper hung up. His jaw was set and his eyes were hard. "I'm beginning to take this personally."

"You and me both." García grabbed his pants off the chair and dug around for the cigarette lighter. When the phone rang again, the detective said, "My turn."

Another Southern voice: "Lucky for you, grease floats."

García slammed down the receiver and said, "You'd think one of us would have the brains to pull the plug out of the wall."

"No," said Jim Tile. He was worried about Skink, and Decker. One of them might need to get through.

"I can't imagine these jerks are actually worried about us winning, not after seeing the boat," García said. "Wonder what they're so damn scared of."

"The sight of us," Jim Tile said. He lay back on his pillow and stared at the ceiling. García lit a cigarette and thumbed through a Lunker Lakes sales brochure that some lady had given him at the barbecue.

It was half-past two when somebody outside fired a rifle through their window and ran.

Angrily Jim Tile picked up the phone and started dialing.

As he shook the broken glass out of his blanket, Al García asked, "So who you calling, *chico,* the Fish and Game?"

"I think it's important to make an impression," the trooper said. "Don't you?"

To get on the dike, Eddie Spurling had to drive to the west end of Road 84, then zig north up U.S. 27 to the Sawgrass Fish Camp. Here the dike was accessible, but wide enough for only one vehicle; at three in the morning Eddie didn't anticipate oncoming traffic. He drove the Wagoneer at a crawl through a crystal darkness, insects whorling out of the swamp to cloud the headlights. Every so often he had to brake as the high-beams froze some animal, ruby-eyed, on the rutted track—rabbits, raccoons, foxes, bobcats, even a fat old female otter. Eddie marveled at so much wildlife, so close to the big city.

It took an hour to make the full circuit back to where the flood levee abutted Lunker Lake Number Seven. When he reached the designated spot, Eddie Spurling turned off the engine, killed the lights, rolled down his window, and gazed off to the west. The Everglades night was glorious and immense, the sweep of the sky unlike anything he'd seen anywhere in the South; here the galaxy seemed to spill straight into the shimmering swamp.

When Eddie looked east he saw blocked and broken landscape,

the harsh aura of downtown lights, the pale linear scar of the nascent superhighway and its three interchanges, built especially for Charlie Weeb's development. There was nothing beautiful about it, and Eddie turned away. He put on his cap, snapped his down vest, and stepped out of the truck into the gentle hum of the marsh.

Water glistened on both sides of the dike. Under a thin fog, Lunker Lake Number Seven lay as flat and dead as a cistern; by contrast, the small pool on the Everglades side was dimpled with darting minnows and waterbugs. The pocket was lushly fringed with cattails and sawgrass and crisp round lily pads as big as pizzas. Something else floated in the pool—a plastic Clorox bottle, tied to a rope.

Eddie Spurling noticed how out of place it looked; obscene, really, like litter. The whole idea of it made him mad—Weeb and his damn Alabama imports. Eddie carefully made his way down the slope of the dike, his boots sliding in the loose dirt. At the edge of the pool he found a long stick, which he used to snag the floating bleach bottle.

He got hold of the rope and pulled it hand over hand. The fish trap was unexpectedly heavy; leaden almost. Must've got tangled in the hydrilla weed, Eddie thought.

When the cage finally broke the surface, he dropped the stick and grabbed the mesh with his fingers. Then he pulled it to shore.

Eddie shone his flashlight in the cage and said, "My God!" He couldn't believe the size of it—a coppery-black bass of grotesque proportions, so huge it could've been a deep-sea grouper. It looked thirty pounds. The hawg glared at Eddie and thrashed furiously in its wire prison. Eddie could only stare, awestruck. He thought: This is impossible.

On the other side of the pond something made a noise, and Eddie Spurling went cold. He recognized the naked click of a rifle hammer.

A deep voice said: "Put her back."

Eddie swallowed dryly. He was almost too terrified to move.

The gun went off and the Clorox bottle exploded at his feet. After the echo faded, the voice said: "Now."

Rubber-kneed, Eddie lowered the fish cage back into the pool, letting the wet rope pay through his fingers.

Across the pond, the rifleman rose from the cattails. By the size of the silhouette Eddie Spurling saw that the man was quite large. His appearance was made more ominous by military fatigues and some sort of black mask. The man sloshed through the marsh and hiked up the side of the dike. Eddie thought about running but there was no place to go; he thought about swimming but there was a problem with snakes and alligators. So he just stood there, trying not to soil himself.

Soon the rifleman loomed directly above him, on the dike.

"Kill the flashlight," the man said.

He was close enough for Eddie to make out his features. He had long dark hair and a ratty beard and a flowered plastic cap on his head. The mask turned out to be sunglasses. The rifle was a Remington.

"I'm Fast Eddie Spurling."

"Who asked?"

"From television?"

"I watch no television," said the rifleman.

Eddie tried a different approach. "Is it money you want? The Jeep? Go ahead and take it."

Without blinking, the rifleman turned and blasted the tinted windshield out of Eddie Spurling's Wagoneer. "I got my own truck, thanks," he said. Then he shot out the fog lights, too.

Eddie was sweating ice water.

The man said, "That's some fish, huh?"

Eddie nodded energetically. "Biggest I ever saw."

"Name's Queenie."

"Real nice," Eddie said desperately. He was quite certain the hairy rifleman was going to kill him.

"You're probably curious what happened to yours."

"They weren't really mine," Eddie said.

The man laughed thinly. "You just came all the way out here to say hello."

Eddie said, "No, sir, I came to let 'em go."

"How about I just shoot off your pecker and get it over with?"

"Please," Eddie cried. "I mean it, I was about to set them fish free. Check the truck if you don't believe it. If I was gonna take 'em, I'd have brung a livewell, right? I'd have brung the damn boat, wouldn't I?"

The rifleman seemed to be thinking it over.

Eddie went on: "And why would I be here three hours before the tournament and risk having 'em croak on me?"

The man said, "You're not one of the cheaters?"

"No, and I don't aim to start. I couldn't go through with it, so screw Charlie Weeb."

The rifleman lowered his gun. "I let those ringer bass go."

Eddie Spurling said, "Well, I'm glad you did."

"Three hawgsters. One must've gone at least eleven-eight."

"Well," said Eddie, "maybe I'll catch him someday, when he's bigger."

The man said: "What about Queenie? What would you have done about her?"

Without hesitating Eddie said, "I'da let her go, too."

"I bet."

"What would be the point of killing her, mister? Suppose I took that monster home and stuffed her. Every time I'd walk in the den she'd be staring down from the wall, the awful truth in those damn purple eyes. I couldn't live with it, mister. That's why I say, you didn't need the gun. I'da let her go anyway."

The rifleman stood there, showing nothing. The sunglasses scared the hell out of Eddie.

"I've got a boy, mister, age nine," Eddie said. "You think I could lie to my boy about a fish like that? Say I caught it when I didn't?"

"Some men could."

"Not me."

The rifleman said: "I believe you, Mr. Spurling. Now, get the fuck out of here, please."

Eddie obediently scrambled up the bank of the dike. He hopped in the Jeep without even brushing the broken glass off the seat.

"Can you turn this thing around okay?"

"Yeah," Eddie said, "I got four-wheel drive." In the dark he groped nervously for the keys.

"The seam of the universe," the rifleman mused. "This dike is like the moral seam of the universe."

"It's narrow, that's for sure," Eddie said.

"Evil on the one side, good on the other." The man illustrated by pointing with the Remington.

Eddie stuck his head out the window and said very politely: "Can I ask what you plan to do with that big beautiful bass?"

"I plan to let her go," the man said, "in about five minutes." He didn't say where, on which side of the seam.

Eddie knew he shouldn't press his luck, knew he should just get the hell away from this lunatic, but he couldn't help it. The fisherman in him just had to ask: "What's she weigh, anyhow?"

"Twenty-nine even."

"Holy moly." Fast Eddie Spurling gasped.

"Now get lost," said the rifleman, "and good luck in the tournament."

After Eddie had gone, Skink hauled the big fish out of the pool. He propped the cage yoke-style across his shoulders and carried it across the dike to Lunker Lakes. He put it back in the water while he searched the banks until he found the two beer cans marking the spot where Jim Tile and Al García had sunk the brushpile.

Skink hoisted the cage once more and moved it to the secret spot. This time he removed the big bass, pointed her toward the submerged obstruction, and gently let her go. The fish kicked once, roiled, and was gone. "See you tonight," Skink said. "Then we go home."

Rifle in hand, he stood on the dike for two hours and watched the night start to fade. On the Everglades side, a heron croaked and redwings bickered in the bulrushes; the other side of the dike lay mute and lifeless. Skink waited for something to show in Lunker Lake Number Seven—a turtle, a garfish, anything. He waited a long time.

Then, deep in worry, he trudged down the dike to where he'd left his truck. To the east, at the dirty rim of the city, the sun was coming up.

At that moment R. J. Decker parked his car behind a row of construction trailers at Lunker Lakes. Dawn was the best time to move, because by then most rent-a-cops were either asleep or shooting the shit around the timeclock, waiting to punch out. Decker spotted only one uniformed guard, a rotund and florid fellow who emerged from one of the trailers just long enough to take a leak, then shut the door.

Decker checked the camera again. It was a Minolta Maxxum, a sturdy thirty-five-millimeter he'd picked up at a West Palm Beach discount house that took credit cards. He was thinking that a Kodak or a Sure-Shot might have worked just as well, but he'd been in such a hurry. He opened the back of the frame and inspected the loading mechanism; he did the same with the motor-drive unit.

Satisfied, Decker capped the lens, closed up the camera, and locked it in the glove compartment of Al García's car. Then he got the boltcutters out of the trunk and snuck up to the supply shed, where he went to work on the padlock.

*   *   *

The blast-off for the Dickie Lockhart Memorial Bass Blasters Classic was set for six-thirty, but the anglers arrived very early to put their boats in the water and test their gear and collect free goodies from tackle reps up and down the dock. The fishermen knew that whoever won this tournament might never have to wet a line again, not just because of the tremendous purse but because of the product endorsements to follow. The bass lure that took first prize in the Lockhart undoubtedly would be the hottest item in freshwater bait shops for a year. There was no logic to this fad, since bass will eat just about anything (including their own young), but the tackle companies did everything in their power to encourage manic buying. Before the opening gun they loaded down the contestants with free plugs, jigs, spinners, and of course rubber worms, displayed in giant plastic vats like so much hellish purple pasta.

The morning was cool and clear; there was talk it might hit eighty by midafternoon. Matronly volunteers from The First Pentecostal Church of Exemptive Redemption handed out Bible tracts and served hot biscuits and coffee, though many contestants were too tense to eat or pray.

At six sharp a burgundy Rolls-Royce Corniche pulled up to the ramp at Lunker Lake Number One. Dennis and Lanie Gault got out. Lanie was dressed in a red timber jacket, skintight Gore-Tex dungarees, and black riding boots. She basked in the stares from the other contestants and dug heartily into a bag of hot croissants.

With an air of supreme confidence, Dennis Gault uncranked his sparkling seventeen-foot Ranger bass boat off the trailer into the water. One by one, he meticulously stowed his fishing rods, then his toolbox, then his immense tacklebox. Hunkering into the cockpit of the boat, he checked the gauges—water temperature, trim tilt, tabs, tachometer, fuel, batteries, oil pressure. He punched a button on his sonic fish-finder and the screen blinked a bright green digital good-morning. The big Johnson outboard turned over on the first try, purring like a tiger cub. While the engine warmed up, Dennis Gault stood at the wheel and casually smoothed the creases of his sky-blue jumpsuit. He squirted Windex on the lenses of his amber Polaroids and wiped them with a dark blue bandanna. Next he slipped on his monogrammed weather vest, and tucked a five-ounce squirt bottle of Happy Gland into the pocket. In accordance with prevailing bass fashion, he spun his cap so that the bill was at his back; that way the wind wouldn't tear it off his head at fifty miles an hour.

Dennis Gault had expected to hear the usual cracks about the Rolls and what a pompous ass he was, but for once the other bass anglers left him alone. In fact, Gault was so absorbed in his own pretournament ritual that he almost missed the highlight of the morning.

It started as a pinprick on the eastern horizon, but it came faster than the sunrise; a strange pulsing light. The bass fishermen clustered on the dock to watch. They figured one of the big bait companies was pulling a stunt for a new commercial. Some stunt it was, too.

Soon the sky over Lunker Lakes throbbed in piercing aquamarine. On a forty-foot screen mounted behind the stage, the face of Reverend Charles Weeb appeared for the morning benediction; it was a taped message (for Charlie Weeb seldom rose before ten), but none of the contestants was in the mood to hear what the Old Testament said about fishing. They were riveted on what was slowly rolling toward them down the road.

It was a convoy of police cars.

Highway-patrol cruisers, to be exact; sixteen of them, their flashing blue lights slicing up the darkness. Dead last in the procession was a garbage truck with a rowboat hooked to the bumper.

Dennis Gault did not like the looks of things. He wondered if the cops had come to arrest somebody, possibly even him. He shot a worried glance at Lanie, who shrugged and shook her head.

The first eight troopers peeled off to one side of the boat ramp and parked bumper-to-bumper; the last eight parked in similar formation on the other side, forming a broad V-shaped alley for Al García and Jim Tile in the garbage truck.

Each of the state troopers got out and stood by his car. They wore seriously neutral expressions, and showed no reaction to the OCN Minicams filming their arrival. To a man, the troopers were young, ramrod-straight, clean-cut, muscular, and heavily armed. They were some of Jim Tile's best friends on the force, and they were white, which definitely made an impression.

The old wooden skiff was lowered into the lake without incident.

Deacon Johnson was up early. The importance of the day weighed heavily, and he had reason to be anxious. He put on his favorite desert-tan leisure suit, buffed his cream-colored shoes, and trimmed his nose hairs. At the breakfast table he chewed halfheartedly on raisin bagels, scanned the sports page to make sure they hadn't screwed up the big display ad for the tournament, then called for the limousine.

He decided to give the VA hospital one more try.

This time, two doctors were waiting at the admissions desk.

Deacon Johnson smiled and stuck out his hand, but the doctors regarded it as if it were a rattlesnake.

"I'm sorry," one said, "but you'll have to leave."

"You've been upsetting the patients," said the other.

"Isn't there one," Deacon Johnson said, "who wants to be on TV?"

"They said you offered them money."

"I had to," Deacon Johnson lied. "FCC rules."

"Money," the doctor went on, "in exchange for lying about their illnesses."

"Not lying—*dramatizing*. There's a big difference." Deacon Johnson folded his arms indignantly. "We run a thoroughly Christian enterprise at OCN."

"Several of the patients became quite upset when you were here before."

"I certainly meant no harm."

"They've discussed violence," said the other doctor, apparently a psychiatrist.

"Violence?" said Deacon Johnson.

"That's why we can't let you back inside."

"But there was one, Corporal Clement. He expressed an interest in appearing with Reverend Weeb today."

The two doctors traded glances.

"Clement," Deacon Johnson repeated, spelling out the name. "The fellow with the trick knees."

The psychiatrist said, "I'm afraid Corporal Clement has been moved inpatient to the sixth floor."

"It appears he got into the pharmacy last night," the other doctor explained.

"He won't be available for television appearances," the psychiatrist added. "Please go now, Mr. Johnson, before we call for Security."

Deacon Johnson got back in the limo and sulked.

"Where to?" the driver asked.

"You know this town?"

"Born and raised," the driver said.

"Good. Find me some bums."

Charlie Weeb would be royally ticked off; he'd specifically said no street people, it was too risky. Lofty standards were fine and dandy, but Deacon Johnson was running out of time. The healing was only hours away.

The limousine driver took him to the dissolute stretch of Fort Lauderdale beach known as the Strip, but there all the bums had bleached hair and great tans. "Too healthy-looking," Deacon Johnson decided.

"There's a soup kitchen down Sunrise Boulevard," the driver said.

"Let's give it a try."

Deacon Johnson saw that the driver was right about the soup kitchen: wall-to-wall winos; sallow, toothless, oily-haired vagabonds, the hardest of the hard-core. Some were so haggard that no makeup artist possibly could have rendered them presentable in time for the show. Worse, most of the men were too hung-over to comprehend Deacon Johnson's offer; the money they understood just fine, it was the part about dressing up and rehearsing that seemed to sail over their heads.

"It's television, for Christ's sake," Deacon Johnson implored.

The men just grinned and scratched themselves.

In desperation, Deacon Johnson selected a skinny bum named Clu, who was in a wheelchair. The driver lifted Clu into the back seat of the limo and folded the wheelchair into the trunk.

As they rode back to Lunker Lakes, Deacon Johnson said: "Are you sure you can rise up?"

"You bet."

"On command?"

"You bet."

Clu wore a mischievous smile that made Deacon Johnson wonder. "So what's wrong with your legs?" he asked.

"Not a thing," Clu replied.

"Then why the wheelchair?"

"I got it on a trade," Clu said. "Three cans of Sterno and a wool sock. Pretty good deal, I'd say."

"Indeed," Deacon Johnson said. "And how long ago was this?"

"Nineteen and eighty-one," said Clu, still smirking.

"And you've been in the chair ever since?"

"Every minute," Clu said. "No need to get up."

Deacon Johnson leaned forward and told the limo driver to pull over.

"Get out," he said to Clu.

"What for?"

"It's just a test," Deacon Johnson said. "Get out and walk around the car."

When the driver opened the door, Clu tumbled facedown onto the pavement. The driver reached down to help him, but Deacon Johnson shook his finger.

He said, "Can you rise up, son?"

Clu tried with all his might until he was pink in the face, but his skinny legs would not work. "I don't believe this," he whined.

"Just as I thought," said Deacon Johnson stiffly.

On the ground Clu continued to grunt and squirm. "Let me work on this a minute," he pleaded.

"Give him back the damn wheelchair," Deacon Johnson snapped at the driver, "and let's go."

Just when he was certain that the grand TV mega-healing would have to be called off, or at least scaled back to a sheep or a cat, Deacon Johnson spotted the blind man.

The man was alone on a bus bench outside the entrance to Lunker Lakes; beneath the big cedar billboard, in fact, directly under the second L. That he would be sitting right there at such a crucial moment seemed like a heavenly miracle, except that Deacon Johnson didn't believe in miracles. Plain old dumb luck was more like it. He told the limo driver to stop.

The blind man did not have a guide dog or a white cane, so Deacon Johnson was hopeful that they could do business.

He walked up to him and said hello. The man didn't move one bit, just stared straight ahead. Deacon Johnson could see nothing but his own natty reflection in the dark glasses.

"May I ask," Deacon Johnson said, "are you blind?"

"I suppose," the man said.

"May I ask how blind?"

"Depends what you mean."

"Can you see what that billboard says?" Deacon Johnson pointed to a big Toyota sign a quarter-mile down the road.

The man said, "Not hardly."

Deacon Johnson held a hand in front of the man's face. "Can you see that?"

The man nodded yes.

"Very good." Thank God, Deacon Johnson thought. For coaching purposes, partly blind was perfect. As a telegenic bonus, the man appeared sickly but not morbidly sunken, like some of the bums at the soup kitchen.

Deacon Johnson introduced himself and said, "Have you heard of the Outdoor Christian Network?"

"Yes," the blind man said.

"Then you've heard of the Reverend Charles Weeb, how he heals people on national television?"

"I watch no television."

"Yes, I understand, but at least have you *heard* of Reverend Weeb's healings? The reason I ask, he's having one today. Right here, inside this gate."

"A healing."

"On live satellite television," Deacon Johnson said. "Would you be interested?"

The man toyed with his beard.

"For five hundred dollars," Deacon Johnson said.

"And would I be healed?"

"Let me say, Reverend Weeb gets excellent results. With the Lord's help, of course." Deacon Johnson circled the blind man and assessed his camera presence. "I think the Lord would probably like us to shave you," he said. "And possibly cut your hair—the braid could be a distraction."

The blind man raised a middle digit in front of Deacon Johnson's face. "Can you see that?" he said.

Deacon Johnson chuckled weakly. "I underestimated you, sir. Let's make it a thousand dollars."

"For a thousand bucks I take a shower," the blind man said, "that's all."

When the man stood up he towered over Deacon Johnson. He pulled on a flowered plastic cap and smoothed it flat over his skull. Then, with thick callused fingers, he pinched Deacon Johnson's elbow and held on.

"Lead the way," the blind man said.

The instant the other bass boats roared away, Al García felt sure that he and Jim Tile would be drowned, that the roiling wakes would swamp the wooden skiff and it would sink upside-down, trapping them both in a cold underwater pocket.

This did not happen. The skiff proved not only stable but also dry. It was, however, maddeningly slow—made even slower by the sloshing heft of the Igloo cooler, which was filled with fresh Lake Jesup water especially. for Queenie. That, added to the considerable weight of the two men, the tackle, the gas tank, the lunchboxes, the anchor, and the bait (several pounds of frozen Harney County shiners, Queenie's favorite) was almost too much for the tired little six-horse Mercury to push.

García puttered down the canal on a straight course for Lunker Lake Number Seven. With one hand he steered the engine. With the other he idly trolled a fishing line baited with a misshapen jangling monstrosity of a lure. "Looks like an elephant IUD," García had told the perky but unappreciative sales rep who'd given it to him on the dock. "Maybe one of Cher's earrings."

It was a long slow ride, and the rhythmic drone of the outboard eventually brought on drowsiness. García was half-dozing when something jolted his hands; he opened his eyes to see the tip of the fishing rod quiver and dip. Remembering what Skink had taught him, he jerked twice, solidly, and a stubborn tug answered at the end of the line. Without much effort the detective reeled in his catch, a feisty black fish no more than twelve inches long.

Jim Tile said, "I believe that's a baby bass."

"I'll be damned," said Al García. "Throw him in the cooler."

"What for?"

"So we can show the governor we got one fair and square."

"It's awfully small," Jim Tile remarked, releasing the bass into the Igloo.

"A fish is a fish," the detective said. "Come on, Jimbo, get in the goddamn tournament spirit."

Then the engine quit; coughed twice, spit blue smoke, and died. Al García removed the cowling and tinkered fruitlessly for ten minutes, then traded places so the trooper could give it a try.

Jim Tile repeatedly pulled the starter cord, but the Mercury showed no sign of life. After the tenth try, he sat down and said, "Damn."

The wooden skiff hung motionless in the canal, not another bass boat in sight.

"We got a long ways to go," García said.

On a hunch, Jim Tile disengaged the fuel line and sniffed the plug. "Something's wrong," he said.

García winced. "Don't tell me we're out of gas."

Jim Tile hoisted the heavy aluminum fuel tank and unscrewed the lid. He peered inside, then put his nose to the hole.

"Plenty of gas," he said dismally, "only somebody's pissed in it."

30

The night had taken a toll on both of them.

Catherine felt gritty and cramped from being curled in the trunk of the car. Her knees were scuffed and her hair smelled like tire rubber from using the spare as a pillow. She had cried herself to sleep, and now, in the white glare of morning, the sight of Thomas Curl's pistol made her want to cry again. Thinking of Decker helped to hold back the tears.

Curl himself had deteriorated more than Catherine had thought possible, short of coma or death. He could no longer move his right arm at all; the muscle was as black and dead as the dog head that hung from it. Gunk seeped from Curl's eyes and nose, and overnight his tongue had bloomed swollen from his mouth, like some exotic scarlet fruit. On the boat he practically ignored Catherine, but murmured constantly to the rictal dog while stroking its petrified muzzle. By now Catherine was used to everything, even the smell.

Thomas Curl had been drinking ferociously since before dawn, and she surmised that this alone had kept the pain of infection from consuming him. He drove the boat slowly, steering with his knees and squinting against the sun. They passed several fishermen on the canal, but apparently none could see the pistol poking Catherine's left breast. If they noticed the pit bull's head, they didn't let on.

"I'm a rich man, Lucas," Thomas Curl said to the dog. "I got enough money for ten of these speedboats."

Catherine said, "Tom, we're almost there." She felt the muzzle of the gun dig harder.

"Lucas, boy, we're almost there," Thomas Curl said.

With this announcement he threw himself against the throttle and the Starcraft shot forward, plowing aimlessly through a stand of thick sawgrass. Catherine let out a cry as the serrated stalks raked her cheeks, drawing blood. The boat broke out of the matted grass, leapt the water, and climbed a mudbank. The prop stuck hard, and there they sat.

"This is the place," Thomas Curl declared.

"Not quite," Catherine said.

"He'll find us, don't you worry," Curl said. "He's got a nose for your little pussy, I bet."

"Cute," Catherine said. "You ought to work for Hallmark, writing valentines."

She used the hem of her skirt to dab the cuts on her face. Half-staggering, Curl got himself out of the boat. The pistol was still in his good hand.

"Don't bother with the leash," he said to Catherine.

"Right," she said. There was no leash, of course. She climbed out of the beached Starcraft and instantly cursed Thomas Curl for not letting her wear any shoes.

While she stooped to pick the nettles from her feet, Curl cocked his head and cupped an ear with his gun hand. "What is it?" he said excitedly.

"What is what?" Catherine asked, but he wasn't speaking to her.

"What is it, boy?"

Somewhere in the deep rotting bog of Thomas Curl's brain, his dog was barking. Curl dropped to a crouch and lowered his voice. "Lucas hears something comin'," he said.

Catherine heard it too. Her heart raced when she spotted R. J. Decker, hands in his pockets, walking along the bank of the canal.

She waved and tried to shout, but nothing came out. Decker waved back and grinned, the way he always did when he hadn't seen her for a while. Grinned like nothing was wrong, like no gangrenous madman was jabbing a loaded pistol into Catherine's nipple while shouting at a severed dog head on his arm: "Heel, boy, heel!"

"Easy, Tom," said R. J. Decker.

"Shut up, fuckhead."

"Did we get up on the wrong side of the bed?"

"I said shut up, and don't come no closer."

Decker stood ten feet away. Jeans, flannel shirt, tennis shoes. A camera hung from a thin strap around his neck.

"You remember the deal," he said to Curl. "A straight-up trade: Me for her."

"What kind of deal you offer Lemus?"

Decker said, "I didn't shoot your brother, but I will say he had it coming."

"So do you, fuckhead."

"I know, Tom."

R. J. Decker could see that something was monstrously wrong with Thomas Curl, that he was a sick man. He could also see that something ghastly had happened to Curl's right arm, and that this might be a cause of his distress.

Decker said, "That a dog, Tom?"

"The hell does it look like?"

"It's definitely a dog," Catherine said. "A pit bull, I believe."

"I used to know a dog like that," Decker said affably. "Lived in my trailer park. Poindexter was its name."

Thomas Curl said, "This one is Lucas."

"Does he do any tricks?"

"Yeah, he chews the balls off fuckheads like you."

"I see."

Catherine said, "You're hurting me, Tom."

"Take the gun out of there." Decker spoke calmly. "Let her go now, that was the deal."

"I'll show you the deal," said Thomas Curl. With his tumid red tongue he licked the tip of the gun barrel and placed it squarely between Catherine's light brown eyebrows. He twisted the muzzle back and forth, leaving a wet round imprint on her forehead.

"That's the deal Lemus got," said Thomas Curl. "Dead-center bull's-eye." He poked the gun back in her breast.

The touch of blue steel on her face had made Catherine shiver. She thought she might even faint; in a way, she wished she would. Falling facedown in the sawgrass would be better than this. And Decker—she could have clobbered him, standing there like it was the checkout line of the supermarket. The one time she wanted to see the hot streak, the dangerous temper. Normally she detested violence, but this would have been an exception; Catherine would have been delighted to watch her ex-husband strangle Thomas Curl with his bare hands.

"I got to kill you both," Curl said. He was fighting off deep tremors. Sweat gathered in big drops on his cheeks, and his breath came in raspy bursts.

Decker knew he could take him, probably with one good punch. If only the pistol weren't aimed point-blank at Catherine's heart. Oh, Catherine. Decker had to be careful, he was so close to the edge.

"A deal is a deal," Decker said.

"Hell, I can't let her go now."

"She won't tell," Decker said. "She's got a husband to think about."

"Too bad," Thomas Curl growled. Suddenly one eye looked bigger than the other. He started rocking slightly, as if on the deck of a ship.

Curl said, "Let's get it over with, I don't feel so good."

He pushed Catherine toward Decker, who pulled her close with both hands. "Rage, please," she whispered.

Curl said, "So who wants it first?" When neither of them answered, he consulted his faithful pal. "Lucas, who gets it first?"

"Tom, one final favor before you do this."

"Shut up."

"Take our picture together, okay? Me and Catherine."

Curl sneered. "What the hell for?"

"Because I love her," Decker said, "and it's our last moment to-gether. Forever."

"You got *that* right."

"Then please," Decker said.

Catherine squeezed his hand. "I love you too, Rage." The words sounded wonderful, but under the circumstances Decker wasn't sure how to take it; guns make people say the darnedest things.

He lifted the Minolta from around his neck. Thomas Curl tucked the pistol under his right arm and took the camera in his good hand. He examined it hopelessly, as if it were an atom-splitter.

"My daddy's just got a Polaroid."

"This is almost the same," Decker said reassuringly. "You look through that little window."

"Yeah?" Thomas Curl raised the camera to his big eye.

"Can you see us?"

"Nope," Curl said.

Decker took two steps backward, pulling Catherine by the elbows. "How about now, Tom?"

Curl cackled. "Hey, yeah, I see you."

"Good. Now . . . just press that black button on top."

"Wait, you're all fuzzy-looking."

"That's all right."

Curl said, "Shit, might as well have a good final pitcher, considering. Now, how do I fix the focus?"

Catherine squeezed Decker's arm. "Fuck the focus," she said under her breath. "Go for his gun."

But in a helpful tone Decker said, "Tom, the focus is in the black button."

"The same one?"

"Yeah. It's all automatic, you just press it."

"I'll be damned."

Decker said, "Isn't that something?"

"Yeah," Thomas Curl said, "but then where does the pitcher come out?"

"Jesus," Catherine sighed.

"Underneath," Decker lied. For the first time he sounded slightly impatient.

Curl turned the camera upside-down in his hand. "I don't see where."

"Trust me, Tom."

"You say so." Curl raised the Minolta one more time. It took several drunken moments to align the viewfinder with his eye.

"Lucas, don't the two of them look sweet?" Curl hacked out a cruel watery laugh. "First I shoot your pitcher, then I shoot your goddamn brains out."

He located the black button with a twitching forefinger. "Okay, fuckheads, say cheese."

"Good-bye, Tom," said R. J. Decker.

There was no film loaded in the camera, only fourteen ounces of water gel, a malleable plastic explosive commonly used at construction sites. For Decker it was a simple chore to run bare copper wires from the camera's batteries directly into the hard-packed gelatin, a substance so volatile that the charge from the shutter contact provided more than enough heat.

As chemical reactions go, it was simple and brief.

At the touch of the button the Minolta blew up; not much in the way of flash, but a powerful air-puckering concussion that tore off Thomas Curl's poisoned skull and launched it in an arc worthy of a forty-foot jump shot. It landed with a noisy sploosh in the middle of the canal.

Catherine was transfixed by how long it took for Curl's headless body to fold up and collapse on the reddening mud; minutes, it seemed. But then, in the pungent gray haze of the killing, every scene seemed to happen in slow motion: R. J. tossing the gun into the water; R. J. dragging the corpse to the boat; R. J. sliding the boat down the bank; R. J. lifting her easily in his arms, carrying her away to someplace safe.

They took turns rowing. Every time they squeaked past another bass boat, they got the same mocking look.

"I don't give a shit," Al García said to Jim Tile. "You notice, they don't seem to be catching fish."

This was true; García and Jim Tile did not know why, nor did they give it much thought as they rowed. Their concern was for one fish only, and they still had a long way to go. As for the other contestants, they might have been interested to know that Charlie Weeb's hydrologist had warned this would happen, that the imported bass might not feed in the bad water. Even had the pros known the full truth, it was unlikely they would have given up and packed their rods—not with so much at stake. Deep in every angler's soul is a secret confidence in his own special prowess that impels him to keep fishing in the face of common sense, basic science, financial ruin, and even natural disasters. In the maddening campaign at Lunker Lakes, whole tackleboxes were emptied and no secret weapon was left unsheathed. The putrid waters were plumbed by lures of every imaginable size and color, retrieved through every navigable depth at every possible speed. By midday it became obvious that even the most sophisticated angling technology in the world would not induce these fish to eat.

As they tediously rowed the skiff through the network of long canals, Jim Tile and Al García detected angst on the faces of other competitors.

"They don't look like they're having much fun," García said.

"They don't know what fun is," said Jim Tile, taking his turn at the oars. "This here's fun."

With each pull the truth was sinking in: even if they reached the brushpile and did what Skink told them, they'd probably never get back to the dock by sunset. Not rowing.

But they had to try.

"Step on it, *chico*," Al García said. "Oxford's gaining on us."

*   *   *

At that moment, on the westernmost end of Lunker Lake Number Seven, Dennis Gault was refolding the waterproof map that his helicopter pilot had marked for him. Lanie was up in the pedestal seat, reading from a stack of *Cosmos* she'd brought along to kill time. Her nose shone with Hawaiian tanning butter.

Dennis Gault breathed on his sunglasses and wiped each lens with a tissue. He tested them against the sun before putting them on. Scanning his arsenal, he selected a plug-casting outfit with a brand-new Double Whammy tied to the end of the line. He tested the sharpness of the hook against his thumbnail, and grinned in self-satisfaction when the barb stuck fast. Then he squirted the lure three times with Happy Gland Bass Bolero.

Finally Gault was ready. He reared back and fired the spinnerbait to the exact spot where the sunken brushpile should have been.

"Come on, mother," he said. "Suck on this."

31

"Explain to me," the Reverend Charles Weeb said from the barber chair, "exactly how that shit got on the air."

"The promo spot?" Deacon Johnson asked.

"Yes, Izzy. With all the police cars."

"It was a live remote, Charles, just like you wanted. 'We interrupt our regular programming to take you to the Dickie Lockhart Memorial Bass Blasters blah, blah, blah. Tune in later for the exciting finish.' "

"Sixteen frigging cop cars, Izzy—it looked like a dope raid, not a fishing tournament."

"It wasn't like we invited them."

"Oh no," Charlie Weeb said, "you went one better. You beamed them into eleven million households."

Deacon Johnson said, "We'd already paid for the satellite time, Charles. I think you're overreacting."

Weeb squirmed impatiently while the barber worked on his bushy blond eyebrows. He thought: Maybe Izzy's right, maybe the cop cars weren't so bad. Might even get viewers curious, jack up the ratings.

"May I bring him in now?" Deacon Johnson asked.

"Sure, Izzy." Weeb was done with his haircut. He gave the barber a hundred dollars and told him to go home. Weeb checked himself in the mirror and splashed on some Old Spice. Then he went to the closet and selected a pale raspberry suit, one of his favorites. He was stepping into the shiny flared trousers when Deacon Johnson returned with the designated sinner.

"Well, you're certainly a big fella," Weeb said.

"I must be," said the man.

"Deacon Johnson tells me you're blind."

"Not completely."

"Well, no, of course not," Reverend Weeb said. "No child of God is completely blind, not in the spiritual sense. His eyes are your eyes."

"That's damn good to know."

"What's your name, sinner?"

"They call me Skink."

"What's that, Scandinavian or something? *Skink.*" Weeb frowned. "Would you mind, Mr. Skink, if today you took a biblical name? Say, Jeremiah?"

"Sure."

"That's excellent." Reverend Weeb was worried about the man's braided hair, and he pantomimed his concern to Deacon Johnson.

"The hair stays," Skink said.

"It's not that bad," Deacon Johnson interjected. "Actually, he looks a little like one of the Oak Ridge Boys."

Charlie Weeb conceded the point. He said, "Mr. Skink, I guess they told you how this works. We've got a dress rehearsal in about twenty minutes, but I want to warn you: the real thing is much different, much more . . . emotional. You ever been to a televised tent healing before?"

"Nope."

"People cry, scream, drool, tremble, fall down on the floor. It's a joyous, joyous moment. And the better *you* are, the more joyous it is."

"What I want to know," Skink said, "is do I really get healed?"

Reverend Weeb smiled avuncularly and flicked the lint off his raspberry lapels. "Mr. Skink, there are two kinds of healings. One is a physical revelation, the other is spiritual. No one but the Lord himself can foretell what will happen this afternoon—probably a genuine miracle—but at the very least, I promise your eyes will be healed in the spiritual sense."

"That won't help me pass the driver's test, will it?"

Charlie Weeb coughed lightly. "Did Deacon Johnson mention that we pay in cash?"

*   *   *

At five sharp, the special live edition of *Jesus in Your Living Room* flashed via satellite across the far reaches of the Outdoor Christian Network. Radiant and cool, the Reverend Charles Weeb appeared behind his pink plaster pulpit and welcomed America to the scenic and friendly new community of Lunker Lakes, Florida.

"We are particularly delighted to be joined by hundreds of Christian brothers and sisters who flew all the way down here to share this exciting day with us. Thank you all for your love, your prayers, and your down payments . . . as you've seen for yourself, Florida is still a paradise, a place of peacefulness, of inner reflection, of celebrating God's glorious work by celebrating nature. . . ."

Camera number one swung skyward.

"And see there, as I speak," said Reverend Weeb, "eagles soar over this beautiful new Elysium!"

The high-soaring birds were not eagles, but common brown turkey vultures. The cameraman was under strict instructions to avoid close-ups.

Camera number two panned to the audience—starchy, contented, attentive faces, except for one man in the front row, who was not applauding. He wore an ill-fitting sharkskin suit, a frayed straw hat, and black sunglasses. He did not look like a happy Christian soldier; more like Charles Manson on steroids. Camera two did not linger on his face for long.

Charlie Weeb didn't call on him for twenty minutes. By that time the audience throbbed in a damp and weepy frenzy. As Weeb had predicted, fat women were fainting left and right. Grown men were bawling like babies.

At a nod from Reverend Weeb, two young deacons in dove-white suits led the blind man to the stage.

"You poor wretched sinner," Weeb said. "What is your name?"

"Jeremiah Skink."

"Ah, Jeremiah!"

The audience roared.

"Jeremiah, do you believe in miracles?"

"Yes, Brother Weeb," Skink said. "Yes, I do."

"Do you believe the Lord is here at Lunker Lakes today?"

"I believe he's here with you," Skink said, reciting the lines, which had been cut drastically due to problems at rehearsal.

"And, Jeremiah, do you believe he watches over his children?"

"He loves us all," Skink said.

"You have been blind, lo, for how long?"

"Lo, for quite a while," Skink said.

"And the doctors have given up on you?"

"Totally, Reverend Weeb."

"And you've even given up on yourself, haven't you, brother?"

"Amen," Skink said, as a Minicam zoomed in on the sunglasses. He was mad at himself for caving in about the straw hat and sharkskin suit.

Reverend Weeb dabbed his forehead with a kerchief and rested a pudgy pink hand on Skink's shoulder.

"Jeremiah," he said momentously, "on this glorious tropical day that God has given us, on a day when Christian sportsmen are reaping fortunes from these pristine waters behind us, on such a day it is God's wish that you should see again. You should see the glory of his sunshine and his sky and the breathtaking natural beauty of his modestly priced family town-home community. Would you like to see that, Jeremiah? Would you like to see again?"

"You bet your ass," Skink said, deviating slightly from the script.

Reverend Weeb's eyebrows jumped, but he didn't lose tempo. "Jeremiah," he went on, "I'm going to ask these good Christian people who are witnessing with us today at Lunker Lakes to join hands with one another. And all of you at home, put down your Bibles and join hands in your living room. And I myself will take your hands, Jeremiah, and together we will beseech Almighty Jesus to bless you with the gift of sight."

"Amen," Skink said.

"Amen!" echoed the crowd.

"Make this sinner see!" Reverend Weeb cried to the heavens.

"See!" the crowd shouted. "See! See!"

Skink was getting into the act, in spite of himself. "See me, feel me!" he hollered.

"See him, feel him!" the audience responded. A strange new verse, but it had a pleasing cadence.

Hastily Reverend Weeb steered the prayer chant back to more conventional exhortations. "God, save this wretched sinner!"

"Save him!" echoed the crowd.

Like a turtle suddenly caught on the highway, Reverend Weeb retracted his neck, drew in his extremities, and blinked his eyes. The trance lasted a full minute before he snapped out. Raising his arms above his head, he declared: "The time is nigh. Jesus is coming to our living room!"

The audience waited rapturously. The Minicam was so close you could have counted the pores on Charlie Weeb's nose.

"Jeremiah?" he said. "Repeat after me: 'Jesus, let me see your face.'"

Skink repeated it.

"And, 'Jesus, let me see the sunshine.'"

"Jesus, let me see the sunshine."

"And, 'Jesus, let me see the pure Christian glory of your newest creation, Lunker Lakes.'"

"Ditto," Skink said. Now came the fun part.

"The Lord has spoken," Weeb declared. "Jeremiah, my dear Christian brother, remove thy Wayfarers!"

Skink took off the sunglasses and tucked them in the top pocket of the suit. A ripple of shock passed through the audience. Skink had not allowed the makeup girls near his face. The Minicams backed off fast.

Averting his eyes, Reverend Weeb bellowed: "Jeremiah, are you truly healed?"

"Oh yes, Brother Weeb."

"And what is it you see?"

"A great man in a raspberry suit."

The audience applauded. Many shouted febrile praises to the heavens.

Beaming modestly, Reverend Weeb pressed on: "And, Jeremiah, above my head there is a joyous sign—a sign invisible to your eyes only a few short moments ago. Tell us what it says."

This was Skink's big cue, the lead-in to the live tournament coverage. Since it was assumed he would still be mostly blind after the healing, Skink had been asked to memorize the banner and pretend to be reading it on the air. The banner said: "Lunker Lakes Presents the Dickie Lockhart Memorial Bass Blasters Classic."

But those were not the words that Skink intended to say into the microphone.

Charlie Weeb waited three long beats. "Jeremiah?"

Skink raised his eyes to the banner.

"Jeremiah, please," Weeb said, "what does the sign say?"

"It says: 'Squeeze My Lemon, Baby.'"

A hot prickly silence fell over the stage. Terror filled the face of the Reverend Charles Weeb. His mouth hung open and his gleaming bonded caps clacked vigorously, but no spiritual words issued forth.

The big blind man with the pulpy face began to weep.

"Thank you, Lord. Thank you, Brother Weeb. Thanks for everything."

With that, Skink turned to face camera one.

And winked.

And when he winked, the amber glass owl eye popped from the hole in his head and bounced on the stage with the sharp crack of a marble. They heard it all the way in the back row.

"Oh, I can see again, Brother Weeb," the formerly blind man cried. "Come, let me embrace you as the Lord embraced me."

With simian arms Skink reached out and seized the Minicam and pulled it to his face.

"Squeeze my lemon, baby!" he moaned, mashing his lips to the lens.

In the crowd, thirteen women fainted heavily out of their folding chairs.

This time it was for real.

"Want a beer?" Lanie asked.

"No," said Dennis Gault.

"A Perrier?" Lanie dug into the ice chest.

"Quiet," her brother said.

He had been casting at the brushpile for a long time without a nibble. He had tried every gizmo in the tacklebox, plus a few experimental hybrids, but returned to the Double Whammy out of stubbornness. It had been Dickie Lockhart's secret lure, everybody knew that, so Dennis Gault was dying to win the tournament with it. Flaunt it. Rub it in. Show the cracker bastards that their king was really dead.

Gault knew he was in the right spot, for the sonic depth-finder provided a detailed topography of the canal bottom. The brushpile came across as a ragged black spike on an otherwise featureless chart; an elliptical red blip shone beneath it.

That was the fish.

From the size of the blip, Dennis Gault could tell the bass was very large.

It did not stay in one place, but moved slowly around the fringes of the submerged crates. Gault aimed his casts accordingly.

"Why won't the damn thing eat?" Lanie asked.

"I don't know," Gault said, "but I wish you'd be quiet."

Lanie made a face and went back to her magazines. She wanted her brother to win the tournament as much as he did, but she didn't fully understand why he took it so seriously—especially since he didn't need the money. At least Bobby Clinch had had good reasons to get tense over fishing tournaments; he was trying to keep groceries on Clarisse's table and gas in Lanie's Corvette.

She spun in the pedestal seat so the sun was at her back, and flipped to an article on bulimia.

Thirteen feet beneath the bass boat, in a tea-colored void, the great fish sulked restively. A primitive alarm had gone off somewhere in its central nervous system; a survival warning, powerful but unselective. The great fish could not know what triggered the inner response—acute oxygen depletion, brought about by toxins in the water—but she reacted as all largemouth bass do when sensing a change in the atmosphere.

She decided to gorge herself.

Loglike, she rose off the bottom and hung invisible beneath the floating shadow. She waited under the boat for the familiar rhythmic slapping noise, and peered through liquid glass for the friendly face of the creature who always brought the shiners. The hunger had begun to burn in her belly.

Glancing at the screen of the depth-finder, Dennis Gault said: "My God, the damn thing's right under us."

"I sure don't see it," Lanie said.

"Under the boat," her brother said. "Right there on the sonar."

The fish was so close that he didn't need to cast. He merely dropped the spinnerbait straight down, counted to twelve, and began the slow retrieve. The lure swam unmolested past the brushpile and rattled up, up, up toward the surface. Its rubber skirt shimmied, and its twin spoons twirled. Its mechanical agitation exuded the fear of the pursued, yet it did not behave like a frog or a minnow or even a crawdad. In fact, it resembled absolutely nothing in nature—yet the great fish engulfed it savagely.

Dennis Gault had never felt such a force. When the fish struck, he answered three times, jerking with all his might. The rod bowed and the line twanged, but the thing did not budge. It felt like a cinderblock.

"Sweet Jesus," Gault said. "Elaine, I've got it!"

She dropped her magazine and went fumbling for the landing net.

"No, not yet!" Her brother was panting so heavily that Lanie wondered if she should get a brown bag ready.

The great fish had begun to do something that no bass had ever been able to do to Dennis Gault—it was taking line. Not just in a few heady spurts, either, but in a sizzling streak. Gault pressed his thumb to the spool and yelped as the flesh burned raw before his eyes. The bass never slowed.

With his free hand Gault turned on the ignition and put the boat in reverse: he would back down on the beast, as if it were a marlin or a tuna.

"What should I do?" Lanie asked, moving to the back of the boat.

"Take the wheel when I say so."

Forty yards away, the fish broke the surface. Too heavy to clear the water, it thrashed its maw in seismic rage, the lure jingling in its lower lip. To Dennis Gault the freakish bass seemed as murky and ominous as a bull alligator. He couldn't even guess at the weight; its mouth looked as broad as a basketball hoop.

"Holy shit," Lanie said, dazzled.

"Here, take it." Gault motioned her to the steering wheel. "Take it straight back on top of this bitch." He stood up and stuck the butt of the rod in his belly, levering his back and thigh muscles into the fight. The fish seemed oblivious. For every foot of line Dennis Gault gained, the giant bass would reclaim two.

"Faster," Gault told his sister, who nudged the throttle. She had never driven a Ranger before, but figured it couldn't be much different from the Vette.

Motoring in reverse, the boat gradually ate up the distance between Dennis Gault and the thing on the end of his line. After several brief surges, the bass bore deep and hunkered on the bottom to regain its wind.

Gault held such faith in his expensive tackle and in his knowledge of fish behavior that he felt confident tightening the drag on his reel. The purpose was to prevent the bass from running out any more line, and for any other hawg the strategy might have worked: the twenty-pound monofilament was extremely strong, the graphite rod pliant but stout. Finally, and most important to Gault's reasoning, the fish should have rightfully been exhausted after such an extraordinary battle.

Gault twisted the drag down so that nothing smaller than a Mack truck could have stolen more line. Then he began to reel.

"I think it's coming," he announced. "By God, the fucker's giving up."

The great fish bucked its head and resisted surrender, but Gault was able to lift her off the bottom. Unlike the wily old lunkers of well-traveled farm ponds and tourist lakes, this bass had never before felt the sting of the hook, had never struggled against invisible talons. She had acquired no tricks to use on Dennis Gault and his powerful noise machine; all she had was her strength, and in the bad water there was little of it left.

Gault savored the feel of the fish weakening, and a faint smile came over his face. If Dickie weren't already dead, he thought, the sight of this monster hanging at the dock would kill him. Gault checked to make sure the landing net was within reach.

Then the line went slack.

For a sickening moment Gault thought the bass had broken off, but then he figured it out. The bass was coming in fast. He reeled frenetically, trying to bring the line tight.

"Elaine, it's running at us—go the other way!"

She jammed the engine in gear and the boat churned forward, roiling the water to a foam.

The great fish came to the top; a big bronze drainpipe, hovering behind the stern. It was dark enough and deep enough to be the shadow of something, not the thing itself. For the first time Dennis Gault realized its true dimensions and felt a hot rush. This fish was undoubtedly a world record; already he could see his name on the plaque. Already he could picture the bass mounted on the wall behind his desk; the taxidermist would brighten its flanks, touch up the gills, put some fury back in the dull purple eyes.

The fury was there now, only Dennis Gault couldn't see it.

When he pulled on the line, the bass obligingly swam toward the boat. "Get the net," he shouted at his sister. "Give me the goddamn net."

Then, with a kick of its tail, the fish sounded.

"Reverse!" Dennis Gault cried.

Lanie jerked on the throttle as hard as she could, and the big outboard cavitated loudly as it backed up. It was then, with the boat directly overhead, that the fish exhibited what little guile nature had invested in her pebble-sized brain. She changed direction.

"No-no-no-no!" Dennis Gault was shrieking.

The boat was heading one way, the bass was going the other. Gault braced his knees against the gunwale. He clutched the butt of the rod with both hands.

The line came tight.

The rod doubled until the tip pricked the water. "Stop!" Dennis Gault grunted. "Stop, you sorry-dumb-dirty-fat-mother—"

The great fish did not stop.

With the drag cranked down, Dennis Gault could give her no line. All he could do was hang on.

"Let go!" Lanie pleaded.

"No fucking way," said Dennis. "This fish is mine."

Lanie watched helplessly as her brother pitched over the transom. The last she saw of him were the soles of his Top-Siders.

The splash was followed by a dreadful low whine, but it was not Dennis' scream. His scream had died when he hit the propeller, which was turning (according to the dash-mounted tachometer) at precisely four thousand revolutions per minute. The propeller happened to be a brand-new turbo model SST, so the three cupped stainless blades were as sharp as sabers. Dennis Gault might as well have fallen facefirst into a two-hundred-horsepower garbage disposal. Grinding was the sound that his sister had heard.

Lanie cut off the engine and stood up to see what had happened.

"Dennis?" Timorously she peered into the cloudy water, darkening from tea to rust.

A rag-size swatch of sky-blue fabric floated up; a piece of Dennis Gault's official Bass Blasters jumpsuit. When Lanie saw it, she knew there was no point in diving in after her brother. She held on to the side of the boat with both hands, leaned over, and daintily tossed her croissants.

A hundred yards away, at the point where Charlie Weeb's canal met the dike, the great fish crashed to the surface, shook its head, and threw the hook.

32

They sat on the hood of the car, parked among the bass trucks. They had a good view of the stage, the weigh-in station, the ramp, and the dock. The sun was starting to slip behind a low bank of copper clouds, and some of the boats were heading in.

"You all right?" Catherine asked. She had showered and brushed out her hair and changed clothes. Decker had stopped at a shopping mall and bought her some slacks and a kelly-green blouse; she'd been touched that he still remembered her size.

"I'm fine," Decker said. His mental lens had preserved Thomas Curl in three frames, none of them pretty.

Catherine said, "James'll never believe all this."

Decker looked at her in an odd way. Immediately she felt rotten about mentioning her husband.

Decker said, "See the excitement you're missing, not being married to me?"

"I don't remember it quite like this."

"I do," Decker said, "just like this." He smiled and gave her hand a little squeeze. Catherine felt relieved; he'd be all right. She slid off the car and went to scout the food at the buffet, which was set up near the stage.

From out of somewhere Skink materialized and stole Catherine's place on the hood.

"Nice threads," Decker said.

"First suit I've worn in years."

"The hat's a treat too."

Skink shrugged. "You missed the show."

"What happened?"

"Preacher tried to heal me."

Decker laughed a little as Skink told the story.

"That explains where the crowd went," he said.

"Scattered like hamsters," Skink said. "Worst part is, I lost the damn eye. Just kept rolling."

"We'll get you a new one."

"Not an owl this time, either. I'd prefer a boar—one of those big nasty bastards."

Up to this moment, Decker had been watching the boats race in. Now he turned to Skink and in a quiet voice said, "I'm in some trouble, captain."

Skink clicked his tongue against his teeth.

"I killed that man," Decker said.

"Figured as much."

"There was no other way."

Skink asked what happened to the body, and Decker told him. "Don't worry about it," he said. "You did good."

"Don't worry about it?"

"You heard me."

Decker sighed. He felt detached and fuzzy, as if he were having an out-of-body experience. He felt as if he were in a tall tree looking down on himself and this hoary character in a straw hat, a bad suit, and sunglasses. From this vantage Skink would have made a fine photographic portrait; like one of those debauched-looking acid dealers at Woodstock. Or maybe Altamont. One of those guys who looked too old and too hard for the crowd.

Decker decided to tell Skink why he'd come back to Lunker Lakes. He was bound to ask, anyway.

"When I found Catherine," Decker said, "I got to thinking about Dennis Gault."

"He's *the* case in New Orleans, the whole thing," Skink repeated. "It's a joke, so forget about it. You're clear."

Decker said, "I wasn't thinking about New Orleans, captain. I was thinking about Bobby Clinch and Ott Pickney and Dickie Lockhart. In relation to Gault, I mean."

"And Catherine."

"Yes. Catherine too."

"True," Skink said, "Mr. Gault is not a very nice man."

Decker took a short breath and said, "I was seriously thinking about killing him."

"Now that you got the hang of it, right?"

Decker was stung by Skink's sarcasm. And a sterling example you are, he thought. "I don't know what I'll do when I see him. Could be I won't be able to stop myself."

"Don't give me that cuckoo's-nest routine," Skink said. "Do you really want to do it? Or do you want yourself to want to? Think about it. Tom Curl was a different story—your girl was involved. That was rescue; this is revenge. Even a one-eyed basket case like me can see you don't have the stomach for it, and I'm glad."

Decker turned away.

"But the best reason not to kill the bastard," Skink added, "is that it's simply not necessary."

"Maybe you're right."

"I don't think you understand."

"Doesn't matter." Decker hopped off the hood. He spotted Catherine on her way back with a couple of chili dogs. "I think it's best if we take off before the festivities," he said wearily.

Skink shook his head. "It's best if you stay," he said. "Besides, I need a favor."

"Naturally."

"You know how to work one of these damn TV cameras?"

Later, when *The Wall Street Journal* and others would reconstruct the collapse of the Outdoor Christian Network, some of Charlie Weeb's colleagues and competitors would say he was a fool not to pull the plug on the Lunker Lakes show the instant Skink French-kissed the Minicam. However, such a judgment failed to take into account the pressure from Weeb's corporate sponsors, who had paid extraordinary sums to finance the bass tournament and definitely expected to see it (and their fishing products) on national television. To these businessmen, the attempted faith-healing was merely a gross and irritating preamble to the main event. The weigh-in itself was attended by no less than the entire board of directors of the Happy Gland fish-scent company, who had flown down from Elijay, Georgia, with the expectation that Eddie Spurling, their new spokesman, would win the Lockhart Memorial hands down. Charlie Weeb had assured them of this in the most positive terms.

So, even after Skink's performance, little thought was given to aborting the program. In fact, there was no time between the church show and the tournament for Weeb to contemplate the scope of the catastrophe, broadcast-wise. He knew it was bad; very bad. Before his eyes the sea of faithful Christian faces had dissipated; the first ten rows in front of the stage now were empty, with some of the chairs overturned by hasty departures. A few people milled around the boat docks, while others hovered at the free buffet. Most apparently had retreated to the charter buses, where they huddled in their seats and recited appropriate Bible tracts. They couldn't wait to get out of Lunker Lakes.

As soon as Skink had leapt off the stage in pursuit of his eyeball, Charlie Weeb had cut to a commercial and gone searching for Deacon Johnson, who had presciently commandeered the limousine and struck out for parts unknown. Weeb's principal inquiry—as enunciated in a gaseous torrent of obscenities—concerned the selection of Mr. Jeremiah Skink as a subject worthy of healing. It was Reverend Weeb's opinion that Skink was more demented than disabled, and that his schizoid tendency toward self-mutilation should have been evident to Deacon Johnson (who, after all, was being paid two hundred thou a year to prevent such embarrassments).

Failing to locate Deacon Johnson, Charlie Weeb returned to the stage and tried to make the best of things. His image as a faith-healer was damaged, perhaps irreparably, but that concerned him less than the mounting specter of financial ruin. Word had filtered back to Weeb that many of the pilgrims who had signed new contracts for Lunker Lakes homesites were having second thoughts—a half-dozen had even demanded their deposits back. Weeb's stomach had churned sourly at the news.

What he now needed—in fact, the only thing that would save the project—was a big warm Southern finish. Specifically: a beaming, tanned, lovable, good ole boy in the person of Eddie Spurling, with a string of lunker bass. That would put the mood right.

So Charlie Weeb seized the microphone and talked a blue streak as the boats roared in. He talked about sunshine, balmy climate, calm waters, central air, adjustable mortgages, bike paths, rec rooms, low maintenance fees, the Olympic-size swimming pool, everything but fish.

Because there weren't any.

Every boat was coming back empty. The OCN sports reporter would stick a mike in front of the angler and the angler would straighten his cap and spit some chaw and grumble about it being one of those days, and then the sports reporter would smile lamely and say better luck next time.

Those gathered dockside—primarily the sponsors and tackle reps and devoted relatives of the contestants—could not recall such a dismal day of bass fishing, even in the weeks after Hurricane Camille had torn up the South.

Skink himself was worried by what he saw, but there was nothing to do but wait. Surely somebody had caught some fish.

As the pattern became clear to Charlie Weeb, he found it increasingly difficult to put a positive spin on the day's events. A weigh-in with nothing to weigh was extremely dull television, even by cable standards. To fill air time until Fast Eddie Spurling arrived, Weeb ordered the director to run some how-to fishing videos supplied by the big tackle companies.

With only ten minutes until deadline, and the winter sun nearly gone, forty-seven bass boats had checked in at the ramp. The empty scoreboard mocked Charlie Weeb. He could no longer summon the courage to look at the Happy Gland entourage.

Where were Eddie Spurling and his ringers?

Backstage the young hydrologist approached Reverend Weeb and said, "Bad news—the water's worse today than ever."

"Get out of my sight," Weeb said. He didn't give a damn anymore about the water—Eddie's fish would be fine, since they were coming out of the Everglades.

With a grave look, the hydrologist said, "You're about to have a major problem."

"And you're about to get a size-ten Florsheim up your ass, so get lost."

Weeb's earpiece crackled and the TV director said: "How much longer?"

"We got three boats out," the preacher said. "Sit tight, it'll be worth it."

It was.

Naturally Skink was first to hear them. He hopped off Decker's car and ambled down to the dock. The other onlookers gave way, recognizing him instantly as the deranged Cyclops whom Reverend Weeb had tried to cure. Skink stood alone until Decker and Catherine came down, holding hands.

312 ■ CARL HIAASEN

"Listen," Skink said.

Decker heard the boat. Whoever it was, he was approaching very slowly—a behavior virtually unknown in professional bass-fishing circles.

"Engine trouble?" Decker said.

Skink shook his head. A mischievous grin split his face.

Catherine said, "This ought to be good."

Suddenly the dock was washed in hot light as the kliegs came on. An OCN cameraman, a wiry young man with curly red hair, hustled across the boat ramp with the Minicam balanced on one shoulder. Without explanation he handed the camera and battery pack to R. J. Decker, and bounded away.

"Prior engagement," Skink explained. Catherine couldn't be sure, but she thought he winked his good eye behind the sunglasses.

Decker got the Minicam focused while Catherine fitted the headset over his ears. In the earphone he could hear the director hollering for Camera Two to get steady.

"This is a breeze," Decker said. A four-year-old could work the zoom.

Skink rubbed his leathery hands together. "Lights! Camera!"

Decker aimed down the lake and waited. Before long a bass boat chugged into view. It was Fast Eddie Spurling, going slow. The reason was obvious.

He was towing two other boats.

"Is it Spurling?" the TV director barked at Camera Two.

"Yep," Decker said.

The word was relayed to Reverend Weeb, who got on the PA system and beckoned all within earshot to return at once to the dock area. Even those who had fled to the buses emerged to see what was going on.

"Go tight, Rudy," the director instructed Decker, and Decker obliged, as Rudy would have.

As the procession of boats tediously made its way up Lunker Lake Number One, a few people in the crowd (specifically, those with binoculars) began to react alarmingly. Curious, Charlie Weeb stepped down from the stage to join his congregation at water's edge.

R. J. Decker was doing quite well with the TV camera. Through the viewfinder everything was in perfect focus.

There was Eddie Spurling half-turned in the driver's seat as he checked the crippled boats on his towline.

The first was the wooden skiff—there were Jim Tile and Al García, sitting aft and stern. They toasted the TV lights with cans of Budweiser.

Charlie Weeb let out a whimper. "Mother of God, it's the Tile Brothers." He had completely forgotten about the spic and the spade. "Get the camera offa them!" the preacher screamed.

Slowly R. J. Decker panned to the second boat, and when he did his knees nearly crimped.

It was the Starcraft, and it wasn't the way Decker had left it.

Catherine said, "Oh no," and moved behind Skink. She leaned her head against his back, and closed her eyes.

The boat was full of buzzards.

There was a ragged cluster of at least a dozen—burly fearless birds; oily brown, stoop-shouldered, with raw pink heads and sharp ruthless eyes. They belched and shifted and blinked in the bright light, but they didn't fly. They were too full.

"Tough customers," Skink whispered to Decker.

Numbly Decker let the TV camera peer into the boat. He ignored the disembodied voice shrieking from his earpiece.

The buzzards stood in a litter of human bones. The bones were clean, but occasionally one of the rancid birds would bend down and pick savagely, as a possessive gesture to the others. The biggest buzzard, a disheveled male with a stained crooked beak, palmed a bare yellow skull in its talons.

"Looks like a dog," Skink said, puzzled.

"It's Lucas," Catherine sighed. "Rage, I want to go home."

As soon as Eddie Spurling tied off the boats, Charlie Weeb barged forward and said, "Why'd you tow those fuckers in?"

"Because they ast me to."

"So where's the fish?"

"No fish," Eddie Spurling reported. "I got skunked."

Weeb sucked on his upper lip. He had to be careful what he said. There was a decent-sized crowd now; the other contestants had hung around just to see how the famous TV fisherman had fared.

"What do you mean, no fish—how is that possible?" Weeb spoke in a low strained voice. He used his eyes to grill Eddie about the ringers—where the fuck were they!

"Damn rascals just weren't bitin'."

"You're in big trouble, Eddie."

"Naw, I don't think so."

The sports reporter from OCN poked his microphone into Spurling's face and asked the star of *Fish Fever* what had happened.

"Just one of those days," Fast Eddie mused, "when you feel like a spit-valve on the trombone of life."

Al García and Jim Tile climbed out of the skiff with the Igloo cooler. Skink was waiting for them.

"We didn't get Queenie," García said.

"I know."

García looked at Jim Tile, then at Skink.

Skink said, "Bet you boys had some engine trouble."

"I don't believe this," García said. He realized what had happened, but he didn't know why.

"What's going on, jungle man?"

"Change of plans," Skink said. "Late-breaking brainstorm."

Jim Tile was thinking about it. "The Starcraft isn't one of the tournament boats."

"No," Skink said, "it's not. Ask Decker about that one."

García said, "That means there's another guy still out on the water."

"Right," said Jim Tile. "Dennis Gault."

Skink looked pleased. "You boys are pretty sharp, even for cops."

Al García remembered what Skink had taught him about the huge fish. "Just what the hell have you done?" he asked.

"It's not me, *señor*. I just arranged things." Skink flipped open the lid of the Igloo and saw García's little bass, darting in the clean water. "I'll be damned, Sergeant, I'm proud of you."

Jim Tile said, "Sir, there's something you ought to know."

"In a minute, Trooper Jim. First let's get this little scupper to the weigh station." By himself Skink hoisted the heavy cooler and elbowed his way through the crowd. "You won't believe this," he was saying over his shoulder to Tile and García, "but I believe you're the only boat that caught fish."

"That's what we're trying to tell you," García said, huffing behind.

Skink climbed the stage and carried the cooler to the scale. He took out the little bass and carefully set him in the basket. Behind them onstage the digital scale lighted up with glowing six-foot numerals: "14 oz."

"Ha-ha!" Skink cawed. He found the stage mike and boomed into the PA system: "Attention, K-Mart shoppers! We've got a winner."

"Shitfire," Charlie Weeb muttered. The voice on the PA sounded just like the blind man. First a boatload of buzzards, and now what?

As the queasy preacher followed the OCN camerman to the weigh station, it occurred to him it wasn't red-haired Rudy, but someone else with the Minicam, someone Weeb didn't recognize. It made little sense, but in the unremitting chaos of the day it seemed a negligible mystery.

The blind man was not onstage when Charlie Weeb got there, but another nightmare awaited him.

The Tile Brothers.

"Hola," Jim Tile said to Charlie Weeb. *"es muy grande* fish, no?"

"Check it out, bro," Al García said.

Charlie Weeb got a bilious taste in his throat. "It appears that you are indeed the winner," he said. The Minicam was right in his face— all America was watching. Somehow Weeb composed himself and raised the puny bass for the camera. Two girls in orange bikinis rolled out the immense trophy, and two more carried out a giant cardboard facsimile of the check for two hundred and fifty thousand dollars.

"That's righteous," Al García said, causing Jim Tile to wince, "but where be the real thing?"

"Ah," Weeb said. How could he go on TV and say that, after all this, the check was missing? That he and Deacon Johnson were the only two human beings with the combination to the safe, and now Deacon Johnson was gone?

Sensing trouble, Jim Tile asked, *"¿Donde está el cheque?"*

"I'm sorry," Reverend Weeb said, "but I don't speak Cubish."

By way of translation, Al García said: "Where's the fucking bread, *por favor?"*

Weeb attempted several explanations, none persuasive and none contradicting the fact that he had promised to present the check to the winners on national television on the day of the tournament. The crowd, especially the other bass anglers, became unruly and insistent; as much as they resented the Tile Brothers, they resented even more the idea of any fisherman getting stiffed. Even the sulking Happy Gland contingent joined the fracas.

"I'm sorry," Weeb said finally, raising his palms, "there's been a slight problem."

Al García and Jim Tile looked at one another irritably.

"You do the honors," García said.

Jim Tile dug a badge and some handcuffs out of his jacket.

Charlie Weeb's lushly forested eyebrows seemed to wilt. A buzz went through the audience.

"Cut, Rudy, cut!" the director was hollering into R. J. Decker's ear, but Decker let it roll.

In perfect English, Jim Tile said, "Mr. Weeb, you're under arrest for fraud—"

"And grand larceny," García interjected. "And any other damn thing I can think of."

"And grand larceny," Jim Tile continued. "You have the right to remain silent—"

Just then a sorrowful cry sheared the dusk. It rose up from the water in a guttural animal pitch that made García flinch and shiver.

Jim Tile bowed his head. He'd tried to tell him.

Decker dropped the Minicam and ran toward the boat ramp.

Skink was on his knees in the shallow water. All around him fish were rising in convulsions, finning belly-up, cutting the glassy surface in jerky zigzag vectors.

Skink scooped up one of the addled bass as it swam by and held it up, dripping, for Decker and the others to see.

"They're all dying," he cried.

"Take my boat," Eddie Spurling offered. "I got six of the damn things."

"Thank you," Skink said hoarsely. Decker and Catherine climbed in after him.

"I hope you find her," Fast Eddie called as the boat pulled away. He would never forget the sight of that magnificent beast in the fish cage; he couldn't bear the thought of her dying in bad water, but it seemed inevitable.

In the bass boat Skink stood up and opened the throttle. First the straw hat blew off, then the sunglasses. Skink didn't seem to care. Nor did he seem to notice the gnats and bugs splatting against his cheeks and forehead, and sticking in his beard by the glue of their own blood. In the depthless gray of early night, Skink drove wide open as if he knew the canals by heart, or instinct. The boat accelerated like a rocket; Decker watched the speedometer tickle sixty and he clenched his teeth, praying they wouldn't hit an alligator or a log. Catherine turned her head and clung to his chest with both arms. Except for the bone-chilling speed, it might have been a lovely moment.

Over the howl of the engine, Skink began to shout.

"Confrontation," he declared, "is the essence of nature!"

He shook his silvery braid loose and let his hair stream out behind him.

"Confrontation is the rhythm of life," he went on. "In nature violence is pure and purposeful, one species against another in an act of survival!"

Terrific, Decker thought, Marlin Perkins on PCP. "Watch where you're going, captain!" he shouted.

"All I did with Dennis Gault," Skink hollered back, "was to arrange a natural confrontation. No different from a thousand other confrontations that take place every night and every day out here, unseen and uncelebrated. Yet I knew Gault's instincts as well as I knew the fish. It was only a matter of timing, of matching the natural rhythms. Putting the two species within striking distance. That's all it was, Miami."

Skink pounded the steering wheel ferociously with both fists, causing the speeding boat to skitter precipitously off its plane.

"But goddamn," he groaned. "Goddamn, I didn't know about the water."

Decker rose beside him at the console and casually edged his knee against the wheel, just in case. "Of course you didn't know!" Decker shouted. He ducked, unnecessarily, as they roared beneath an overpass for the new superhighway.

"We're running through poison," Skink said, incredulously. "They built a whole fucking resort on poison water."

"I know, captain."

"It's my fault."

"Don't be ridiculous."

"You don't understand!" Skink turned around and said to Catherine: "He doesn't understand. Do you love this man? Then make him understand. It's my fault."

Shielding her face from the cold, Catherine said, "You're being too hard on yourself. That's what I think."

Skink smiled. His classic anchorman teeth were now speckled with dead gnats. "You're quite a lady," he said. "I wish you'd dump your doctor and go back—"

Suddenly, in front of them, another boat appeared. Just a flat shadow hanging in the darkness, dead across the middle of the canal. Someone in a yellow rain slicker was sitting in the bow of the boat, hunched in the seat.

Skink wasn't even looking, he was talking to Catherine, who had opened her mouth to scream. Desperately Decker leaned hard left on the steering wheel and drew back on the throttle. Fast Eddie's boat nearly went airborne as it struck the other craft a glancing mushy blow on the stern. They spun twice before Decker found the kill switch that cut the engine.

Skink, who had been thrown hard against the engine, got to his feet and took a visual survey. "This is the place," he said.

The other boat had been bumped up against the bank. Decker waited for his heart to stop hammering before he called to the person in the yellow slicker: "You all right?"

"Screw you!"

"Lanie?"

"Always the vixen," Skink said. He was stripping off the cheap sharkskin suit that Deacon Johnson had given him for the healing.

"Who is that woman?" Catherine asked.

"Gault's sister," Decker replied.

"Screw both of you!" Lanie shouted. She was standing in the bow, pointing angrily at them.

"So, where's Dennis?" Decker asked.

"Change the subject," Skink advised. He was naked now. He was on his knees, leaning over the side of the boat, unwittingly mooning Decker and Catherine. He slapped the flat of his palm on the water.

"I hope your fish croaks," Lanie shouted at Skink, "like all the rest." Her voice broke. "Like Dennis."

Catherine said, "Have I missed something?"

Skink furiously pulled a dead yearling from the canal and heaved it to shore. He slapped and slapped, but no fish rose off the bottom, no fish came to his hand.

Decker rummaged through Eddie's boat until he found a spotlight, which plugged into the boat's cigarette lighter. With Skink still hanging over the side calling and slapping for Queenie, Decker worked the beam along the shoreline. Once he inadvertently flashed it in Lanie's direction; she cursed and spun around in the pedestal seat to face the other way.

Decker spotted the body floating at the end of the canal, near the flood dike. He lowered the twin trolling motors and steered Eddie's boat along the yellow path of the spotlight.

Catherine craned to see what it was, but Decker put his hand on her shoulder.

Dapper Dennis Gault was in shreds. He floated facedown, snarled in twenty-pound fishing line.

"The rhythm of confrontation," Skink said. "In a way, I almost admire the sonofabitch."

Decker knew there was nothing to be done.

"This is some sport," Catherine remarked.

Skink and Decker saw the great fish simultaneously. She surfaced on her side, feebly, near Gault's bloated legs. Her gills had bled from red to pink, and her flanks had blackened. She was dying.

"No, you don't," Skink said, and dove in. For a big man he made a small splash, entering the water like a needle.

Catherine stood up to watch with Decker. Their breath came out in soft frosty puffs.

"I got her!" Skink shouted. "But damnation!"

Somehow he had become entangled in Dennis Gault's body. For several moments the water churned in a macabre one-sided duel, stiff dead limbs thrashing against the living. Catherine was terrified; it looked as if Gault had come back to life. Skink was in great pain, the foul brackish water searing his raw eye socket. All at once he seemed to be slipping under.

R. J. Decker picked up Fast Eddie's fish gaff and stuck it hard in the meat of Gault's shoulders. He pulled brutishly at the corpse with all his weight, and Skink kicked away, free. He cradled the sluggish fish in his bare arms. He swam with his head out, on his back, otter-style. He was fighting to catch his breath.

"Thanks, Miami," he wheezed. "Take care."

With four kicks he made it to shore, and carried the great fish up the slope. Decker didn't need the spotlight to track him—a naked white Amazon running splayfooted along the embankment. He was singing, too, though the melody was indistinct.

Decker gunned the engine and beached the bass boat with a jolt. He jumped ashore and reached out his hand for Catherine. Together they jogged toward the flood dike, but Skink was far ahead. Even toting the fish, he seemed to be running twice as fast.

From the canal behind them, Lanie Gault called Skink's name. Decker heard two shots and reflexively he dragged Catherine to the ground. They looked up to see two small flares explode overhead, drenching the night in vermilion. In a strange way it reminded Decker of the warm safe light of the darkroom. He had no idea why Lanie had fired the flare gun; maybe it was all she had.

They got up and started running again, but by this time Skink had already crested the dike. When they reached the other side, he was gone, vanished into the seam of the universe. As the flares burned out, the red glow drained from the sky and the crystal darkness returned to the marsh.

A washboard ripple lingered on the quiet pool. Frogs peeped, crickets trilled, waterbugs skated through the bulrushes. There was no sign of the great fish, no sign of the man.

"Hear it?" Decker asked.

Catherine brushed the insects away and strained to listen. "I don't think so, Rage."

"Something swimming." The gentlest of motions, receding somewhere out in the Glades. Decker was sure of it.

"Wait," Catherine said, taking his arm, "now I do."